MW01050015

PRAISE FOR THE CONSULTANT
BY ALEC DONZI

"Very exciting and compelling.
Donzi's thriller is certainly action-packed!"
—G. K. Hendricks, *Pocket Books*

"*The Consultant* is an engaging story."
—S. Ross, *Crown & Crown*

"I read it with great interest."
—S. Mehta, *Alfred Knopf*

"I enjoyed reading this."
—W. Malloy, *The Mysterious Press / Warner Books*

"Compelling."
—C. Marino, *HarperCollins*

"Intriguing."
—M. Friedrich, *Aaron Priest Agency*

THE
CONSULTANT

— A Novel —

ALEC
DONZI

scherf.books™

www.scherf.com

Published by scherf.books
a division of Scherf, Inc.
PO Box 80180
Las Vegas, NV 89180-0180, USA
www.scherf.com

Library of Congress Control Number: 00-135036

ISBN 1-887603-04-2

Cover design by Scherf Design Studio
Cover and author photograph by Patrice Rech

Printed in the United States of America

First Edition: X/MM

But those who want to get rich
fall into temptation and a snare
and many foolish and harmful
desires which plunge men into
ruin and destruction.

—1 TIMOTHY 6:9

CHAPTER

1

JOHN FARNSWORTH watched the Dallas skyline disappear as the Gulfstream banked north, climbing to twenty thousand feet. A flight crew of five, including two flight attendants, accompanied the Nicanor Industries CEO on his trip to North Korea.

Farnsworth found it strangely disquieting that the other parties scheduled for the trip had canceled at the last minute. Something about prior commitments.

"Care for a glass of champagne before lunch, Mr. Farnsworth?" one of the flight attendants asked.

"Sure, sweetie," he said, his eyes locked between her legs.

She smiled, aware of his horny gaze, and not disliking it at all.

Farnsworth accepted the glass and stared out the window. Below, he could see Wichita Falls and the barren West Texas panhandle beyond. The attendant began serving lunch and Farnsworth shelved his apprehension about the sudden cancellations for later.

After lunch Farnsworth had an attendant bring his laptop so he could work on revisions for his North Korean proposal. Two hundred miles off the California coast, the CEO for Nicanor clicked off the computer and leaned back satisfied.

From the ground, against the backdrop of a cloudless and perfect blue sky, an imaginative observer may have mistaken the Gulfstream for a polished, shiny silver bullet advancing in slow motion.

Suddenly, a massive explosion over the Pacific, not audibly noticeable for anybody on the ground or in the air, except for Farnsworth and the flight crew of the doomed Nicanor jet. The aircraft transformed into a ball of fire instantly. The Gulfstream disintegrated into thousands of tiny burning pieces seconds later. Simply ripped apart by powers as violent as an erupting volcano.

With one bang the noise from the engines had been forced into a deadly silence. Nothing anymore. No screams, no laughter, no happy toasts of gentle colliding champagne flutes, no friendly chiming noise from active silverware, no chirps from computers and other high-tech gear, no swish of thighs wrapped in nylons softly rubbing against each other, no rustle of a garment. No sound at all. Silence shattered only for a moment as the debris hit the waters. With its immeasurable yawning gulf and much like an anticipated dessert, the gigantic ocean swallowed the crushing fragments of the jet and of charred bodies within minutes.

Ten minutes after the explosion every ounce of debris had been sucked down into the deep. Sure, a few small segments still floated here and there, but it wouldn't take much longer until these were lost at sea too. Vanished, gone forever.

The only apparently positive aspect in this whole ordeal was the fact that the victims didn't have to suffer—no pain at all. It ended in a one-second tick.

2

PEARLS OF sweat formed on his forehead whenever he squeezed his two-hundred-seven-pound body into the tight Recaro seat of the Jaguar convertible. Exiting the car was an even more strenuous experience, producing soaked armpits instantly. The Jaguar was his wife's car. Birgid Birchner liked convertibles, especially for the type of climate they enjoyed year-round in this part of Florida. Jerome Birchner on the other hand wasn't enthusiastic about cabriolets. Not that cabriolets weren't any fun, but he was a little paranoid. In fact, Jerome Birchner had good reasons to be paranoid. Someone could shoot him in the back of his head, or some crazy dude may perceive the cabriolet an easy carjacking target.

On this scorching day in July as asphalt patches softened and rare spots of connecting asphalt strings melted, Jerome stashed away his fears and phobias. The convertible stood readily available and he was in the mood to feel the wind blow through his thinning hair and smash against his face and swerve around his ears. His wife had gone shopping and she cruised around town in the new Navigator they had just bought a week ago.

Every time he slid into the driver's seat of the Jaguar, he felt sporty and healthy. Several years ago, his weight was high up there at two-forty. It had been unbearable as his movements had slowed, the wardrobe didn't fit anymore, and perspiration had increased to bathtub levels. The current poundage was somewhat stabilized by a daily NordicTrack-exercise routine and a disciplined health diet. He hadn't been sick in years, eating his Kiwi fruit and strawberries every morning, and he'd mix garlic juice and cayenne pepper into almost every dish. For himself he kept a Porsche in the garage, but very rarely ever drove it. The Porsche had the same problem like the Jaguar: it was an athletic exercise to get in and out of the driver's seat. The one thing Jerome really enjoyed on the Porsche was the incomparable rush of several Gs as his body was violently forced into the Recaro whenever he stepped on the accelerator and the car snatched from zero to sixty in less than five seconds, as the smoking tires left plenty of rubber on the asphalt. The Porsche was a toy, just like his triple-engine forty-three-foot Scarab. But like the sports car, Jerome even less frequently roved around in the Scarab. Both of these toys had become collectibles—more so than anything else. His favorite car, though, was the roomy S-Class Mercedes. He bought a new Benz every three years—always a white one with beige leather interior.

SINCE HE had first hung out his shingle as a corporate consultant, some twelve years ago, his career had taken off without a break from day one until recently. It was hard work though, especially during the mid-nineties, and as long as he could make a fortune at what he did, he didn't mind routine jobs. These days things were pretty relaxed for Jerome Birchner. Having just turned thirty-nine with a net worth of sixty million dollars, Jerome could've retired already—he gave it some serious thought recently.

Occasionally, he still longed for the excitement of new business ventures. Every deal was a challenge and the money was always very good. He welcomed manageable difficulties and took great pleasure in overcoming those. But Jerome didn't like the odd stuff anymore, deals that were too sophisticated and almost always resulted in major headaches. Therefore, he was no longer interested in these complicated and risky deals. But he also knew that the really big bucks weren't that easy to come by, instead, really major dough could only be hatched from these cumbersome deals—high-risk deals filled with intricacies that would often produce sleepless nights.

THE BLACK Jaguar turned right and coasted slowly toward the remote controlled cast-iron gates of Whitecaps Island, a new development. The remote control was voice activated and verified the identity of the speaker as it communicated with the receiver built into the left pillar on which one of the gates was hinged.

"Me," Jerome said into the mic of the remote control, and the stately gates opened without a squeak.

Two surveillance cameras peered from the gate pillars—one camera in each pillar—producing digital recordings of the immediate area around the gates, around the clock.

Will Smith's *Wild, Wild West* blared through the car stereo.

Situated on nearly fifteen acres, four Mediterranean-style mansions of generous proportions were on display. Located at the northern city limits of Naples, connected to the Gulf Shore Boulevard and near Mooring Line Drive, this luxurious residential development stood out amid the other developments in the area. There were plenty of multimillion-dollar homes everywhere, but Whitecaps Island was a notch above the rest as it had been graciously crowned with a rare long private beach front. Even at auction this parcel of land sold for a small fortune. Jerome had purchased this chunk of paradise together with a friend, Walter Kalkmeier, four years ago.

A couple of yachts were anchored at the northerly end of the property where a wooden pier ran straight into the Gulf. A few exotic imports decorated the driveway of Walter Kalkmeier's estate. Two of the four homes seemed vacant with empty driveways.

Valerie Kalkmeier emerged from underneath a weeping willow, storming into the driveway.

"Hi, Val!" Jerome waved.

She ignored him. With her high heels Valerie slid over the loose gravel and almost fell. Her short skirt barely covered her derriere—Jerome couldn't help but notice. And Valerie's scanty tank top didn't provide much protective cladding either, baring her breasts more than was usually acceptable even in this generous part of Florida where almost anything was tolerated—her Gucci shades seemed bigger than the tank top.

She jerkily opened the door to a yellow Ferrari. Her mind was obviously preoccupied as she didn't pay any attention to her surroundings. Without even as much as a glance, Valerie backed the car out of the driveway, rocks kicking from the rear end, the fat tires squealing and leaving marks on the asphalt as she raced toward the main gate. She was only inches away from ramming into the Birchner Jag. She didn't notice a thing, and neither did Jerome.

Jerome's mansion was the last house on the left near the pier where his Scarab rested in the calm waters. A huge circular drive crowned the exorbitant front entrance which was heavily populated by tall columns. The circular drive had been directly attached to the cul-de-sac. Left to the circular drive was a straight driveway to Jerome's six-car garage. One of the garage doors opened quietly as Jerome lightly pressed the button on the automatic garage-door opener in the Jag.

Once the car was in the garage and the engine killed, Jerome lifted his frame—adorned with two hundred-plus pounds of raw meat—out of the Jaguar. It was truly an arduous task. The temperature had climbed to over a hundred degrees and the humidity rating issued a reading in the high nineties. Both of these factors aided an even higher level of perspiration—his shirt was soaked. Dressed in a black silk shirt drooped loosely over his ivory cotton shorts, Jerome's appearance was typical for the area. Through the garage, Jerome headed for the rear entrance to his mansion.

At only five-eight Jerome wasn't a standout and could get easily lost in a crowd. He certainly had no resemblance to the typical six-foot-plus German stereotype, like so many of his fellow countrymen. And he was a far cry from resembling massive muscle pack Arnold Schwarzenegger who incidentally was born in the same sleepy little town in which Jerome first saw the light of the world.

But then, Jerome's family tree was traced back to a Jewish heritage, even though he grew up a Roman-Catholic. His mother's maiden name was Rosenthal—such a last name left no doubt about his origin. His grandfather had been taken away to a labor camp by the Nazis during World War II. Through some odd circumstances, Mr. Rosenthal didn't end up in a concentration camp, but instead was released by Hitler's armies a month later.

The two hundred-plus pounds showed a little, but Jerome wasn't preoccupied with losing weight.

CHAPTER

3

"ANYBODY HOME?" Jerome hollered as he entered the living room. "Hello!"

Nobody was home. Their two teenage kids were in school and Birgid had gone shopping. He knew the whereabouts of his kids, but expected to find his lovely wife somewhere around the house.

"Hello! I'm home." He searched the kitchen area and the lanai.

It was an exquisite, luxurious home with marble flooring. Eight thousand square feet of extravagant living space sprawling two stories. All bedrooms were upstairs, except for an additional guest room which had been installed at ground level. This additional bedroom on the ground floor was actually never used for visitors, but instead served as a huge walk-in closet for Birgid's extensive wardrobe. Almost ninety-nine percent of her clothes in this storage facility had never been used, not even once. For visiting friends and family they had two larger, more lavishly furnished guest rooms prepared on the top floor.

The entertainment facilities with its own home movie theater and a fully isolated music room, the main kitchen and a kitchenette for convenience sake, and both dining rooms were all located at ground level. It had cost Jerome less than two million dollars to build this mansion and he enjoyed the spaciousness and the superb location. This was the place he called home.

Throughout, the house had been furnished in a contemporary style. It remained comfortably homey though and even cozy in several important areas. White was evidently the dominant color for walls and ceiling elements. Natural maple had been generously applied to cabinets in the kitchen, the bathrooms and in most other rooms downstairs and upstairs. The wood brought lots of warmth to the place. At its lowest point the ceiling was still twelve feet high. A twenty-four-foot cathedral ceiling in the foyer supported the spaciousness and elegance of this particular mansion.

The plantation shutters were kept in white too, and elaborate arrangements of tropical plants brought color and an attractive habitat to the place. Some areas in the house appeared like the part of an authentic jungle. A few scattered originals by Friedensreich Hundertwasser and similar paintings by various other lesser-known artists produced an optical sensation of vibrancy along the walls throughout the home.

He gave it one more try, "Hello!" But to no avail. Nobody was home.

After he fetched himself a can of iced Nestea from the fridge, Jerome fell into a fluffy, beige leather sofa in the living room. He fumbled with the multifunctional remote control in his right hand. When Jerome finally succeeded in turning on the television, he switched back and forth between CNBC, CNN and Bloomberg. For half an hour he caught a glimpse of this and that.

The stock market had become boring with no major movements in either direction, even though high volatility could be found in isolated stocks.

"Internet IPOs are still hot," reporter Ron Sanford said on CNBC. He explained how one of these money-losing companies with supposedly high potential had shot up 211% on its first trading day.

Jerome was somewhat interested, but wouldn't invest a dime into these risky offerings. At this time he only owned a few shares in Dell, Microsoft, Cisco and Intel. All four stocks had the potential to double or even triple in price within a year or two . . . *maybe,* he thought. Investing only a few hundred thousand dollars in Dell shares half a decade ago, Jerome's initial investment had ballooned into several million dollars.

For a season, Jerome had once actively traded stocks, and it continued to be somewhat of a habit to casually follow the market. But generally speaking, Jerome had lost his interest in the tension and action of trading stocks on a daily basis. He had made enough money in the early nineties, and then again with the first wave of Internet stocks during the Internet craze of '97 and '98. Now, his time was much better spent, he reasoned.

The domestic economy had slowed down a bit, but remained vibrant underneath the surface. Aside from the few millions he had invested in his favorite stocks, he kept most of his wealth liquid in money-market funds. Before taxes these funds yielded four and a half percent annually, with virtually no risk exposure to a volatile marketplace.

Jerome surfed amid the two hundred channels when on VH1 he caught the TLC music video *No Scrubs.* Disney showed a *Growing Pains* rerun from the late eighties and TNN rebroadcast a Trisha Yearwood concert. Then he caught a report on CNN Headline News about a private jet that had supposedly crashed into the Pacific.

"About eighteen hours ago, two hundred miles off the coast of California, a corporate jet owned by Nicanor Industries disappeared from radar screens. It is surmised that the aircraft has crashed into the Pacific Ocean. On board were the flight crew of five and Nicanor president John Farnsworth, who are all unaccounted for at this time.

"The U.S. Coast Guard, aided by Search & Rescue teams from the U.S. Navy, will continue their search-and-rescue mission in the area. Investigators from the National Transportation Safety Board flew over the suspected crash site earlier today. In a first briefing, officials from the U.S. Coast Guard confirmed that so far no bodies or parts of the airplane wreckage have been found.

"A spokeswoman for the FAA said that a thorough investigation into the presumed crash will provide the necessary clues and answers to what may have caused the fatal accident of the brand-new Gulfstream aircraft. And that it would take anywhere from nine to eighteen months before a final report of the investigation would be released." The anchorwoman Lynn Romero reported the news in a solemn manner.

Miss Romero continued to report speculations regarding the possible cause of the crash, and details why officials from the FAA and NTSB thought it very likely that the jet had actually crashed. The network showed a video feed with a map in the upper right corner of the TV screen from the presumed crash site. They also showed pictures of John Farnsworth, the Nicanor headquarters in Texas, a Gulfstream V, and a C-130 rescue plane.

While the CNN report was still in progress, Jerome stood up hastily and went into the study to retrieve his notebook computer. He quickly returned to the sofa in the living room. For immediate Internet access he connected the notebook to a separate cable outlet next to the TV.

Jerome searched for *Nicanor* and the search engine yielded over four thousand hits within seconds. After checking through the first ten sites, he had the idea to send an e-mail to Randy Dermont of APL (Aerospace Precision Laser) in Baltimore. Perhaps Randy Dermont would be a competent source for an inside scoop on the Nicanor story, Jerome thought. The e-mail read:

> *Dear Randy,*
> *How are you? I just saw the Nicanor thing on CNN.*
> *Do you know anything about this company?*
> *Please let me know if you do. How is everything else?*
> *Your friend,*
> *Jerome :)*

He clicked the *Send* icon, and then returned to continue his search on the Web for more data on Nicanor. He found plenty of information about the company.

U.S. COAST GUARD helicopters, various ships and cutters from the USCG and the U.S. Navy, and a C-130 rescue plane from the National Guard searched the surface of the ocean in the presumed crash area extensively. Earlier in their search efforts, neither the USCG nor the FAA or NTSB had any kind of substantiations to the fact that the plane had actually crashed. Because of far distance out on the sea and frequently erratic weather conditions in the region, the Gulfstream could've been just simply lost from radar screens.

But their trepidation was fortified when neither the crew nor Farnsworth had checked in by phone with Nicanor headquarters upon the scheduled arrival time in North Korea, which would've been regular procedure. Also, the aircraft left no further radar hits nor had it been spotted anywhere along the designated route. Therefore, the general assumption was that the jet had crashed indeed.

The U.S. Coast Guard had searched until late in the afternoon yesterday and again since the early morning hours. They hadn't found anything, not even a hint of some debris of the crashed airplane. Of course, the sea was rough so far out there in the ocean. Sometimes the cutters had to conquer twenty-foot waves. Within hours, floating debris would've been scattered over an area measuring at least a few hundred square miles, enlarging the circumference virtually by the minute.

With highly sophisticated sonar equipment, the U.S. Coast Guard assisted by the U.S. Navy made every effort to find at least the two black boxes—the cockpit voice recorder and flight data recorder. If the plane had truly crashed, the find of the black boxes would've confirmed their worst fears. One major problem existed though, namely that the ocean floor of the Pacific was thousands of feet deep in this area and for humans absolutely unreachable.

Every shred of evidence had been sucked below the surface shortly after impact. Even if the black boxes made it undamaged to Davy Jones's locker, chances of receiving the locator signals from these boxes were practically nonexistent. And in the case that these black boxes were somehow miraculously located, it would've been downright impossible with current available technology to recover them.

CHAPTER

4

NICANOR INDUSTRIES used to be one of the largest defense contractors in the world. In the early nineties, when the Democratic President came into office, he cut defense spending drastically. Nicanor had been left standing in the cold. The Cold War was over and no longer was there a need for heavy-duty defense weaponry, the White House argued. They didn't acknowledge that behind the scenes Russia was highly unstable and had the weirdest guys running for office—it was only obvious to the rest of the world. The Administration finally got a hint of Russia's troubles when Russia went almost bankrupt in 1998. The ballyhooed up Russian stock market crumbled within days and the Russian currency collapsed overnight.

Under the leadership of the Democratic administration, the White House followed a strange foreign policy. Much was going on around the world. Virtually all of Africa had problems, the former Yugoslavia, Russia, China, North Korea, Haiti, and especially the Middle East and occasionally a few hot spots in Latin America were of great concern. It was like several active volcanoes in the final stages before massive eruptions. The ground was already shaking.

Jerome remembered the extensive research he had conducted on Nicanor in 1990, when he planned to purchase a few thousand shares in the company. Back then there was the crisis in Kuwait, because of the Iraqi aggression and invasion of that

Saudi Arab nation, with the culmination of Desert Storm. The defense business yielded billions of dollars in profits for Raytheon, Northrop, Grumman, Martin Marietta, Nicanor and hundreds of other companies.

Now, on the Web he quickly obtained an update on recent developments concerning Nicanor. He received a broad overview regarding their current projects and activities. Jerome found out that over the past few years, Nicanor had been forced to shut down several manufacturing plants. They had to lay off twenty-eight thousand people to avoid bankruptcy. After nearly two decades, John Farnsworth, who led a consortium to acquire Nicanor Industries in the late seventies, and who took the company public in the late eighties, was still Nicanor's president and CEO. According to many reports it was a tremendous challenge to change the course of the company into the direction of peace related products and services.

Jerome recalled that during the Cold War, Nicanor had manufactured the widely used W-78 331-kiloton-yield nuclear warheads. Each Peacekeeper (LGM-118) Intercontinental ballistic missile was armed with ten W-78 warheads. He was baffled by the fact that they called the nukes *Peacekeeper*—a term Ronald Reagan had invented, in hopes of making the controversial nuclear weapon more palatable. Dropping a nuke guaranteed immediate peace in the region where it detonated—meaning, everything was burnt to the ground in a flash. In 1945, hundreds of thousands of civilians were burned alive by the nuclear blasts in Hiroshima and Nagasaki. Back then the U.S. government decided to drop an atomic bomb on these two Japanese cities. Detonating nuclear warheads caused total destruction.

By all means, Jerome Birchner wasn't a pacifist, and he hated what Hitler had done to his kindred folks decades ago. But he also held the position that the nuclear holocaust in Japan was nothing short of the atrocities Hitler committed during the

Holocaust of World War II.

Jerome pictured in his mind how in a nuclear blast babies and little children were burnt alive. He could hear their screams. In slow motion he saw their little bodies fried like hot dogs on a barbecue as their skin burst and the insides fell out. Just a second or two later, these little bodies were smoking little bundles of black coal, without even as much as a hint to their former humanity. And the others who didn't die in the blast had blisters, boils and open wounds all over their bodies, and they were eaten alive by the cancer, with much pain day by day. Some were dead in a few days, others in a few weeks, months and years. He could only stand by and watch helplessly as they died. Such atrocities were truly abominable.

Nicanor manufactured tens of thousands of nuclear warheads. Under the START agreement, the number of these nuclear warheads had to be reduced to 4,900 worldwide. It was a multibillion-dollar business for Nicanor, which suddenly vanished overnight. U.S. arms sales dropped from fifteen billion dollars to only six billion dollars annually. All of a sudden, France became the world leader with sales in weaponry of eleven billion dollars. No lobbying helped. The U.S. government had turned a deaf ear to all suggestions, pleas and complaints and had simply cut funding for the defense industry substantially and immediately.

5

A FEW minutes after three o'clock in the afternoon, the phone rang. Jerome made himself ready for a swim in his Olympic-sized pool. At eighty-two degrees the water was refreshing. In his bright green Speedo trunks, Jerome moved slowly into the water, which now splashed against his kneecaps. He had a thick layer of forty-five Banana Boat sunscreen covering his upper body, arms, legs and face. The lotion left white streaks on his nose as it had been especially embalmed. Amid the tender breeze of the Gulf and in the quiet of this relaxing Florida afternoon, the buzz of the phone seemed disturbing, almost like a nasty alarm clock going off at four A.M. He reached for the cordless phone next to the pool and pressed the *Talk* button.

"Is Jerry there?" a male voice demanded at the other end of the connection.

"Yeah, I'm right here," Jerome said, momentarily not recognizing the caller.

"Hey, Jerry, it's Randy from Baltimore," the caller said enthusiastically.

"How are you? Haven't heard from you in awhile."

"I'm fine, I'm fine. Listen, I just got your e-mail. How're you doing? Are things going well with you and your family?"

"I can't complain . . . life is good."

"I have something for you. It's strictly confidential, though, . . . whatever that means." Randy Dermont sneered. "You know

Nicanor is a customer of mine . . . has been for a few years," he whispered into the receiver as if to conceal himself turning his head to the left and to the right, afraid that someone might be able to hear his splatter of secrets. After a short pause, he chuckled.

"That's something. So you know the management, and you know whatever Nicanor does?" Jerome asked, as he continued his descend into the water, which now surrounded his pelvis.

"Matter of fact, I do. They're a little panicky down there right now . . . you can imagine. I've talked to their headquarters this morning. And you saw the news about the crash and so on."

"Of course, I did, as you know I'm a news fanatic. It's because of the crash that I wrote you the e-mail. I just need a little bit more inside info to update my files. Do you know anything about this company? So far, whatever I got on Nicanor is pretty compelling. I just don't wanna miss anything."

"You know I met Farnsworth several times. Also his wife—well, at least I saw her once," Randy Dermont said.

"That's interesting." Jerome frowned.

"It took awhile to close the deal, but they placed a major order with us for drilling some laser holes a year ago. It's a custom order, you know." Randy Dermont got all excited just thinking about it.

"That sounds interesting. Is this finally the big break you were waiting for?" Jerome inquired as he vaguely smirked.

RANDY DERMONT and Jerome had been good friends for nearly a decade. Jerome met Randy Dermont in Maryland when the Birchners were still living up there. He recalled Randy Dermont desperately trying to make deals for years.

Randy Dermont owned a small company named APL, which operated out of several converted farm buildings in Hunt

Valley, Maryland. With two dozen employees they drilled micro holes with lasers for the aerospace industry—at least that was Randy Dermont's official APL story. Years ago, Jerome had stopped trying to figure out what APL was really up to. In their storage facilities thousands of used computers were stacked above each other. Randy Dermont frequently explained that in the not too distant future, these items would be very useful. According to Jerome's perception, this junk was only scrap metal and maybe not even that.

Randolph L. Dermont was the founder and president of the company. One APL expertise was to burn micro holes for various fuel systems in the Space Shuttle. Randy Dermont was especially proud of his contract with NASA and Hughes.

APL's promotional gimmick was a shiny penny with a tiny laser hole shot through Abe's pupil. The hole was only visible when the coin was held against a source of light.

Randy Dermont didn't get rich with his business, even though it paid for a generous upper middle-class lifestyle. It allowed Randy Dermont to purchase a gracious suburban home with a Mercedes and a BMW in the driveway. At least he was able to pay his bills, and most importantly, Randy Dermont never complained about anything—he appeared to be absolutely content.

His employees were mostly retired engineers and some were former CEOs of major corporations. Some worked for APL at no charge and just wanted to feel useful in some way—they just needed something to do in their spare time. Others were asking for a few hundred bucks a month to justify spending their time at APL. But all APL employees were experts in their particular field and as a result, APL was able to distinguish itself against the competition in a variety of ways.

Adding another bright color to complete the makeup of APL was Randy Dermont's flamboyant wife, Mary Anne. She was

an unforgettable blonde—an aging Marilyn Monroe type. Together with Mary Anne he attended several trade shows annually—that's when the famous Dermont parties took place.

"I HOPE so. They've placed an order for fifty thousand holes.
It'll take us another six months to bring this job to completion.
They'll pay us close to a million bucks," Randy Dermont said,
revealing some anxiety.

"Sounds great. Congrats! I guess, soon you'll be needing
some investment advice?"

"No . . . well, you know what, that's not a bad idea . . . maybe
later. As I think of it, a week ago I was in a meeting with
Farnsworth down in Dallas. They talked about offshore corporations and stuff like that. They've asked me if I see a problem
in getting paid through an offshore account. They've also asked
me not to invoice them through APL. They suggested that by
going offshore we'd save a bundle on taxes and paperwork. I
don't understand a thing about this offshore stuff. So, when they
approached me with this, I had already thought about gettin' in
touch with you. This might be something interesting for you too,
Jerry. You're still into this, aren't you?" Randy Dermont asked.

"Well, I'm still somewhat involved with things like that, and
Offshore always sounds good to me. You just have to be very
careful so that the IRS won't lock you up. But who wants to pay
taxes all the time? I think these guys in Dallas are on the right
track. It's somewhat odd though, please forgive me for saying
this, but it's very unusual that they would ask a relatively small
subcontractor like yourself to use offshore accounts. Seems like
they're not having the right people doing the job . . . but of
course, I don't know.

"What is Nicanor doing now anyway? I've read all kinds of
things about them on the Internet. Something that they're

working on nuclear reactors and things like that? Or are they selling computers and automotive parts?" Jerome was eager to find out a little more inside info on Nicanor's current business dealings.

"No cars or computers, Jerry. But you're right, they're manufacturing all kinds of equipment for nuclear power plants. During the past few years, Nicanor has become the number one nuclear power plant construction company in the world. They did the right thing. Why don't you come up here to Baltimore for a day or so and we'll chat about it? You know, we've expanded our facilities and I like to show you around. Besides, it would be nice to see you again."

"Sorry Randy, but you know I hate airplanes. I make most of my money on the phone and on the Web. Of course, in case you can get me hooked up with Nicanor somehow, I might be willing to take a trip. I wanna see you too, you know that, right? Why don't you come down here with Mary Anne for a weekend? By the way, how is she? Down here it's hot, but we love it, and it's beautiful . . . the Gulf, the beach, the sun, very relaxing, even romantic." Jerome preferred to stay around the comfort of his home. He very rarely went on a trip unless he really had to.

"Well, sounds good. I'll think about it. I haven't had a vacation in ages. And I'm sure Mary Anne would love to come. But for the next few weeks I'm pretty busy and I won't be able to take a weekend off. Jerry, let me make some phone calls about that Nicanor thing. Maybe I can get you in the door somehow. I just finished all my stuff down there last week. But whatever, I'll try to arrange a meeting for you. I've gotta check with them. I'll let you know by tomorrow, okay? I can't make any promises though, but maybe something will work out."

"Sure, let me know. I appreciate that you're thinking of me. Maybe you can get me into a meeting with their financial guys. It appears that they could use some input. Maybe I can get a piece of the action, you never know." Jerome thought about the possibilities of getting involved in a deal with Nicanor. Since these guys were already talking *Offshore*, it automatically eliminated the usual prep time. With Jerome's expertise in the area of international finance he could easily sway clients whose minds already contemplated alternatives within this amplitude.

Nuclear power plants were certainly a multibillion-dollar business, especially on an international level, Jerome thought. There would be plenty of money to go around, and perhaps it would be easy to make a few million bucks on the side, he continued the thought.

Jerome was already absentminded when the conversation with Randy Dermont ended through the exchange of a few niceties.

6

JEROME AND his family lounged by the pool and devoured chicken teriyaki sandwiches. Dennis put a couple of steaks on the barby and Vivian opened a bag of hot dogs, which she and her mom lusted after at this moment. Jerome and Birgid had two kids, Dennis and Vivian. Dennis was sixteen and Vivian had just turned fourteen a month ago.

Birgid bugged him every now and then to have another baby, but Jerome always kindly declined. Several years ago, when the subject of additional kids had been constantly on Birgid's mind, he almost gave in to the subtle pressure. He even prepared for the event by purchasing a Chevy Suburban, just in case.

They had planned cross-country trips year after year, but never went on one. Jerome finally sold the Suburban and bought the smaller Lincoln Navigator which was more than sufficient for a family of four. The whole family business was a lot of action, but Jerome and Birgid enjoyed every minute of it. He was glad that the kids were now teenagers and grew up fast through adolescence.

During the early evening hours, the phone rang.

Without waiting for Jerome's usual *Hello*, Randy Dermont said, "Jerry, it's me, Randy."

"Just a second," Birgid answered the phone.

"It's Randy," she said as she handed the cordless to Jerome.

"Well, this was quick," Jerome said. He once again was just

about ready to slip into the pool with his ankles already immersed.

"Can you come to Dallas on Monday? I've told them all about you. They really wanna see you. I didn't talk to Juliet Farnsworth directly, who runs the show at Nicanor now, but that's not important anyway. You've gotta meet these guys. They're in charge of the financial stuff down there. One of their VPs told me to bring you along."

"That sounds great. I'm surprised. You know it's very crucial that the meeting is really with someone who is in charge down there," Jerome said. He didn't count on Randy Dermont's ability to pull off arrangements for a meeting with a competent figure at Nicanor that fast. He had known Randy Dermont for too long to believe it, and in the past most such things had never worked out. It was always just a lot of hot air.

"Jerry, you're the hotshot consultant and you know everything about this offshore business. Like I said, I haven't talked to Juliet Farnsworth, because I've only met her once, and she's probably not gonna talk to me anyway. Her financial guys take care of all the money stuff. I told them a few things about you, so that they basically know who you are. They had to know a little something about you. You understand that, right?"

"Sure, Randy, whatever you say, that's fine with me. I'm definitely interested to meet these guys. I just don't wanna waste my time in a meeting with someone who isn't in charge."

"No, no, Jerry, trust me, you're going to meet the people in charge," Randy Dermont persisted.

"All right. No problem. I appreciate it," Jerome replied.

"Well, let's get down there for a day or two. I'm sure we'll have a great time and we'll meet some interesting characters. We can meet at the airport in Dallas on Monday morning? I'll send you an e-mail about my arrival time."

"Yeah, I think that'll be fine. But I can only stay for a day, because I have to be back in Florida by Monday night. They're an hour behind, this should give us plenty of time to do the job down there. Just e-mail me your schedule. Let's plan to arrive in Dallas around nine or ten in the morning," Jerome suggested. He wasn't really in the mood to take a trip. But then for the sake of nourishing his friendship with Randy Dermont, and out of curiosity, and because there was a remote chance of making a few million bucks in the process, he agreed somewhat reluctantly to the meeting.

Jerome was torn between two desires: on one hand Jerome wanted to make some money and get some action going, but on the other hand life was so comfortable without all the hustle and bustle of wheeling and dealing. He couldn't make up his mind just yet.

Due to his appointment with the Nicanor guys, Jerome had to prepare himself accordingly, which meant that he had to indulge himself into extensive homework on Nicanor before he went to Dallas. He had to know everything that was important about the company.

"I'll probably take Southwest or American. If there's a problem give me a ring. Okay?" Randy Dermont said.

"Southwest or American sounds good to me. We can meet at the baggage claim. Make sure to catch an early flight, direct if possible," Jerome suggested. He was trying to nail down a time and the schedule for the meeting. He knew exactly how chaotic Randy Dermont could become in respect to banal details.

"Sure, no problem, Jerry. It's going to be all right. Trust me, some day you'll thank me for this. I'll meet you in Dallas Monday morning. Okay, see ya, buddy!" Randy Dermont hung up.

* * *

JEROME COULD'VE chartered a Learjet, but so far the whole thing was rather an adventurous leisure trip than a serious business prospect. That's why first class was just fine with him for right now. He usually began most of his deals on a casual note. Once a deal became solidified by signing a contract, securing a retainer, and a specific budget had been established, money was spent rather generously to make sure the deal didn't lack anything.

Customer satisfaction and quality workmanship were always utmost priority on Jerome's list of objectives. He strongly believed in the apothegm of doing things right the first time or not even bothering to begin a work at all. Mistakes could've been very costly for Jerome and his clients. Therefore, before he accepted a contract, every potential deal was meticulously evaluated. Once a deal had been approved, he made sure that each contract was completed on schedule and in the most professional way he knew how.

7

BOTH RANDY DERMONT and Jerome Birchner arrived at DFW airport around ten o'clock on Monday morning. Everything worked out fine. Jerome waited only a few minutes at the agreed upon meeting spot at the baggage claim until Randy Dermont emerged from the direction of the rest rooms.

"Good to see ya!" Randy Dermont was hollering as he approached Jerome.

"How's it goin' Randy?" Jerome said as the two men embraced. "What's the plan?"

"I guess we just walk over to a rental place and get us a car. Or you wanna jump into a cab?" Randy Dermont asked.

"You know what, I already took the liberty and made reservations at Hertz, right over there. Is this all right with you? I usually like to drive myself, but whatever you say is fine with me." Jerome had the visit well planned, especially concerning such details. Any element of chance regarding banal particulars had to be eliminated. Jerome suggested the rental car company by pointing through the exit doors of the terminal. All rental cars were located in the parking garage across from the terminal.

Randy Dermont nodded in agreement. "Sure," he said. He was dressed in his usual dark blue pinstripe suit. Randy Dermont had two of the same kind. His white shirt was decorated with a bright yellow tie—certainly one of Mary Anne's delicate choices.

Jerome was clothed in a sandstone silk suit. It made him look a little flamboyant, especially with the big shiny Breitling Chronograph flashing on his left wrist. His tie was still rolled up inside the leather portfolio which he had squeezed between his left elbow and chest.

Outside the terminal they walked across four lanes to the parking garage. At the Hertz rental counter the keys to a silver Lincoln were promptly handed to Jerome. Both men opened the door to the vehicle simultaneously. Jerome put his leather portfolio on the driver's seat. He adjusted the right combination to unlock it and to pry out the tie.

"I really hate these things," Jerome commented as he proficiently slung the slice of silk around his neck. He hated wearing neckties with a passion. Jerome avoided putting these things on as much as he could. But whenever he was forced to wear a tie he delayed binding it around his neck for as long as possible.

THEY HEADED several miles southeast to Irving where the headquarters of Nicanor Industries were located. At the entry gate, security was tight and at first it seemed as if Jerome and Randy Dermont wouldn't even be let in.

"Hi, gentlemen. Do you have an appointment?" one security officer asked through an open window in the booth.

"Sure do," Randy Dermont answered as he leaned over to Jerome's side, so that the security guard could get a better look at his face.

"May I ask with who?"

"It's with the big guys up there. Fred Hancock and Mrs. Farnsworth." Randy Dermont hesitated to name Mrs. Farnsworth. He wasn't sure if she'd be attending the meeting.

"Okay, sir, it'll take us a minute to verify. Your driver's licenses please," the officer requested.

"Mine too?" Randy Dermont asked.

"Yes, sir," the guard replied.

Jerome made a face and removed the driver's license from his wallet. It took two guards ten minutes to authenticate their identities and to confirm their visit. While the one guard was on the phone checking with the visitors desk, the other was hammering wildly on a PC.

The PC was hooked up to a high-tech ID system. With today's technology it was possible to verify the identity of virtually every legitimate person living in the U.S., Canada, and in Western Europe. Every person that had ever applied for a credit card, or had been issued a driver's license, or was registered somewhere with a phone number including wireless devices, or had a social security number, or had once obtained a passport, or only set up an e-mail address, it was a sure bet that this person's ID had been stored in the system.

After approval, both Randy Dermont and Jerome had to sign a visitor's sheet. The security guard handed two already pre-printed sheets on a clipboard to Jerome. Their driver's licenses were also attached to the clipboard. They were asked to park their rental car at a small parking lot to the right near the entry gate. A white minivan followed them. The minivan chauffeured the two men to the main entrance of the stylish Nicanor HQ building.

The facade was made out of a blend of symmetrically arranged dark blue and silver mirrored glass squares. The entrance steps were solid light gray marble. Some areas of the inside walls around the lobby also featured sections of inlaid marble. All wall elements and staircase railings were accentuated with brass inlets and applications.

"Is this a new place?" Jerome asked.

"They just built it a couple of years ago. They sure don't hold back on the buck, wouldn't you say?" Randy Dermont answered with excitement.

As they entered the building they had to pass through a metal detector. Randy Dermont's attaché case floated effortlessly on a belt through the X-ray machine, which was located just next to the metal detector, and appeared similar to security checkpoints at most airports. Jerome left his leather portfolio in the Lincoln and only carried a small notebook in his left hand. Beyond the metal detector a security guard checked both men for hidden handguns or other potentially dangerous devices.

Once they had passed through all the security checks they stood in front of a desk with a rather small *Receptionist* sign bolted to the top. The receptionist didn't smile, and she requested IDs in a very official manner. She took their driver's licenses and photocopied or scanned these documents quickly on a desktop device. Then she handed Randy Dermont a guest book of sorts.

"Please put your name in there and sign right next to it," the receptionist commanded in her sweet little Texan twang. She stretched out her index finger, settling it forcefully on a prepared line.

"Both of us?" Randy Dermont inquired while searching for a pen inside his jacket.

"Please, if you would," she requested now politely with a vague smirk on her face, tilting her head slightly to the left. She produced a pen and placed it on the guest book.

"Thanks," Randy Dermont said.

Jerome and Randy Dermont put their names into the *Visitors* book. After they completed this procedure, the receptionist took her pen back and added information to the entries. Then she returned their driver's licenses as she waved with her left hand lightly through the air. Promptly a security guard walked across the entrance hall to the receptionist's desk.

"Show them to the executive suite," the receptionist ordered the security guard.

He showed them to an elevator in the back of the foyer. The

guard stepped into the cabin after Jerome and Randy Dermont had entered the elevator.

"Is this always such a hassle?" Jerome asked Randy Dermont.

"Yeah, sure is, unless they give you their special ID. And even then it's not much easier. They don't trust anybody. So far, I haven't been issued a special ID and I'm not in a hurry to get one either. I'm only a small supplier and I only come here once in a while, so I don't really care if I have one or not," Randy Dermont explained.

"Why wouldn't you be interested in getting a privileged Nicanor ID?" Jerome placed the question with a grin.

"Yeah, yeah. You know the book of Revelation talks about the mark of the beast. And that's exactly what this is. They implant some sort of infrared chip on the back of your right hand. 'It doesn't hurt,' they say, and it only takes a second. It's actually some type of lasting impression in or under your skin, and it's invisible to the naked eye. It's a pretty new thing and they say it can store all kinds of data. The information can also be updated in seconds with certain machines. There's supposedly nobody on earth that has the same chip, something like your very own artificial DNA. They've just started doing this a couple of months ago. I guess you wouldn't join the club either? Huh?" Randy Dermont produced a short cough-like chuckle.

"You got that right, but it's sure interesting," Jerome didn't hesitate with his response.

Security guards were everywhere, and all of them exposed a reliable Austrian-made Glock 21 (caliber .45 ACP) in their holsters.

8

ALL EXECUTIVE offices were on the top level of the seven-story building. The security officer stayed in the elevator when the cabin door of the elevator opened. One of many Nicanor vice presidents, Fred Hancock, welcomed the two men. He escorted them to Mrs. Farnsworth's office.

"Great to see you, gentlemen," Hancock said. He was pretty relaxed. And while he didn't shake their hands, Hancock appeared to be outgoing and friendly as he smiled and was soft spoken.

Dressed in black, Juliet Farnsworth stood in the rear right corner of the office, next to the somewhat hidden kitchenette. She held a glass of bourbon. Mrs. Farnsworth appeared to be absentminded for just a minute as she stared through a window.

"Mr. Dermont and Mr. Birchner are here," Fred Hancock announced their visit calmly.

Juliet Farnsworth emerged from the back of the room and approached Jerome and Randy Dermont.

"Welcome gentlemen," she said like a grand duchess in a professional manner. "Have a seat," she continued as she showed them to the black leather sofa in the center of the room. Mrs. Farnsworth didn't shake their hands either. Once a very important gesture, it was very obvious that handshakes had become too intimate, at least here at Nicanor.

"I'd like to offer my sincere condolences, Mrs. Farnsworth.

I'm very sorry about your husband," Randy Dermont said with an uncertain shaky voice to open the conversation on a formal note.

"Thank you, Mr. Dermont, it's truly a tragedy. John was an excellent businessman," Mrs. Farnsworth replied with the typical Texan drawl common to the area.

"And you are . . . Mr. Birchner, I assume? Did I pronounce it right?" she inquired as she turned to Jerome locking her eyes with his.

"Nice to meet you, Mrs. Farnsworth," Jerome said with a smooth but definite tone as he nodded slightly.

"Let's get right down to business, gentlemen. Should we? I can assure you, Mr. Dermont, not much will change here, at least not for now. Sometimes suppliers have the fear that they'll lose their contract when there are changes at the top. But this won't be the case here.

"While we've never met personally, Mr. Dermont, I've looked over your file this morning, and I must say that everything looks good to me. You probably also know from the press releases that I've actively participated in the management of Nicanor Industries for the past several years. I've run the company with John together as a team. I'm also proud to say that I'm a hands-on executive, so I pretty much know everything that's going on around here." Mrs. Farnsworth didn't waste any time to establish her authority and leadership precipitately.

"That's good to know, Mrs. Farnsworth. You sure have a great company here. It's always a pleasure to do business with you," Randy Dermont assured her with a sigh of relief.

She was right, suppliers often feared that their contracts were in danger of termination whenever changes took place at the top. Randy Dermont was no exception and he knew very well that more often than not it meant cutbacks—streamlining they called it. Usually the new CEO had to prove himself to the board and the shareholders. This was easily accomplished by cutting unnecessary costs, which meant the implementation of drastic measures to eliminate certain employment opportunities and the proficient act of renegotiating contracts with suppliers. That's how they superficially added to the bottom line, at least on paper, and in the early phase of their executive appointment.

Randy Dermont had seen it over and over again. Of course, in the case of Mrs. Farnsworth, she didn't have to prove her expertise because she had already been the Co-CEO for several years. Now she was the only boss at Nicanor. In the perception of many it was still more difficult for a woman to fit the role of such a powerful position than it would've been for a man. But then they hadn't met Juliet Farnsworth yet.

"Thank you, Mr. Dermont. Nicanor is truly a great company and we want to keep it that way. We all know what it means to work hard to reach our goals. It's a team effort and we must all work together. When I graduated from Yale, not too long ago, and got married to John, I've made it my mission in life to support him in his efforts to spruce up Nicanor to one of the finest companies in the world." The saying about Yale wasn't so much as to underscore her qualifications to run Nicanor with credibility, but rather a blatant effort to deceive both men regarding her true age. She was certainly not interested in revealing this little detail to them.

Juliet Farnsworth had a slender body. Her long dark hair fell like silk in a stylish flow over her tender shoulders, reducing her age at least in appearance by a decade. She seemed to be in her early thirties rather than her actual early forties. In fact, she had already graduated as valedictorian from Yale some fifteen years ago.

Early in their marriage, Juliet had accidently conceived a child by John. Abortion was out of the question, even though a baby didn't suit their plans. Virtually every night, during the first six months of her pregnancy, Juliet cried herself to sleep. One day John had had enough as he no longer was able to just stand by and look at Juliet's psychological deterioration. He didn't know where to turn, so he arranged for a female yoga instructor to visit Juliet several times a week. As the delivery date neared, Juliet actually became very excited about the new life in her womb. And when the baby girl was finally born, she adored her dearly and catered to her every wish and need with abundant motherly love.

It was a sad morning in the Farnsworth household when only a couple of months after her birth the apparently healthy little girl was found dead in her crib. The doctors attributed the death to SIDS. It was a shock for Juliet, and for a season bitterness had overcome her. During this difficult time she was never seen smiling. Instead, Juliet had become dead serious about every little thing and often erupted fiercely angry, throwing all kinds of handy articles after employees in the Nicanor offices. She cried for hours every day, desperately trying to blame herself, John, the doctors and everybody around her about the tragedy. In the end she couldn't find anyone to accept responsibility for the death of her child and Juliet used God as the ultimate scapegoat.

She desperately attempted to rid herself of the oppressive grieve by plunging herself wholeheartedly with all her energy, creativity, and capacity into the tough business world of Nicanor Industries.

It was Juliet Farnsworth who had a secretary, not John, because she alone was John's very personal assistant, she insisted. Before somebody was able to get through to John, they had to pass her much dreaded interrogation process.

"NEVER BECAME a lawyer . . . there was no time for it.

Especially not after we had to change the course of the company," Juliet continued. The sorrow was gone and a decisive businesswoman emerged.

With just one turn she seemingly changed her look from a mourning widow to support the appearance of a successful Fortune-500 CEO. In her black suit with just above-knee-length skirt she projected a seductively attractive image. "Sex sells," was the prevalent aphorism in the highly competitive world of marketing. The black thigh highs added flavor and underlined such a first impression forcefully.

"I've heard that you're very knowledgeable in the field of international finance, Mr. Birchner. In fact, I just received your book last Friday. So far, I couldn't find the time to read it though, but at least I was able to scan through it. Sure looks interesting. Are you are tax lawyer or something, Mr. Birchner?" Juliet Farnsworth began her skillful inquisition of Jerome Birchner as she only occasionally looked at him.

Her southern accent sounded kind of cute, Jerome thought. Without further ado he replied, "No, I'm not a lawyer. I'm a corporate consultant in the area of corporate efficiency."

"What exactly is it that you do for your clients, Mr. Birchner?"

"I help companies save money and lower their tax burden. For our clients we take care of all the paperwork and arrange for the financial intricacies. We do lots of things differently than your average tax lawyer, and in fact, you won't find too many firms that are as experienced as we are. I also help 'em put together the deal as we prepare the research and assist in the negotiations. And, if a client so desires, we also help 'em invest their profits later on." Jerome paused for a few seconds and shrugged his left shoulder.

"Everything is top professional work and we only use proven methods . . . and we're low profile. No fancy press and things like that." He looked at her like a puppy. Even though he still had this kind of salesman approach, at this moment, he really didn't care if anything would come out of this trip or not. The whole experience was already worth the journey.

"As you may know, Mr. Birchner, and I assume you've done your homework, Nicanor Industries is the premier nuclear-power-plant construction company in the world. During restructuring we had to lay off a lot of people. It was really a struggle in the mid-nineties, but for the last few years we've been involved as lead counsel in this megadeal in Korea." Juliet explained some details.

"Pardon me, Mrs. Farnsworth, is it North or South Korea, or are you not at liberty to say?" Jerome interrupted as he was curious regarding this issue.

"It's the North, Mr. Birchner. The U.S. government approved the project and has put Nicanor in charge of it. Actually, because John has a lot of friends in Washington. You must know that the folks in Congress had known my husband for years and they trusted his judgment completely. He had extensive experience in this area.

"Originally, it was supposed to be a ten-billion-dollar deal, but according to our latest figures we're a little over budget and we're edging closer to sixteen billion now. Not everybody likes that.

"Oh, by the way, while some of the information I'm telling you is public knowledge and has been floating around in the press for quite some time, I must remind you, Mr. Birchner, that nothing of what we discuss within these walls can ever leave this room. It's for your ears only. I can trust you for that, Mr. Birchner? It's all classified," Mrs. Farnsworth said, strongly emphasizing this point with an inquiring frown.

"Of course, Mrs. Farnsworth, you can trust me. I've been in this business too long not to know any better and I've never let a client down. It's all strictly confidential and as you know we signed the 'Confidentiality Agreement' at the front desk," Jerome answered in an attempt to assure her of his integrity.

"Okay, I just had to throw this in as I don't know you that well, Mr. Birchner. Maybe we should discuss everything over lunch. Let's catch a ride down to the Hyatt. They have a great restaurant on top of the Reunion Tower," Mrs. Farnsworth said abruptly to end the conversation for now.

All four stood up.

"Mr. Dermont you come with me. I'll show you the labs. That'll be more interesting to you and I'll introduce you to some of our technicians and engineers," Fred Hancock said to Randy Dermont.

"You'll be all right?" Randy Dermont asked Jerome.

"Sure. I think I'm in very good hands," Jerome answered with a grin. He turned to follow Juliet to the bank of elevators.

All four stepped into the same cabin one by one. In the gigantic foyer Randy Dermont waved goodbye to Jerome. A Nicanor limousine waited for Mrs. Farnsworth and Jerome to drive them to downtown Dallas.

9

ON THE way to the Hyatt, Jerome mentioned to Juliet that two percent of the population in Dallas was of German descent. He gave her a few other stats, some even comical in nature, so that she would loosen up a bit as she acted rather stiff. She may have carried on mourning the loss of her husband, which happened only a week ago, and this was certainly understandable, he thought.

A memorial service was held over the weekend at the Farnsworth mansion in Tarrant County near Dallas. It was a funeral without a coffin. Only an enlarged photograph of John Farnsworth in a picture frame stood in front of the temporary altar amid generous flower arrangements. His corpse hadn't been recovered yet. In fact, no bodies were found and slowly the brutal reality set in as last glimmers of hope evaporated.

JEROME FOLLOWED always a highly professional approach. Each deal was carefully selected based on a sophisticated formula for success. Each complexus and situation was unique. While the money was the driving force behind his occupation as a corporate consultant, he also immersed himself into each case with proficiency in the pursuit of perfection to avoid costly and often devastating mistakes. Over the last several years Jerome had been involved in less than a half dozen deals.

There were other guys just like him that were far more popular than he was. Most of them had an education from an Ivy League college, which Jerome didn't have. Often, these guys would write bestselling books on tax avoidance and receive hefty fees by touring the seminar and conference circuit as keynote speakers. Frequently, even in public, they proudly identified Fortune-500 companies on their client list—that's a thing Jerome frowned upon. There were too many confidential and sensitive issues at stake.

Due to the fact that the clientele usually consisted of high-profile tycoons with their well-known publicly traded companies, it wasn't easy for these corporate consultants to keep a low profile. They were as visible as trial lawyers when it came to a major court case. Some of these consultants had become celebrities themselves as they were frequently interviewed on national radio and television shows.

Jerome went the other way and had put a lot of effort into reducing his exposure over the past couple of years. No longer did he participate in the distribution frenzy of exaggerated press releases and PR articles with chichi pictures of his extravagant lifestyle. At the brink of retirement, Jerome had no need to be ostentatious to obtain wealthy new clients. In fact, he didn't even want any new clients.

In recent years, most of his deals were around a hundred million dollars. For his involvement, Jerome could easily pocket two million dollars in customary fees, and in the end his take was often twice or even three times that amount, depending on the individual contract.

He completed his most recent deal about nine months ago. He had been hired as lead counsel by a German conglomerate to take one of their international divisions public in the U.S. With virtually one sweep he arranged a joint venture for the German company to open a manufacturing plant in North

Carolina for their optical precision products. It took him nearly six months of hard work, day and night, to wrap up the deal, but things had worked out just fine. After all his independent associates and research specialists were paid off, his net profit was almost twenty million dollars. It was the largest fee he had ever collected until now. His net worth received a substantial boost because of this particular deal.

Jerome wasn't eagerly hunting the dream of becoming a billionaire, but a few hundred million in the bank were certainly better than sixty million, he thought. The desire, and yes, even the lust to have more money and to perhaps hit the jackpot some day, kept him on his toes looking for potential megadeals. And he only considered megadeals. Everything else wasn't even worth looking at.

A net worth of sixty million wasn't enough to own a personal Gulfstream V, he argued with himself. When put into a money market fund, sixty million yielded only about $2.1 million p.a. in interest after taxes. Almost every day Jerome reflected upon these numbers and concluded that while sixty million wasn't that bad of a nest egg, it was simply not enough—at least not for him.

After every deal he'd say that this one was now the final one. But half a year later he again contemplated the possibilities of participating in just one more deal, which would definitely be the last one, he promised himself and Birgid.

THE REVOLVING restaurant atop the Reunion Tower had a romantic touch to its ambience. The lights were turned way down low and the tinted windows promised intimacy, accentuated by flickering candles at every table. At this time of the day the restaurant was supposedly a place for business luncheons, but Jerome observed plenty of couples holding hands like lovebirds, drinking wine, and even pecking each other on the cheek—one couple was even lost in each other's mouth.

Juliet Farnsworth had loosened up and enjoyed the company of charming Jerome Birchner. Jerome was only a few years younger than Juliet and their chemistry appeared to be intact. The reflection of the candles on their table produced a sparkle in her eyes. Juliet put her elbows on the table, and folded her hands in a vertical position as if in prayer. Occasionally, she rested her chin lightly on top of the folded hands and gazed into his eyes as she listened to his amusing little stories, which were even more entertaining because of Jerome's German accent.

Mrs. Farnsworth had a few secrets she wouldn't dare share with Jerome. In fact, she knew quite a bit about him. The chief of security at Nicanor had handed her a dossier about Jerome Birchner just a few hours after Randy Dermont had initially called to inquire about the visit to the Nicanor headquarters. And then, before the weekend she received an even thicker folder inspissated with over five hundred pages of comprehensive information about Jerome Birchner. She fervently studied report after report and was intrigued by his somewhat mysterious persona.

The folder encompassed a considerable amount of files and a series of briefs from various government agencies. The INS, SEC, IRS, FINCEN and the CIA all had files on Jerome Birchner. Only the FBI didn't have anything aside from his finger prints. Those were filed with the FBI during his immigration proceedings a few years earlier. Because of his extensive immigration documentation, the INS had virtually volumes on Jerome Birchner. The first documents in their database dated back to the early eighties.

The SEC established a *Birchner* file when he once headed an offshore investment group in the early nineties. Some third-party information about supposedly awkward securities transactions involving U.S. investors had surfaced. Nosy as the SEC was, they couldn't resist taking a closer look at this piece of highly interesting lowdown. They investigated Jerome vigorously, twice ordering a search of his home office. No substantial evidence turned up though. After they couldn't find anything incriminating and no illegal activities were reported or discovered, the SEC reluctantly withdrew. They thought they could cash in on Birchner. The SEC was hoping for at least a million-dollar fine for some ridiculous minor violation of the Securities Act.

But the SEC was out of luck and tapped around in the dark like a blind man. Jerome made certain that his corporate structures and deals were configured in the most proficient and sophisticated manner. If someone had the crazy idea to go after him, he sure wouldn't make it easy for them to nail him. Pursuing such a tedious task would've been very hard work indeed as Jerome had placed booby traps and dead ends everywhere.

The IRS, of course, couldn't stand the guy. They hated Jerome Birchner, especially because of his provocative publications regarding tax avoidance. Over the years, he had been actively involved in helping a number of corporations and wealthy individuals to legally avoid paying hundreds of millions of dollars in income taxes.

Once, several years ago, when the IRS had been first made aware of Birchner's activities, they wanted to charge him with conspiracy in aiding one of his clients to defraud the Federal government in a highly popularized tax-evasion scheme. Based on a number of recommendations by influential politicians, the IRS had been asked to back off. In the end they decided not to prosecute Jerome Birchner on the intended charges and dropped the case altogether. Jerome was forced to pay a lot of money to a team of top-notch Washington lawyers to fend the IRS off.

These lawyers distributed several hundred thousand dollars in campaign contributions to candidates of both political parties. Fighting guys like Birchner was nothing less than kicking against the pricks, the IRS eventually concluded. He would initiate a media circus and this was simply too risky for the IRS at that time as such a rumble in the press would've ruined or at least tainted their new nice-guy image campaign. They were desperately trying to portray themselves as a friendly and helpful government agency.

FINCEN, based in Arlington, Virginia, had been watching Birchner for years. His name was associated with several massive money transactions. But all transactions were properly filed according to legal requirements. Foreign corporations incorporated in exotic locations were often named in these dealings. The wires originated in all kinds of countries around the globe. Often sums of tens of millions of dollars were just passing through accounts in the U.S. and were immediately channeled to other accounts in Canada, Switzerland or England. FINCEN couldn't find anything criminal yet, but they were watching.

The CIA couldn't figure him out. Jerome had dual citizenship. He was an Austrian citizen and had obtained U.S. citizenship a couple of years ago. He didn't hide his lifestyle of a multimillionaire. The file stated that Jerome resided at least fifty weeks of the year in the United States, but paid only nominal income taxes in the U.S. His 1040s indicated that he derived very little official income from sources in the U.S.

Of course, Jerome owned numerous foreign corporations and most of these existed only on paper. Nobody really knew for sure and the CIA had its own theory about such things. Outside the U.S. he only owned insignificant real estate in Canada. The little farm in Alberta served as an emergency refuge, just in case. It was more of a mental backdrop than anything else for Jerome. Since he had bought it some three years ago, he had visited the place only once for a few hours. He was seriously considering selling it now.

Instead of the small farm in Alberta, he was eyeing a premier piece of ranch real estate near Jackson Hole, Wyoming. It was located just across from where Harrison Ford had his 800-acre estate. Since he became a U.S. citizen, he felt more comfortable to invest in U.S. property. But Jerome was still not motivated enough to go through with the purchase in Wyoming.

He argued that it was simply too cold up there and he would probably end up spending only a week or two each year at such a remote location. Jerome wasn't interested in spending money on things he wouldn't use adequately. The asking price for the Jackson Hole ranch was just below seven million dollars. It was something to think about and a precipitated decision was certainly not the appropriate approach, he thought.

The CIA files noted that from 1991 through 1997 he left the U.S. with his family once a year. Jerome Birchner supposedly traveled around the globe, often within less than a week. Birchner had money and neither the CIA nor the IRS were able to figure out how exactly his net worth had legally accumulated. They estimated his net worth somewhere in the neighborhood of ten to twenty million dollars. And since it wasn't that much money after all, they didn't bother to pursue an investigation into the origin of his wealth.

Based on the FINCEN records, they speculated that he had most of his fortune outside the U.S. They figured that he perhaps transferred funds here and then to the U.S. as needed. The CIA concluded that most of his fortune had been family money from Europe, but they didn't know for sure.

Birchner posed as a corporate consultant and private investor. As a private investor he never surfaced in any SEC filings. This wasn't that awkward because he himself never bought sizeable equity positions in the measure that would require filings with the SEC. For his deals that demanded SEC filings, he customarily used only offshore corporations. In such a case no ownership disclosure of the actual owners of that certain foreign entity was required.

The CIA and IRS knew that he was the author of several books on the subject of tax avoidance. But they also tracked the annual sales figures of his books and those numbers were insignificant as he rarely ever sold more than a few thousand copies in any given year. Based on his 1040s he seemingly derived virtually all his income from such meager book sales, and some royalties as an orator at occasional speaking engagements.

When Jerome had spent a couple of weekends in Japan a few years ago, with trade embargoes and sanctions in effect, the IRS in cooperation with U.S. Customs and the CIA was hoping to nail Birchner for espionage or some other violation. He had helped a few U.S. companies circumvent the trade embargo, utilizing foreign corporations aided by entities within the European Union.

Once again the IRS was left in the dark and couldn't prove a thing. Neither investigators from the IRS nor the CIA were able to come up with anything substantial. Instead, while not discarding the file entirely, they had to put the file away to let it gather some more dust.

Juliet Farnsworth was enthralled by what she read in this exhaustive folder. Jerome was her man—he was the right one for the job.

10

AS OF now, Jerome still had to learn the exact details of Nicanor's pending deals. His interest was especially centered in this certain megadeal in North Korea. He also had to find out more about the financial state of Nicanor. Nuclear power plants were fine with him and he didn't have an ear for these wacky environmentalists—weirdos who preached that cars were the curse of the earth.

Mrs. Farnsworth began to make sense in the conversation, explaining sketchy particulars about the construction site in North Korea.

"John told me that our financial affairs were set up in Switzerland and some preparations were made in Uruguay. But nobody really knows for sure. He took care of it and he had made most of these arrangements. Especially over the past couple of years, John had educated himself extensively in these things. Even though the U.S. government trusted him blindly, he in return didn't trust the U.S. government at all. He'd always put some money aside, just in case."

"Are you aware of any offshore companies that you may have right now, or a trust or something else?" Jerome inquired.

"All I know is that we have a numbered Swiss bank account and that's it. I've got access to it and I just checked the balance earlier this morning. Based on those numbers, I don't think any money had been removed or transferred to Uruguay or anywhere else. It seems that all the money is in Switzerland. Of course, we do have a couple of brokerage accounts here in the U.S., but that's just for the record. And these are official accounts. I don't think you care much about those.

"You must also consider that we didn't have a major deal since we had to close down our production facilities for the warheads several years ago. The government had canceled all our contracts. We were forced to discontinue our warhead operation immediately. As you know we almost went bankrupt. All our private arrangements were dissolved to save the company, except the Swiss bank account which didn't have a lot of money back then anyway," Juliet said. Somewhat incensed from reflecting on the past, she inhaled an extra portion of smoke from her cigarette and released it all at once in a long sigh of relief toward the ceiling.

Jerome listened intently as Juliet continued with her narrative.

"In fact, this Korea deal is a considerable chance to establish Nicanor as the industry leader on a global basis, and at the same time guarantee its survival for years to come. The Koreans have already paid us half of the bill and the project is near completion. We have to finish it up quickly though, so that we can get the other half, which includes our profit. We desperately need the final payments to boost our cash flow.

"On this contract Nicanor is going to net about two billion dollars. It may sound like a lot, and I'm sure it is, but if everything would've worked out perfectly, we could've made at least a billion more. To be blunt, Mr. Birchner, from the remaining payments I need at least half a billion dollars for my own account. I want to play it safe this time. 9-1-1 won't take my call if something goes wrong. Do you understand me, Mr. Birchner?"

"Sure, I do," Jerome said with assurance while Juliet

executed a short breather.

"This time around I won't be left in the cold like last time. If something happens, at least I'll be able to continue my lifestyle. You know the ranch, the jet, the yacht, the vacation homes in Bermuda and in Vail, and all the other nice little things in life. It wasn't easy, you know. It was very hard work and it still is," Juliet said with some bitterness. But she was tough and calculated every move.

Juliet Farnsworth was a fighter and the world champion title was up for grabs. Nothing could stop her now. Jerome Birchner arrived at the scene at the right time. He was sent from heaven and he would seal her sinister plan, she thought. Juliet was convinced that he was the guy who could apply the necessary skill to make her subtle and vicious scheme successful.

Nice little deal, Mrs. Farnsworth. That's exactly what I was dreamin' of: half a billion bucks in the bank . . . this sure makes for a sweet retirement, Jerome thought to himself as Mrs. Farnsworth shared her intentions.

Jerome never asked his clients if their deals were legit throughout, unless it appeared that drugs may have been involved, or if it smelled like fraud, robbery, or Mob money. In such a case he wouldn't have touched the assignment. But regarding Juliet Farnsworth, things sounded basically all right. Here was a big company and a widow working very hard to establish her nest egg. *Half a billion bucks . . . some nest egg,* he continued the thought.

"Okay, if you want me to get involved in this, we can start right now. All we need is a few offshore corporations, at least that's what I'd suggest. Within less than a week you're on your way to your five hundred million bucks, or even more if you like. Just let me know if you want your name anywhere or if you prefer some anonymous third parties, which I'll arrange. I mean, I have a few good friends that can act as the officers and shareholders of these offshore companies, and your name will never appear on anything. And my friends don't mind making a little bit of money on the side."

"But can strangers be trusted?" She asked concerned.

"Of course, they can be trusted, don't worry, I've worked with them before. Trust me, Mrs. Farnsworth, it's gonna be perfect. That's the least thing we have to worry about. But let me ask you this: How much do you think we'll have to run through the accounts? If I understand it correctly, you want at least half a billion stashed away? I'm just asking for your guess because you know your business better than I do. I need to know what your comfort level is," Jerome inquired.

He was curious and already had an idea about how much dough he had to process to move half a billion aside. Within another ten seconds he'd have the right figures for his fee together. The total was rapidly adding up in his mind.

"I'm not really sure, Mr. Birchner . . . haven't figured it out yet. You should know, that's your job, Mr. Birchner. You have to come up with the numbers. Give me an estimate. I'm at a loss right now. All I know is that we still have about eight billion to play with. But I'm also aware of the fact that we won't be able to touch all of it." She paused and took her time to light up another cigarette, inhaling the first drag slowly.

"My guess is that in order to get a hold of five hundred million without attracting too much attention, we probably need to consider a flow of something like three to five billion. From the eight, we have access to about five. We should probably use all five. The rest comes directly from the U.S. government to Nicanor and we won't be able to touch any of that. So you tell me, Mr. Birchner," Mrs. Farnsworth said with no uncertain gesture. She was enjoying her smoke, watching his response intently.

Jerome's mind was racing. He smiled. "That's a lot of money. But I think your guess is pretty much on target. The more money we handle the easier it will be to get a hold of your cut. A flow of three billion should do, but if you want more we need to float another billion or so.

"Depending on the final amount that I must handle, my fee will be a minimum of, let's say forty million bucks, and perhaps as much as eighty million all fees considered. The fees alone are usually one percent of the total money flow. You must take in account that the banks charge at least a quarter of a point for each deposit and another quarter point for the transfers. It's better to work with a full percentage point to make sure all transaction fees are covered. I'd say eighty million should do," Jerome answered. He was excited, and he played with open cards. On this deal he'd make a fortune, no doubt about it, he thought.

His net worth would increase by over fifty percent and who knows, maybe there's a bonus somewhere, he contemplated. It was a lot of money and it was rather easy to make an extra ten million on a deal of this magnitude. Finally, retirement at forty with a hundred million in the bank was no longer out of reach.

"Well, Mr. Birchner, it's worth it. I need my five hundred million. I don't really care how you'll pull it off . . . just get me my money. I'll guarantee your fee of forty million plus the applicable transaction fees as you say, which brings the total to about eighty million. I figured about a hundred million for everything.

"That sounds good to me and we still have some room to play with. If things work out as planned, and if in one way or the other you, Mr. Birchner, can get me another hundred million, I'll appreciate it. In this case I'll guarantee you that you'll pocket at least a fifty-million-dollar fee tax free just for yourself. How is that? Mr. Birchner." Juliet smiled, and winking as if initiating a flirt.

"Sounds good to me too, Mrs. Farnsworth. I guess, you've

got yourself a deal," Jerome said.

"When we get back to the office, I'll make arrangements for let's say ten million bucks? Is that sufficient to get you started, Mr. Birchner? You'll have the money by tomorrow."

"Ten million is fine. That'll get us things going with no problem."

"As for timing, everything must be completed before the end of the year. My schedule is actually set for a four-month period for everything. You, of course, will act independently, and you'll never use my name. Mark that down, Mr. Birchner. Only on the account where my money is going to end up, you must use my name. Matter of fact, I must be the sole signatory on this account. I want all of the six hundred million in this account . . . that's a good idea," she commanded. Her eyes froze as she looked directly at him.

"You have to set it up so that nobody else but me can touch the money," she continued. Then Juliet leaned toward him and lowered her voice, "That includes you, Mr. Birchner. You can set it up, but I don't want you or anyone else but me, to have access to it. Have I made myself clear? Just keep me posted on how things are progressing. Never tell anybody under any circumstances about this arrangement. You'll only report to me personally. Do you understand, Mr. Birchner?" Mrs. Farnsworth insisted.

"Sure, ma'am, of course. It's our little secret so to speak." Jerome wasn't about to be intimidated by her big numbers and bossy attitude. He could handle her. She could trust him.

"I'll get you all the necessary details regarding the payment schedule from the Koreans and the U.S. government in a few days. You'll see it's going to be easier than it may sound right now. Let's talk about the general procedures on the way back to the office. Enjoy your lunch, Mr. Birchner."

* * *

A SHORT pause followed as both stared in each other's eyes intently.

"One more thing, Mr. Birchner. Don't ever think for a moment about double-crossing me," Mrs. Farnsworth issued the deadly warning.

Slightly incensed, Jerome interrupted her immediately. "Mrs. Farnsworth, I've told you that I act with absolute integrity. I don't rip my clients off. But in the process, lots of things will happen that under normal circumstances may look awkward to you. But that's the way things work. You've gotta trust me.

"In your specific case I depend on you to pay me. Usually I deduct my fee during the transaction, but in this deal I can't even do that, I've gotta trust you to pay me." He emphasized this point with a gesture of his right hand. "And I expect you to always pay me on time. I have to sleep at night and I don't need trouble. These are the only deals that I can accept. It has to be smooth and I don't wanna worry about certain essential things like trust, payment, and so forth. You know what I mean, Mrs. Farnsworth?" Jerome issued his own warning.

"I didn't want to offend you, Mr. Birchner. You're a very capable man, and I know I can count on you. But with all that has been going on in the past and now the death of my husband, you have to understand that I don't trust too many people anymore. I'm sure you can follow, right?" Juliet pleaded with her lips and with somewhat teary eyes for him to comprehend her fears. Then she put her hand gently on his as a gesture of affirmation.

Jerome replied with an effort to comfort her. "Mrs. Farnsworth, I understand. But you've gotta trust me in this. My business is based upon trust, and you can check my references. Every client will tell you that I did excellent work for them and I've never ever ripped anyone off. That's why my clients are longtime customers and most have become my friends. I'm in this business for the long term. It's very important that you're comfortable with me, Mrs. Farnsworth. Otherwise we should break it off right now. I'd rather not get involved if you have any doubts."

Even though Jerome suggested that Juliet check his references, in actuality there weren't any references she'd be able to investigate. Because of confidentiality reasons he would never dare provide his clients as a reference. The books he published completed his promotional efforts and these were his references.

While most of his clients were obtained by word of mouth, his clients usually never discussed this type of business with any third party anyway. They were advised by Jerome not to do so. Too much was at stake. Of course, Juliet Farnsworth had the dossier, and it contained plenty of references to Birchner's style of business.

"I'm certain that you're the man for this job and I like you, Mr. Birchner. Honestly, I like you. But it's a lot of money and a lot is at stake. It's almost scary, wouldn't you say?" she softly said on a solemn note. Juliet was friendly and almost apologetic.

Without another word they finished their lunch with strawberry shortcake desserts. Frequently, as they went ahead to deepen their comfort level, they looked at each other almost like lovers would.

11

AN HOUR later they returned to the Nicanor headquarters discussing several particulars of the deal in the limo.

Juliet Farnsworth didn't tell Jerome the whole story, though. It wasn't only she that was after the six hundred million bucks. There were other parties and entities who considered the money their own. These folks weren't necessarily blessed with the gift of patience and more often than not displayed their violent predisposition even in public surroundings. They would do anything, literally, to get a hold of not only the six hundred million, but more than that, they had their eyes set on a wholesome two billion dollars.

Juliet didn't even realize the danger she was in. They needed her alive for now, at least until the final payments from the Koreans were released. But her fate was already sealed—she was history. Jerome Birchner didn't fit into their plans at all as he was hired by Juliet without their permission. They knew about him, but they couldn't play or use him. He was too clever to become a part of their evil pursuits.

RANDY DERMONT sat alone on a sofa in the lobby near the entrance of the building. He gawked through the air, checking for Juliet's and Jerome's arrival every fifteen seconds. Through the large windows in the lobby, Randy Dermont observed a limo run straight through the gates, passing the security checkpoint on the right. When he saw Juliet and Jerome emerge from the limo, he swiftly went outside.

"I just finished the tour. Once again, I must say, you really have a great company here, Mrs. Farnsworth. Congratulations," Randy Dermont commended her, stretching out his arm in an attempt to shake her hand.

"Thank you, Mr. Dermont. It was a pleasure to have you visit," Juliet said as she clutched his hand with a rather firm grip.

"Mrs. Farnsworth, it was very nice meeting you. I'll send you an e-mail later tonight about the few things that we've discussed," Jerome said.

"The pleasure was on my side. I look forward to doing business with you, Mr. Birchner. Thank you for coming." She sweetly and cordially concluded their meeting.

Juliet felt the urge to hug Jerome, but it would've been inappropriate at this time. Therefore she restrained herself. Besides, someone was watching.

Jerome Birchner and Randy Dermont were chauffeured back by the white minivan to their rental car in the parking lot near the main gate.

"You've made quite an impression on her," Randy Dermont said when they were back in the Lincoln as they fastened their seat belts almost concurrently.

"Well, it's a huge deal, and she's a lonely woman. That's all I can say. So I was very kind to her. We're gonna make big bucks on this one, Randy. I can feel it. Thanks for making the connection. I'll make sure it's gonna pay off for you too," Jerome replied, shaking Randy Dermont's hand in agreement.

Jerome was excited and already pictured in his mind his net worth soar above the one-hundred-million dollar mark—all by the end of the year.

* * *

BEFORE BOARDING their separate planes, Jerome expressed his deep gratitude to Randy Dermont about his friendship. He also promised him a hefty finder's fee for his effort for making the connection with Nicanor. They didn't discuss any details, but only some general stuff regarding the new contract.

Jerome was very secretive and discreet about his business. The dealings with his clients had to remain absolutely confidential. It was part of his job to be tight-lipped about the affairs of his customers. There was simply too much at stake. Not even his clients knew everything. In fact, they only knew the basics of the process, and most certainly they wouldn't be filled in on the intricacies.

Once Jerome fulfilled his end of the deal he would leave the intimate personalizations and modifications to his clients. This was another key component to protect them against Jerome's insight in the specifics of an individual situation. His interests were preserved too, by lacking information about exact particulars Jerome made it virtually impossible for himself to be a competent source of information in a particular case, if, for whatever reason, a government agency or an adversary would go after him to press for details regarding one of his clients.

THEY LEFT Dallas shortly after five P.M. Jerome headed for Florida, and Randy Dermont flew back home to Baltimore.

Jerome swore to himself that this was absolutely the last contract he'd take on in his life. He looked forward to his retirement at age forty which he would celebrate in the new year. Maybe he would become a writer, he thought. But then, perhaps this could compromise some of his clients, because eventually he would divulge one or the other confidentiality in a novel. No, this wasn't a good idea—he had to take all the secrets with him to the grave. Nobody could ever know—the welfare of too many people was at risk.

12

TREVOR GATES was the CIA Special Agent in charge of surveilling the Nicanor project in North Korea. It wasn't an easy surveillance task. One major obstacle to this endeavor was the North Korean secret service, who didn't cooperate with the CIA. Eavesdropping was therefore out of the question as the CIA was incapable of wiring any Nicanor sites inside North Korea. They couldn't obtain a firsthand record on any of the important negotiations and meetings that initially took place in Pyongyang, the capital.

The proposed construction site for the Nicanor nuclear power plant was supposedly located in the vicinity around Yongbyon. Yongbyon was situated some sixty miles north of Pyongyang at the locus with the specific coordinates of N39°48' E125°48'. Yongbyon was also the most controversial location during the crisis of 1994. Back then the North Koreans didn't allow officials from the International Atomic Energy Agency to inspect several key sites in the area.

For years Yongbyon had provided accommodations for the Radiochemical Laboratory of the Institute of Radiochemistry, the Nuclear Fuel Rod Fabrication Plant, and to a storage facility for nuclear fuel rods. Most nations around the world distrusted North Korea and suspected that Yongbyon was home to North Korea's secret nuclear missile operations. Together with China, the North Korean government had deployed an estimated staff of two thousand to these key facilities in Yongbyon who labored at the nuclear factories. But no physical evidence existed that supported any claims or speculations of nuclear weapons activities.

North Korea was a poverty-stricken communist nation. People were starving and by itself, North Korea didn't have the financial means to build any sort of expensive nuclear facility. Of course, China, which was North Korea's closest ally, could have provided resources for such purposes. But so far no spy satellite had detected a massive building complex or construction site at the supposed Yongbyon location.

Among the wild rumors, the U.S. and some vocal NATO countries circulated speculations that a Soviet-era nuclear power plant was perhaps developed underground. In 1994, North Korea signed an agreement with the U.S. that no such developments had taken place and that North Korea would freeze any existing nuclear weapons program at once. According to the agreement, in return the U.S. would provide North Korea with the necessary funds to build two civilian nuclear power plants, each with 1,000 MW light-water nuclear reactors. Those facilities would help boost the supply of electricity for the country. The agreement brought calm to the crisis for four years.

In November 1998, while impeachment hearings had begun against him in Washington, the Democratic U.S. President during his Asia trip, once again urged North Korea to put a halt to its nuclear weapons program. North Korean officials assured the world that all allegations were false and unwarranted. They strongly denied that North Korea was involved in any secret nuclear weapons program. Officially, North Korea denied that even a nuclear power plant for civilian use was under construction. And they never mentioned the Nicanor project.

Of course, the speculations weren't that unfounded, just the location was a little off. The actual Nicanor facility was twenty-five miles northeast of Yongbyon in a remote mountainside area. And yes, it was an underground complex, like many other special projects in North Korea. But this industrial site was supposed to be a simple nuclear power plant for civilian use. Construction of the reactors had been subsidized with billions of dollars from the U.S. government. The actual construction of the project was supervised by the IAEA. But the U.S. Department of Energy was very reluctant to confirm any speculations about the Nicanor project for years. The DOE began a substantial misinformation campaign to quiet any suspicions from story-hungry journalists. After all, the Nicanor nuclear-power-plant project in North Korea was still a secret undertaking by the U.S. It was considered classified information for the most part. U.S. government policy throughout all departments had been issued that the Nicanor project in North Korea was to be kept secret.

From a diplomatic viewpoint it was somewhat of a success. The U.S. cooperated with China and Japan to finance and construct this nuclear facility in North Korea. It was a dangerous and unstable undertaking which could've failed at any time. A simple political fallout or whatever would have jeopardized all efforts for a successful outcome of the agreement amongst all participating countries. But a successful consequence of the cooperation would result automatically in enhanced and secured relations between China and the U.S., the White House argued and hoped for. It would have also added another stepping stone toward reconciliation between North and South Korea.

And having a major U.S. corporation, namely Nicanor Industries, do the job was an additional guarantee for a successful mission.

Another benefit was the watchful eye of the IAEA. The IAEA was a U.S. controlled entity, but headquartered in the

UNO City building in Vienna, Austria. It basically controlled and managed all details regarding the project. But the IAEA was only able to do so in close cooperation with Nicanor. Together with USEC (an U.S. organization whose task it was to keep uranium and plutonium out of the hands of terrorists) the IAEA managed all nuclear components for this new power plant. It deployed dozens of its own inspectors, scientists and engineers to the location so that even a remote possibility for foul play by the North Koreans or China was absolutely eliminated.

THE CIA committed two agents, James Brighton and Hank Taylor, to assist Trevor Gates with the Nicanor assignment. For over two years they had tried to tape negotiations between John Farnsworth and the North Koreans. They never succeeded. They had attempted several times to bribe North Korean officials to place a few bugs in various important locations; again, they were unsuccessful. As a routine procedure the CIA had wired the executive offices of Nicanor headquarters in Texas, the two Nicanor Gulfstream jets, and a few company cars.

Based on CIA orders, no significant emphasis was put on surveillance efforts of Nicanor in the U.S. It would've been a waste of time and resources, the CIA argued. Nicanor handled this deal with considerable secrecy and virtually all key negotiations took place in North Korea. The only exception were the talks with various department heads and political figures in Washington. Such conversations and arrangements were not recorded for obvious reasons. In most cases the CIA had no knowledge of these conversations and nobody bothered or ordered the CIA to get involved.

When rumors of a proposed Nicanor deal in North Korea initially hit the airwaves there was a rampant media rumble. This was usual and it didn't extend over a two-week period. A familiar crowd consisting of the vets, the pacifists and Green-peace members held a rally in Washington—less than a thousand showed up.

13

AFTER BRIEFING Gates about the Farnsworth incident over the Pacific, Brighton flew back to L.A. for further investigations. Taylor, meanwhile, was waiting for orders in Seoul, South Korea.

Tuesday morning, Trevor Gates met with CIA Director, William B. Tish, at the CIA headquarters in Langley, Virginia.

"Gates, what in the world is going on with this Nicanor thing?" the CIA Director asked. "Is this getting out of hand? Are we missing something here? It has been over a week now and we don't even have a clue, no leads, nothing at all. Fill me in, Gates, would you?"

"I don't think we're missin' anything, boss. There's nothing left—no bodies, no debris, and the plane is gone. We've been working around the clock—" Gates answered before he was abruptly interrupted by Tish.

"What happened to Farnsworth? Where is he? Isn't he a billionaire? Didn't he have a parachute? Didn't the Coast Guard find the bodies or parts of it, or something?" He was irascible, swinging both of his arms wildly through the air.

"Chief, they found nothing. At first they weren't even sure if the plane had really gone down, or had just flown off into the sunset. As you know the plane was wired. But our reception is always bad once they're getting too far out there. The last thing we heard was just the regular interruptions in the transmission because the signal was fading. Then suddenly the transmission was discontinued, and initially we assumed the plane just got out of range. That's not unusual, sir. I've got a copy of the tape here. The original is still in the lab." Gates handed a copy of the cassette tape to the director.

"Yeah. Yeah. What's your theory, Gates? You know, the FAA got in touch with the FBI, one of our guys at the Bureau told me yesterday. And they're asking all kinds of questions." Tish wasn't very happy about the FBI snooping around in the Nicanor matter.

"Why is the FBI involved? I didn't even know about it."

"It's not really standard procedure, because when such an airplane disappears, the Coast Guard normally contacts only the FAA and the NTSB. But because some idiot spread a rumor suggesting suspicious circumstances and then they found out who Farnsworth was, they notified the FBI. Anyway, as soon as I heard about it, I called the FBI.

"Earlier this morning I had a talk with the new FBI Director, Steve Schuhmacher, and I told him to back off because we got it all under control. Surprisingly, he didn't mind, and offered to help if need be, just in case. He's a nice guy. Too nice if you know what I mean. I'm sure he has assigned a couple of his boys to the case. He's not goin' to back down that easily. I know these guys.

"Tell me, what's the story with Farnsworth? Was there anything unusual going on?" He leaned back in his chair, and chewed on the back end of a pencil. Slowly the director calmed down, but still somewhat upset and obviously uncomfortable with this unpleasant and unplanned situation.

"Well, dealing with the North Koreans was never a walk in the park. They're very difficult to deal with as you know, sir. But, from what we understand, Farnsworth was never threatened, or anything. The project was on schedule and should be completed by the end of the year, they say. Actually, everything was fine until now. Of course, they went over budget and spent a few billions more than what they had initially anticipated. But that's nothing new with such a project, and honestly, if you ask me: who cares?

"Of what we know, Washington will foot the bill anyway. They'll cover any amount over budget as usual. The Undersecretary of State, Robert Baxter, as you know, kept a close eye on the whole thing. In fact, he initiated and introduced the project to Farnsworth a few years ago," Trevor Gates explained.

"The White House, the Pentagon, Congress, the Defense Department, the DOJ, the DOE—nobody had a problem with the deal. Only we had some concerns initially, if you remember, sir. But it was only routine stuff and nothing serious."

"What are your thoughts about it? Was it an accident?" The director asked. He was dead serious, looking Gates deep into his eyes. Tish removed the pencil from his mouth and placed it with a snap on his desk.

"Sir, at this point I really don't know for sure. Agent Brighton briefed me earlier this morning and that's what it seems to be. It sounds simple, but at this point we don't have any other indications."

"What about witnesses?" the director asked. "I heard from Schuhmacher that there were a couple of elderly folks who supposedly saw something."

"Brighton interviewed the elderly couple that allegedly witnessed the explosion from their yacht. They were the only eyewitnesses. But they didn't even see an airplane. All they saw was a big ball of fire falling out of the sky. Seconds later it supposedly disbursed into thousands of tiny pieces, crashing into the Pacific at high speeds. One piece apparently hit their boat and left a scratch on top of the bridge. Forensic is checking out a paint chip right now. They should have the results pretty soon. I'll check with them later today.

"The elderly lady called the Coast Guard to report the incident. At first, they thought it was a UFO or something. Both have very bad eyesight, and actually only the wife had been wearing her glasses at the time of the incident.

"Very vague. But aside from the tape, it's the only thing we have so far. Honestly, I don't think that their account is anything that we can use. Their statement though seems to confirm that the Nicanor plane actually exploded and went down, unless it was something else . . . another plane, or a piece of a satellite, or a meteorite, or whatever. I'm sure that Forensic will find that out in a few hours. We'll see.

"Brighton is now back en route to L.A. As soon as he finds anything else or something important, I'll let you know, sir." Gates was anxious to conclude this briefing on a positive note, even though he wasn't very hopeful that the investigation would turn up anything significant.

"What about the tape? I mean, airplanes don't explode or disappear just like that. And this ain't the Bermuda triangle we're talking about." Tish was concerned, and frowned, trying to think of some alternate answers and a reasonable explanation. He tilted back with his chair, grabbed the pencil and clenched it between his teeth again. Nothing made really sense. It was virtually a brand-new jet and an experienced flight crew. No serious threats existed and the crash took place over safe U.S. territory in most favorable weather conditions. All kinds of thoughts rushed through his mind. "What about the plane?"

"They took delivery of a couple of brand-new Gulfstreams a year ago. The Gulfstream V is one of the best jets around, at least they're the most expensive. I wish we had one. The Undersecretary of State joined Farnsworth on a recent trip. In fact, if I recall it correctly, just a month ago or so," Gates explained as he looked at his notes.

"It was the same plane that is now history. Security at

Nicanor is very tight and it would've been extremely difficult and I would dare to say, even impossible for an outsider to find access to the planes," Gates said.

"What about insiders?" The director asked.

"Even an inside job would've been easier said than done. We already thought of it. If someone had tampered with the plane, our files were unable to identify a potential suspect within Nicanor. I just ran another search and cross referenced a lot of stuff this morning.

"And from the outsiders, only environmentalists didn't like Farnsworth, but there weren't any serious threats. There was peace, so to speak, over the past four years. He didn't have any real enemies. Practically speaking, Nicanor had no competitors in the U.S. who would've envied them regarding this project.

"There were only a couple of companies overseas that could've perhaps handled this kind of a deal in North Korea. But it was our contract, and no German, no Frenchman, no Swede or Brit could've done it. Their governments are absolutely unable to subsidize deals of such a magnitude. We considered that possibility extensively, but we didn't turn up any quality leads."

"You know, Gates, remember this and never forget it: wherever there's lots of money I know there's someone who has a motive. You should've learned that in the academy." He gave it a moment's thought.

"Somebody must've hated Farnsworth. But then I don't understand the timing. I mean, this thing is a done deal. Who in the world could get anything out of it at this juncture? I mean, it's too late to get a piece of the action now. There must be something else. Who runs the show in Dallas now?" The director lifted his eyebrows as his curiosity grew.

"Well, his wife and an army of VPs," Gates answered.

"How is she? Was she hurt by this thing? Does she have

something going with a VP or some other guy?" The director was blunt in an attempt to find a motive by throwing all kinds of suspicions in the air.

"No, chief, she seems to handle the situation all right. Of course, she's hurt, but I don't think she has anything to do with it." Gates paused for a moment as he once again took an inquisitive look at his legal pad.

"They had the funeral on the weekend. Of course, there was no casket, just a picture of Mr. Farnsworth. But otherwise a normal memorial service, nothing appeared to be aberrant." Gates paused for another moment.

Trevor Gates casually scanned once more through his notes. "Oh yeah, yesterday, Jerome Birchner, the German tax guy, stopped by for a few hours. I don't think it's important though. Based on our records John Farnsworth and Birchner had never met, at least not in the last four years or so. And I don't think Juliet Farnsworth had ever met Birchner before. Mrs. Farnsworth and Birchner had lunch at the Hyatt. We were only able to pick up general conversation in the limo, but nothing of interest . . . just the usual stuff," Gates continued to explain.

"Who is Birchner? A Nazi or what? Sure sounds like it." The director was a little irritated and fumbled with the pencil wildly in a circular motion through the air.

WILLIAM B. TISH was of Jewish descent and a German with the name *Birchner* sounded genuinely German to him. But then, obviously, this wasn't his best day, and at fifty-five, retirement wasn't too far away for Tish.

He didn't really enjoy his job anymore. The enthusiasm and excitement had long since died. He'd seen it all. Especially in his early years when he was with the FBI and later with the DEA. The drug lords, the street gangs, the S&L crooks, the mob and the nutcases of serial killers, child molesters and rapists.

And he hated homosexuals—those perverts, faggots. Of course, he loved the death penalty. Tish told his officers never to bargain with an offender, but shoot 'em and he won't tell. The Agency would stand behind their men and always protect them no matter what.

He had told Internal Affairs more than once to back off and stop bothering his people. Once, Tish even protected a major spy inside the Agency for years. They finally caught up with the guy and convicted him and his wife on a whole array of counts from espionage to murder and everything else in between. Tish never thought for a moment that one of his men could be a spy. He thought it was an unjustified witch-hunt.

When the spy got busted, IA implicated Tish too and it almost cost him his job and pension. But in the end, the President, a good friend of Tish, bailed him out by arguing that it was a case of bad judgment on Billy Tish's part. Tish hated Internal Affairs because they were suspicious of everybody, even of their own buddies.

"SIR, BIRCHNER is a financial consultant. I checked his file. There was nothing substantial. In the past the IRS had requested more than once that we'd take him out. And several years ago we actually worked together with the folks from the IRS on a case, but it was a dead end. The guy doesn't do anything wrong. He pays his taxes, travels the world and races his boat down in Florida." Gates casually supplied the information on Birchner to the director, and discarded it as meaningless.

"Why would Mrs. Farnsworth see this Birchner guy just days after her husband dies?"

"I guess just regular business. The Farnsworths are wealthy folks and she probably had to bring the financial affairs in order.

To involve a numbers guy like Birchner makes sense, at least to some degree . . . nothing unusual.

"He came in with a Nicanor supplier, Dermont, from Baltimore. I checked him out and he's clean. The Pentagon faxed us some confidential stuff on Dermont and his company, APL. Lots of black though on his report, but then, they've got a lot of useless stuff on all these defense contractors and their affiliates. But looks all right to me."

"Gates do me a favor and check every single thing. We need to close this case," the director said.

"Of course, sir, we'll be checking some more as we get to it. Right now we're working within the proximity of the indicated crash site. We're also checking up on everybody who perhaps was capable of tampering with the plane.

"Sir, if you could spare a few more agents, I'll be happy to send them on their way to check out Birchner and Dermont, if you want me to. But only if you think it's really important. I personally don't think these guys have anything to do with this," Gates persisted. He felt like a novice. He also knew that the Agency was short on personnel and he'd be lucky to get one or two more agents to help him out.

"Gates, I hope this plane crash was just another accident, because we have no leads, no evidence, no suspects, no nothing. Let's call the FAA and the NTSB, and tell 'em to officially rule it an accident due to some technical defect, or heck, whatever. This will keep the FBI out of it.

"And you go ahead and check in with Mrs. Farnsworth, maybe there's something we aren't aware of. We also need some background checking on the ambitious young guys at Nicanor . . . you know, the VPs, management, et cetera. Maybe we've overlooked something or somebody there.

"I'll assign you two more agents to help you out on the case, at least for the next two weeks. But you'd better come up with something, Gates. If this crash wasn't an accident, make sure you have a suspect in custody by then. I don't want this to drag on forever. Do you understand me, Gates?" The director began to busy himself with tons of other things.

Russia once again was a hot spot; and lots of tension existed between Japan, China and the U.S., in addition to the unstable condition in Yugoslavia. And there was the usual noise in the Middle East, especially in Iran and Iraq. Then there were also the terrorist camps in Libya, Afghanistan and Sudan who recruited actively on a global basis.

A plane crash of a wealthy industrialist was one thing, but terrorists preparing to kill thousands or perhaps millions with Anthrax or some other chemical weapon was of much greater relevancy. In fact, the latter was an immediate danger as it was a time bomb waiting to explode somewhere in the U.S. on any given day.

14

TREVOR GATES was thirty-two and not yet married. Perfect teeth, an athletic body and short black hair. Measuring just over six feet in height, he could've easily passed for a male model in *GQ* or even made it into the NBA.

He broke up with his fiancée six months ago. There was always friction in the relationship, even some fighting. She couldn't handle his schedule anymore, and she consistently complained about everything. It wouldn't work—they both agreed. After several months of arguments and going back and forth it was Gates who gently told her to take a hike.

Aside from the initial tears she handled the breakup pretty well. The same day he told her to leave, she moved out of the apartment they had shared. They hadn't seen each other since. She was still a student at Georgetown working toward her law degree. He didn't miss her. His convictions became solidified when he realized that he most certainly didn't wanna share his future with a nagging wife.

After the academy, Gates worked his way up in the Agency's hierarchy in record time. He was sent around the globe as an assistant agent gathering experience in the field. Then they gave him a couple of assignments as officer in charge domestically. He completed those successfully.

The Agency was in desperate need of guys like Trevor Gates. They provided Gates with one promotion after the other. The purpose behind all those promotions was to get him hooked for life. The Nicanor job was his first major assignment as officer in charge outside the U.S. He felt honored to assume this responsibility since it was the largest U.S. deal ever under way in Asia.

The pay, though, was terrible. Until recently he had rented a studio apartment in Washington, D.C. Shortly after the breakup with his fiancée he'd moved to the suburbs. In the suburbs he bought a four-bedroom colonial in a quiet family-oriented neighborhood. Nothing fancy, but still a very nice place for a single guy.

He paid eighty thousand down for the nearly four-hundred-thousand-dollar home. The Agency knew about his purchase, but never investigated his resources for the down payment. They hadn't even questioned Gates as to how in the world he was able to afford the monthly mortgage payments on his salary.

But then, Gates didn't own a fancy car, nor did he do anything extravagant—no strange or expensive hobbies whatsoever. He hadn't had a vacation in years and only visited his mom in Maine occasionally. Trevor Gates seemed to be a sold out CIA agent. And in private he appeared to be an honest ordinary guy, someone everybody would love to have as their next-door neighbor and date their daughter.

He drove the dark blue Agency-owned Ford Taurus to his office in Langley. And he was allowed to use it off duty too. A year ago they replaced his Crown Victoria with the smaller Taurus. Initially, Gates didn't like that too much, but there wasn't any alternative. They sure wouldn't furnish him with a Town Car, a privilege reserved solely for the director.

Gates had no close friends that anyone knew of. The CIA didn't really care about the private lives of their agents that much, as long as everything seemed normal—whatever that meant in each specific case.

* * *

THE NICANOR task involved only basic surveillance to ensure national security interests. This was according to the official instructions of the assignment. The CIA was supposed to snoop around a bit just to keep informed about the progress of the deal.

Nicanor was aware of it and this was part of doing business in this industry. Nicanor had a very good track record from its time as a defense contractor. Nothing ever appeared suspicious enough worth investigating. The CIA never detected any strange behavior and Nicanor passed as a meticulous company.

The State Department moved rather quickly to approve the deal for the nuclear power plant in North Korea. John Farnsworth was very good friends with both the Secretary of State and the Undersecretary of State. Whenever their busy schedule permitted, all three played golf together. Sometimes they were joined by the President, some members of Congress and other government appointees—the typical Washington clique. Deals were done, or at least initiated and put together on the *Green*. Friends met friends, and everybody received a piece of the action. It was the same game all over the world.

The CIA by nature had to be somewhat suspicious of everybody involved in global trade. This was especially the case when it concerned nuclear facilities and countries like North Korea who didn't have the best relationship with the United States. For safety reasons the National Security Advisor requested that the CIA would keep a close eye on Nicanor's activities, especially regarding the project in North Korea.

At the time when the Nicanor deal with North Korea was signed, the U.S. didn't even have an embassy or any other representation in North Korea. Based upon all available facts and gathered intelligence, and the individuals from the State Department involved, Nicanor had been a routine assignment for the CIA until now.

So far, they only had to hang around and to sniff a little here and there just to keep in the know. But since the plane crash, things had changed dramatically. The CIA was in a difficult position as the White House and everybody else demanded answers. Unless specific leads were identified, the CIA was incapacitated to operate within its full measure of global law enforcement. They had to consider the incident a tragic accident for now. Evidence or something else of substantial consequence had to emerge to mobilize and justify a massive effort by the CIA in this matter.

15

JEROME BIRCHNER faxed the order forms for three new corporations to the incorporation agency in Road Town, Tortola, British Virgin Islands. The incorporation agency was an outfit owned by a well-known British accounting firm, Spencer & Lithgow. This firm also operated offices in Boston, New York and Los Angeles. The three new corporations would be incorporated the next day.

Jerome had visited the British Virgin Islands only once. Most offshore business was handled by fax and courier services. It was not necessary to travel to the islands in the flesh, as it was still kind of complicated to get there. Usually, a traveler would board an island hopper in Miami—this was an experience by itself. After a few hours and a couple of stopovers the customary two-engine aircraft would land in Road Town on the island of Tortola.

Regarding the opening of a bank account in Switzerland, Jerome used to travel to Zürich in person, until a few years ago. But now he was familiar to the bankers there, he thought, and business was regularly conducted via phone, fax and e-mail.

These days a tiresome trip to Europe was no longer required for such undertakings. Still, in the case of Nicanor, he wouldn't take any chances. Within a week he once again would engage in this arduous journey and travel to Zürich. Too much money was at stake. Even small mistakes could become very costly.

* * *

"YOU WANNA come over?" Walter yelled through the phone. Walter Kalkmeier was also an Austrian citizen. He owned the luxurious mansion next to Jerome's house in this affluent neighborhood. Kalkmeier was a real estate developer. He'd built mostly luxurious condominium complexes and million-dollar homes in the southwestern part of Florida along the Gulf coast.

"Sure, I hope you have a steak ready." Jerome grinned.

"Of course, I do. We'll have a great time. Bring Birgid and the kids," he suggested.

The tantalizing odor from the barbecue of freshly grilled steaks and salmon would lure anyone. The seasoned smell engulfed half of the fifteen acres of Whitecaps Island. It was a hot summer evening. Even at night, the temperature wouldn't drop below eighty.

JEROME, BIRGID and their two kids loved to live in Naples. At times though Birgid would become highly emotional. This always really ticked Jerome off. She would go through her phases of homesickness year after year until reality finally woke her up again.

Here in Naples were palm trees, the turquoise waters of the Gulf, and the offer of a lifestyle that millions of people only dreamed about. Austria on the other hand had a harsh climate. The uncoordinated narrow roads ran aimlessly through the misty cities and countryside.

For whatever reason, once every year, Birgid was over-whelmed by her yearning to move back to Austria. This usually happened around Christmas. Maybe because there wasn't any snow in Naples while Austria was plagued by treacherous avalanches.

On her side of the family tree she didn't even have next of kin left in Austria. Her parents had passed away several years ago and she was the only child. There were no other siblings. The only family she knew and could be part of was Jerome's family. Jerome's parents were in their late sixties. His brother with his family lived in Austria, and also some of Jerome's aunts and uncles and cousins. Somehow Birgid had this illusion that life across the big pond in Austria was better than in America. Jerome hated it when she went through this homesick cycle. It was almost like a monomania and he couldn't stand it.

During the early nineties they lived in Fallston, twenty-five miles north of Baltimore. After the heavy winter storms of '93 and early '94 everyone in the family agreed to move to Florida. They finally moved in July of '94. It never snowed around Naples and life was much more relaxed down South than up North.

WALTER KALKMEIER was married to Valerie and they had two children. The boy and the girl were the same age like the Birchner kids. Jerome and Walter had first met in the summer of 1993. They were introduced to each other by Hubert Neumann. Mr. Neumann was a Swiss native who owned the third mansion on the property. Hubert's home was white on the outside, just like the vacant fourth house in Whitecaps Island. Jerome's place was painted in a light peach pastel with white accents, and Walter's luxurious mansion was kept in a richer, darker peach pastel.

Walter was only thirty-seven and the youngest of the property owners in Whitecaps Island. His initial wealth, a couple of million bucks, came from his in-laws. With a lot of hard work he had been able to quadruple his fortune over the past seven years—mostly with various real estate deals.

* * *

AS THEY frequently did, they sat in comfortable chairs on the lanai around the pool, relaxing and enjoying the abundance of food. The teenagers were swimming their hearts out between watching movies on the big screen television in the living room. Walter had a swimming pool that extended partially into the living room.

Softly, jazzy music by Kenny G, Kirk Whalum, Yanni and other artists rained from the speakers in the background. It accompanied the casual conversations. The ladies were chin-wagging about fashion, crafts, cooking, the latest heroes in the soaps and so forth. Walter and Jerome kept their chat within the realm of cars, boats and movies.

"I have a deal for you," Jerome said to Walter later that evening. "We'll all make some good money on this one. You can play a director again. It's an offshore deal. You'll make a hundred or maybe even two-hundred grand. Does this sound interesting to you?"

"If I don't have to kill somebody, I might be interested," Walter said, laughing openly as he ran the fingers of his left hand through the last remaining strains of his oily hair.

In his right hand he held a Cuban cigar without which he was rarely ever seen. For Walter it didn't matter if the cigar was lit or not, the cigar was an image thing and increased his self-esteem. A psychiatrist told Walter about this observation once, and from that day on a Cuban was always around.

In his comments, Walter Kalkmeier frequently revealed the typical Austrian pessimism and scepticism. He was often neutral, but basically he was a kvetcher. And then on rare occasions he'd express the opposite extreme. He would splatter a type of superficial optimism about his future ventures which were completely unrealistic for his financial situation at that time.

Walter was wealthy with a net worth of over eight million, but he had hardly a six-figure amount in the bank. Almost all of his money was tied up in often illiquid real estate investments. In addition, he had spent over a million dollars in toys over the past few years. He'd purchased several exotic automobiles, a yacht, a double-engine turboprop and an obligatory Harley. His mansion was furnished with inexpensive furniture, even though it looked stylish. Walter had a knack for knockoffs when it came to these things. But regarding cars, boats and motorcycles: they had to be the genuine brand name product.

Because he was a developer, he himself selected all the materials for his house. He also billed his customers a little extra for time spent by his workers to construct his own lavish palace. Therefore he was able to save a bundle on his mansion which, when everything was totaled, had cost him only three quarters of a million.

"Walter, it's easy. Just one trip, or maybe two to Europe, a few signatures and that's it. Everything's legit. You know that, right?" Jerome attempted to convince him.

"Well, I don't know . . . " Walter ran the tip of his tongue over both his lips and smacked them.

"C'mon. What's wrong with you? We've made money in the stock market, we've made money in cars, we've made money in real estate and in lots of other deals. This isn't a hard one. All you've gotta do is sign a few papers and that's it. There's no risk. It's simple and you'll get at least a hundred grand."

"You said two hundred," Walter said with a smile.

"All right, two hundred." Jerome stretched out his hand to get Walter's approval on the deal.

Walter reluctantly clutched Jerome's hand in agreement— the money was simply too much of a temptation to say *No*. "Okay, that sounds good to me. But once the deal is done you must remove me from the corporate papers immediately. I can't take any risks right now. All right? I don't wanna be caught up in some offshore scandal . . . you know what I mean."

"Of course I understand. Everything's gonna be fine. I'm a pro . . . you should know that by now. Have I ever let you down or done anything stupid to you?" Jerome said, demanding a reply from Walter.

"No, no. It's not a problem. I just have a lot of things on my mind right now," he said.

Walter Kalkmeier wanted the two hundred grand, of course. And he knew that he could trust Jerome in the details. It was also true that while Walter was often sceptical of Jerome's business dealings, that so far, all deals had worked out just fine. He'd made quite some easy money doing virtually nothing—all thanks to Jerome.

"I'll fix the papers tonight. Next week we'll fly to Zürich for a day or two. You can visit your friends in Austria if you like. But if you don't wanna go right now, just sign a Power of Attorney and we're all set."

Jerome was relieved when Walter agreed. He had already indicated Walter as director on two of the offshore companies which he had ordered for incorporation in the BVI earlier this morning.

There wasn't anything to think about, Jerome thought. In fact, he did Walter a favor, who certainly could use the money. Currently, vacation homes just under a million weren't selling that well in Florida.

Not too many retirees liked the heat in this part of the country. Another fact was that they were rarely ever spending a million bucks for a single-family home, or three quarters of a million for a three-bedroom condo. Europeans used to be the big buyers in the area, but the rising U.S. dollar and a soft landing of Europe's economy had curtailed sales significantly in recent years. More and more Europeans preferred to purchase property within the EU or in Eastern Europe. Along the coast of Spain there were plenty of attractive investments for wealthier

Europeans.

Interest rates were still low in the U.S., but the real estate market in Naples had slowed down dramatically. Prices though remained in the loftier levels and there were no indications that these would come down anytime soon. Walter did most of his own financing, and between existing and new projects there wasn't much cash left to play with.

"I'll sign a Power of Attorney. Just fix the papers. I can't go to Europe next week because I have a few clients from Germany and Italy coming in. When do I get paid?" Walter was all business. After posting the question he extracted a heavy dose of smoke from his cigar. Then he blew the smoke skillfully in the shape of a thick circle into the evening air.

"Walter, do you need money right now?" Jerome inquired.

"Well . . ." Walter grimaced, and shrugged as he placed his left hand toward the back of his sweaty skull, scratching his neck.

"You'll get paid as soon as the deal is done. But I can give you twenty grand now, if you're desperate. Or if you need fifty that's all right with me too. Just let me know." Jerome offered the money jokingly. He chose the wording carefully. He knew Walter didn't want to appear desperate and therefore wouldn't demand money up front.

"You know it's not that I need the money, it's just a routine question," Walter said. Walter really needed the money, just to free him up a little bit with some liquid dough.

"I know, I know," Jerome said. He wasn't interested in arguing. "Tomorrow when you sign the papers I'll have a check for you. Is that okay?"

"Sure, no problem. I appreciate it," Walter responded nonchalantly.

16

"HELLO, THIS is Vicky Darnell from the State Department. I'm looking for Mr. Birchner. Are you Mr. Birchner?" A gentle voice introduced herself on the phone.

"Yes, I'm Mr. Birchner." Jerome was surprised, but not speechless, as he had not a clue what to expect from the State Department.

"Sir, the Undersecretary of State would like to meet with you in Korea. He's going to be there in about ten days. Are you available, Mr. Birchner?" Vicky Darnell asked.

At first he couldn't think of anything smart, then of course, it had to be concerning the Nicanor deal. For a moment it took his breath away. He couldn't think of what kind of an important role he could play in this thing, if any at all. Jerome only had an arrangement with Mrs. Farnsworth, he thought, which was something that wouldn't be officially discussed.

Nevertheless, Jerome was curious. "I'll be honored to meet with the Undersecretary. Next week I'll be in Europe, but by the end of the week, I can catch a flight to Korea. I guess that should work out. Just let me know where and when. I've never met with the Undersecretary before. By the way, may I asked what this is in reference to?"

He liked rubbing shoulders with government officials. So far, he personally had never come really close to U.S. politicians, as he never really cared much for them anyway. But now, when it would happen out of the blue, the adrenaline rushed through his veins. His hopes soared that maybe, just maybe, he would find an inroad into the Washington establishment. Some folks would still remember his generous donations a few years ago, he contemplated, but hopefully nobody would recall the bad stuff—the thing with the IRS.

He loved to meet the rich and famous. In the past Jerome had entertained people from the movie industry, powerful investors from Wall Street and all kinds of wheeler-dealers, but never politicians.

Some years ago, during campaign activities in Maryland, he was offered an opportunity to chat for five minutes with presidential hopefuls Ross Perot and Steve Forbes. But since he wasn't in the mood back then to get involved in any kind of political activity, he declined.

Also some years ago, Jerome thought about starting his own political party back in Austria. But it would've been too much of a hassle and dealing with the media on a daily basis would produce more than a headache. No, politics wasn't for him. He rather enjoyed his millions and a relaxed lifestyle in privacy. He definitely desired to be far away from public scrutiny.

"Sir, the Undersecretary mentioned that it had to do with an important facility in Asia. And he said that you would know what this is all about. Anyway, sir, so may I put you down for a meeting with the Undersecretary in Korea?"

"Sure, that'll be fine."

"I'll fax you the schedule and the details by the end of the week. If there are any questions, or if you can't make the meeting for whatever reason, simply give me a call on our toll-free exchange. You can dial that number from anywhere in the world." Vicky Darnell helpfully instructed Jerome. She didn't sound at all like one of these bureaucratic idiots, but rather like an executive secretary of a Fortune-500 company. She was very professional with a personal touch.

He was impressed. Jerome thanked her and ended the conversation after supplying her with his fax number.

"HONEY! HONEY!" he yelled through the house searching for Birgid.

"What? What is it?" Birgid came running down the stairs from the terrace on the first floor. She never became used to him calling her in this panicky manner as she perceived it. It always seemed as if something bad had happened—maybe a heart attack or whatever, when in fact, it was always something good.

"I'm gonna meet the Undersecretary of State. His office just called." Jerome beamed all over his face.

"Oh. Don't scare me like that. You always scare me when you yell that way. I thought something had happened," she said with relief, but a little crossly.

"Well, something did happen. I'm meeting with one of the Washington power guys. I'll meet him in Korea after the trip to Zürich. This works out fine. I mean, I don't have to go to Korea, but it can't hurt to be there for a couple of days, just to arrange everything. Of course, this really makes sense now," Jerome explained.

"I thought you're retired. I didn't know you're involved in another deal." Birgid suspiciously crossed her arms.

"Don't be upset, honey. This is really the last one and it's goin' to double our net worth. It's your money too, sugar."

"You've said that many times before, but it's never the last one. You're not kidding anybody. Not that it matters to me, but I thought you want to write books, play golf or do something else. We've got plenty of money, Jerome, we don't need another million." A little frustrated, she shook her head.

"When is it enough? I mean I love you and I'm a hundred

percent with you, but is it never enough? Just be careful," Birgid said approaching him with a hug.

"Sure, honey, of course. I'm always careful. It's not a matter of enough though. It's never enough. You should know that by now. It's the last deal, I promise. But it's easy money. The only thing I don't like is that I have to be away from you for a few days." He caressed her arms.

"I hate to travel, you know that. But I guess that's part of the deal. I promise, it's the last deal, really, and it's so much money I just have to do it." Jerome made the promise as he stroked her cheek gently with the back of his hand.

JEROME LOVED his wife. Birgid was attractive and responded passionately to his initiations. Today was no different. Having time always provided them with an opportunity to enjoy each other. He gently took her in his arms and lost himself in her mouth. They spent the better part of the afternoon in each other's pleasure. He would cherish these moments and remember them when he was alone at night the following week.

Birgid didn't like for Jerome to travel alone. She wanted to see him every day and she desired to be close to him. But she had been aware of the fact that his trips were usually very short. Even though just a few days apart felt like an eternity to both of them.

Always, when Jerome returned home from a journey, he said that this was definitely the last trip he would go on without her. This promise only lasted until the next trip came about. Birgid was just glad that these trips had become very rare in recent years. When he left she already prepared herself mentally for his return.

Sex would be especially pleasurable and intense the first night he was back home again. Their sex life was fabulous, but a few days apart could really fire it up a notch and catapult them both beyond this certain edge into that cherished realm of the senses. They enjoyed sex virtually every day. It was a rare week when they only made love three or four times in any given week. Neither Birgid nor Jerome had ever gone out on each other. They were simply faithful and old-fashioned. Both agreed that cheating wasn't even an option. They were also germ freaks. This helped deaden any potential temptation that made itself available. They couldn't fathom that anyone would make love with someone other than their respective spouse.

17

JEROME WASN'T very fond of Europe. Most of all he hated the long flights to get there. But this time around, because of his involvement in the Nicanor deal, it was imperative that he put all reluctancy aside and engage himself vigorously in this laborious journey overseas. Bank accounts had to be established in Switzerland and he had to take care of it in person, just to be on the safe side.

On Tuesday morning he drove a rental car to Miami. He didn't want to leave any of his own cars parked at the Miami airport. It was almost a written guarantee that cars parked in the long-term parking garage would receive multiple dents and scratches. And this wasn't the worst case scenario. Chances of theft were even higher, especially if a car was left there for several days.

In Miami he boarded a plane to New York. At 1800 hours the Swissair airliner was ready for takeoff from JFK. Swissair was perhaps the safest airline in the sky. Until the fatal crash along the coast of Nova Scotia in 1998, Swissair had a nearly perfect track record without a fatal accident for well over two decades. Before Jerome booked a flight he always checked the latest safety ratings of available airlines.

The flight to Zürich took forever. He could've made reservations on the Concorde to cut the actual flying time to Europe in half, but then it would've required boarding another plane from

Paris to Zürich. This was too much of a hassle and in the end it wouldn't have saved him any time at all.

On this trip too, he only had carry-on luggage, which was his preferred way to travel. He had brought two bags with him. He wasn't interested in wasting valuable time waiting at some baggage claim, and the possibility of perhaps losing the luggage was something absolutely foreign to Jerome—he avoided such circumstances at all cost.

The ride had been smooth aside from the customary turbulences around Halifax, and some bumps and shakes when they entered European air space over Ireland and especially more severely over Scotland.

It was nine A.M. on Wednesday when he arrived in Zürich. During the winter season the city would've been a depressing sight: rain, snow, and gray buildings. But in the summer things were almost appealing and left a positive impression on most tourists. Lake Zürich, the gorgeous flower arrangements all around town, and the buildings appeared in light and fresh colors.

It was hot, around twenty-eight degrees Celsius with high humidity. Rarely any home, public building or business facility was equipped with the luxury of an air-conditioning system. As in most parts of Europe, people on average enjoyed a shower only once or twice a week. The public transportation system of buses and trams smelled intensely of stale sweat in the heavy air—salty, like the stench of rotten eggs combined with the symptoms of athlete foot. Women rarely shaved their armpits or legs.

Disgusting! it screamed through Jerome's head by just thinking of it.

Additionally, most of the population smoked heavily. And alcoholic beverages of all sorts were consumed in high quantities. They offered schnapps, whiskey, a martini, or vodka at every business meeting, or when simply just visiting somebody's home. Europeans consumed their *Mittagessen*, which was the main-course meal, at noon. It was traditionally served with a gigantic mug of beer or a bottle of wine. And the salad wasn't served at the beginning of the *Mittagessen*, but at once with the main course.

And a *Jause*—a lunch break—was often concluded with cognac. While most Europeans didn't make any claims to be endowed with an outgoing proclivity, a lot of people there were usually amicable.

Outside the airport Jerome obtained a cab.

"Paradeplatz 6, bitte," Jerome spoke to the cab driver in German.

The cab driver nodded. With his right hand he retrieved a pack of cigarettes from the center console. He offered Jerome a fag before he got ready to hit the road.

"Care if I smoke?" The cab driver asked in German.

Care if I die? Jerome thought, but didn't say it out loud. Instead he distastefully answered, "Thank you, but I don't smoke. If it's absolutely necessary, please open your window if you would. I personally can't stand any smoke."

The cab driver stashed the pack of cigarettes back into the center console and didn't light his fag either which he had habitually placed between his lips. On the way to Paradeplatz the cabby neither smiled nor said a word. He didn't even mention the total of the fare once they arrived at their destination. The Mercedes taxi stopped at the main entrance of the Swiss Bank Corporation. The fare came to thirty-three Swiss Francs and some change.

"It's okay," Jerome said as he handed the cab driver two twenties. He had both of his bags next to him on the rear seat. He dragged his bags across the rear bench to expeditiously exit the vehicle.

Paradeplatz was an intersection. It was a type of plaza in the *City* which downtown Zürich was called as downtowns were called *City* in most other European cities too. Paradeplatz was the banking center of Zürich. The headquarters of most Swiss banks were located in the surrounding area.

18

WHEN JEROME entered the *Schweizerischer Bankverein* build-ing, he immediately knew his way around and turned right to the desk of the receptionist.

"Grizi!" a stocky man, who could've easily passed as a Danny DeVito look-alike, greeted him in the typical Swiss dialect. The man wore a dark burgundy uniform-like jacket and black trou-sers. His shiny black shoes were only visible when one was leaning awkwardly over the desk, or when the stocky man would emerge from behind the protective desk.

"Do you have an appointment?" The stocky man posted the question in German.

Jerome also spoke in his native German, "I'm looking for Mr. Heinz Richter."

"Let me check. Do you have an appointment with Mr. Richter? What is your name, sir?" The stocky man asked as he turned around, ready to pick up the handset from the phone which was affixed to an ancient column behind him.

"No, I don't have an appointment. But please let him know that Mr. Birchner, Jerome Birchner, from America is here."

The clerk now fetched the handset and turned his back to Jerome. He spoke into the receiver in a manner so that no one standing around the desk could hear a word he said.

"Third floor." The clerk pointed Jerome in the direction of the elevator. "The elevator is right there," he added.

The elevator was in the corridor running to the rear of the building. Several elevators had been installed in the rather wide hallway.

"Danke!" Jerome headed down the corridor and stepped into an empty elevator. Without hesitation he pressed the *3* button. It was a jerky ride and the cabin groaned and crackled as the elevator made its way at a snail's pace with much travail to the third floor.

HEINZ RICHTER had left his office the moment the visitor was announced. He approached Jerome the second he stepped outside the elevator.

"Mr. Birchner?" Heinz Richter placed the question to confirm that it was Jerome Birchner indeed.

"Yes," Jerome answered shaking Heinz Richter's hand with a firm grip.

"It is so good to meet you face to face, finally. I am Heinz Richter," Richter said this in English with a heavy Swiss accent as he put a vague smirk on his face.

They had met some twelve years ago for the first time when Jerome had opened his first account at the Swiss Bank Corporation. They had also met a few times since then. Heinz Richter seemingly didn't remember and Jerome didn't bother to correct him. The voice of the other was the valid identifier, and the voice was often the only identification used to transact business over the phone. On occasion faxes were sent too, especially when written confirmation of larger or multiple and complicated transactions was required.

Still, in most European courts in the case of a dispute a fax was considered a copy and did not qualify as a genuine legal document. And in the rare case when a fax was admitted as evidence, the signature on the fax was always disregarded. Only an original signature would make a document authentic.

Strange though, on the other hand business laws from previous centuries were still in effect under which a verbal agreement was recognized as an absolutely binding contract. Verbal communication was frequently used to avoid traces. Such an agreement was legally binding and concerning legitimacy almost carried as much weight as a written contract, especially if there was at least one witness to the pertaining agreement. Most recently, next to verbal communication, e-mail had also become common practice. But like the fax in the case of a dispute, most European courts did not admit e-mail notices as liable evidence.

"Nice to see you, Mr. Richter. It's certainly good to be here. By the way, would you like to speak in English or in German?" Jerome inquired of him politely.

"It doesn't matter to me, but English is better for me. I like to practice it," Heinz Richter responded with a shrugging motion. Heinz Richter showed Jerome to a conference room.

HEINZ RICHTER left Jerome waiting in the conference room for almost fifteen minutes. Then he returned with a colleague. It was regular procedure to have two bank officials present at a meeting. Even on the phone it was customary that another bank employee would listen in. The purpose of this process was to ensure the presence of a qualified witness to all conversations and negotiations in case of a future dispute. But of course, the other reason was to guarantee the continuous integrity of all bank employees. The legitimacy of all transactions had to be secured to preserve the well-established reputation of the bank.

The colleague was introduced by Heinz Richter. They didn't shake hands and Jerome was unable to catch his name. This small detail wasn't of importance to him anyway. Jerome didn't even want to meet anyone else but Heinz Richter and expressed some discomfort with the other guy in the room.

They sat down at a long table which was suited to seat at least twelve or fourteen people. Jerome chose a chair on one side of the table across from the two bank guys. The gentlemen from the bank wore ties and suits, while Jerome was dressed casually in khakis, a black polo shirt and some dark brown Loafers.

"What can we do for you, Mr. Birchner?" Heinz Richter asked.

Jerome put his two bags next to his chair. He then produced several letter-sized booklets and documents from his leather portfolio, which he had just removed from one of his bags.

"I'd like to open a few accounts for one of my major clients. Her husband died a couple of weeks ago . . . a plane crash. To make things easier for her future business needs, we've decided to take steps in this direction." He handed the booklets and documents to the two bank officials.

"Three companies? All are new British Virgin Islands incorporations," Heinz Richter said, prying through the material.

"Yes, that's correct. Three companies and we need US-Dollar and Euro accounts for all three," Jerome answered and waited for a moment before handing Heinz Richter the Power of Attorney. Walter Kalkmeier had signed the Power of Attorney a couple of days ago. Kalkmeier was the director on two of those companies.

The two bankers took a close look at the Memorandum of Articles and the Certificate of Incorporation for all three entities. The one associate scanned through some of the pages of the Memorandum of Articles and then put it aside.

"Did you bring a Power of Attorney, Mr. Birchner?" Heinz Richter requested.

"Sure did . . . here it is. I'm the corporate and financial consultant for all three companies."

"Okay, Mr. Birchner, it'll take us about an hour for the

paperwork. Is it possible for you to wait here, just in case we have any questions? Otherwise, there's a coffee shop across the street. We can give you a walkie-talkie so that we can keep in touch if need be?" Heinz Richter suggested the coffee shop alternative.

"No, it's not a problem, I'll stay right here. If you have any questions just ask me. Okay?" Jerome answered.

He hated wasting time for bureaucratic nonsense, but he didn't show his aggravation. He initially had planned for the whole process to take no longer than maybe fifteen to thirty minutes, but an hour—*what's that for?* he asked himself. Jerome didn't ask for a line of credit, but only desired to open three simple bank accounts. And it was he who brought the money and entrusted the bank with the moolah.

"Coffee?" the colleague asked.

"Mineral water would be better, if you have some, or a Pepsi is okay, too, but no coffee. Thanks."

"Certainly," Heinz Richter said, immediately nodding to the colleague.

Both bank officials left the room with all the documents. They closed the door, leaving Jerome sitting there by himself. This was a crucial time, because now these guys would check if the documents were authentic. They would also inquire if these companies truly existed. But more than that they would also investigate if there had been any criminal charges filed against Jerome or against any of the companies. They would search databases to see if negative remarks against these entities existed, and if by chance a warrant had been issued on any person indicated as director. All Jerome could do was wait patiently for the result.

FROM THE sixties to the eighties, hundreds of billions of dollars were laundered through Swiss bank accounts. Most of it was pelf. They called it black money—money off the records, from under-the-table transactions, simple tax free dough. But there were also huge sums of dirty money. Illegal fortunes were laundered through these accounts. They considered real dirty money, dough from illegal drugs deals, lucre from unethical weapons sales, and stolen fortunes from various fraudulent endeavors.

Dictators too, hoarded billions in numbered Swiss bank accounts. With much effort FINCEN had urged governments around the world to sign treaties and to allow international prosecution of financial criminals. Still, tax cheats would not be prosecuted by foreign countries.

One of the most popular IRS fugitives was Marc Rich, who fled with his former partner Pincus Green to Switzerland in the early eighties. They had made billions with their U.S. corporations in the commodities trade. Rich and Green were indicted in the U.S. with more than fifty counts of wire fraud, racketeering and income tax evasion. Some fifteen years later they were still on the run and on the FBI's *Most-Wanted* list. Switzerland was their safe haven.

Switzerland was a phenomenal place to launder money. Under ongoing pressures from the U.S., at one point the Swiss government caved in for a short period of time. In 1998 they charged a few individuals from certain Swiss banks with accessory in money laundering schemes. Of course, nobody was ever sent to prison. They only received a slap on the wrist and were back on the job days later. It was more of a publicity stunt by the Swiss to appease the concerns of U.S. authorities, than anything else. They just wanted to be left alone and desired very much to rid themselves of these annoying bureaucrats from overseas.

The Swiss had a disdain for any kind of interference into their affairs. They treasured and demonstrated their independence by not joining the EU. Switzerland also continued to use the Swiss

Franc instead of the Euro as their primary currency.

JEROME'S EXPERTISE was mainly focused on taking advantage of sophisticated loopholes in the tax code of various countries. Early on in his career he made it his mission to help wealthy folks and corporations to legally avoid income taxes. An array of corporate structures served its purpose well. It kept billions of potential income taxes in the pockets of all kinds of individuals. He put his advice with specific methods and strategies into a couple of books that were sold around the world. Most of his books were sold over the Internet.

The Offshore *Fan Club* grew rapidly, especially when the EU expanded. In the U.S. alone, two million entities—individuals and corporations—had been using offshore provisions.

AFTER KILLING time with nothingness for half an hour, he gave the suggestion about the coffee shop across the street some serious thought. A rich cappuccino and some fluffy pastry would've been a delight. But he was still hoping that these guys would return with the paperwork earlier than the one hour they had originally indicated.

Finally, after an hour and twenty minutes, the two bank employees returned to the conference room where Jerome was patiently waiting. He stood by the window and stared at the busy intersection below. When the door opened, Jerome, hands in his pockets, slowly turned and walked casually toward the two men.

Heinz Richter's assistant stretched forth his right hand instantaneously and shook Jerome's hand to say goodbye. Then he turned his body in the other direction and left the room speedily.

Heinz Richter sat down at one end of the table. He returned the original paperwork to Jerome before he was firmly seated in the chair. In addition, Heinz Richter slipped three small folders to him.

"Here are your new accounts. We need a few signatures." Heinz Richter pointed with a pen to a couple of areas on each form at the top of each folder.

"If you'd like to make a deposit right now you can do this downstairs with the cashier. This year our required minimum balance on each account has increased to fifteen thousand Swiss francs. By the way, I've gotta make a note here, just for our basic reference. How much money will be placed into each of these accounts, Mr. Birchner?" Heinz Richter continued.

"It's hard to say, but I guess we're talking tens of millions of dollars over the course of a year," Jerome replied nonchalantly as he completed signing the three forms.

"Yes, this should be sufficient, but please provide me with a specific amount, just so that I can put down a number."

"Mr. Richter, put down whatever you think is appropriate. If you wanna write down ten million it's all right with me. And if you wanna put down fifty million that's okay with me too," Jerome answered. He didn't know how much money would flow through these accounts altogether, and if he told him the truth right now, Heinz Richter would probably become suspicious causing a significant delay regarding the establishment of these new accounts.

"You know that it's usually a requirement by our bank that the minimum balance is deposited into each account upon opening the account. And I understand that in your case you may simply transfer the initial balance into each account by telegraphic wire during the next few days," Heinz Richter explained.

"Don't worry, Mr. Richter. That's exactly what I'll do. I

don't run around with a lot of cash these days. I mean we've got millions of dollars in our other accounts right here at your bank. You know that, right? I guess the initial balance for these three new accounts shouldn't be a problem after all? If you insist, I'll arrange for the wires today," Jerome said somewhat offended. They basically treated him like a new customer who wasn't familiar with the ritual. Jerome had opened hundreds of accounts for his clients at this bank, and also maintained his own account right there.

Jerome didn't appreciate this kind of treatment, but he kept his cool and picked up the three folders. He also realized that in a sense it was actually much better not to be too familiar with these guys. In the rare case that something went awry, there was always a good chance that these guys wouldn't even remember his face. They probably wouldn't recall any particulars of the meeting and therefore it was, in fact, very beneficial to be anonymous.

Anyway, Jerome put all his paperwork back into his leather portfolio. Then he stashed the leather portfolio back into one of his bags. He clutched both bags and walked into the corridor. Heinz Richter escorted Jerome to the elevator. Jerome sealed the deal with Heinz Richter and said goodbye. When the elevator hit ground level, Jerome left the building in a hurry. He was glad to be out of there. Once outside he didn't look back.

19

JEROME BIRCHNER moved around the corner to a Hertz rental-car agency. Before he left Florida he had made reservations over the Internet for a luxury sedan to be made available to him at this certain rental location. For some reason, Hertz was unable to confirm the specific make or model that would stand ready for his use on that day. It could've been a Mercedes, an Audi, a Volvo, or a Bimmer.

"Grizi!" the sexy blonde behind the desk said in *Switzerdütsch*, which was the colloquial Swiss dialect. She was very courteous, yes, even flirtatious with a salacious leer on her lips and she smiled continuously. It relaxed Jerome momentarily. Her white blouse and short black skirt were wrapped tightly around her slender body. The silky black thigh highs were a perfect fit too. Her Hertz nameplate which was pinned high up unto her left chest area read *Gudula*.

The majority of the female gender in Europe didn't take advantage of a bra to hold their breasts in place. They preferred their tits to swing loosely in all directions. Occasionally these were exposed carelessly. Frequently though, not all of it was bared, but only bits and pieces, so to speak, for everyone to gawk at. This was especially the case with a low cut top during the warm spring and summer seasons.

Gudula was no exception—she didn't wear a brassiere either. Her blouse didn't allow for the auspicious dekko. Only if she had been bending forward, Jerome would've been in luck. But Gudula continued to stand upright.

At first, Gudula appeared somewhat flat-breasted, but when she moved her shoulders a little backward similar to a shrugging motion, her contours became explicitly evident. Her firm nipples sculptured a sensuous relief on the surface of the translucent fine textured fabric of her blouse. These emerged like peaks of dangerous icebergs, ready to rupture Jerome's Titanic.

Jerome beheld this sensual sight only for a brief moment as libido waves shot uncontrolled and rampantly through the air, charging the atmosphere of the tiny office. It felt like a jolt of electricity before reality brought him back to earth. An indescribable sensation that had occurred to Jerome only at the sight of his wife.

Then Jerome remembered in a flash that he had experienced this specific sensation with such a high intensity once in his life aside from his wife. And now this pleasure became reality for the third time. It was the lust of the eyes.

The first such incident took place when he met Birgid. The sensation continued to this day. In Birgid's case it had become even stronger, because it would result in the ultimate fulfillment of his desire. The second one occurred in the early nineties when he went shopping for a copier. The gal in charge of corporate sales came over for a demonstration of the many features of the copy machine. She too had many interesting features, Jerome thought, and a similar feeling came over him. For a brief moment he indulged himself with these memories.

Now he was just hoping that he wouldn't be attacked with nasty bureaucracy from Gudula, which was often the case when renting a car in Europe. Jerome was put at ease when the pretty blonde made things real simple for him. She only inquired about the desired insurance coverage, and asked for his credit card, passport and driver's license. Best of it, she only requested one signature and a couple of initials on the rental agreement.

"Would you prefer a BMW or a Mercedes?" she asked in German with a Swiss dialect as she slightly slanted her head to the right.

"If it's a seven-fifty then I'll take the BMW," Jerome replied, expecting at least a seven-forty. His German had a touch of American accent.

"I have a seven-forty," she said.

"Okay, that's very good. I'll take that one," he answered, satisfied with the choice.

"Is the dark green seven-forty ready?" Gudula put the question through the speaker system by pressing a button on the phone unit in front of her desk.

"*Ja!*" it came back loud and clear through the small speaker in the phone.

"The car will be in front in a minute," she said in a friendly, but professional manner. She continued her efforts to stimulate a flirt now with a lubricious look in her eyes.

She returned his driver's license and the AMEX Platinum card. Then she put the rental agreement into an envelope. Gudula moistened the envelope tenderly with her tongue until she realized that this envelope wasn't gummed and wasn't supposed to be sealed. She just giggled and handed Jerome the envelope together with the car keys. Her fingers touched his hand—a moment of arousal.

Jerome thought that she was really cute, even though for just a millisecond the *bimbo* thought crossed his mind. He refused to receive it though because her gestures and her voice had truly a soothing effect upon him. He certainly welcomed all of this at this juncture. He also enjoyed the fact that no one else came into the storefront office while he transacted his business there.

"See ya," he said softly in English as he swiftly moved through the front door to the Bimmer. He put his two bags into the trunk and only extracted his passport, just in case border controls would stop him for a random passport check. With one more look at Gudula through the glass door he slid into the driver's seat and sped away.

20

WITHIN AN hour Jerome had crossed the Swiss border to Austria. To reach his desired destination, Jerome had to drive all the way across Austria from Tirol to the southeastern region of the country. That's where his folks lived, in the province of Styria where he was born. Altogether, the 625-mile trip took about eight hours. Included were a couple of stops along the way to gas up and to check into the Men's room. The traffic sign at the entrance of the Autobahn indicated a speed limit of 130 km/h. At times he was gutsy enough to close in on about 225 km/h, but only on some straight stretches of asphalt. Occasional rain hindered the thrill of speeding and kept him somewhat safely within and around the permitted speed limit.

He arrived shortly after eight P.M at his parents' house, which was located about fifteen miles east of Graz. He had a day to spare and was eager to visit with his folks. They traveled to the U.S. only once every other year to spend a couple of weeks with the family. And Jerome hadn't visited Austria since the early nineties.

He planned on staying only for a day or so. Just before he left Florida he announced his visit as he called his parents from the airport in Miami. When Jerome left Zürich he once again gave them a holler to inform them about his departure from Zürich. He verified his estimated arrival time for later that evening. His father and mother were anxious to see their son.

The BMW came to a halt in front of the cast iron gates. Jerome got out and rang the bell. His father came down the stairs and opened one gate manually.

"Servus," Jerome's father said.

"Hello, how're you?" Jerome replied in German. Then he drove the car into the driveway and parked it in front of the two-car garage.

His mother was also standing there. They embraced. Only his parents lived in this three-bedroom 1800 sq.ft. bungalow. The cozy house offered some upgraded amenities. It was embellished with heated marble floors. Handcrafted woodwork stretched across the ceiling from the hallway into the kitchen. By no means was it a cheap place. They had worked for over a decade on building and furnishing this luxury house. The appraised value of the home had soared to an equivalent of half a million bucks.

All three went into the kitchen area. His parents were in their late sixties. Mom had prepared a traditional supper for Jerome of cooked beef and onions immersed into a fantastic rich marinade of vinegar and pumpkinseed oil. He relished this exceptional dish which was served cold. The pumpkinseed oil made all the difference. Only pumpkinseed oil of locally grown and harvested pumpkin seeds, that had been filled into glass bottles by small independent farmers in the province of Styria, offered this sought-after special flavor.

In the U.S. pumpkinseed oil was very hard to come by. Sometimes Mom had sent him a half-liter bottle which would last for a month or two. Aside from this dish called *Saures Rindfleisch* which Birgid prepared for him once in a while, Jerome frequently poured the black *Kürbiskernöl* over salads. To the casual observer unfamiliar with this delicious seasoning, pumpkinseed oil resembled motor oil as it indeed looked just the same.

Fresh baked dark bread was also served. He ripped the bread into several small pieces and added those into the bowl in front of him. He was hungry. The last meal he ate was on the Swissair airliner. He had eaten all of it as the food in first class was always a notch better than in coach. Since he left Zürich he only had a Mars chocolate bar and a Pepsi along the way.

Among the other delicacies served by Mom were pretzels from the *Murbrücke*. The Murbrücke was the main bridge in Graz that crossed over the Mur river. Right on that bridge the *Pretzelmann* stood five days a week selling his most delicious pretzels. Earlier on that day, Jerome's father had driven down to Graz to purchase two dozen pretzels. For Jerome these were the best pretzels in the world, and they tasted the best when freshly baked. That night these pretzels were fresh and tasty like never before.

To conclude the supper a homemade strawberry shortcake with newly harvested strawberries was the dessert of choice. He was stuffed. This meal compared easily with any feast prepared at Thanksgiving, he thought, and tasted even better right now. His parents weren't eating, but only watched their son gain a few more pounds as he enjoyed some real food. They chatted in their native language covering the usual topics from the kids to Birgid, to their next scheduled visit to Florida, how the business was doing and about his journey to Asia, and the good life in Naples.

Jerome's Dad didn't waste any time to pull out a Cadillac brochure from a stake of magazines. He expressed once again his strong desire to own a brand-new Cadillac by the end of the year. He'd said the same thing over and over again for the past five years, but never followed through on his plans. Jerome had offered more than once to buy him a Cadillac in the U.S. and to ship it over, but so far, for whatever reason, it had never worked out.

This year he would make his dream come true, Jerome assured his Dad. On small notepad he wrote down the desired choice of exterior and interior colors. Jerome promised that he would buy a brand-new Cadillac for his father immediately upon his return to the U.S. Jerome would register and insure the car in the U.S. for six months and store the vehicle in one of his garages. Then, whenever he shipped the car to Austria, after the six-month period, the automobile was exempt from all import duties, customs and taxes. Such fees would normally increase the cost of the vehicle by fifty percent. Even with tens of millions in the bank, Jerome wasn't about to throw some twenty grand in unnecessary fees out the window.

The hours vanished quickly and the clock had turned past midnight. Jerome was at work on his fourth or fifth piece of the scrumptious strawberry shortcake. He turned around and reached for the old-fashioned phone behind his chair. He placed a call to Birgid to see if everything was all right.

"Hi, how are you?" Jerome tenderly asked Birgid.

"What time is it?" She replied half asleep.

"It's just after six o'clock in the afternoon in Naples. It's midnight over here, and I'm ready to go to bed. Did I wake you?" Jerome asked.

"I must've fallen asleep again," Birgid said as she continued to listen in her state of drowsiness. She would often zonk out in the afternoon when watching a crafts show on TNN or HGTV. Not that she was sick, but just tired so she repeatedly napped in the afternoon for an hour or two.

She had this ritual of getting up at five-thirty every morning. Not that she had to get up that early, but she loved beholding the sunrise. Birgid also studied the scriptures on a daily basis and the morning hours were usually the best time for such a thing, she said frequently. She would sit outside on the lanai and observe the burning sun rise out of the water on the horizon while quietly reciting a Psalm. This exercise brought peace to her soul—memorable moments in unity with God and creation.

"Can I talk to her?" Jerome's mother asked.

"No, I don't think it's a good idea. She's not quite awake right now," Jerome answered his Mom.

Jerome only continued the conversation with a few more sentences to let Birgid doze off again. Jerome assured her that everything was all right and that he missed her a great deal already.

Birgid echoed his niceties and they ended the conversation with both of them saying in unison, "I miss you. I love you."

Jerome spent Thursday with his parents gabbing about this and that. They gazed at childhood pictures and ate lunch at the village's only *Gasthaus*—an old-fashioned country restaurant. They had a rich time of fellowship enjoying the most precious things in life. That evening he went to bed early.

21

LATER ON Friday morning, after a hefty continental breakfast prepared by his mother, Jerome said goodbye. He stopped by his brother's home which was just down the road from their parents' bungalow. His brother, who was a year younger than Jerome, was a chemical engineer and taught chemistry at the University of Graz. He was married and with his wife he had three children.

Contrary to Jerome, Anton, his brother, was not the adventurous type and lived a rather dull lifestyle in comparison. One thing they had in common though, namely that Anton wasn't fond of traveling the planet just as Jerome was hesitant to go on a trip. Anton spent most of his time at the university and he invested any spare time in his family.

Financially, Anton wasn't wealthy at all. With the meager salary from his teaching position at the university he was only able to make ends meet. His wife also helped out a bit by working as a part-time or substitute teacher at an elementary school. Some years ago they had visited the U.S. with their three kids. It was Jerome who footed the bill for the trip. For years Jerome had provided Anton with investment tips in the stock market, but he never took advantage of his advice.

Anton was an active member of the local Greenpeace chapter and had supposedly put special emphasis on an alternative lifestyle. Jerome couldn't figure it out: *Did it mean that all environmentalists had to appear poverty stricken?* he argued with himself. It started with all these ridiculous concepts and ideas. While Anton owned a minivan, he still rode his bike around town most of the time. He used soap with only every third or fourth shower, and neither he nor his wife applied deodorant. They ate wild rice and lots of veggies. Anton, of course, had a beard and long hair which had been braided into a ponytail. But his wife's hair was short—very short.

At first, Jerome didn't even want to go and see Anton, but then upon the urging of his mother, he agreed to a quick visit to say *Hi!* since he'd been in the area.

In Jerome, Anton and his wife saw the personification of a capitalistic villain who was busy at work destroying the planet. And Jerome considered his brother to be the perfect example of an environmental wacko. Anton still couldn't understand that the hole in the ozone layer had remained virtually unchanged in size for dozens of centuries. Anton didn't get it and had desperately clung to his believe that global warming was a reality, even after it was a proven fact that no such thing as global warming existed. The global warming hype was only a public relations stunt by some wacko scientists in the sixties to extract some endowments, Jerome remembered a Rush Limbaugh sound bite as he once scanned through some AM stations in the early nineties.

"Hi, how are you?" Jerome asked when Anton opened the door.

"What a surprise to see you around," Anton answered rather sarcastically.

They shook hands. Apparently nobody else was home.

"The kids are in school," Anton said. "Would you like to come in?" he continued.

"No, thanks, I just wanted to say 'Hi!' and I'm actually already on my way to Vienna. I've got a plane to catch," Jerome explained. He didn't want to go in and sit down and listen to all kinds of weird theories. He had no desire to be indoctrinated by a pessimistic outlook for planet earth with a gloomy future for mankind saturated with doomsday religion.

He sure couldn't tell Anton about his current involvement in a nuclear power plant. This would've potentially infuriated Anton in a split second. As a teenager, Anton was already a participant in the largest anti-nuke protest march in Austria. That certain march, that had ended in a riot, prevented the start-up of the only nuclear reactor ever built in Austria. The government of Austria had spent well over a billion dollars for the construction of the Zwentendorf nuclear power plant. Later the government was forced to shell out another hundred million or so to dismantle the nuclear components of this monument of *Schildbürgertum* (Gothamitery).

"Too bad," Anton said.

Before they finished their initial handshake, the conversation that lasted for only about fifteen seconds, was abruptly terminated as the *Hi!* turned almost simultaneously into a *Goodbye*.

It made Jerome sad to see that he had no cordial relationship with his brother. Through all kinds of creative means he had invested years in building such a relationship, but seemingly to no avail. They had drifted farther and farther apart over the years. The gap had become noticeably unbridgeable.

Jerome hated scepticism and negativity. He feared that he would be bombarded with all these decadent philosophies if he would invite Anton and his family to the States once again. Sure, Jerome would have to foot the bill for the tickets anyway, which wouldn't have been a problem, but since Anton was very critical of the U.S., the whole notion screamed disaster before the idea was even conceived. He had given it his best shot with countless chances for this relationship to work, Jerome assured himself in an attempt to appease his conscience. But some things just weren't meant to be. This afterthought was a balm for his mind to take away the lingering anguish.

CHAPTER

22

ENJOYING THE Autobahn, he raced to Vienna, sometimes doing a hundred and forty miles per hour. The BMW was glued to the asphalt moving as on rails even through the most conical bent curves. On a long straight stretch along the turnpike near Sebenstein, the needle of the speedometer closed in at 150 mph.

It was about noon when Jerome reached the outskirts of Vienna. He maneuvered the Bimmer skillfully through heavy traffic right into downtown Vienna toward the *Wiener Börse* (Vienna Stock Exchange). Across from the Exchange was a Hilton, where he checked in to his reserved room. This hotel was one of the rare buildings in town which was equipped with quality air-conditioning.

"*Guten Tag.* My name is Birchner and I have reservations," Jerome said in German.

"One moment please," the clerk said as he punched a few keys on the keyboard.

"Yes, Mr. Birchner. Your passport or a picture ID please," the clerk requested.

Jerome handed his Austrian driver's license and a credit card to the clerk. The Austrian driver's license had no expiration date and it was a valuable document. He once used it in Florida when he was stopped for speeding. Jerome handed the State Trooper only the Austrian driver's license. The State Trooper argued that he couldn't write a ticket on an Austrian driver's license and let

Jerome go free.

At first, the guy at the front desk took only the driver's license, and then, a few minutes later, reached for the credit card. It took a fifteen minutes until the clerk returned the driver's license. Then he handed Jerome the credit card together with the key to the room. The room key was in the format of a credit card with a magnetic strip on the back. The clerk wasn't very communicative and didn't even provide Jerome with instructions on how to get to his room. It didn't really matter to Jerome. It was always the same procedure anyway. The first two digits would indicate the level and the two or three digits thereafter, the room number.

"Where can I park my car?" Jerome asked as he already moved away from the front desk with a couple of steps.

"Drive around the building and into the parking garage. The room key will open the gate," the clerk instructed calmly.

Jerome expected somewhat of an apology. But no such thing from this cocky little weasel, Jerome complained to himself. The weasel just turned around after he provided Jerome with the instructions. It was obvious that the behavior of this receptionist didn't fit the decorum of personnel in his position. Jerome exited the Hilton and drove the BMW to the designated spot in the parking garage. Then he stepped into the elevator to go to his room.

When he opened the door to the room his eyes convinced him that five hundred bucks a night wasn't necessarily a bargain for this kind of accommodation. But at least it appeared to be comfortable and clean. It'd be all right for a night, he cheered himself up. He'd rather be back home in his mansion gazing at the sunset over the Gulf and enjoying the luxurious ambience of his home in the much desired company of his lovely wife.

Later in the afternoon he strolled through the tiny streets of Vienna, along *Kärntnerstrasse* and the *Graben*. Friday was always busy along the promenades of the *Innenstadt* where thousands of people had made window shopping their favorite pastime. Pantomime groups, portrait artists, and street musicians freely interacted with the various crowds on every street corner.

"Hi, honey, how are you?" Jerome phoned Birgid around 1800 hours *MEZ*. It was noon in Naples.

"Pretty good. At least I'm awake today," Birgid replied.

"That's great. Things are fine here and I'll be off to Korea tomorrow morning."

"Be careful, honey. I miss you," she said.

"Me too. I'll call you from Korea when I get a chance to. I love you," Jerome said. The confab ended. He didn't want to stretch the dialogue. Due to the nature of the Nicanor contract he was aware of the probability that someone could've been listening. In the case that someone was listening, he made sure that they would get as little material as possible. Jerome and Birgid used to communicate in German to each other, but for over a year now they had adopted English as their primary language. Occasionally, German was still spoken in the Birchner home in everyday conversations, especially when the kids were around.

"HE CAME alone. He's staying at the Hilton across the Exchange," a suspicious looking character of Middle Eastern origin placed a call from a phone booth outside the Hilton. A man in an IAEA office located on the twenty-sixth floor of the UN building in the UNO City in Vienna was on the other end. The swarthy individual was a man leisurely dressed in dark colors. He wore a black T-shirt, black cotton trousers, dark sunglasses and a black baseball cap. His face revealed contempt—the corners of his mouth pulled down, and his lips curled into a wave, his chin bullied firmly forward. He obviously hadn't shaved in a week. A violent aura beleaguered this man with his typical Arab features.

"Very good. Just keep a close eye on him. Is the phone bugged?" The voice from the IAEA office asked rudely. "Nobody told me, boss. I've just been waiting for your orders . . . and you didn't tell me." His sarcasm manifested mounting stress. "It's kind of late now, unless he leaves his room again." "What are you waiting for?" his contact snapped. "Of course we need his phone bugged. I thought you were a pro." Incensed, the IAEA man was wondering if he had made a mistake by using the Arab for this kind of work. After all, the Arab wasn't a private eye or a detective, but a cold-blooded killer and that's what he did best.

"You want me to take him out now?" the Middle Eastern character pressed the inevitable question carelessly through the receiver.

"Of course not!" the male voice yelled, now obviously unsettled by the inquiry. "We need him in Korea, stupid!" he spit out. "You should know . . . that's the plan," he continued to scream through the phone. "Just keep a very close eye on him. He's smart, he's been around the block. Make sure he doesn't see you. If he suspects anything, we must kill him immediately. But I don't want that to happen right now. It's perfect. In a few days he won't be a problem anymore." He tersely continued to explain the situation much calmer now, but still with notable aggravation. The phone clicked and the telephone connection was broken.

The sinister man in the phone booth looked at the receiver and shook his head. He shrugged his shoulders before he put the handset back in place. He left the phone booth and slowly slid into the driver's seat of a black Mercedes with dark tinted windows. He dangerously turned the car around, cutting off oncoming cars, tires squealing as he crossed the busy boulevard in front of the Hilton. He moved the Benz into a public parking space across the hotel. His behavior was obviously suspicious and strange.

THE MERCEDES was parked until Jerome emerged from the hotel around six-thirty the next morning. Jerome climbed into the back of a taxi, refusing to put his bags in the trunk. He had already made arrangements for the BMW to be returned to the Hertz rental-car agency. The hotel would take care of it whenever the Hertz office opened for business a couple of hours later, the front desk assured him. The taxicab chauffeured Jerome to the airport where he was scheduled to catch a flight in first class to Seoul on a KAL airliner.

Wide awake now, the dubious swarthy goon followed the cab in his Mercedes to the airport terminal. He parked his wheels a few cars behind the cab. He observed as Jerome exited the taxi at the terminal and swiftly vanished through the automatic sliding doors of the *International* departure building. His job regarding Jerome Birchner had just begun. Half-closing his eyes, the thug reminded himself of the work ahead.

23

THE KAL airliner landed in Seoul on schedule. Two men in suits awaited him. As soon as Jerome walked off the aircraft through the door in the front, the two men approached him instantly. Both produced shiny badges.

"Mr. Jerome Birchner?" the man to the right in the brown suit asked.

"Yes," surprised Jerome replied, indicating the *Who are you?* question with his countenance. But initially no response came from either one of these guys.

"Who are you? CIA?" Jerome inquired.

"The State Department has sent us to pick you up, Mr. Birchner. This is Special Agent Taylor, he's with the CIA and I'm with the Air Force." The gentleman from the Air Force made the introduction, but failed to introduce himself with a name. "Please follow me. A chopper is waiting to fly us to Pyongyang right away. We'll handle immigration for you," he continued with his instructions.

Their extremely formal air forced Jerome to comply. "Okay, let's go," Jerome said as he didn't know what else to say. The badges seemed authentic and the helicopter would quickly reveal if these guys were for real or not. He handed one of his bags to the guy in the gray suit, who had been identified as CIA Special Agent Taylor. Agent Taylor hadn't said a word yet and apparently wasn't about to change the course of his intentions.

Reluctantly, Taylor took the bag from Jerome. He followed both men through the exit to a separate immigration booth. The Air Force man showed his badge to the South Korean immigration officials and said something in Korean.

Then the Air Force guy turned to Jerome. "Sir, your passport please," he requested.

Jerome handed the passport directly to one of the two Korean immigration officials, but the Air Force guy intercepted the transaction. He took the passport from Jerome and flipped it skillfully open to the page of the mug-shot. Then he disclosed the document to the immigration official who barely glanced at it.

Another immigration official emerged from behind. Agent Taylor flashed his badge to all three immigration officials. The three men were waved through the immigration post without a hassle. Jerome followed the man who only identified himself as someone with the Air Force as fast as he could. First through a small corridor down a flight of stairs made out of steel. Then through a glass door to the outside where a U.S. Army helicopter waited.

The Air Force man directed Jerome to enter the chopper. Jerome climbed into the aircraft through the rear opening behind the pilot. After Jerome had boarded the helicopter, both guys boarded behind him. Agent Taylor threw Jerome's bag carelessly through another rear opening into the chopper. Once the blades began to turn, conversation was impossible. Jerome hated helicopter rides. He was hopeful that it wouldn't take too long to get wherever they were going. Both men in the suits didn't smile once during the flight. They simply stared through the window into the sky. This thing was really moving and an exhausted Jerome fell asleep.

When the chopper arrived in Pyongyang they had to wake Jerome Birchner. He had moved on into la-la land.

"Mr. Birchner, time to get up. We're here," the Air Force guy firmly said, trying to wake him as he gently shook him by the right shoulder.

Jerome woke up, but was groggy. With a shaky voice he said, "Guys, it was a nice ride, but now I have to find me a hotel. And I don't know a thing about this place, so maybe you can help me out here?" Jerome just looked at these guys, hoping they'd be able to assist him with some advice. Jerome had been unable to book a hotel room in North Korea in advance. He'd searched the Internet and contacted various travel agencies, but it had led nowhere. Originally he'd planned on staying in Seoul until he made contact with the U.S. Embassy in Pyongyang to arrange the specific time for the meeting with the Undersecretary of State. These were actually the instructions he had received from Ms. Vicky Darnell.

"Sir, you're in North Korea. Sorry to say, sir, the bad news is that there aren't too many hotels in Pyongyang to choose from. They don't have a Holiday Inn here. But the good news is that you, sir, won't have to worry about it since you're a guest of the U.S. government. A suite has been made available to you in the American embassy." The silent man had just spoken his first few sentences since meeting Jerome in Seoul.

"I like that. Is Mr. Baxter . . . I mean, the Mr. Undersecretary, in Pyongyang yet?" Jerome wanted to know.

"Sir, the Undersecretary will arrive tomorrow. His visit had been delayed for a day. But the ambassador will be at the embassy," CIA Agent Taylor explained.

A HEAVY duty white Suburban came speedily toward the chopper. The State Department and the CIA used three-quarter-ton Suburbans with four-wheel drive. These Suburbans were basic models with cloth interior and no particular luxury features to speak of, except that all were furnished with bullet-proof glass and armored on every side.

Looks like a CIA vehicle to me, Jerome said to himself. It was customary for the CIA to use either white, dark blue, or black vehicles in foreign territories. Jerome's luggage was put through the cargo doors in the rear of the SUV. He was asked to take a seat in the second row of the bulletproof Suburban. Agent Taylor too, squeezed himself into the second row next to Jerome. The Air Force guy sat in front next to the driver.

They crossed over dirt roads and drove through what appeared to be a slum area. The driver, a uniformed soldier employed by the U.S. Army, apparently knew his way around. He maneuvered the vehicle proficiently through confusing turns which sometimes didn't even indicate a continuation into a certain direction. It did, however, guarantee disorientation to a stranger. When they later reached the heart of Pyongyang the road widened. The Suburban had the road to itself as the city showed obvious characteristics of a ghost town. No cars, but only a few people here and there on bicycles. Even without motorcycle escort, the adventurous thrill ride to the U.S. Embassy lasted only about twenty minutes.

Jerome was tired and all he desired was a phone to call Birgid before he would search for a bed for his holy eight-hour sleep.

"Is the ambassador here?" Jerome inquired.

"No, sir. May I show you to your room?" Agent Taylor answered courteously. He gestured for Jerome to go first. He bent a little forward much like a British butler would, which was absolutely atypical behavior for a CIA agent.

The Air Force man didn't enter the embassy but remained standing next to the Suburban in the courtyard. Agent Taylor accompanied Jerome to his room. An elderly Asian woman appeared from around a corner. She seemed to be the house-keeper or maid at the embassy. She smiled and was polite, helping Jerome and Agent Taylor to schlep the luggage up the stairs to the suite.

"If you need anything, let the maid know. She'll have dinner ready for you soon. Don't expect a steak though . . . this is still a third-world country," Taylor said, smirking.

"I need a phone. I need to call my wife," Jerome said, and anxiously searched the room with his eyes.

"Sorry, there's no phone in your room, sir. And all the other phones don't work. They still have the old analog system from way back when, if you know what I mean. And the lines are pretty rough once you do get through," Taylor attempted to clarify the situation for Jerome. Once again another smirk revealed either a friendly or a sarcastic disposition. Jerome wasn't sure yet what kind of propensity Taylor really had.

JEROME CARRIED a handheld satellite phone in one of his bags, just in case. But he preferred using it only in emergency situations, whatever that meant. Somehow in the back of his mind he still thought that the seven-dollar-a-minute charge was a pretty stellar rate. This usually hindered him from using his satellite phone more often. Jerome liked all kinds of gadgets and this $3,000 device was just another toy in his Byzantine collection of high-tech toys, which he truly treasured quite a bit.

On this trip he didn't feel the need to take his new sleek lightweight notebook computer. It was loaded with a whole array of portable capabilities for cable, Internet and even satellite connections. He considered the notebook a treasure too, and rarely ever used it. Since the late eighties Jerome had bought a new PC every three years. He bought one simultaneously with the obligatory purchase of his Mercedes. Usually within a year of launching a new upgraded Microsoft Windows version, he ordered his custom-built Dell PC.

The notebook though was his first portable computer unit. He had hesitated for years to buy either a laptop or a notebook computer. During those years, he had purchased one magazine after the other and scanned through hundreds of reports about this product. On the Web he compared the features of the available units. Until recently, Dell Computer hadn't manufactured something he liked. And because he owned Dell Computer shares, he wouldn't buy any other brand. This was a matter of principle, even though products from Toshiba, IBM and Gateway often appeared to be attractive alternatives. Jerome wasn't fond of the touchpad which Dell Computer placed in their notebooks. Instead he preferred the AccuPoint pointing device which was predominantly featured in units manufactured by Toshiba and IBM.

At last he was willing to shell out the five grand to purchase the notebook because he had already contemplated writing a novel soon. In such a case he had to be mobile, he thought. Jerome imagined that he would travel for research purposes. Perhaps he would search out an inspirational retreat at some remote mountain lodge in Montana, Colorado or Wyoming. He thought about going away for perhaps a couple of weeks or so, here and then. It would require portability and access to a PC or a notebook. And a complete PC equipment package would've been too cumbersome to carry around all the time. It was also an issue of not breaking the valuable gear. Jerome was more of a convenience guy and a notebook was the perfect solution.

He waited and waited, year after year, to go through with the purchase of such a unit because he also wanted his notebook to be stuffed with the latest features and toys. A DVD-ROM drive was an absolute necessity. That's how he was able to watch movies on the go, he argued. For Jerome watching movies was not only an important hobby, but even more than that it was a very significant tool for research purposes.

Even as entertainment was most likely the first and foremost objective of any motion picture, a great majority of filmmakers had also engaged in extensive research regarding the subject matter of their films. They always communicated a message in every movie because they had analyzed the topic of their films and had certainly come up with certain conclusions, which they were eager to communicate with the audience. The desire for most filmmakers was to bring viable stories to the screen with a cast of authentic characters that developed into a great movie. Frequently, they communicated in a film the result of their research very effectively. Authors of novels and nonfiction books practice the same thing. Jerome learned from movies and absorbed them.

By purchasing the notebook, Jerome was at least prepared to be mobile. It afforded him with the advantage of engaging into such undertakings as writing a book, watching a movie, doing research on the go, and other interesting stuff, just in case, if a change of location was required.

Jerome had put a lot of effort into preparing for all kinds of various scenarios. These were often things that could only happen by chance, but as long as the potential possibility existed, Jerome was interested. Frequently, certain specific issues wouldn't leave his mind. In some situations, he surely acted like a monomaniac.

The Y2K thing, for instance, was a good example for that. At first he was all excited about it and was on his way to becoming a proponent of the Y2K hype. Jerome had decided to write an extensive research report about it and the potential catastrophic consequences. In his mind he painted pictures of all kinds of cataclysmic events. For a week or so he was mesmerized by the presentations of the fearmongers.

But then he came back to earth and saw the reality of the problem as he researched the subject thoroughly. In his research

Jerome found evidence that the Y2K thing was nothing but hype and so extremely overdone that it was disgusting. No matter which camp the facts would lead him to in the end, he accepted the result of his research. Objectivity was the key to successfully researching a topic. Once he found out the facts about the Y2K issue, he consequently attempted to convince his friends and clients of the truth of such things.

"BY THE way, I'm Agent Taylor, Hank Taylor." The agent officially introduced himself now and extended his right hand for a handshake.

"That's what the other gentleman said. Anyway, nice to meet you," Jerome responded and clutched his hand. "Are you guys always this official?"

"Yes, sir, most of the personnel here is. Nobody really likes to be up here in the North. They'd rather be in the South, which is more like back home, you know. You can't trust too many people up here. If you need anything let me know. I live in the compound behind the embassy, room twenty-one." Taylor pointed in the direction of his compound.

"Are you always around?" Jerome inquired.

"Just press two and the one and then the *Talk* button on the intercom over there." The antiquated speaker made out of cheap gray plastic was mounted on the wall to the right of the only door in the room.

Jerome nodded as Taylor swiftly turned around to exit the room. The suite looked comfy enough and featured traditional Victorian decor. The double-sized bed though was not firm at all. It was so soft that it was virtually a written guarantee for severe back pain in the morning.

24

DINNER THAT evening consisted of a filled chicken breast with vegetables on the side. It didn't taste that bad at all—in fact, Jerome devoured the food with relish. The dinner was delicately prepared and was simply delicious. The presentation was similar to any quality restaurant, but with somewhat of homey touch to it. Jerome sat alone at the large dining table that easily could've seated sixteen. The Asian maid was friendly, even though she didn't say a word. But she carried a big smile on her long oval face. A few times she motioned with a wooden spoon pointing to the saucepan to inquire of Jerome if he wanted more of her cooking. To please her, he accepted one additional portion of mashed potatoes. She enjoyed serving the foreigner her exquisite cuisine.

He asked her in English for a telephone gesturing with his right hand, thumb and pinky stretched out. She led him into a room next door which was like a secretary's office. It was nine P.M. and since Korea was thirteen hours ahead of Eastern Standard Time it was eight o'clock in the morning back in the U.S. Contrary to what Agent Taylor had said earlier, the line worked surprisingly well.

"It's me," he whispered.

"Hey hon, so good to hear your voice. I was waiting for you to call me. I haven't heard from you in a couple of days. I miss you," Birgid responded softly, almost inaudibly at the other end of the connection.

"Miss you too. You can speak up, it's only me that doesn't wanna make a noise here. You know it's not that easy to call you from here. It's a strange place. But guess where I'm staying? Right in the U.S. Embassy in Pyongyang, the capital of North Korea. Seems like nobody is here. I can't wait to get home again. I wanna hold you, squeeze you and cuddle." Jerome's imaginations ran wild. So did hers.

Suddenly, the door slammed open and a man in a dark suit approached Jerome. "Who are you? Hold it right there," the man demanded, screaming.

Jerome was surprised as the calm atmosphere had been shattered in the twinkling of an eye. He was snatched out of his dreams and his desires to be with Birgid. The harsh reality of thousands of miles away from her in some strange country catapulted him violently back to consciousness.

"I'm Jerome Birchner with Nicanor," Jerome said slowly and stuttering a bit as he looked at the man, not knowing what to expect.

The man appeared to be lost in thought for a moment. He fumbled around for the light switch, desperately trying to turn on the lights in the room. When he succeeded he turned to face Jerome. He had taken a few seconds to calm down. "I'm sorry . . . I'm the ambassador, Jo LeJeune." The ambassador was still not fully aware of who this intruder was. But he felt more comfortable now, able to muster Jerome.

Jerome was seated in an office chair behind the desk and still held the receiver in his hand.

"Everybody seems a little tense around here, if I may say so," Jerome replied still kind of shaky. "I was just calling my wife."

"That's all right. No problem, young man. Go ahead. I'm sorry, but we're extremely cautious around here. Lots of things are going on." The ambassador went through the room and then opened a door and turned around to take one more inquisitive look at Jerome. "This is my office," LeJeune said. "Please come in as soon as you finish that phone call of yours. I really want to apologize, Mr. . . . Mr. . . . "

"Birchner, Jerome Birchner," Jerome said to help LeJeune remember his last name.

"Thank you, Mr. Birchner, I'm sorry," he continued with his head down as he entered his office.

"What's going on Jerome?" Birgid had been asking at least a dozen times while holding the line during the incident.

"Nothing, really nothing. The ambassador just crashed through the door and for a second he didn't know who I was. He probably thought that I was a burglar, a thief or something. Everybody is really tense around here," Jerome explained.

"Please take care of yourself. I wish you were here, right now. I haven't seen you for so long. It seems like an eternity. I miss you," Birgid's voice evaporated.

"I know, I know, I hate these trips too. But I'll be back soon. Remember, it's my last trip without you," he assured her. "I love you. I must hang up now, baby. Maybe this phone is bugged. I don't want them to hear our private conversations. I can't wait to get home again. I wish I could be there right now. We could cuddle and do so many beautiful things. I have to stop thinking about it. I love you, I really do. Bye sweetheart. Take care."

"Bye. Love you too," Birgid said with a heavy sigh. She wanted him home. She desired to lay in his arms and enjoy his gentle ways of stroking her, caressing her and kissing her all over her body. Love had matured and she was now more in love with him than ever before—even more than on the day they got married many years ago.

This was the beauty of genuine love. Yes, there were arguments and disagreements at times, but love had matured. Now she was able to really love him for who he was. She could trust him in everything. All infatuation had disappeared—marriage laid everything bare. With true love at work, it would've been very difficult to hide dark secrets. She knew how he would respond and react in certain situations. Jerome didn't have to verbalize his wishes, she was now able to look at him and know exactly what he wanted. Genuine love was beautiful and so fulfilling. It was pure and an overwhelming experience to be lifted up by one's soul mate. It was magical. She was in love with him, and he was in love with her. It was real, genuine love. She missed him, plain and simple.

JEROME ENTERED the U.S. ambassador's office slowly. The room was furnished with blue tapestries and looked a bit like the Oval office. The only difference was that this room wasn't oval, but instead it had four corners.

"Have a seat, Mr. Birchner," the ambassador offered, trying to be polite. "Some coffee?"

"Thank you, but no thanks. I just had a fabulous dinner," he replied. Jerome sat down in a chair in front of LeJeune's desk. "I don't wanna be unkind, ambassador, but why is there so much tension around here?" he inquired.

"You've got that right, Mr. Birchner. The North Koreans are very difficult and we've got a lot of things going on. All these new businesses from all over the world are moving in here now. Especially since we opened our embassy in this godforsaken country, everybody wants to be here. They all think they're going to hit it big this time. I can't figure it out. Everybody is poor and the Koreans haven't gotten the slightest grip on capitalism." The ambassador shook his head while reaching for a bottle of whiskey to pour it into an empty glass. "Want some?" he asked.

"No thanks." While the ambassador spoke, Jerome was already aware of the ambassador's alcohol tainted breath. "So you have your hands full I imagine?"

Joseph LeJeune nodded. "You can say that out loud. It's a full-time job. We don't even have parties like in other embassies around the world. They don't have a social scene here if you know what I mean. It's no fun spending your life here, believe me." The ambassador paused. "I heard you're with Nicanor, huh?"

"Yeah, they just hired me, so to speak. Do you know anything about their project in Yongbyon?" Jerome asked.

"No, not really. They're very secretive about it. But lots of people are involved. On his last Asia trip our President came across the border for a quick unofficial visit. He just checked up on them, I guess. He toured the plant and stayed for less than an hour. The media was kept at bay in Seoul and hadn't been invited to come along for the visit. The White House had ordered them not to mention a word about it. Nobody did. It was an unofficial private trip, that's why. I don't care what they do with this project up there, but a lot of U.S. tax dollars are being thrown out the window, if you asked me. It's our country that's paying for it." The ambassador took a long, slow sip.

"What?" Jerome was astonished.

"It's all U.S. taxpayers' money pickin' up the tab. You should know that, you're with Nicanor. Besides, it has been all over the press. They're over budget already. It's several billion dollars as I understand it. But that's nothing new and it keeps the North Koreans happy. Based on that ninety-four treaty they've agreed to abandon their interest in manufacturing any nukes as you probably know." He swirled the ice around in his glass. "But who really knows? We can't control it and we don't know what they're up to." LeJeune was obviously not very happy about the White House's policy toward North Korea.

"That's interesting." Jerome listened intently. All kinds of thoughts raced through his mind. U.S. taxes of ordinary citizens

THE CONSULTANT   139

were used to pay for this venture and he should help to put hundreds of millions of dollars aside for a beautiful, relatively young widow? Well, it was like stealing it in a sense, but maybe not. He didn't want to think about things like that anymore. He knew all along that the U.S. had subsidized North Korea with billions of dollars based on that certain 1994 agreement. The fact though that U.S. tax dollars were used to do so, sunk in with him just now. It bothered him a bit.

Juliet Farnsworth hadn't filled him in on these particulars, as she hadn't said much about where the money for this project really came from anyway. Based on his evaluation, it was all just a regular business deal. He hadn't wasted too much thought about the actual source of the capital until now. But now, thinking about it, this deal was a borderline thing, that was for sure. He didn't feel too comfortable with it at the moment and it would take a day or two to clear up his mind to reach a certain comfort level again. But after all, it really wasn't an issue because he didn't really care where the money came from. His contract was to siphon six hundred million dollars off the top for pretty Juliet Farnsworth.

"What about your wife and kids, do they live here?" Jerome asked LeJeune, kind of nosy.

"No, they're back in the States. Who wants to be here?" LeJeune complained, somewhat sneering at the thought, as he twitched the right corner of his mouth into a faint smirk. "I wanna get outta here too. Wanna go back home to Louisiana." Jo LeJeune was disillusioned. The pay was okay. But most certainly this was the very last territory in the world anyone wanted to be an ambassador in. He did the President a favor when he was asked to come here. His appointment was for a five-year term. He regretted his decision within a few weeks after arriving in Pyongyang. His wife and kids returned home to New Orleans after just a couple of weeks. Considering the unacceptable conditions of this locale, her decision to move back to the States was absolutely understandable.

"As I understand it, my guess is that I can get out of this assignment within a year or so." LeJeune wasn't at all convincing. "Then I'll go back home or maybe they'll give me another post in a more reasonable country. But we'll see." He shrugged, displaying little optimism.

Jerome didn't wanna be sentimental and saved himself and LeJeune the agony of going through all the routine questions. Questions such as it must have been hard to be alone here without his family, did he miss the kids, and so forth. His dilemma had been kind of obvious anyway.

25

THE NEXT morning, Jerome strode around the embassy looking for the ambassador. The diplomatic mansion once again seemed deserted. LeJeune was nowhere to be found. He couldn't even locate a secretary and he doubted that one was even employed by the embassy at this time.

In an effort to reach Agent Taylor, he pressed buttons two and one on the speaker unit in his suite, just as Taylor had instructed him to. But there was no response and Jerome concluded that Taylor too was either still asleep or had left the compound early. The only person Jerome encountered this morning was the nice little elderly Asian lady from last night. She smiled and appeared to enjoy serving Jerome her home-made breakfast.

Jerome was surprised to find the breakfast comparable to the American tradition of bacon and eggs, toast, grits, sausage, cheese, blueberry jam, and butter were offered. Instead of the traditional orange juice though, apple juice was served.

After the delightful breakfast, Jerome didn't even bother to ask for a rental-car agency. If he looked hard enough, he could probably find shop that rented bicycles, but a car rental was certainly out of the question. Neither Budget, Hertz or Avis had even considered entering North Korean market yet.

At the front gate the checkpoint had been staffed with well-armed guards equipped with automatic weapons, bulletproof vests and helmets. A wire fence surrounded the area. Surveillance cameras and infrared beams formed a tight web of additional security. This high-tech equipment made the U.S. Embassy an impenetrable fortress—it seemed.

From a window upstairs he spotted what appeared to be a café or bar across the street. Jerome pocketed his passport and walked nonchalantly through the checkpoint. He then opened one door and trekked through a narrow, short corridor till he reached the gate.

Surprisingly, when he walked through the gate, nobody took notice of him or even looked at him. Once outside on the sidewalk, he took a deep breath. He expected a polluted industrial stench, possibly a mixture of rotten eggs and gasoline. That's exactly what he had encountered in Eastern European cities during the eighties. To prepare himself for the worst, he recalled that certain odor to his senses, just in case, he thought. Jerome was baffled by the unexpected rush of clear, refreshing, mountain-like air. The lack of industry and cars surely had a very positive impact on the air quality. The pleasant atmosphere was complemented by a cloudless blue sky, and a tender breeze created a comfortable climate as the sun began to warm the ground.

There weren't many people walking, and only a few on bicycles. In all, it was a quiet morning as he entered the café.

"Hi, how are you?" Jerome spoke loudly to a Korean bartender as he approached the bar. He hoped that the bartender would understand at least a few basic English words.

The bartender nodded as to greet him.

"A Coke please," Jerome requested.

"Yes, sir, Coca-Cola," the bartender said with a big smile across his face. He was friendly and curiously looked over the gaijin.

There were a few older guys sitting around a table in the

corner playing some kind of board game. They didn't pay any attention to the stranger. Jerome sat down on a stool at the bar handing the bartender a U.S.-dollar bill. He didn't have any Korean currency and hoped that as usual, U.S. dollars would be accepted in this place too, as almost everywhere else in the world.

"Is this enough?"

"Thank you, sir. Yes, sir." The bartender nodded twice and placed the Coke in front of Jerome. Then the bartender leaned with his back against the counter behind him. A row of mirrors decorated the wall along the bar.

The Coke was served in a classy old Coke bottle made out of glass. Jerome would've preferred Pepsi, but he didn't bother to ask for it. The café advertised with Coke and Coca-Cola signs everywhere. For a moment this café appeared to look similar to some good old drinking hole in Texas back in the forties or so. The wooden floor moaned with every step a customer or the bartender took. A black dog crawled through an opening in a door in the rear of the café and even his movement produced the familiar moaning noise as in an old house. Jerome enjoyed himself.

It was so humorous to hear Neil Young sing *My My, Hey Hey* as the song screeched through an antiquated little red-and-white Sony radio on the counter in the back near the wall of mirrors. As he sang the line *It's better to burn out than to fade away*, Jerome felt the urge to chuckle. The thoughts that rushed through his mind were interesting in comparison. This place would probably never fade away and was here to stay, and on the other hand it didn't appear that anyone in this bar was getting burnt out either. These folks were all so relaxed it was as if the world had stopped turning and had come to a standstill decades or maybe even centuries ago. One of the old guys at the round table tapped his foot to the rhythm of the tune as he continued to play the sui generis board game without interruption.

Neil Young's classic anthem was followed by the Willie Nelson oldie *I Can't Find The Time* which was ironic because seemingly everyone in this tavern had plenty of time. After the Willie Nelson tune some local chirp aired for less than a minute—maybe it was only an announcement or a commercial, Jerome couldn't tell what is was. Things became really hilarious when right afterwards *Time Is On My Side* by the Rolling Stones took to the airwaves. Jerome was unable to control himself any longer and had to genuinely laugh out loud. Nobody in the room except the bartender noticed. While the bartender didn't pay any attention to it, Jerome himself kept grinning from ear to ear. *This wasn't real,* Jerome said to himself, *it's like out of a movie.* He smiled and closed his eyes for a moment as he drank the Coke out of the bottle. The soda, true to its name, created a refreshing, exciting sensation as it ran down his dry throat with prickly bubbles. It cooled his upper body from the inside out, much like a block of ice melting within the torso shooting sharp splinters of ice through the veins as he felt goose bumps forming on his arms. The soda had a much greater cooling effect than a cold shower would've had at this very moment.

26

EARLY IN the afternoon, two military men on motorcycles escorted the white Suburban through the gates of the U.S. Embassy. Jerome was back in his room when he heard the commotion from down below. The Undersecretary of State, Robert Baxter, had arrived. The ambassador too, was apparently awakened from his nap. LeJeune entered the hallway from his office. He carried a near empty bottle of Jack Daniels in one hand. His shirt hung halfway out of his trousers. His necktie swayed loosely from one side to the other. It was quite obvious that the ambassador had had more than one too many under his belt.

"Hi, Bob," the ambassador yelled across the corridor.

"Jo. What happened to you?" The Undersecretary said, concerned. "Gee, you're all drunk. What's wrong with you? C'mon let's go into your office."

Robert Baxter gave the ambassador a helping hand as LeJeune tottered and almost fell to the ground. Both men vanished behind the doors of the ambassador's executive office. Inside, behind closed doors, Baxter confronted the drunkard.

"Jo, you can't do that. The President has put you in charge to represent the United States of America in this country," Baxter said.

"What? The United States? What's that all about? Don't preach to me, Bob. All right?" LeJeune slurred his words.

"Nobody is giving me a helping hand. I wanna go home, Bob. I don't wanna be here anymore," he muttered and kvetched.

"Jo, I'll get you home. Just hang in there a little while longer, buddy." Baxter helped LeJeune to a chair. "Give me a few more months and I'll get you outta here. But you can't get drunk every day. That's not good, Jo."

"Bob, please get me outta here. I wanna be with my family. I miss my wife and the kids. I'm all alone here. I can't stand it any longer," the ambassador said, desperation recognizable through his whining.

"I promise, Jo, as soon as I get back to the States I'll talk with the President and we'll get you outta here," the Undersecretary said, realizing that the ambassador would soon be worthless at his post.

BAXTER ASKED Jerome into a more or less comfy waiting area, normally reserved for appointments with LeJeune. Of course, the ambassador had rarely any appointments and he was thankful for that. Baxter offered Jerome a seat on a couch next to him.

"So, you're Mr. Birchner?" Baxter articulated the question more like a statement as he firmly shook Jerome's hand.

"Yes, sir, that's me," Jerome answered as he sank into the sofa. He sat there like an applicant for a government job, recalling feelings of job interviews from decades ago, it seemed.

Robert Baxter and Jerome were alone in the room. The Asian maid brought coffee for Baxter and tea for Jerome. Also, some type of homemade Korean Danish, cake and pastry were served. Baxter and Jerome engaged into meaningless small talk. They talked about their places of birth and their individual upbringings. They also chatted about their families and other little things in order to get somewhat acquainted. Jerome though was reluctant and divulged little information about his personal life. But Baxter was all gung ho and rattled on and on about one private matter after the other. With one breath he went from one thing this minute to the next topic in the next minute. They also mentioned the Nicanor project in Yongbyon. Juliet Farnsworth and Nicanor Industries were also subject to discussion.

"It's sad what happened to John," the Undersecretary said thoughtfully about the John Farnsworth accident over the Pacific. "He was such a great guy. I had known him for over twenty years."

"What happened to the plane and what is going on with the investigation? Did they find the bodies or anything else?" Jerome asked, concerned.

"As you know CNN made sure that the whole world knows about the plane crash." Baxter shrugged.

Jerome nodded with approval. "It was on the news for days."

"But in reality they haven't found anything yet, at least not that I know of. The plane just disappeared. Gone." He snapped his fingers. "Just like that. You know, I was scheduled to go with John on that trip. But lady luck was very kind to me that day. Just a few minutes before I was ready to fly to Dallas on that fateful day, the President called for me. It was supposed to be an important meeting, according to the note that I'd received from his office. When I got there the President and I played a short round of golf and that was it. This made all the difference in my life. I'm alive and regretfully . . . John is dead." Robert Baxter expressed a mixture of relief and sadness, pressing his lips together, staring through the room, perhaps reflecting on his friendship with John Farnsworth and imagining the Gulfstream crashing into the ocean. Evidently he had spent hours thinking of their fate and how he had avoided an untimely death.

"I'm glad you're here, Mr. Baxter," Jerome echoed his feelings with empathy. "On another note: why is everybody so secretive about this Nicanor project? I mean, I do know that there has to be some sort of secrecy, but to the people that I've talked to, even the existence of the whole project has been denied. The other night the ambassador told me that the U.S. government is virtually funding the Yongbyon venture. I guess that means that the public should have access to some sort of information regarding this facility."

"Well, Mr. Birchner, Jo talks a lot and he shouldn't have. In any case, I'm sure you'll see the truth about this project up there soon enough. In 1994, the President made a contract with North Korea as we all know by now. We, the U.S., helped North Korea out with several billion dollars to get their infrastructure going. Who knows and who cares what the President thought of when he was doing this. He was probably distracted by thinking more about messing around with his gals in D.C.," Baxter said, amused by the thought.

Baxter chuckled, then continued, "In an effort to keep peace in the region and in an attempt to make China happy, I guess, they made this treaty with North Korea. Japan was all for it and they've also put some money into this project. Of course, as always, Japan only made a very small investment. They just wanted to pat themselves on the back to assure the world that they, too, were dedicated to a global peace endeavor. At the same time, the Japanese were scared to death of what China could do through North Korea in the region. By pitchin' in a few bucks, the Japanese hoped that this gesture would buy them some sort of insurance against China. But that's wishful thinking on their part, at least in my opinion. And we . . . we just have to be everywhere. Don't forget, we're the world police. At least we have a need to snoop around everywhere and we're trying to control things as much as we can, I guess," the Undersecretary explained. While he meant several of his comments to be received dead seriously, some of his other remarks were of the lighthearted sort, uttered solely for entertainment purposes.

"Sir, if you don't mind me asking, I'd really like to know why you've askcd me to come here? It's a rather remote location. I suppose there's a specific reason for that. Not that I mind coming here, because I really wanted to see the Nicanor plant anyway, but there must be a particular reason why you've asked me to come here," Jerome inquired.

"Mr. Birchner, we've gotta talk. Not now, but I have to discuss with you something very important. Maybe tonight. Maybe there's a chance for us to sit down and go through the details step by step. Mrs. Farnsworth told me a lot about you." Baxter was somewhat hesitant with his answer.

"You probably know that I've met Mrs. Farnsworth only once in my life so far. That was in Dallas a couple of weeks ago or so." Jerome was surprised and shrugged. "What did she tell you much about me?" Jerome was curious.

"This is a long story, and I can't get into it right now. But tonight, I'm sure we'll have an opportunity to relax in a nice club in Yongbyon. There we can talk about it. Get your things, if you please, Mr. Birchner. I know it's on short notice, but we're actually scheduled to fly up to the plant in half an hour. I apologize for not telling you earlier. I got carried away with our little chat. But anyway, this gives you a chance to check out the plant for yourself and to see everything with your own eyes. I'll give you the tour. Are you ready to go, Mr. Birchner?"

"Sure, let me grab my bags. I'll be downstairs in a minute." Jerome arose and walked expeditiously to his room to get his things. Another helicopter ride, Jerome thought, already feeling uneasy about it.

HE MET the Undersecretary in the lobby of the embassy. Both Jerome and the Undersecretary headed for the courtyard within the walls of this diplomatic facility. Outside in the courtyard, Agent Taylor opened the door to the white Suburban. Baxter and Jerome climbed in the second row.

"Why aren't they using the helipad in the back?" Jerome asked.

"They don't let us," the Undersecretary replied. "They're paranoid. No aircraft whatsoever can fly at a low altitude over Pyongyang. Their President is the only one who could, but he doesn't take advantage of his privilege either. Instead he takes his limo to his private airport just outside the city limits. The presidential airport is part of the Pyongyang military air base and is actually directly attached to the complex. The Korean military has strict orders to shoot down everything that invades the immediate airspace over Pyongyang," Baxter continued to explain.

"They're really paranoid," Jerome said, somewhat surprised, lifting his head to look at the perfect blue sky.

"Since the old guy died and his son took over, they're now more crazy than ever. They don't trust anyone. Of course, we can't trust them either. It's worse than Russia in the old days and during the Cold War . . . they're unpredictable. A few years ago they killed their own babies, just like the Chinese did. Birth control after the fact, if you know what I mean? I guess if you don't believe in God, you become the devil himself." The Undersecretary seemed outraged about these charges. He, too, showed some signs of disillusionment, but not as bad as Jo LeJeune. One of the biggest differences was that in comparison to LeJeune, Baxter didn't run around with a bottle of booze clenched under his arm.

"I thought things had changed in recent years and now they're embracing capitalism with open arms. IBM, Coke and Nicanor are already here. And what I've heard many other major corporations are opening offices in Pyongyang."

"Mr. Birchner, the big companies are here. They wanna suck 'em dry. The only problem is that the Koreans don't have any money for themselves. All the money comes from our government and goes right back to the big guys. It's the old money-making scam, if you know what I mean. Free enterprise and capitalism at its finest," Baxter said, clasping the back of his skull with his hands as he glanced to the ceiling.

"Every U.S. taxpayer pays for it to make the rich richer. It's been the same old game forever. It was the same in ancient history as it is today in our high-tech new world order. It's the same old scam all around the world. You should know about that, Mr. Birchner," Baxter elaborated.

"That's what the ambassador told me, too." Jerome looked at Baxter.

"Don't believe everything he says, but this one thing is true: back home nobody really cares. They think it's another Thailand, Singapore or South Korea. They think that this time the U.S. will cash in on it big time from the beginning. But my gut feeling tells me it will crash before it even gets really started." He pointed out the window. "Look at them . . . they all ride bicycles. They don't want cars. 'It's too dangerous,' they say." Baxter waved toward the bicyclers outside on the street. They hurried by continuously—sometimes alone, but more often in droves.

Baxter continued without interruption in the presentation of his essay. "They all have a job in some government-owned factory. I have a feeling that communism will never leave this place. They're all comrades and they're crazy. They all run around with big smiles on their faces, but on the inside they don't care. Well, that's at least my opinion, if you know what I mean. I don't think I'm wrong on this one though. But of course, everybody is entitled to his own opinion. I'm sure you have one too, Mr. Birchner," the Undersecretary gave Jerome the floor.

"I don't know. Every person has a soul and we all have

essential desires. How can anyone hide these things on the inside forever? It has to come out some day," Jerome replied. He was somewhat disturbed by the statements and observations of the Undersecretary.

"It's a whole different ball game over here, Mr. Birchner. I'm telling you. For example: did you know that when they're born their marriages are arranged immediately? They grow up and their jobs, their lives, everything is already planned. And worst of it, they don't wanna change it. These are their traditions. Don't touch their traditions. They actually get mad if you're trying to change anything or if you wanna do away with their way of life." Baxter gave it his best shot to win Jerome over to his viewpoint and philosophy. He even attempted to convert him.

Sure, everybody is entitled to his own opinion. Freedom of thinking and even freedom of speech are essential liberties of human individuality and creativity, Jerome thought. Was this truly the reality though regarding the people of North Korea? Jerome pondered the statements with which Baxter had just confronted him. In some circles his assertion and conclusions regarding this subject may have been considered total heresy.

This time the white Suburban arrived at the airport via a modest freeway. The route was certainly a shortcut as they reached their destination in just a little over ten minutes. The SUV stopped at a U.S. Army helicopter. The aircraft had been waiting for the men and was ready for lift-off. The Undersecretary, Jerome and Agent Taylor boarded the chopper. Jerome carried his two bags. The Undersecretary had only one garment bag which he had draped over his left arm. Hank Taylor carried a small white plastic bag which he had probably gotten from a grocery store. They threw their luggage, each for himself, into a compartment in the rear of the chopper.

27

THE MEN headed toward the crucial site of the Yongbyon plant. As they were nearing the area it initially didn't look much like a sophisticated industrial site, at least not from the air. In fact, virtually nothing hinted at the reality that at this location the most advanced nuclear power plant in the world was under construction. There wasn't even any source of water—a lake, a canal, or something for the cooling process.

Along the mountainside the front of a modern mirror glass building reflected in the afternoon sun. Almost like a monolith from another planet, it was cast into the mountainside. The structure was an architectural masterpiece and had been skillfully placed in a precise angle at exactly the right location. Therefore the building wasn't easily detected at first glance as it was somewhat camouflaged. The helicopter landed on a helipad right in front of the main office complex at the plant.

From the ground the appearance of the glass building was similar to the Nicanor headquarters in Texas, except that this structure was a few floors taller than the building in Irving and that this building was not a stand-alone construction, but built right into the mountainside. Also, instead of the color blue, they had used a bronzite coloration of tinted glass to obtain the camouflage effect to fit in with the colors of the surrounding area.

No cars were in sight anywhere. From the air, Jerome

couldn't even locate a parking area. A straight black strip indicated a possible access road to the site, though. Here and there a few golf carts moved silently around the premises. "This way," Agent Taylor said. He showed the Undersecretary and Jerome the way to the main entrance of the mirror-glass building.

"What do you think? Are you impressed?" The Undersecretary asked Jerome.

Jerome hadn't entered the edifice yet and not much had been visible from the outside. Sure, the architectural gem was imposing, nobody could deny that. He made an effort to be polite, "Well, I'm intrigued. I must admit, I've never been at a nuclear power plant before, but it sure looks interesting."

"Wait till we're inside," Baxter said, raising his eyebrows.

Agent Taylor stood in front of an oversized glass panel near a sliding door. He said his name slowly. It took a few seconds for the automatic door to open and to invite the guests to come in.

"It's a speech recognition device," Taylor explained as Jerome looked at him curiously.

Once inside they were required to pass through the obligatory metal detector. Then, an Asian man dressed in white overalls led the men into an area which was a type of locker room. White overalls were already nicely prepared for all three men. The odor in the building was comparative to typical chemical labs or even hospitals, similar to a mix of odors such as disinfecting agents, cleaners, and detergents.

"It's a very clean environment. That's why everybody runs around in stuff like this," the Undersecretary commented. With a grin he looked at Jerome as he lifted one of the overalls in the air for everyone to see.

"To date, this is the most advanced nuclear facility in the world," Baxter made this statement acknowledging a degree of pride in his underlying tone.

"Very impressive," Jerome said. He thought that the size of the facility actually very impressive, but he was reminded of a hospital, more so than of anything else. It appeared to be a futuristic, highly advanced environment. Almost something not from this planet, but rather a piece from another world if there would've been such a thing. Jerome had no doubt that this structure was man-made and that it wasn't a spaceship or something extraterrestrial. He didn't believe in the existence of life on other planets, nor in UFOs which he believed were purely an invention of the human mind. But whoever designed this Nicanor plant must've been into sci-fi movies and literature, and most certainly had an extraordinarily vivid imagination.

"Sign this, Mr. Birchner," Taylor said loudly as he suddenly stood behind him. He handed Jerome a piece of paper fastened onto a translucent clipboard.

The headline of this paper read *Confidentiality Agreement.* Jerome scanned it quickly. *Nothing new,* Jerome thought as he was reminded of the same paper at the Nicanor headquarters in Dallas. The agreement said that the person signing this paper couldn't tell a soul that he or she had ever been to this facility. Everything a person saw or heard at the Nicanor plant was classified information, and it was strictly prohibited to communicate anything about this facility to anyone outside the plant. On the bottom of the piece of paper under the designated signature area, a U.S. National Security advisory had been attached. It indicated that any person found in violation of the agreement is subject to criminal prosecution under U.S. law and is punishable with imprisonment of up to ten years and/or fines of up to $500,000.

"Where do I sign? Right here?" Jerome asked Agent Taylor, pointing with his index finger to the lower right hand corner of the paper.

"Yes, sir, right there," Baxter replied before Taylor could

answer. Jerome signed the agreement.

The men slipped into the prepared overalls and put on white rubber boots. For the purpose of covering their heads, each man received a white and blue cotton cap dressed with the Nicanor logo in front. The Nicanor Industries logo consisted of a modified *N* in italics with an *i* slapped creatively in the middle on top of the *N* somehow. The outfit resembled typical lab gear.

BAXTER LED the way ahead of Jerome. Jerome tried very hard to keep up with the swiftly moving Undersecretary. Taylor followed the two men like a security guard. They stepped into a nearby elevator and moved effortlessly to the twentieth floor. The elevator was noiseless—not even a squeak or rattle, simply nothing, an eerie silence.

All three men engaged in the common elevator posture by looking up to the elevator ceiling. Only as Baxter said a few words did Taylor and Jerome change their position and glance at the Undersecretary.

"First I want you to meet a few people," the Undersecretary said as they neared their arrival at the twentieth floor.

"This is the IAEA office. The International Atomic Energy Agency, you know that, Mr. Birchner, right? They tell us exactly what we can do and what we can't. It's like a little devil whispering consistently into your ear. In a place like this it means that they're checking on you constantly, twenty-four hours a day. They wanna make sure you don't screw up, if you know what I mean. If something does go wrong, it's a written guarantee that lots of people have messed up all at once. The engineers have to file reports with the Agency on a daily basis. This includes psychos."

Jerome thought about that for a few seconds. "Psychos? What do you mean, Mr. Baxter? Nutcases?" Jerome inquired.

That thought made Jerome a little nervous.

"Well, yes, to some extent if you wanna call 'em that. It's more like an incident of some type of phobia with a crew member. Sometimes they get crazy or reactionary. Usually it's just a bad day. But you can't have that around here," Baxter emphasized, without having to explain.

"For the U.S. engineers, scientists and all the other folks who work here, the pay is usually double what it is back home. Even a regular guy in maintenance makes at least a hundred grand a year. The scientists get half a million and often a lot more. But they can't have their families here and they can't talk about this place to anyone back home. So some of the new guys develop various phobias after awhile, something like a cabin fever. We just have to make sure they're kept in check. That's why you had to sign the *Confidentiality Agreement* like everyone else. Theoretically, you can't even tell anyone that you've ever been here." The Undersecretary acted like he was running this Nicanor project in Yongbyon himself.

Through automatic glass doors they entered a huge office—at least 5,000 to 7,000 sq.ft. in size. Computers, quiet laser printers, peeps and hums from servers and other high-tech gear played together in the manner of an orchestra. A stocky guy, balding on top, in a white overcoat was busy with something and moved jerkily around the rear of the humongous office.

"Hey, Mr. Kensington. Kensington!" Baxter hollered across the wide open space.

The stocky guy apparently got on his toes and glanced over a partition to the three men. He waved a short *Hello!* and slowly moved through the maze of desks to meet the men.

"Hi, Mr. Kensington. I want you to meet someone," the Undersecretary said as he introduced Jerome Birchner. "This is Mr. Jerome Birchner. I'm just giving him the tour," Baxter explained.

The short guy greeted the small delegation. "Nice to meet y'all," Kensington said in a southern drawl, making no effort whatsoever to hide his native place of upbringing. He shook Jerome's hand. Kensington didn't wear an overall nor a hat. Instead, underneath his white overcoat he was dressed in gray dress pants, a light blue button-down Oxford shirt and a dark blue tie. He wore classy, shiny black shoes.

"Nice to meet you, too," Jerome said quietly. He smiled slightly and lightly nodded, attempting to look Kensington straight in the eyes.

With his left hand Kensington played with a coin. He tossed the penny into the air and skillfully caught it again with his left hand. He performed the fling several times. Jerome followed the coin casually with his eyes and unconsciously registered the tiny hole in the penny as it passed a source of light on the way up toward the ceiling. Although he had a strange feeling, Jerome couldn't place the item. He only knew that he had seen it somewhere before.

Kensington turned his head jerkily to the Undersecretary. "Sorry, chief, I've gotta run. I've got lots of work to do. But maybe after the tour y'all stop by again for some coffee and a drink. All right?" Kensington said and clutched Baxter's hand. All of sudden he was apparently in a hurry. His movements became hectic.

"Sure, no problem, Kensington. Let's do that," Baxter replied.

Kensington turned and swiftly returned to the area in the rear of the office.

The three men exited the IAEA office. Next stop for the three men was four floors down. This was the designated level for the Nicanor executive offices. This floor was dominated by a bright dark blue carpet. Not a soul was there. Hundreds of computers, servers, laser printers and other high-tech gear peeped here and there, similar to the IAEA office upstairs. It sounded like a causerie of some birds in the trees.

"Does anybody work here?" Jerome inquired.

"This is Juliet's office back there," Joseph Baxter answered as he waved toward the rear section of the office. "The whole floor is Nicanor operations. Most of the work is handled by computers though. Up here we don't really need a lot of personnel. Computers don't lie and when something is wrong they tell us what's wrong with 'em. With people you always need a shrink around to find out and even then you don't know for sure. Right? Nowadays, with virtually no training, any idiot can fix these machines. Computers aren't moody and they don't have affairs. They don't smoke, they don't drink and they don't use drugs, if you know what I mean, Mr. Birchner. Best of all they don't need a vacation either." Baxter was elated about his insight. He offered a big grin across his baggy face and looked at Taylor as he continued to elaborate his philosophy regarding the benefits of PCs vs. humans.

"Well, that's true, but I guess somebody has to be around, I mean—" Jerome commented.

"Sure, we still need some folks to maintain this stuff. Several guys are down there in the buildings below, see?" Baxter went to the window and looked down on some flat buildings constructed into the mountainside. "They monitor the whole operation. Doesn't take a genius to do that. Still, each one of them makes at least a hundred grand a year, and most of them probably twice as much. I lost track of the payroll some time ago. Doesn't concern me, but it's interesting, isn't it?" the Undersecretary said. He stood there with his arms crossed, still looking down to the *barracks*.

"This is fantastic. I love it. Is this the future for all of us?" Jerome somewhat sarcastically verbalized the thought.

"Mr. Birchner, that's what it is. Here we are in a third-world country in which the natives are happy about getting their bowl of rice every day. And we're in this plant, a facility that indicates what the future of our planet will probably look like in some twenty years from now. Most North Koreans couldn't even handle an environment like this. They are farmers and are still using manpower to plow their fields. Once this plant is up and running, they'll have electricity a hundred times over what they'll ever need. Remember, that right now, most of them in the countryside don't even have electricity," the Undersecretary explained in detail. He was excited about it. "Let's go down to the reactor." He couldn't wait to show Jerome more high-tech installations and futuristic innovations.

While Jerome was somewhat interested, he could've cared less about this tour. The men stepped again into the noiseless elevator and the cabin sank to ground level. Once they arrived, they headed toward a type of station.

"There we go," Baxter said as he led the way once again.

At the station, several golf carts just stood there for someone to board these vehicles. Baxter motioned to Jerome to enter first. The Undersecretary squeezed himself next to Jerome. Agent Taylor sat in the back. The golf carts had limited independent steering capabilities as these were fastened onto rails. Baxter pressed a red button and the cart began to move. Just like the elevators, these vehicles moved almost noiselessly. The vehicle carried them through a long white corridor to the actual reactor facility of the plant.

Arriving at the reactor was the equivalent of entering a city through its city gates. Dozens of levels were built all the way up to the top. This part of the premises was the super high-tech area with flat-screen monitors everywhere. Tiny lights in colors of amber, red, green and blue were blinking or just stayed lit. It was a gigantic industrial site with hundreds of small integrated labs at every level. Everything was squeaky clean.

In the center of this domelike edifice were several silos that were apparently part of the reactor. Until this day, Jerome Birchner had never seen a nuclear reactor up close. He didn't know what a reactor would look like in real life. He'd only researched information about what such a thing was supposed to look like. But even if he would've seen one before, in recent years technology was changing quite rapidly, thanks to Nicanor, so that no nuclear reactor looked the same anyway, even though there may have been certain basic similarities.

They stopped the golf cart next to an elevator. The elevator cabin was fully enclosed in glass. They ascended approximately halfway up the building. Then the three men walked around a perforated steel bridge to a type of control center. Jerome looked through the holes in the steel bridge and while he wasn't afraid of heights, an eerie feeling succumbed his body. His feet became heavy as if someone or something was pulling him down. He heard voices that lured him to the ground. Only for a moment, his vision blacked out and he was dizzy. Jerome reached for the railing and got a hold of himself. He looked at Baxter in front of him, who didn't notice Jerome's momentary struggle. When Taylor stood right next to him, he continued to follow Baxter.

From the bridge the three men were able to overlook the site. It wouldn't have made much sense to just go down to the actual floor of this building. The chances of getting lost in this maze were great. From up here they received a much better picture of the facility's gigantic dimensions.

In the control center an engineer, who Baxter seemingly knew from a previous visit, offered extensive explanations about this and that. The engineer was of Asian origin and he hadn't yet mastered understandable, articulate pronunciation in English. He rambled for about fifteen minutes. Jerome was courteous and indicated with his facial expressions interest in his lecture, but he didn't understand a word the gentleman said.

After the class in high tech about nuclear reactors, which none of the three men understood, they went back over the bridge to the transparent glass elevator. At ground level, Baxter, Jerome and Taylor once again boarded one of the funny carts to explore more of these futuristic premises.

28

THE CART carried them through a long corridor. It was the opposite direction from where they had come earlier. When they arrived at the end of another long corridor, they found themselves in the midst of some type of marketplace. There were plants, fountains and a playground for kids. People sat on benches and were talking to each other. Most of these people weren't dressed in overalls, but were simply clothed in casual garments. The scene looked pretty Americanized. Most of the men and women wore tight jeans, and colorful T-shirts were popular. Some men wore black slacks and white shirts with colorful ties. Sure there were also several folks in their white overalls with their Nicanor caps, but they were in the minority at this location.

"That's unique, looks like the Enterprise," Jerome noted.

"C'mon, Mr. Birchner, over there is a nice restaurant. They've got pizza, very tasty greasy hamburgers, and donuts. Would you believe it, we also have a fabulous recreation facility in the back over there. Tennis, golf, a fitness center and a gigantic pool," Baxter said, pointing in the direction of the supposed recreation area. Baxter loved this part of the tour. He was grinning from ear to ear. He lit up like a child playing with his favorite toy and entering the playground at a McDonald's. He appeared to be a changed man and seemed to get younger by the minute. "Let's have a bite to eat," he suggested with enthusiasm.

It was obvious to Jerome that this facility was built right into the mountain. Aside from the artificial light, there were also bursts of daylight here and there—probably channeled from the outside through mirrors to these specific areas. They ordered pizza and bacon cheeseburgers, which when served looked so picture perfect that they looked almost to good to be true. Nevertheless, all three men were hungry and enjoyed their meal.

"Mr. Birchner, enjoy the food," Baxter encouraged Jerome as he got ready to stuff a hamburger violently into his mouth.

"Thank you, Mr. Baxter, you've been very kind to me. To come up here is certainly an experience," Jerome said as he too grabbed his bacon cheeseburger for the first bite. This thing not only looked good, but also tasted delicious, Jerome thought. He enjoyed every bite of it as he devoured french fries in between each mouth-sized portion.

Taylor indulged himself with a simple pepperoni pizza. It was greasy. He became jerky when a piece broke off and glued itself to his nice, clean shirt. "Jeez," that's the only word he said. He was trained well enough not to react in public to small mishaps like this. It would've been unprofessional to do so, they were taught at the CIA academy. With a napkin he made several desperate attempts to clean off the mess. When the stain didn't come out, he tipped one end of the napkin into his Sprite and gave a few more tries to wipe it off. Then he excused himself and went to the Men's room.

A TYPICAL Korean, thin and short, stood in the rear section of the restaurant. The light was dim in that certain area and the features of his face were barely recognizable. As soon as Taylor had entered the rest room, the Korean came over to the table where Baxter and Jerome continued to devour their lunches.

"Mr. Robert Baxter, there's a phone call for you. The phone is right over there next to the bar," the Korean said facing Robert Baxter. He pointed to the rear section of the restaurant from where he'd just emerged. The man spoke fluent English with only a touch of an oriental accent. Somehow the voice seemed familiar to Jerome, which for a moment took him off guard. But he dismissed the impression when he couldn't place the voice in his memory and the subconscious innuendo didn't make any sense.

"For me? Are you sure?" Baxter inquired.

"Yes, sir, Mr. Robert Baxter," he repeated.

After he said what he had to say, the Korean turned and left through one of the exits.

Baxter went to the phone and stayed only a few seconds on the line. Then he returned nonchalantly to the table. Meantime, Agent Taylor had come back to the table, too. He was much more relaxed now as the oily pizza stain had disappeared from his shirt. Instead, a huge wet spot of water decorated his shirt.

"Mr. Birchner, that was Kensington. The ambassador left a message for me to get back to Pyongyang tonight. I guess they can't do anything without me. All the preparations for the arrival of the delegation tomorrow is a big thing for them. So we need to fly back within the hour," Baxter explained, breaking the news solemnly.

"Too bad, I'm beginning to like this place," Jerome commented, absorbing the view around the marketplace.

"You know what, Mr. Birchner, I have an idea. In fact, Kensington suggested it. If you like, you can stay overnight. I'll be back tomorrow around noon. At lunch we can then talk about the very important confidential stuff I've told you about earlier today. Remember? Tomorrow afternoon, we need to meet with these big-cheese people from the States . . . several scientists, bankers, and a congressman are among them. I mean you don't have to meet them, but I do. That's why I'm here, you know. Anyway, it's because of this top-secret stuff, which I must discuss with you in detail, that I've asked you to come here in the first place. It's very important. I need your opinion on it," the Undersecretary said.

"That's great, Mr. Baxter. I'm not very fond of helicopter rides anyway. Actually, I hate them," Jerome answered.

"You can stay and glance into the future for a night. Too bad you can't tell anyone about it though," Baxter said, exposing his dentures with a big smile.

This was a great offer that Jerome accepted without hesitation. He hated these helicopter shuttles.

"Sir, I like to remind you that we've gotta stick to our security policy. I can't leave either one of you up here by himself," Taylor addressed the Undersecretary in a firm fashion. Until this moment Taylor was just staring across the marketplace observing people pass by like robots.

"Haven't we got at least one agent up here who could protect Mr. Birchner?" Baxter inquired.

"Sir, no, not at this time. They're all in Seoul for the arrival of the delegation tomorrow," Taylor explained.

Jerome interrupted, "Mr. Undersecretary, it's not a problem for me. If this is against your policies it's no big deal. I'll just fly back with you. Really, it doesn't matter to me." This solution was less desirable to Jerome, but if necessary, then acceptable.

"No, no, I want you to stay here, Mr. Birchner. I want you to enjoy this once-in-a-lifetime experience," the Undersecretary demanded facing Jerome. Then he turned away from Jerome and looked Taylor straight in the eyes.

"He doesn't need protection in this place. It's a fortress for crying out loud. It's a hundred times safer up here than in any state pen back home that I know of. Furthermore, nobody even knows who he is. There's nobody here who wants to harm our friend," Baxter, trying to persuade Taylor, said it all without taking a single breath. He patted Jerome lightly on the shoulder.

"Sir, if you'll sign a release, I have no problem with it either. But you must understand that I have to follow procedures, as you know. I just need a release from you, sir, and I can call Kensington to accommodate Mr. Birchner and I guess it'll be all right," Taylor replied, shrugging his shoulders.

"That's what I call good thinking, Hank. Let's get rid of this stupid bureaucracy. We're not in the Pentagon, but we're on vacation. Right, Mr. Birchner?" The Undersecretary said, slapping Jerome on the shoulder.

"Well, it's beginning to feel like a vacation." Jerome answered. He was excited to stay at the Nicanor plant in this virtual Utopia. As a child he had always dreamed about building spaceships and cruising the Milky Way. He loved watching *Star Trek* on television. Visiting the Yongbyon plant was the closest thing he would ever get to experience a futuristic space-station-like environment. It was an adventure.

Baxter wrote on a napkin:

> *Release for Mr. Jerome Birchner to stay at the YB Nicanor*
> *facility for one night. Today's date.*
> *Signature, Undersecretary of State, Robert Baxter.*

"Is this all right?" he asked Taylor. After signing the piece of paper the Undersecretary handed it to the agent.

Agent Taylor took a casual look at it and said, "Sure, sir. I'll call Kensington to meet us at the main entrance in thirty minutes." Taylor went over to the phone next to the bar and phoned Kensington.

"TAKEOFF WILL be in half an hour. Get ready." Kensington

ordered the hit through the phone and hung up.

The Arab listened through the speaker in the Hummer. He moved the vehicle slowly around the outside of the facility to the east wing of the plant. As he left the vehicle, he chewed a piece of tobacco and spit it on the ground seconds later. A few feet away was the farthest easterly corner of the building. By leaning his body slightly forward, he was able to glance around the quoin. With his night-vision gear he was now looking westward. He focused in on the main entrance, which was several hundred feet ahead at a 60° angle to his right. The visibility for the helipad was a much better one as the chopper was straight in front of him. The routine takeoff position of the aircraft would lead the chopper away from the plant and the mountainside, and take it in its predetermined course to his left in a southerly direction.

After they had finished their lunch, Baxter, Birchner and Taylor boarded a cart. The vehicle transported the three men through another long corridor back to the station from where they had originally departed. The three men trotted to the locker room.

"You can stay here," Baxter said to Jerome as he opened the door to the locker room.

"All right."

"You just keep the stuff on," he instructed Jerome.

Taylor and the Undersecretary quickly changed out of their overalls back into their own clothes. From there they walked over to the main entrance. It was the same entrance where they had entered earlier that day. Kensington stood there in the lobby, wrapped in his white cotton overcoat. The automatic door opened and all the men went outside. Because of heavy clouds higher up in the atmosphere no stars or moon could be seen in the night sky, even though it was a clear night over the immediate airspace of the Nicanor facility.

"You be a good host, Kensington," the Undersecretary said to Kensington.

"Don't worry," Kensington replied.

"We talk tomorrow, Birchner. I'll come early . . . a few hours before the delegation arrives. Plan on meeting me for lunch. Sleep tight, Birchner!" The Undersecretary smiled, turned around and gave a quick wave. Baxter and Taylor ran to the chopper which was ready for takeoff.

"Good night," Jerome said and also waved.

Jerome and Kensington turned around. They headed for the station inside the building where the small carts were waiting. The door closed electronically behind them. It kept every noise outside where it belonged. Inside, classical music quietly played in the background. It had a soothing and relaxing effect on Jerome. He was tired.

THE ARAB knelt on the ground. His position afforded him to aim precisely and the helicopter would make a perfect target. He was dressed in dark overalls. He was equipped with a FIM-92A Stinger portable antiaircraft missile. The Stinger weighted only thirty-five pounds and was very effective and very destructive. It was a favorite tool of Middle Eastern terrorists. The infrared sensor locked onto the aircraft's engine exhaust. Once the trigger was pulled, the missile blasted from the launch tube reaching a speed of Mach 2 within seconds. The 6.6 pound highly explosive warhead was able to completely destroy the targeted aircraft within a three-mile range.

As planned, the helicopter took off in a southerly direction. Suddenly, the quietness of the evening was interrupted by an outrageous bang as the Arab gently squeezed the trigger. The hulking aircraft disintegrated instantaneously into thousands of tiny pieces. About a mile and a half away from the plant, the burning debris scattered quickly into a desolate field. The chopper exploded only about a minute after takeoff. This wasn't just a minor burst, but a rather immediate and massive explosion. The missile ripped the aircraft apart in an instant. It was a precise unit that didn't allow for any mistakes. None of the parts hit a building on the premises of the Nicanor plant. Many tiny pieces simply dropped from the sky like fire raining to the ground. Nobody saw anything. It happened so quickly. There was no need to confirm the death of the passengers their death was sudden and certain. It was all over now.

Satisfied, the Arab watched the scenario to make sure he'd once again completed a job superbly. Then he took the Stinger, which was still hot, and secured it to a steel plate in the back of the Hummer. With skill he swerved the Hummer around as the four fat tires kicked rocks through the air. He returned to the base inside the mountain. The base was a storage facility for all the vehicles, weapons and other sophisticated gear on the Nicanor premises. Because it was underground, no spy satellite had the ability to look into the mountain and discover the explosive cave. The base could never be detected from the outside. If Baxter knew about this special storage facility, they sure hadn't visited this part of the Nicanor plant on that fateful day.

29

THE U.S. AMBASSADOR to North Korea, Joseph LeJeune, paced frantically like a madman through the U.S. Embassy in Pyongyang. On this morning he was sober and fully alert. His shirt was neatly tucked into his trousers, even though it was already soaked under his arms and around his back. His necktie was fastened properly. He'd rolled up the sleeves of his shirt. LeJeune held two phones in his hands: with one hand he seized the receiver of a desktop unit; in his other hand he clutched a portable phone. Alternately he talked into each telephone.

He spoke loudly and even screamed once, "What are you talking about?" Saliva gathered in both corners of his mouth and hit the receiver.

Nobody around LeJeune knew to whom he was talking. But then, everybody was very busy with their assigned tasks to solve this crisis situation as quickly as possible.

The embassy bustled with U.S. Army personnel. Phones were ringing constantly and LeJeune had his hands full. Water dripped from LeJeune's face as if the air-condition unit wasn't working. They didn't have air-conditioning at the American Embassy in Pyongyang. It was the beginning of orchestrating a sizeable search-and-rescue operation.

The Undersecretary of State, Robert Baxter, a U.S. Army chopper with two pilots and CIA Special Agent Hank Taylor had apparently disappeared from the face of the earth. The alert began to take shape in the early morning hours. LeJeune, the U.S. Army and various other U.S. government agencies and departments were unable to locate Baxter. A call to Kensington confirmed that the Undersecretary had left by helicopter the previous evening. While not yet confirmed, a potential tragedy was a foremost probability. It was cause for immediate concern and demanded action at once. LeJeune promptly contacted the State Department in Washington. The State Department in turn informed the CIA headquarters in Langley, Virginia.

CHAPTER

30

TREVOR GATES was stuck in traffic on his way home to his residence in the Washington suburbs. His digital PCS phone rang at precisely 1900 hours.

"You've gotta come in. We've just received a report about a situation in Korea," the female voice urged Gates to return to the office at the CIA.

He immediately placed a flashing blue light in the center of the dashboard of his Ford. Gates switched on all available emergency lights—the same kind the cruisers from the Highway Patrol and State Troopers were equipped with. All lights were now blinking rapidly. In his attempt to cross the median, the Ford jerked across the grass and slid through the mud to the other side of the road. When the car reached the asphalt, the tires squealed and burned white smoke. Trevor Gates wasn't the best driver on the force and he had a hard time regaining control of the vehicle. With a panicky effort, he got the cruiser back on track.

Because of traffic jams he frequently swerved into the emergency lane on the way to the CIA headquarters. Gates hadn't yet turned the sirens on because he hated their annoying sound. He considered the flashing lights sufficient enough to alarm motorists of his reckless high-speed maneuvers. The Ford was weaving rapidly through traffic from one lane to the other.

When a Cadillac, driven by a senior citizen, didn't move out of the way, Gates almost crashed into it. A hard last-second push to the brake pedal prevented the accident. The elderly couple in the Cadillac was shaken wondering who this maniac could've been. Even when Gates passed them they didn't realize that it was a law-enforcement vehicle. The CIA headquarters was located about seven and half miles from the White House.

Nearing the CIA headquarters, Gates received another call from the director's secretary. He fumbled with the phone attempting to avoid collisions as his speedometer hit 90 mph.

"Where are you?" she inquired impatiently.

"I'm, I'm . . . " he stuttered, "I'm right here. Give me a minute, okay?"

One of the last turns was a tough one as he rallied without stopping across a three-lane stretch of oncoming traffic. The stunt went without incident. As he entered the CIA premises though, Gates was simply driving too fast and rammed into a parked automobile. The crash resulted in a significant dent and an array of scratches on the parked car. The right front fender of his Ford had been demolished. Sharp edges of the damaged fender punctured the right front tire. When he arrived at the front entrance of the building, only bits and pieces of the tire were still glued to the rim. Gates got out of the car and glanced at it for just a second.

"Nice job," a fellow agent commented as he passed by.

Gates didn't pay any attention to the smart remark and barely heard it. He hurdled over the barricade and ran up the steps into the building. In the process he almost knocked down an elderly lady who was coming out. There was no time to apologize as he hurried to reach his destination.

CIA DIRECTOR William B. Tish was still at the office when he heard about the panicky phone call from LeJeune. The CIA was already busy at work pulling all its resources when Trevor Gates arrived. A weather satellite indicated some atmospheric turbulence in the area between Yongbyon and Pyongyang. But it was the National Security spy satellite which surveyed the area between Seoul and the Chinese/North Korean border that registered and spotted an explosive incident near Yongbyon. At first, it seemed to be weather related, perhaps a severe lightning bolt. CIA experts sat in the lab, replaying the digital recording of the occurrence several times over. By focusing and enlarging the frames of the incident one by one, CIA surveillance experts came to a shocking conclusion as they all leaned forward in unison. It was now a fact that the recorded phenomenon must have been a powerful explosion. It was probably caused by a missile or some other potent explosive projectile.

Gates arrived at the director's office breathless. He was wet under his armpits and sweaty all over.

"Gates, where the heck were you? Get your rear end to Korea at once." Tish was furious. When he saw Gates he sprang out of his chair like a teenager, steaming, he confronted Gates.

"Yes, sir, I'm on my way," Gates didn't hesitate with his answer. The tension in the room made it hard for him to breathe.

"You'd better be. Someone is blowing up our guys, one after the other like it's going out of style. And we're sitting here like idiots watching it like a bad football game. Let's go, Gates, let's get going. Let's get on the ball," he screamed at Gates, motioning with his right hand for Gates to go. The director was red-faced and ready to explode.

"Sir, everything is in motion," Gates replied in an attempt to calm the director. It didn't seem to work.

"Yeah, Yeah, you're telling me this. You just waltz in here while we've been working on it for the last half hour! I thought I put a competent man in charge of this operation!" The director stormed around the office. "But I can't have this, Gates. I can't put up with stuff like that. Don't you understand? The President is gonna freak out when he hears about it. I sure don't need any of this stupidity before I retire," he hollered. No way that Tish would slow down now. The war was on—it had just begun. The enemy was loose and unidentified at this time. But this foe wasn't invisible. Somewhere the perpetrator must've made a mistake. Most certainly somewhere a mark was left and a trace would ultimately surface and lead to the identification of the adversary. Tish was positive that they would catch the perpetrator in no time.

"We have an Air Base near the Korean border and an aircraft carrier in the East China Sea." The director surveyed the map he'd ripped from the wall and had spread out on the table. "Navy SEALs are on their way to the scene. The State Department is running wild. They're all gung ho about mobilizing everything possible. I've put Special Agent Chuck Osteen in charge of the operation." He turned to Gates, "You report to him. Is that clear, Gates? He's taking over for now," Tish explained. Adrenaline was rushing through the director's body, making him short of breath. He was agitated enough to have a heart attack.

"Sir, all right, but why Osteen? I don't think it's a good idea. He isn't familiar with the case," Gates said without thinking.

"Shut up, Gates," Tish spat out. "I don't care what you think, Gates. You blew it. Can't you see it? I've assigned you to a top-notch case and there you are. The two most important people in this get killed right under your nose. They didn't die of a heart attack, remember? Did you expect a medal for this?" He was in Gates's face. "Boy, if I didn't need you right now, I'd pull you off the case altogether," Tish, voice raised and red-faced, was losing his composure quickly.

"Okay, sir, I see," Gates backed away from Tish. He was at a loss for words.

"Well, what are you waiting for?" the director yelled. "Get

outta here. Get down to Andrews. A plane is already waiting for Osteen and you. Fly to Korea and make sure you solve this case right away. I don't care how you do it." Tish ran a hand through his hair and paused. Unsuccessfully he attempted to regain his composure. "Look, I need a suspect so we can hunt 'em down. Then everybody is happy again. You get it?" He made himself speak slower. "I've assigned thirty men to help you out. All our resources are available to you. It surely can't hurt to work with a guy like Osteen . . . he's done this many times before. Don't forget he's a Navy SEAL. If you're smart you'll learn something from him."

Tish leaned wearily on the table. "You're second in command, that's not that bad. It's your chance to prove yourself. So, please do your best and work together with Osteen. You won't regret it," the director made an attempt to encourage Gates now in a much quieter voice.

This didn't go well over Gates' ego and it didn't fit into his plans. *But whatever,* he said to himself, *let's make the best out of it. Let's work it to our advantage.*

"And Gates, one more thing," the director spoke directly at him, "let's keep the whole thing quiet. The press can't know about this yet. We've gotta name a suspect first. I don't wanna see your face on the eleven o'clock news. Do you understand, Gates? Did I make myself clear? No fancy talk to the press. We've plenty to do, we don't need them right now. We may have to do some covert operations over there. I don't want all the terrorists knowing about it. No leaks this time, Gates," Tish was enforcing his position on the zip-locked policy to the media, which he had upheld for decades.

But some secretary or some agent would always leak things to the press, or to the office of some political candidate. Then they would make a big issue out of it and create a stir. The whole world would know about it before the CIA could act. Suspects would go into hiding for years and the trace would trail off and run cold. It happened more frequently in recent years and Tish was angry at that. Usually, they'd never catch the informer as it wasn't always the same guy or gal.

It was regular procedure that the press secretary of the White House would give a statement once the accident was confirmed. And Tish was hoping once again that it was just an unfortunate accident. But his gut feeling told him otherwise. This time it wouldn't be that simple, he thought.

31

UPON ARRIVAL, the delegation of scientists, bankers, a congressman, and quite a group of media representatives were escorted by U.S. Army troops to a hotel in downtown Seoul. They arrived with a chartered airliner at Kimp'o International. Initially, the plane was scheduled to land at Osan Air Base. But after the disappearance of Baxter had become a certainty in the morning hours, plans were immediately changed to redirect the destination of the aircraft to keep the delegation at bay in a hotel in Seoul. It was clear to the CIA and to the office of the National Security Advisor that nobody from the delegation would be allowed to visit North Korea on this trip. Instead, they'd be sent back to the U.S. the next morning. Just the folks of the delegation didn't know it yet.

All members of the envoy were packed into the usual Suburbans and with motorcycle escorts were chauffeured expeditiously to the hotel. It was an awesome sight as eight white Suburbans and eight motorcycle escorts formed a convoy and raced through the streets of Seoul. Two lanes of traffic had been blocked off, otherwise they all would've been stuck in the heavy traffic congestion.

At first, CIA Director Tish suggested they should send the delegation back to the U.S. at once. But this would've created even more curiosity, especially among the media folks in the delegation, some argued. So they came up with the alternative plan.

The CIA Special Agent in charge of the protection of the delegation offered the people a legitimate excuse for the delay. He announced to all members of the envoy that the preparations for their visit weren't completed in time. Therefore their visit to North Korea had been postponed for a day. All members of the delegation understandably acknowledged this circumstance. They had been made aware of the possibility of delays before they had left the States. They were also informed about the fact that North Korea wasn't an easy country to deal with. The journalists didn't mind the postponement. For them it meant a night out on the town. The congressman was the most agitated by this circumstance and offered his apologies to the high ranking bank officials and the scientists over and over again. They assured him that it was all right and that he shouldn't worry about it.

A U.S. NAVY surveillance jet, deployed from the U.S. aircraft carrier in the East China Sea, located the intact signal of the flight recorder near the Nicanor project. From the time of the discovery it took less than an hour before the first U.S. Air Force helicopters with a search-and-rescue team arrived at the Yongbyon site. Several more choppers with such search-and-rescue teams on board followed. A transport aircraft from the Osan Air Base in South Korea near the North Korean border was already in the air on its way to the site. It was loaded with half a dozen U.S. Army Hummers and at least fifty U.S. troops.

Altogether 37,000 U.S. troops were stationed in South Korea. The U.S. maintained two Air Force Bases there, the Kunsan Air Base, home to the 8th Fighter Wing and the 8th Supply Squadron, and the Osan Air Base, home to the 51st Fighter Wing which flew the A-10 and F-16 fighter aircraft.

The search-and-rescue teams searched the site extensively, leaving no stone unturned. And it didn't take much time to find debris of all sorts. Hundreds of small helicopter pieces left plenty of indicia. Even some fractional charred bodily remains, a part of a finger, ear, burned skin, a piece of a shoe were found. The black box was discovered within minutes upon arrival at the site. It was immediately flown back to the Osan Air Base.

Forensic experts and bomb squad professionals were on the scene. The evidence was collected at breakneck speed. It was a race against time. Included in the bags and trunks of evidence were some samples of scorched dirt from the ground where the tiny bits and pieces of the incinerated helicopter hit. Several video cameras recorded the scene, the evidence, the mission as a whole, and hundreds of photographs were taken.

The North Korean government projected itself as a major problem. They weren't at all cooperative. They were extremely displeased about this invasion of U.S. troops. At first they wanted to conduct the investigation themselves. But this would've taken months and perhaps, may have never taken place at all. Heavily armed North Korean troops had also arrived at the site. They monitored the situation and kept an attentive eye on the activities on the ground. They took their own still pictures and videotapes.

U.S. ambassador LeJeune had spent an hour on the phone negotiating with the North Koreans. They finally agreed to allow restricted access to a limited number of U.S. military forces. And the permit was strictly limited for the purpose of search-and-rescue efforts on the site of the specific accident scene. Nicanor's own airstrip, which ran through a field near the Nicanor premises, was used by the planes for landing and takeoff. The allocated time limit graciously provided by the North Korean government was eight hours. After the ultimatum expired, all U.S. military forces had to be out of North

Korea. It was a take-it-or-leave-it kind of situation. There wasn't any time to negotiate better terms. Evidence had to be collected quickly and it was better to accept this deal than none, the State Department argued.

Based on international treaties, a country had every right to refuse or limit and restrict access to foreign military forces. Especially communist countries like North Korea were reluctant to allow even a friendly foreign intrusion of its territories for whatever purpose or reason.

32

AS GATES left the CIA building, he witnessed CIA mechanics tow away his damaged Ford. The CIA repair shop had already parked an older Crown Vic cruiser as a temporary replacement vehicle in the spot from where they towed the wrecked Taurus.

"They've put a new agent in charge of the operation, at least for now," Trevor Gates said through his digital PCS phone. He was on his way to Andrews Air Force Base. From his locker at the Agency he had retrieved a bag which contained some clothes and toiletry items. He always kept that bag ready for such emergency situations. It was too late to stop by his house to get some things. The colonial was too far out and it actually lay in a different direction from where he was heading.

"Is he going to be a problem?" the female voice asked in her familiar cute southern twang at the other end of the connection. She expressed some concern, but she wasn't terribly worried about it. There was nothing in the world she couldn't handle, she thought. She had all the necessary assets to make it work: brains, beauty, money and dedicated slaves who would do anything she bid. They would even kill for her if necessary and they had already done so under her command.

"No, I don't think so. He'll be out of the picture in no time. It's just routine procedure," he answered.

"You want me to take care of him?" she asked.

"No, it's all right. I can handle it. Don't you worry," Gates replied.

"All right then. I'll keep our men on standby, just in case. If you need help, let me know. Take care of yourself, Trev. See you soon," she said and hung up.

IT WAS in the middle of the night when the CIA Learjet landed at the Osan Air Base. On board were Osteen, Gates and four special agents that Osteen had brought with him. When Gates stepped out of the aircraft, he was glad to see Agent James Brighton.

Brighton had arrived a few hours earlier at the Base. According to orders, he'd boarded a commercial airliner in L.A. It was important that he made it to Korea as soon as possible. In Seoul, he was picked up by a U.S. Army helicopter and was immediately flown to the Osan Air Base. James Brighton was black and only twenty-eight. He began working as an assistant to Trevor Gates just a couple of months ago. Brighton wasn't filled in yet, and perhaps would never be.

"Good to see ya," Gates said.

"I'm glad the timing worked out," James Brighton replied. "We sure got a mess here, boss. From what I've heard it's not a pretty sight."

"It's gonna be all right, Jim. Don't you worry, we'll take care of it—we always do," Gates assured Brighton in a professional manner. He expressed confidence.

Charles Osteen was forty-five. His hair was silver and thick around the sides of his head, but he was balding on top. He maintained a mustache, also silver. While Gates was still dressed in a suit and tie, Osteen was ready for combat. His muscles and excess fat were squeezed into desert camouflage fatigues. Recently, he hadn't worked out that much and it showed a bit around the waist. Osteen was a short guy. As soon as he put his face through the exit of the Lear, he stuck a cigar between his teeth and clenched it tightly. But he waited a minute before he lit it. First he had to reach solid ground at the bottom of the gangway. Osteen hadn't shaved in days. His appearance was one of a mercenary. And to some degree he probably was one. A most genuine mercenary. His background was perfect to fit the cliché exactly.

They had a few hours till daybreak. Then they would fly to the crash site. The search-and-rescue teams had completed their job during daylight. Osteen suggested they proceed with briefing the teams at this late hour. Theoretically, it would've been possible, but Gates explained to him that there was no rush and it could wait a few hours. Osteen drank one coffee after another on the plane. He was quite awake and ready to roll. Gates, who had napped a bit on the Lear, was exhausted. Four hours of rest would help a lot to get him back on his feet, he thought. Osteen reluctantly gave in to Gates' suggestion as he also understood that the teams were exhausted and needed their rest. It wouldn't have made much sense to do something right now anyway. They were all taken in a Jeep to the barracks to get at least a few hours of sleep.

33

AT FOUR-THIRTY the search-and-rescue teams were gathered at Fellowship Hall. Grits, bacon and eggs, cornflakes and watermelon tasted very good this early in the morning. Most of the men at the Base were used to rising early, even though four-thirty was still about an hour earlier than normal. Gates and Brighton were a few minutes late for the meeting. But Osteen had already everything under control. After the one-hour briefing, Osteen, accompanied by his four soldiers, was led to a hangar where the gathered evidence had been spread out. U.S. Army personnel with assistance from several forensic experts of various U.S. government agencies had already begun with the tedious task of logging the inventory of items from the crash site. Brighton followed Osteen to the hangar, while Gates took it kind of easy.

"Listen, if you're unhappy about coming here, then it's better for you to get outta here," Osteen suggested harshly to Gates, indicating a choleric predisposition.

"What is that supposed to mean?" Gates gave Osteen a sidelong glance.

"It means precisely what I just said. Get outta here, if you don't wanna do this thing."

"He's probably just tired. He'll be all right in a second," Brighton said, attempting to calm Osteen.

Osteen was wired. He looked at the scenario as absolute

combat. Terrorists were probably out there and real men like him and his soldiers were needed to deal with the situation. Osteen intended to add a few nasty words, but decided to back off in the last second. He had to stay focused to resolve this case quickly.

TWO CHOPPERS took off from Osan Air Base at six A.M. One hauled Osteen and his mercenary crew of three, the other helicopter carried Brighton and Gates as well as one of Osteen's soldiers and an U.S. Army captain. The ride didn't take very long.

Suddenly, well into North Korean airspace, two Migs closely investigated the two choppers. It didn't appear that the Migs were on a friendly mission, instead it seemed that they had hostile intentions. One of the Mig pilots addressed the choppers in Korean. He was screaming—at least it seemed that way. The pilot in Osteen's helicopter replied in Korean. It wasn't a positive exchange. The two Migs came even closer which was already dangerous territory as the air turbulence caused by the Migs could've easily grounded the helicopters instantly.

Osteen requested to speak to the Mig pilots. He was handed a headset with a microphone. In perfect Russian he told them something. Everybody in both choppers could hear what he said, but of course, nobody understood a thing. They looked at each other with a loss for words, shrugging their shoulders, not knowing what was going on.

"This should do," Osteen said afterwards in English into the microphone.

The two Migs took off and were cautious in their maneuver as they left the nearby airspace. Nobody questioned Osteen. His soldiers knew better anyway and they were confident that their boss was doing the right thing. They all looked up to him and desired to follow in his footsteps some day. He was a true soldier, ready to deal with every combat situation.

"Nice job," a helicopter pilot complimented Osteen as he showed him thumbs up.

"Do we have Rambo with us?" Gates said jokingly to Brighton.

Brighton didn't offer a verbal reply, but only a short-lived grin to acknowledge hearing Gates' comment.

THE HELICOPTERS first landed at the crash site. Osteen and his men were led by the U.S. Army captain to explore the immediate area. The captain held a map in his hands and informed them about important locations of crucial discoveries of evidence from the wreckage.

While Osteen and his band searched the crash site, Brighton and Gates went over to the Nicanor power plant. It was about fifteen minutes away. They walked to the end of the desolate field and arrived at the only road that promised potential access to the premises. The rest of the plant was protected by a barbed wire fence. Land mines had also been placed around the barbed wire fence to protect the facility from unwanted and uninvited intruders.

They stood at the gate. Gates leaned into the guard house to search for the guard. An Asian security officer emerged from a small area in the back of the booth, seemingly from the bathroom, and was visibly surprised to see the two men. He was dressed in a uniform with the Nicanor logo woven on the chest over the heart.

"Kensington. We're looking for Mr. Kensington." Gates flashed his CIA badge. "We're with the CIA."

The guard looked at Gates and Brighton unsure what to do. Then he reached for the receiver and called the plant. He showed them where to wait near the gate. A golf cart made its way slowly to the gate. Brighton and Gates stepped into the vehicle and were chauffeured to the main entrance of the Nicanor plant. They entered through the automatic door where Kensington waited to greet them.

"Does he know?" Gates inquired of Kensington.

"Not really. I just explained to him yesterday that he had to stay another day. I don't think he suspects anything, but he's growing impatient," Kensington answered.

"All right, I talk to him," Gates said.

Gates and Brighton walked across the lobby into a corner and broke the tragic news to Jerome Birchner.

"Mr. Birchner, I'm Special Agent Trevor Gates with the CIA, and this is Agent Brighton, also with the CIA," Gates officially announced as he flashed his badge and introduced himself and Brighton.

"There has been a fatal accident. The Undersecretary, Mr. Robert Baxter, and CIA Special Agent Hank Taylor were killed in that crash the other night. I have to ask you a few questions, if you don't mind. Just regular procedure." Gates addressed Jerome in a solemn manner.

"Baxter? Taylor? That's sad . . . I didn't know." Jerome was shaken, but not taken completely by surprise. All kinds of thoughts crossed his mind. "What happened?"

"We don't know yet. The helicopter crashed about a mile from here. U.S. Army troops were over there yesterday. Matter of fact, they're over there right now to search for some more clues. Anyway, I suggest that you get outta here as soon as possible."

"I can't wait to get home."

"I have to ask you a few questions, though, sir."

"Sure. I don't know if I can be of any help to you. You're the first one to tell me about this. Did Kensington know anything?"

"I'm not sure, but that's not the issue right now." Gates began his bogus inquisition. "Did you see or hear anything, Mr. Birchner? This is just for the record," he said in an attempt to assure him of this common procedure.

"When exactly was the accident?" Jerome inquired.

"Two nights ago. I don't know the exact time, but apparently whenever the Undersecretary and Agent Taylor left. Why weren't you on the chopper?"

"Good question. Regarding your other question, I didn't hear anything. I was with Kensington after the Undersecretary left. And later that evening I went into my room. I watched a movie and fell asleep. And yesterday, I was down at the square most of the day and read a book," Jerome answered.

"What did you do before Mr. Baxter left?"

"We toured the plant. Then we had some pizza and hamburgers down in one of the food courts," Jerome replied.

"Was there anything out of the ordinary? You came up here with Baxter, but didn't leave with him. Why is that? Can you give me a few details or something?" Gates grilled Jerome.

"I don't have the answers to all your questions, Mr. Gates. All I remember was that Mr. Baxter received a phone call and suddenly he had to leave. He said something about going back to the U.S. Embassy in Pyongyang. Agent Taylor insisted that I should come along, but Mr. Baxter arranged for me to stay. Thank God."

"Do you know who called the Undersecretary?" Agent Brighton inquired.

"I'm not sure, but maybe it was Kensington. The Undersecretary mentioned something about Kensington, but I'm not certain of that, I didn't pay any attention to it," Jerome said.

"Well, 'twas sure good for you that you didn't have to fly with them," Gates commented, and paused for a few seconds before he continued. "All right then, Mr. Birchner. If you remember anything or think of something in particular, let me know, all right?" He concluded the conversation. "One more thing. Do you know anybody here, Mr. Birchner?"

"No, of course not. It's my first time here."

"I know. But I mean, is there anyone here that looks familiar to you. Maybe someone you may have met before?"

"No, sorry, I don't know anyone here. What was your name again?" Jerome asked. Even though he addressed him as Mr. Gates already before, he couldn't remember his name at this very moment.

"I'm Agent Gates, and this is Agent Brighton. All right then, thanks. By the way, here's my card. If you remember anything just call me. Every little thing that you remember could be of significance and may help us," Gates said politely.

Brighton also handed him a card. Then Gates and Brighton turned around. They intended to walk back over to Kensington.

Jerome seized both cards, the one from Gates and the other from Brighton. He put those in his pocket. Still somewhat distracted he headed for the exit. Then he turned to Gates and Brighton. "Agent Gates. Excuse me," Jerome said with his voice raised so that they could hear him. "I don't know where you're going, but is there a chance that I can hitch a ride with you all? I really need to get outta here."

Gates looked at Jerome. "Well, let's see. I've gotta check our seating capacity in the chopper, but I guess it shouldn't be a problem," Gates replied.

"You know I'd really appreciate that, because I'm a little lost in this place and I really don't wanna get stuck here. Somehow I need to get back to Seoul to catch a plane back home," Jerome explained. He wanted to get out of this place without delay. He very much desired to be back in the quietness of his mansion in Naples. What a hassle, he thought. People were dying everywhere and he was drawn into the midst of this fiasco.

While Jerome didn't regret coming to North Korea, he was no longer excited about staying there for another minute. This was certainly the last deal, he thought and made the promise quietly to himself. That's it, no more deals after this one. It was time to enjoy life to the fullest. Life was too fragile and too short to take unnecessary risks like this.

When Gates was ready to leave from the Nicanor plant, he invited Jerome to come along. A Hummer was waiting outside to transport the three men to the chopper at the crash site. The Arab drove slowly at first, until he reached the gate. Then he ran the vehicle through the mud across the desolate field toward the chopper. The windows of the black Hummer were darkly tinted except for the windshield. Nobody said a word inside the vehicle. Once the three men had left the Hummer, the Arab sped away.

"WHERE HAVE you been?" Osteen snorted at Gates.

"Doing my job, all right," Gates answered with arrogance.

"Well, we're done here," Osteen said.

"Then let's go home," Gates suggested.

Jerome was glad that he could hitch a lift with these CIA guys to the Osan Air Base in South Korea. During the flight to the Base he didn't say anything. Jerome thanked Gates for the ride after they got off the aircraft. Gates was now more relaxed and helpful. He even ordered Brighton to inquire for Jerome to get him somehow back to Seoul. Brighton walked into one of the U.S. Army offices and made the arrangements.

34

A FEW hours later a U.S. Army helicopter flew Jerome to the international airport in Seoul. Nobody accompanied him aside from the two pilots. When they arrived in Seoul one of the pilots handed Jerome a piece of paper. It was like a type of U.S. Army authorization for him to enter the regular air terminal from the airfield. Jerome walked over to the international terminal and booked the first available flight to the U.S. This one was headed to Los Angeles. Every day, several flights were scheduled from Seoul to the West Coast, usually two to Vancouver B.C., one to Seattle, two to San Francisco and three or four to L.A.

When he arrived in Los Angeles, he quickly bought a ticket for the next leg to Miami. No nonstop flight was available, therefore he had to go through a change of planes in Atlanta. It was already late at night when the aircraft from Atlanta landed in Miami.

He'd called Birgid from L.A. and wished very much that she'd pick him up at the airport in Miami. She would have done so without hesitation. But he knew that she was afraid of driving into the big city. Jerome didn't wanna risk her getting lost, or think about whatever other unfortunate circumstance could happened to her. Birgid preferred to stay within the vicinity of Naples. So Jerome rented a luxury car at the Miami airport. It wouldn't take him too long to be back home in Naples, he contemplated.

The speed limit wouldn't matter that night. On I-75 he raced at a speed of over a hundred miles per hour through the Everglades. Thousands of insects, all in different colors, sizes and shapes, hit the windshield of the rented Cadillac. The stereo had been tuned to a country station which was relaxing. It reminded him of the classy old café in Pyongyang. In his mind he saw the faces of the bartender and the old guys sitting around the table, playing their board game. The Coke and Coca-Cola plaques seemed to light up on the windshield as images of that place flashed through his mind. Now, it seemed so unreal. It was like watching a movie. It was a different world over there, that was for sure. But it was unique to see, to experience and be confronted with the contrast between these almost ancient depictions and the futuristic exploitations at the Nicanor plant.

So far the station had only played pure country. Suddenly, instead of the country version, the original song *I don't want to miss a thing* by Aerosmith blared through the speakers. Just as the song came to its climax he heard a loud bang. Initially it came from the right front underbody of the car. Then there were several hollow blows along the right side of the vehicle—all in a matter of seconds. In this area it could've been either a lost alligator which was frequently the case, or a huge piece of a torn truck tire. It was obvious that he didn't have a blowout, because the automobile kept moving firmly across the asphalt. Jerome didn't bother to stop and check out the situation. The radio played a variety of country greats. Country music was very soothing. The cute little stories relaxed his mind.

It was after midnight when he arrived at his Naples mansion. Jerome was glad to be back home again. He'd missed these comfortable surroundings. The beautiful palm trees, the kind breeze from the Gulf as the moon was reflected on the surface of the water. The freedom to go to the fridge and retrieve an ice cold Pepsi. Small things, but precious and not to be taken for granted, he thought.

While she was waiting for him, Birgid had fallen asleep. She was cuddled up on the sofa downstairs in the living room. He was exhausted. Jerome kissed her lightly on the forehead. She woke up. They embraced and moved without talking slowly upstairs, step by step, into the bedroom. It was too late for a shower or anything else, he thought. Birgid silently agreed. Within minutes he was lost to a sleep filled with many dreams.

The next morning Jerome checked out the area on the car from where he had heard the weird noise the night before. He found several wide black scratches along the lower part of the vehicle. From this it was clear that he'd run over just a big chunk of tire and not an alligator. Later in the morning a guy and a gal from the local rental car office dropped by to pick up the Cadillac.

"DID BIRCHNER leave the country all right?" Kensington questioned the Arab.

"I dropped them all off at the helicopter, and I'm pretty sure he went with them. I didn't wait for them to leave. You haven't given me any orders, boss. I thought you just wanted him gone," the Arab answered.

"It's all right. I still need some information from him. But for now, it's all right. I'll take care of it. Just keep me posted, all right?"

"Should I get a hold of him in the States, boss? Do you want me to take care of him?" the Arab asked, offering his deadly services.

"No, we've got someone else there. I have a different plan. You've gotta lay low for awhile. Right now, you have to be out of the picture until everything has calmed down a little bit. Maybe it's best if you fly to Vienna and stay there for a couple of weeks or so," Kensington suggested. "But make sure that nobody recognizes you in Seoul," he warned. "The airport is probably loaded with agents from the Secret Service and the CIA. Take it easy for a week or two, okay. Go ahead and fool around with the girls in Austria—they like guys like you. Then get back on standby. I'll let you know if we need you to do anything about Birchner, but I think we're all set for now. It's all gonna be over very soon anyway. We just can't make any mistakes." Kensington took a deep breath. "So far so good. Things are going according to plan."

The Arab listened and with his teeth he broke off another piece of tobacco to chew on.

35

"HI," SHE softly answered through her satellite phone. "Is everything ready to go? Has the setup been completed?"

"Yes, Mrs. Farnsworth. Can I talk to you about it in detail on this line?" Jerome asked the question to make absolutely sure that it was safe to communicate intricate details over the phone. Nobody else was supposed to hear this conversation.

"You're okay, Mr. Birchner. It's scrambled, but don't talk numbers, all right."

"The accounts are all established and we're ready to roll, Mrs. Farnsworth."

"Good job, Mr. Birchner. Good job," she complimented him.

"The money can move through the accounts immediately. As agreed upon, the one personal account for you has been established, too. Once the money is in this one, you're the only one who can access it. Nobody can take anything out of it but you alone, Mrs. Farnsworth," he explained.

"Great, sounds good to me. You're sure nobody can touch it?" She needed to be absolutely certain.

"Absolutely sure. Nobody, but you, Mrs. Farnsworth. That's the deal. Still, I suggest that you designate someone in your will or whatever to allow them access in case of an emergency or in the event that something happens to you. Of course only if you care to do so," he quickly assured her. "We should move the money as soon as possible. With the first tranche I'll also need some money for my own account. There are several expenses that we need to cover," he said. Jerome needed plenty of dough just to pay fees and commissions for such huge transactions.

"Sure, no problem, Mr. Birchner. Just tell me how much and consider it done. Don't tell me the figure over the phone though. I heard you were in Korea?"

"Yes, I just got back last night. You probably already know about the tragic accident with the Undersecretary and the CIA agent. I was supposed to join them on that flight, did you know that?" Jerome was still shaken about the possibilities.

Mrs. Farnsworth knew about the whole ordeal. "Yes, I heard about it. Mr. Kensington called me yesterday. I think you met him when you toured the plant?"

"Sure did. He showed me around. He doesn't talk much, but I guess it comes with the job. You sure have an excellent facility over there in Korea."

"Thanks, Mr. Birchner. I don't want to be rude, but I really have to go now. I'll be back in Dallas tomorrow. Then I'll get you the details for the first tranche by e-mail," she said. "We'll be in touch tomorrow, Mr. Birchner." She hung up before Jerome was able to say goodbye.

SHE UNBUTTONED his shirt and pressed her head into his chest. Gates held Juliet in his athletic arms. She had just emerged from the shower. A bath sheet was wrapped around her tender body. Her hair was wet and wild.

"Do you love me?" she asked.

"Of course I do," Gates replied.

"I mean, it's not just the money, is it?" She didn't look at him when she phrased the question candidly, as she continued to rest her head on his muscular torso.

"Honey, I love you," he said with emphasis on the word *you*. He kissed her on the forehead.

"But I'm so much older than you are. We can never have kids," she argued gently.

"We don't need kids. We have each other." He held her tighter. "You're so pretty," he assured her whispering into her ear.

Then they kissed as lovers do. She pulled off his pants. With a gentle but skilled motion, he unwrapped her as they moved toward the bed. They made love in the suite of a hotel in downtown Seoul. Nobody was supposed to see them. But somebody was watching. She came only for a few hours. The Nicanor Gulfstream was hidden in a desolate hangar at Kimp'o Airport. Trevor Gates had picked her up in a cab from the hangar.

After the sexual encounter they ordered room service. The generous late-night dinner consisted of a little bit of everything. Thin slices of various types of meats; even salmon and fresh trout; and all kinds of vegetables and fruits. When she put a piece of eel into her sensual mouth, Gates told her what it was and she spit it out in disgust. Both laughed. Juliet drank a glass of champagne to rid herself of the disgusting taste. While sex was physically exhausting, it often awakened a strong craving for food.

At the conclusion of this engaging evening, Juliet Farnsworth left the suite alone. She left the hotel through a somewhat hidden staircase that led her to the ground level of the parking garage. Her high heels produced a loud clacking noise on the steel covered steps. The tight, short black skirt hindered her ability to prevent the annoying noise as she hurried along.

She wore a black overcoat that reached just below her knees. The coat was left open. Underneath, Juliet was wearing a white blouse. She had left every piece of lingerie behind in the hotel as she was unable to find the stuff in the hurry. Gates would look for it later and bring it with him to the States, he assured her. They joked about it how funny it would be if someone at customs would go through his belongings and find these feminine items. Gates came up with several explanations, one funnier than the other. They laughed a lot that evening.

Juliet hiked swiftly through a few rows of cars, then up the ramp and into an alley. For a moment she was disoriented, but turned right toward what appeared to be a wide avenue. The street wasn't busy at all and she couldn't spot a taxi anywhere.

It was well after midnight. She walked back nearing the main entrance of the hotel, where usually a few cabs were parked, waiting for customers. She finally flagged down a taxi that came from the opposite direction. The cabby was available to take her to the ominous hangar. In the cab she put on some makeup and remembered that she didn't wear any panties. Every so often the taxi driver glanced into the rearview mirror to check for potential traffic from behind. But he never looked at her and didn't see anything unusual. When the vehicle came to a halt in front of the hangar, she handed him a hundred-dollar bill as she requested that he stay in the car. She didn't need any help to open the door, she could manage herself. He thanked her profusely bowing his head at least a dozen times. The Gulfstream was ready for departure and took off within minutes of her boarding the jet.

36

JULIET FARNSWORTH listed the exact details for the wire of the first tranche in an e-mail to Jerome. He sent her a reply via e-mail that things were looking good. In his e-mail he'd also mentioned that he needed at least ten million, but preferably even twenty million to cover expenses for the transfer. The job had to be done right, especially on this first transaction, he explained. This first tranche concerned the churning of almost a billion dollars. This sum had to be directed and groomed properly.

Juliet wanted to see Jerome in action. She desired to be in the know regarding the exact steps and particulars on how Jerome would handle the money to extract her portion. She didn't trust anyone, not even Jerome.

Mrs. Farnsworth had enough from business deals. Nicanor stock had been in the doldrums for years. And not even the exciting new business in North Korea brought it back from the dead. This was her last deal, she'd promised to herself hundreds of times in the past year or so. Six hundred million in the bank—that was her initial goal, but she wanted much more than that.

Nicanor could go bankrupt afterwards—she didn't care. Thousands and thousands of workers would lose their jobs, but she wouldn't worry about such minor details. Nobody really cared about her either—she'd learned it the hard way. *When you're rich and famous, people only see the mighty dollar in you, not the person that's behind it, and they don't see who you really are,* she often said this to herself. Juliet herself wasn't any different though. When she met John Farnsworth she only saw the money in him, too. John wasn't attractive because of his physical appearance—he was twenty years older than Juliet—but rather only because of his enormous wealth was Juliet attracted to him. Money and riches are sexy. Money is power. It's like a magnet. People are in awe when they come in touch with the moolah. Everybody wants a piece of the action. Once they get the taste of it then greed takes over and they want more and more. In the end, it's never enough. Money is a drug. Men and women alike would easily lose their self-respect. Somebody once said, *When it comes to money, people get funny.* How true this apothegm was. Women would sell their bodies for a few bucks. Guys would rob banks and kill people, just to gain a few dollars. They would do anything to get ahold of this valuable printed paper.

For Juliet Farnsworth, her objective wasn't too far away anymore. Only a couple of months or so and she would reach her dreams. She would revive the lifestyle of the genuine jet set. Parties in Cannes during the annual Cannes Film Festival. To Park City, Utah in January. In between short stints in Jackson Hole, Wyoming, and in Vail and Telluride, Colorado. Of course, she wouldn't forget to enjoy the cruises to Alaska and into the Caribbean. A nice retreat in the spring or in the fall in Argentina had been scheduled, too. She would buy a ranch there, maybe. Regular trips to Miami, Paris, London, New York, Tokyo and Hong Kong wouldn't be left out either.

No children were around to hinder a truly classy jet set lifestyle. Only a committed and faithful lover, who was available for sex at any time she wanted to, she hoped. A guy who didn't complain, but loved her just for who she really was, she convinced herself and dreamt about it. She saw herself as a sensual women, a princess, tender and loving, in need to be treated like a queen—caressed by a strong man of valor. Yes, Trevor Gates was her Romeo, she assured herself often.

Juliet Farnsworth reached for the stars and if anyone could touch them, it was she. Old John was dead, thank God. Baxter and John wanted to bail out from the deal and mess it all up, self-righteous as they were, she thought. John Farnsworth didn't understand that it was all just about money and it wasn't at all about patriotism, creating jobs, nourishing friendships, and all the other crap he talked about.

She wanted it all—she was already in her early forties. Not enough time was left to waste another minute of her life with stupidity. Now she was in charge and she would make her dreams come true. Somebody dead here and there didn't matter. To Juliet Farnsworth it didn't even matter if nations were going to war against each other, just because of her greed. In fact, it would've been flattering, she entertained the thought occasionally. It was sad though, but the mighty green buck was smiling in a big way at Juliet Farnsworth. Over half a billion and maybe even more, much more—she would kill for it, again.

CHAPTER

37

THE FIRST billion-dollar transaction went well. Jerome was able to siphon two hundred million dollars into Juliet's personal account. Twenty million landed in Jerome's own offshore account, and about twelve million were consumed by various banking fees. The majority of the money was credited to the main bank account of Nicanor Industries at Citibank in Dallas. This was an easy tranche because the dough came directly from Asia. It went through Swiss accounts and was perfectly laundered there before it was sent on to the States. Things went smoothly and he considered it a successful beginning for greater things to come.

There was only one more tranche that would come directly from Asia. Most of the other billions would originate in the U.S. and were derived from various U.S. governmental departments and agencies. These transactions were more difficult and much riskier. Jerome planned on siphoning the greater chunk of the money off of the Asian transfers.

In the end, still about a third of the desired funds had to be extracted from wires that emanated in the U.S. Mistakes could've been costly, but even if obvious errors were made, perhaps nobody on the outside would detect them in a timely manner. It would take an outsider at least a couple of years to figure the whole thing out. Nicanor Industries was subject to audits by the General Accounting Office. Eventually the GAO would perform an audit of Nicanor Industries and then bloopers would surface rather easily.

Therefore, the art of the deal was to arrange everything within a believable common structure. It was absolutely prohibitive to mess up on a single key component in these transactions, or the scheme would unravel by itself. Certain *genuine* mistakes were purposely planted by Jerome to lead suspicious auditors and investigators onto a false hot trail, but after many laborious twists and turns these would eventually empty into a dead end. The objective was to cause a diversion and plenty of confusion. With this technique, Jerome was able to achieve the proper effect. The officials of the GAO were happy to prove their investigative skills and justified their work as they would find a few minor errors here and there, which were in actuality meaningless and insignificant. But they would call it success and pat themselves on the back.

The financial arrangements that Jerome had made for Nicanor weren't perfectly ethical in the opinion of most moral individuals. But according to the tax code, things only had to appear legal and be in compliance with the rules and regulations established. Based on the bureaucratic provisions found in the extensive and ridiculous tax code, and with a little bending of the rules, sometimes to the edge of the maximum extent, though, it wasn't that difficult to still remain within the legal boundaries of the applicable laws.   .

Most major international companies did a lot of bending anyway, and most of them got away with it decade after decade. And even if a company was caught, at times the common practice was to simply fire the accountant and to pay a relatively small fine to appease the authorities for the next few years. It was never really a problem, but rather only another part in the process of doing business.

When it came right down to the heart of the matter to make

a determination, it was usually the IRS that made the final decision what would be accepted as legal tax avoidance and what was illegal tax evasion. And such a verdict was always negotiable for the better, especially when a company agreed without much hassle to pay a fine and perhaps a comparatively modest sum in back taxes. That's why everything had to be carefully planned to ensure that no grounds of suspicion for serious tax evasion existed. Everything had to look perfectly legal, even though it was on the edge.

In Jerome's opinion his clients only wanted to save on income taxes and rightly so. In good years the IRS would take their share of taxes, but in bad years when a company failed in generating profits, nobody would come along to help unfortunate entrepreneurs out. Instead, often they would be laughed at and even made a mockery of for having missed the mark in any given year. They had praised Donald Trump in the highly successful eighties, but turned their backs on him in the early nineties when things looked dim and an apparent odor of bankruptcy surrounded the quoin of Trump Tower. Of course, honor, praise and glory returned when in the mid-nineties he was once again on top, and he was the celebrated and undefeated comeback kid.

"I'M VERY pleased with your performance, Mr. Birchner," Juliet Farnsworth complemented Jerome.

"I'm glad you are," Jerome replied. "We're ready for the next one. This one went really well."

"Jerome, do you mind if I call you Jerome?" She inquired, pronouncing his name explicitly in a heavy Texan drawl as in *Jeeerooome*.

"Sure, Mrs. Farnsworth, no problem, call me Jerome if you like. Matter of fact, call me whatever you want," he said, jesting.

It was all right with Jerome to be called by his first name. But he also knew that often this would lead to familiarity down the road.

One of his general professional rules had been to avoid a too personal contact with his clients. He came across very much like a good old friend, though—this was his intended strategy so that customers would trust him. But personally, he wouldn't cross the line for good reasons. Once a client had crossed the professional line, they would often take his services for granted and this was never good for a business relationship. In such a situation, customers would frequently expect that certain advice and even actual work be provided at no charge—simply just as a favor because they were *friends*. They would call him on Sundays to discuss business and so on. Of course, in the case of Juliet Farnsworth, it was his last deal—he could live with it, he thought. And she paid him a lot of money. Therefore it wouldn't really matter what she'd call him, he continued the thought.

"Well, then, my friends call me Jewels. Would you call me Jewels, Jerome?" she was very friendly.

"Jewels it shall be," he answered, chuckling quietly to himself.

"Jerome, I need to meet with you as soon as possible. We have to discuss a few more things, and I'd feel much better if we could do that face to face," Juliet insisted.

Without verbalizing the thought, he considered that this *Jewels/Jerome* thing had already started with the wrong approach. *Why did he give her that liberty?* He now questioned his actions. But he politely answered her without hesitation, "Sure, let's meet. As long as it's in the country I don't mind. You can imagine, after this crazy trip to Korea, I'm not really in the mood to fly anywhere right now. I really hate flying."

"How about your place? I can make time on Friday or Saturday. Is that convenient for you?" She was persistent.

Now she invited herself to check out how he lived. Normally this wouldn't go through and it was too personal, he thought. But then he just made the mistake himself by his honest, but careless remark about boarding another plane.

Only on very rare occasions would Jerome have clients visit him at his house. Usually these clients were trusted individuals who had a longtime relationship with Jerome. Anyway, he attempted not to worry too much about it. It didn't really matter anymore. And Juliet was someone who would soon have six hundred million in the bank. She was ready to retire herself— maybe she just wanted to chat a little bit, he contemplated. Juliet wasn't a threat, he carried this notion for a few seconds. It's good to have wealthy friends, he continued to entertain the thought.

"That sounds like a great idea," Jerome answered promptly as he fixed himself a glass of ice tea. "I'll pick you up at the airport."

"Well then, let's say that I'll be there on Friday afternoon, around three? I call you if my schedule gets messed up for whatever reason. But I think it's going to work out. I can't wait to see you."

"Sure, let's do it. Well, Jewels, I'll let you go and I'll see you in a few days." For some reason, Jerome wasn't too excited about her announced visit.

"Bye, Jerome."

NICANOR'S GULFSTREAM touched down in Naples precisely at three P.M. Jerome waited in front of an improvised, newly opened Butler Air Terminal. All corporate and private jets that arrived in Naples were anchored at this certain facility. After a flight attendant opened the door, Juliet Farnsworth emerged first from the jet. She exited the plane in her professional, graceful grand-duchess-like manner. But this time her attire was casual. Juliet was dressed in tight white denims. A gentle breeze rushed momentarily through the generous openings between the buttons of her comfortable white cotton blouse. Her hair flew sensually in the manner of a banner in the wind, then returned to rest around and over her fragile shoulders. White sneakers supported the desired appearance of a trendy, sporty outfit.

In private, Juliet wouldn't wear high heels anymore—that was a thing of the past. After her last Korea trip all high heels and dress suits vanished in some spacious walk-in closet at her Dallas mansion. It was bothersome, and many times even painful to run around all dressed up in classy accoutre at Nicanor headquarters, she argued.

Little by little she began withdrawing from the office. Except for a few signatures and occasional meetings here and there, her physical presence at Nicanor headquarters was no longer necessary. Her staff would take care of the day-to-day business. She'd rather manage things from her lavish estate in the Dallas suburbs. Even without her physical attendance, she carried enough clout, that at least in spirit, she was almost omnipresent. Virtually every employee at Nicanor was aware of this mystical circumstance. They had all learned to take her very seriously. Nobody would give in to any foolish jesting or a careless remark about Juliet Farnsworth. She hated gossip, and Juliet was quick to fire anyone who crossed her path with even only a minor negative connotation.

THE GULFSTREAM crew of three followed her down the gangway. Jerome drove his Lincoln Navigator close to the aircraft. He got out of the SUV and moved around to the front of the vehicle. As he prepared to shake Juliet's hand cordially, she instead clasped him gently with a hug and put a fat, wet smooch on his cheek. No doubt that her rich red lipstick left significant visible marks on his face. Birgid most certainly wouldn't approve of that, he thought. It only took a little gesture like that to make Birgid jealous. In this regard, she was a possessive type without exception.

"Did you have a nice flight?" Jerome inquired.

"Thank you, Jerome, I sure did. I look forward to a fabulous weekend with you here in Naples," she said as she hooked her right arm through his left elbow.

"Does the crew wanna go somewhere in particular, or are they staying here at the terminal?" He asked Juliet. Jerome opened the passenger door to the SUV for her and helped her climb into the massive vehicle which had higher than usual ground clearance. Jerome was dressed very casually. But no shorts this time, instead loose khakis and a burgundy polo shirt drooped over his pants subtly concealed his growing waist line.

"No, they'll be all right. They can take care of themselves.

Let's get outta here," she said. Juliet made herself comfortable in the generous four-wheel drive.

One of the crew members put a couple of oversized leather bags into the cargo area of the Navigator.

Juliet pressed the power window button on her side and said loudly, "I'll call you guys." She addressed the crew without giving it much thought if they even heard her remark.

Jerome drove off with Juliet. They exited the terminal through a nearby gate.

"It's nice here, Jerome. I wish we had a few palm trees in Dallas. Maybe I'll buy me a place around here. Nothing big or fancy, just something for an occasional weekend in the sun. What do you think, Jerome? Isn't that a precious idea?" She made her comments and didn't really care what Jerome's response to her questions were. Juliet was herself. She was excited and she would do whatever she wanted anyway—no matter what other people said.

"It's sure a nice place. Of course, it gets pretty hot in the summer though. And it's not such a metropolitan area like Dallas. Naples is more like a small town. We even compare it to a little fishing village on the coast. Everybody knows everybody," he explained.

"I think I would like that," she said gazing at the turquoise waters of the Gulf. "I can't wait to live a normal life again."

"I don't wanna be nosy, Jewels, but may I ask what you're going to do after you have all this money? I mean, it's a lot of dough," Jerome phrased the question carefully.

"It's kind of personal, Jerome. You shouldn't ask questions like that." She looked at him and smiled slightly. "But I can tell you, because I don't mind you asking me this, Jerome." She now turned her head and gazed out the window. "I'm gonna sell all my Nicanor shares and I'm going to live. For the first time in a long time I'm going to live life the way it's supposed to be. I'm gonna travel the world. I've worked enough in my life. I'm tired, you know." She turned to look at him again. "It's time to party, Jerome. No more business . . . no more stress . . . no more aggravation. Do you understand what I mean?"

"Sure, I'm with you a hundred percent. I know exactly what you mean. It's gonna be my last deal too. I already told my wife. This is the last one," he emphasized.

THEY DROVE to Jerome's estate first, with plans to go out for dinner in the evening. Jerome wasn't certain yet how to work this out with Birgid. As long as they were married, he had never gone to lunch or dinner with a female client alone. But with Juliet he already went to lunch once and now an evening dinner had been announced and scheduled by Juliet. He imagined that Juliet wouldn't appreciate Birgid's presence because they had to discuss intimate business dealings. Birgid, of course, would be furious if he went out with this woman alone. Everything was so unexpected and Jerome hadn't prepared for such a scenario in advance. On one hand he didn't wanna incense Juliet; on the other hand he had no interest whatsoever to create a war zone at home either. It didn't concern a life-and-death decision, but it was just another minor detail that presented itself as some sort of dilemma. He hadn't prepared mentally for a character like Jewels.

Juliet enjoyed the gracious Birchner mansion and took the liberty to inspect every room. She took off her sneakers and ran around the house barefoot. Birgid wasn't home yet, but was still out shopping with the kids.

Jerome showed Juliet to a guest room upstairs. "My wife will be home soon. If you'd like to freshen up in the meantime or take a shower, feel free to do so. I'll be downstairs if you need anything. By the way, would you like an ice tea or anything?"

he asked.

"Sure, a martini would be great," she answered, apparently already in the process of undressing as she plucked her blouse out of her white denims.

"Sorry, Jewels, no liquor in this house. But maybe a soda, or I have an idea: how about an ice cold Starbucks cappuccino?" Jerome offered.

"All right, the coffee will wake me up. Can you bring it up here, Jerome?" she requested. "I'm heading into the shower right now."

Jerome didn't offer a verbal reply immediately. Instead he took the bottle of Starbucks upstairs into her room. "I've put the coffee on the nightstand, Jewels," he hollered as he heard the shower turned on to full capacity.

"What's your wife's name?" Juliet shouted from inside the shower.

"Birgid. She's Austrian too."

"Is she coming to dinner with us?"

"Depends on you. Whatever you prefer. She's very understanding when it comes to business," Jerome said, knowing that he'd just placed a definite lie.

"Let's go all three of us. We've got plenty of time to talk about business tomorrow," she said loudly with every intention to spend the night at Jerome's luxurious place. "You don't mind if I sleep here tonight? Do you?" she added.

"No, not at all. That'll be great," relieved, Jerome answered loudly again through the open bathroom. This was perfect. Birgid wouldn't get angry and Juliet was in a vacation mood. That was great, it would work out just right, he thought.

"You gonna take a shower too," Juliet inquired of him.

Seeing where this could lead, he answered without hesitation, "I just had one before I picked you up from the airport, and I swam a few rounds in the pool—that's plenty of water for me today."

Juliet seemingly accepted his justification for not taking a shower at this time. She was in a seductive, sensual mood, even licentious—ready to commit an act of sin. She was salaciously deceptive.

39

"WE'LL BE out to eat. You can make your shots from the air when we're gone. I guess only the two kids will be home. Don't be too obnoxious though. All right? Just fly a few times over the place, that should do," Juliet whispered through her satellite phone.

AS JULIET entered the kitchen area, Jerome introduced her to Birgid.

"Nice to meet you," Juliet said. She stretched forth her hand, her arm almost straight, to greet Birgid. Her voice was gentle and warm, and still seductive.

"Me too," Birgid answered as she examined Juliet's appearance. She had only wished to be as slender as Juliet. But Birgid was unable to keep her weight down. Too many Hershey kisses day after day, and several snacks in between guaranteed her at least twenty pounds over her ideal weight.

Juliet was dressed in a black cocktail dress which lacked fabric in many places and therefore evinced lots of flesh around the shoulders, bust, back and legs. She accentuated the dress with stylish Fendi slippers, which weren't her first choice. But since she'd grounded her high heels, it was the only viable alternative. *Who cared anyway?* she thought.

Birgid wasn't fond of formal wear and she hated dresses with a passion. Juliet felt much better with her somewhat odd slippers when she glanced at Birgid's casual outfit. Her choice of attire for the evening was a pair of silky black pants and a red silk blouse. Jerome's outfit complimented both ladies, as he wore natural linen trousers with wrinkles all over, and his favorite black silk shirt this time neatly tucked into his pants. It was still daylight when all three left in the elegant white Benz at seven P.M. They drove to an exquisite Italian restaurant on the water. Everything was so perfect. All three observed the beautiful sunset, and they enjoyed the excellent cuisine and a lovely atmosphere. Juliet drank a couple of glasses of red wine. Birgid enjoyed herself too, chatting with Juliet about women related issues. Juliet tried her best to be a nice girl. Only here and there she had a slip of the tongue, especially as the evening progressed and the wine increased. Juliet began cracking jokes, but stopped in the middle of telling one when she realized that it wasn't appropriate for this party. Jerome kept to himself and enjoyed watching Birgid and Juliet.

At eleven o'clock they were back at the mansion. All three converged to the lanai and gathered around the pool. Juliet relaxed on a chaise and Birgid obtained another sun lounger, while Jerome made himself comfortable in an armchair. They continued to talk about this and that. Juliet inquired a few times about alcoholic beverages. The Carr's crackers, as good as these were, caused her throat to desiccate. As she requested the booze, she slapped her tongue against the sticky gums in her dry mouth.

At first, Jerome couldn't think of having anything like that in the fridge. Then Birgid reminded him of a case of French champagne he'd acquired during a charity fund raiser at auction many years ago. It took him about ten minutes to recall where he'd put the carton of champagne bottles. The whole case was stored in an oversized refrigerator in the back of an isolated storage room. It took Jerome awhile to get to it and to dig it out.

The original seal was still intact as the box had never been opened.

Juliet loved it. Jerome placed a couple of glasses on the table in front of her.

"You're goin' to join me, Jerome, aren't you?" she almost demanded enticingly.

"No, Jewels. I don't drink—not even a little bit, as I've told you," he replied.

"Why did you put out two flutes then? What's that for?" Juliet inquired curiously.

"They're both for you. In case you wanna gulp it down. And it just looks better to have two glasses. No big deal though, Jewels," Jerome said, as he poured the liquid into both flutes.

Juliet only shrugged without saying another word. She reached for the first glass and gulped it down. As soon as it was empty she reached for the second one. Birgid didn't pay too much attention to the vain chatter, but she placed a wide-eyed look at him as Juliet emptied the second flute rapidly after the first one. Jerome shrugged. He added a quick fake smirk with the left corner of his mouth after he raised his eyebrows for a second. Juliet didn't notice the exchange of gestures between the lovely couple.

"Once, when I was about eighteen, I got really drunk. And that was it. I swore to myself back then that I would never ever have another drop of alcohol in my life. I was completely whacked. I laid there, partially in my own vomit, for a full day as sick as I could be. I never became violent or anything, but this utter intoxication, this one time, served its purpose." Jerome shook his head. "It just brings back bad memories. I don't condemn you for drinking this stuff, Jewels. It's not a problem to me, because everybody can make his own decision in this regard. But I'm sure you can understand my specific situation why I don't even wanna touch it. No offense, Jewels, okay?"

"Oh, I didn't know. This stuff is just so good, I can't stop. You don't mind, do you?" Juliet addressed Birgid. She couldn't care less about Jerome's stories or opinion. She wanted to get stimulated by the drinks—just a little bit to loosen up. "You enjoy it Jewels. I had it waiting for you for all these years," Jerome said reluctantly. He would've preferred if she didn't drink, but maybe it was better that she did. She'd probably doze off in no time, he thought.

IT WAS around three o'clock in the morning. Jerome and Birgid had already gone to bed two hours earlier. When they retired to their bedroom, Juliet requested that she be left alone on the lanai. It was a warm night and the stars sparkled brightly. She said that she wanted to enjoy the nice night out in the open.

Initially, as she slowly got up from the chaise on the lanai, she was a little bleary-eyed. With the help of an ice cold Starbucks frappuccino coffee drink from the fridge, her sleepiness vanished within minutes. The mocha flavor had been very effective. She became especially awake when she realized that she had a job to do. Juliet quickly ran upstairs into the guest room. She threw her Fendi slippers into one corner. The dress was tight. She opened the short zipper of her dress from below the middle of her back all the way down to her buttocks. This gave her a little more space and freedom to move around. It was also a reasonable excuse if someone would find her running through the house at this hour. There was no time to change her attire at this juncture.

From her things she retrieved a photo camera and a small video camcorder. Sporadically she turned on lights in the various hallways and rooms here and there. In one dark spot near the foyer, Juliet bumped a decorative pillar with a potted plant on top of it. It shook her for a moment, but the heavy object only wavered a little and didn't fall to the ground. This would've been a mess for sure and been noisy enough to perhaps wake everybody in the house. Thank God that the object balanced itself back into position, she thought. She made several pictures of these types of objects throughout the house that could've been devastating obstacles for any intruder.

Within thirty minutes she'd put a good fifteen minutes on tape and had shot over a hundred pictures. Especially the area around the lanai was of interest to her, but also the foyer. After she did what she had to do, she quickly went back to her room, satisfied with the assurance of a job well done.

The temperature in the house was around eighty degrees as the digital thermostat for the air-condition was set precisely for this certain level. Juliet wasn't used to this high level of humidity and she was hot. Perspiration had formed on her forehead, in her armpits and in some delicate places of her body. She was aware of the nasty body odor, but it was too late for a shower, she argued with herself as she undressed and fell asleep naked.

CHAPTER

40

ON SATURDAY morning breakfast was served at the familiar site on the lanai next to the pool. Jerome and Birgid had been up for an hour when Juliet came slowly downstairs.

She's been in the shower for at least an hour, both Birgid and Jerome thought to themselves. Juliet's slender body was wrapped in some nifty red jersey shorts and a white tank top. It didn't escape Birgid's or Jerome's careful visual examination of their guest that no undergarment was worn underneath her scanty tank top. Her body was firm and in this outfit she could've passed for early thirties at the max. Most women would've envied her physical appearance. Birgid did so to some degree.

"Good morning, Jerome," she said, as she attempted in vain to hide a yawn behind her hand.

"Good morning, Juliet," Birgid replied.

"The same to you, sweetie," Juliet said quickly to make sure that she didn't appear as to ignore Birgid.

"Did you sleep well?" Jerome asked.

"Sure did. Thank you for last night. I rarely get to enjoy myself like that," Juliet continued. "I'm hungry . . . I'm really hungry," she said, when she glanced at the deliciously prepared breakfast on the table before her.

"Are you goin' to stay around for a few more hours, or are you in a hurry?" Jerome asked Juliet.

"To be perfectly honest: it's too early to say, right now, I just got up," she said, giggling. "If you know what I mean. I'm not all here yet. But I guess if you don't kick me out right away, I sure would love to hang around you folks for a little longer. It's so pretty here." Juliet cherished the panoramic view of the Gulf as she turned from the right side to the left. The sun smiled at her and the salty breeze, which was tender this morning, instigated a vacation mood. The atmosphere was inspirational. The urge came over her to relax and read a book or just simply do nothing—to be lazy for a day. Juliet hadn't had such a time in years. Even at home she always worked on some project for Nicanor.

After swallowing bacon and eggs, Juliet ate watermelon and drank freshly squeezed orange juice made out of oversized fruity oranges from Florida plantations—the best in the world. The juice must've tasted much better than the champagne the night before, Jerome thought, as he observed her gulping down three glasses of the delicious fruit juice. She didn't go for the French toast though, but instead reached for a couple of pieces of sapid Oroweat twelve-grain bread.

"You like boats, Jewels? Would you like a quick ride in my runabout over there?" Jerome asked, waving in the direction of the pier and pointing to his anchored Scarab.

"That sounds like fun. But the breakfast . . . it won't bother me if we do that?" she inquired. "I sure don't want to throw up after what you told me last night about vomit and stuff."

"No, not if you have a good stomach. It gets a little bumpy out there sometimes. But this morning the water looks pretty calm. It doesn't appear that we'll encounter any rough sea. Birgy, you wanna come along?" Jerome implored her with his eyes to say yes, but Birgid wasn't looking.

"I have a few things to do. How long will it take?" Birgid now glanced at Jerome.

"It's not goin' to be that long. Maybe for an hour or two.

C'mon," he encouraged her. "It's gonna be fun. Usually you never ride with me anyway. It won't hurt to enjoy life a little bit." He noticeably desired Birgid to come along for the excursion. "Let me think about it."

"Jerome, if you don't mind, may I take a few pictures of your house? It's so gorgeous and so inspiring. I like your style. I want to show my interior decorator what I'd like for my new place," Juliet said.

"Jewels, it's all yours. Take as many pictures as you want," he cheered her on. "I still have to get the boat ready, which is going to take me about fifteen minutes anyway." As he stood up, he grabbed two slices of the twelve-grain bread and put scrambled eggs and bacon in between. He hadn't touched his high fiber, rich in Vitamin C Kiwi fruit this morning. But Jerome couldn't resist to hastily drink another glass of the freshly squeezed orange juice.

"Jerome, I haven't brought a swim suit with me. Do I need such a thing?" Juliet was curious.

"Only if you wanna go for a swim. I don't think you need one. Even if you do get wet, the sun and the breeze are gonna make it dry again before you know it," he answered. "Beware, there are sharks out there . . . and they're not only in the water," Jerome posted the warning with a vague smirk, teasing her.

Birgid had just left the lanai and was on her way into the kitchen area. She overheard the little flirtatious remark and frowned at Jerome. *"Very funny,"* she gestured with a motion of her lips without speaking the words out loud.

"Let me take some pictures and then I'm ready to go. By the way, can I borrow some sun lotion, I didn't bring any. I didn't think of it. I had no idea about all of this." Juliet apologized for her obvious oversight about bringing these various necessary articles along on this trip.

"Sure, let me get you some," Birgid answered.

Juliet filmed the Birchner mansion extensively on the inside and the outside. She shot an additional four rolls of film. Before they left, Vivian and Dennis also made Juliet's acquaintance briefly, and she took a few pictures of the kids, of course.

Dennis couldn't help but gawk at Juliet's cleavage.

"Isn't he cute?" Juliet noted, tilting her head.

Most men are enticed and aroused by the sheer glimpse of an attractive female body and its movements. Juliet was well aware of her affect on men. Most ladies would probably not arouse a man intentionally. Not Juliet though. She knew exactly what she was doing. She wanted to deliberately produce an erotic charge in the men around her, particularly in a young, virginal lad.

And for a sixteen year old who lived a very sheltered life at the Birchner mansion, the surprise of Juliet's uninhibited presence was even more of a challenge to remain calm and take his eyes off her chest. It was successfully accomplished as Dennis left the scene as soon as he was introduced to her, and she had shot the few pictures of him and Vivian. Sure, in school, some girls would run around sparsely dressed, but not in such a lewd fashion as was the case with Juliet's scanty outfit that morning.

IT WAS already noon when Jerome left with Juliet for the excursion at sea. Birgid didn't come along for the cruise. She let Jerome and Juliet know that she had too many things to do around the house. Jerome had invited the kids too, but neither Dennis nor Vivian were in the mood to go on a cruise that day.

Juliet seemed to enjoy herself on the trip. Not many words were exchanged, but lots of smiles instead, as the wind rushed violently through their hair, and slapped hard against their faces pulling the skin around their cheeks backward. At full throttle the powerful engines were deafening. At one point Jerome let

Juliet take over the bridge. It was fun, she expressed her excitement by screaming into his ear. Initially, she couldn't keep the boat straight, but instead caused wild swings to the left and to the right, and finally steered a circle. Jerome helped her to get the powerful boat back on track. The emerald waters of the Gulf with its whitecaps seemed to transfer each passenger into an imaginary world—a magical world beyond reality.

They ran ashore at a small uninhabited atoll. Jerome anchored the boat not even a hundred feet away from the beach. He waded through the warm Gulf waters and encouraged Juliet to do the same. Suddenly, she took off her tank top and jumped from the bow of the boat head first into the clear and clean turquoise ocean. Jerome heard the splash and turned around, but didn't see her maneuver. He saw her swim toward his position and then she stood up next to him. The water rippled down her body over her bare breasts. He didn't dare to glance any lower than her head, but of course, some things couldn't escape his view. Jerome took especially notice of her firm nipples which invited some fooling around. He was thankful for his oversized trunks which for the most part hid the obvious sign of his arousal.

Jerome looked at her, trying not to show his surprise. The more he got to know Juliet Farnsworth the less he was shocked by her actions. He had brought two folding chairs and he went back to the boat once more to get the sunshade.

"Jerome, please bring the sun lotion too," she said as she sank into one of the beach chairs.

He had no intentions to stay at this atoll for very long. Because of his very sensitive skin, Jerome wasn't fond of sunbathing. Fifteen minutes or so would be plenty, he thought. Jerome was just interested in showing Juliet the good life, giving her a taste of what retirement could be. For Juliet this was a memorable experience to just sit there on a beach on a remote island far away from a phone, fax, e-mail and the worries of business. She sure didn't have too many moments like that. It was a priceless gift, he thought.

She placed a bath sheet on the ground. She asked if he could rub some more sunscreen on her back. Before they left the house they had already applied a thick layer of forty-five sunblock lotion. He agreed reluctantly to do so, but didn't feel comfortable with this request. Juliet seemingly enjoyed the gentle rubbing and even massaging as she closed her eyes, and released an occasional sigh of relief.

"This feels good, really good," she said quietly several times. Small waves rolled slowly unto the beach and splashed between her legs.

All of a sudden, she turned around. In the last second Jerome managed to pull his hands off her body. Otherwise he would've inevitably touched her well-sculptured breasts. He knew his weaknesses. It was a handful just to look at certain things, but touching her firm nipples would've meant that he would lose control of his libido instantly. He would be forced to give in to his essential human desire and have sex with her in a heartbeat. And she would've loved it, he was convinced. At this moment Juliet was highly attractive. The location, the posture, the circumstances—all this made it the more dangerous.

He realized that a situation in a setting like this was a treasured fantasy for most men, and at times during a weak moment it was even one of his. Jerome had the chance to make such a dream come true right now. Nobody would see them. If she and he didn't tell, nobody would ever find out and it would remain their very own little secret, he thought.

Jerome was still on all four hunched over her. Her tiny shorts were partially unzipped, but remained in the place where they belonged. With big lubricious eyes she stared into his as she sensually parted her lips. Then Juliet ran the tip of her tongue

over her upper lip as to say, *Take me, let's make love.*
In a flash he remembered Gudula from the rental car agency
in Zürich. If she'd been here in place of Juliet things may have
turned out differently, Jerome contemplated. He pictured her
blond hair covering her tender breasts as she stood there on the
beach catching the breeze. And they would make love passionately. Such an episode would've changed his life forever. Eventually he would tell Birgid about the affair. He couldn't keep
such secrets from her. She would divorce him immediately, no
doubt about it. For several seconds wild thoughts and images
rushed through his mind.

Jerome was flabbergasted. "I guess we should go," Jerome
gathered his composure. He'd played long enough with fire.
This was dangerous, he convinced himself. No, he'd never
cheated on his wife, why should it start now, Jerome asked
himself. Everything happened so fast.

Juliet was full of surprises. "Why?" she asked with a tender
voice as to further seduce him. She smiled. "No one would ever
know."

For a moment, it was the same voice of his own conscience.
He took a deep breath. "I don't think it's a good idea," Jerome
replied as he moved away from her to take a seat in the folding
chair next to her.

"Let's just stay a little longer," she requested.

He granted her request for an additional fifteen minutes.
Then they grabbed their stuff and cruised back to the Birchner
mansion. Neither Jerome nor Juliet said a word on the way
back. It was a little after two P.M. when they arrived at the
house.

"Thank you Jerome. This was really fun," Juliet said as she
entered the lanai.

Birgid heard her comment and glanced questioningly at
Jerome. He didn't pay any attention to her. He'd behaved—he'd

been a good boy. No, there was no need to answer Birgid, he thought. But she better never find out about Juliet's behavior, and not about his secret thoughts either.

Juliet got dressed. She squeezed herself into white denims, and a red silk blouse was the top of choice this afternoon.

CHAPTER

41

"JEROME, I almost forgot, I still gotta talk some business with you. Just a couple of things." Juliet approached Jerome in the living room which by means of sliding doors opened to the lanai. "Sure, what is it?" he said. "Let me grab a soda. Let's take a seat over there." He pointed to his favorite sofa in the living room. "Care for a soda, too, ice tea, or something else?" Jerome continued to play the role of a gracious host.

"Yes, I'll take a Pepsi," she answered as she wandered over to the designated sofa.

Jerome brought two glasses with ice cubes and straws, and a two-liter bottle of soda.

"What's wrong with you, Jerome? It seems as if you don't have any hang-ups, habits or whatever. You don't even sin . . . and you don't even have caffeine in your house." She took the caffeine-free Pepsi bottle and looked defiantly at this thing. "You probably don't even drink coffee." She laughed.

From the lanai, Birgid stared at the two when she heard the laughter.

"It's not like that at all, Jewels. We all have our little things, and I have my secret little sins too. Matter of fact, I actually like coffee a lot—I just love the smell and taste of it. But I rarely ever get a chance to drink a cup, except the cold Starbucks in the bottle which is my favorite. But sorry, if you prefer, I've got a can of regular Coke in the fridge too," he offered.

"No, that caffeine-free Pepsi is fine with me. I'm just a little surprised. You're so different than what I had in mind. In many things you don't fit the profile of the guys that I've met over the years. You don't drink, you don't smoke, and apparently you don't party. It's obvious you don't fool around either. And all I can see is that you love to spend money, but even that you do in moderation," Juliet said half jokingly.

"Well, I like it that way. And as I said, I'm in retirement mode. I just wanna enjoy life. No more hassles. I wanna sleep good at night and for as long as I want to. No more annoying phone calls, e-mails, or things to do. Soon you'll have the same. You'll see, life is much better that way. And with your money you'll be set forever anyway," he responded with confidence.

"Let me ask you this: How exactly do you transfer the money from these wires? I mean, how do my six hundred million end up in my account?"

"It's not that easy. In fact, it's a little complicated. But you don't have to worry about it, Jewels, you hired me to take care of it, and we'll do it right. The U.S. wires will be more difficult, but it's goin' to work out fine. Trust me, you'll be happy with the result," Jerome assured her.

"You couldn't tell me just a little bit how it works. I'm so eager to learn, you know," she begged him.

"Okay. As you know we've set up several offshore corporations and opened accounts in Switzerland for these companies. To make it simple, one company bills Nicanor or one of these offshore companies a certain amount for all kinds of things. It could be licensing fees or an advertising charge, or a franchise agreement, or for that matter, it could be even some type of supplies, or expenses for travel services or basically anything else. It really could be almost anything. The key is to get the money off the table outside the U.S. before it's credited to Nicanor's bank account in Dallas," Jerome explained to her the procedures vaguely. "I've done this for over a decade and of course, we've caught on to some pretty creative ideas along the way. But it's nothing you should worry about, because that's why you pay me."

"You're right. That's your job. So far so good. The next transaction will take place next week. I think it's another billion or so," she concluded the conversation. Juliet's work with Jerome was finished.

Birgid said goodbye to Juliet, embraced her and pecked her on the cheek. Birgid stayed at the house while Jerome drove Juliet to the airport. The crew had been waiting for hours at the Butler terminal. But it was their job to be patient and to serve her. They too, were her slaves. She paid them well, though, and they didn't mind working for her and putting up with her eccentric behavior. It was those rich folks—they all had their own way of doing things.

She embraced Jerome and thanked him for the weekend. "Thanks Jerome. It was nice visiting with you," she actually sounded as if she honestly meant it.

"Sure, anytime Jewels. It was a pleasure to have you," Jerome answered, quite relieved to have her off his hands.

"I'll see you soon," she added as she turned around. Juliet put her hand in the air and waved goodbye without looking at him as she continued to stride toward the Gulfstream.

He returned her gesture of the goodbye, but she didn't see it. As she walked up the gangway and just before she retreated to the inside of the plane, she turned her head around once, but only for a short glance to scout for Jerome's whereabouts. He stood there leaning against his car and now repeated the wave as he saw her head turning. She released a faint, but seemingly genuine smile. Then with one more step she disappeared.

Jerome got into the car and left the airfield. He didn't wait for the plane to take off. Thoughts of compassion shot through his mind which tore on his heart. Juliet probably wouldn't appreciate his thoughts. But he couldn't help it, somehow he felt sorry for her. A lost soul. She was all alone crying out to be loved. Or was it just a stint? Then Juliet would be better off in Hollywood, he argued with himself. He couldn't figure her out yet, and Jerome wasn't sure of his assumptions. But one thing was certain, Juliet Farnsworth was a live wire.

42

"THIS IS the FBI," a deep voice declared through the rolled down window of the cruiser into the intercom. "We need to ask Mr. Birchner some questions," the agent in the driver's seat growled.

Jerome looked at the color monitor near the kitchen sink. He was trying to figure out if these guys were the real McCoy or if someone was just playing a bad joke on him. "Put your badge about ten inches in front of the camera, would you please?" he asked.

"We're the real deal, Mr. Birchner. But here it is," the one agent said as he reluctantly put his FBI ID in front of the rather hidden camera lens. But he didn't remove his dark sunglasses.

"All right, officers, come on in. It's the last house on the left," Jerome said through the intercom. He pressed the *Open* button beneath a label titled *Main Gate* next to the intercom. From a small printer he received a printout of the picture frame with the FBI ID and the license plate of the vehicle. Then Jerome sprinted into his office to run a quick ID check on the one agent over the PC. Within seconds the computer spit out the result. The agent was real. His name was Oliver Bushwell. He was forty-one years old. Bushwell was Afro-American and had thick black hair and it appeared to be his own. The license plate on the car too, checked out all right. The car was positively identified as a genuine FBI cruiser.

These FBI agents still drove a dark blue Crown Vic which was a few years old. Jerome stood in front of the house and watched them park the car in his driveway. Both agents were dressed in dark blue suits. They could've played a part in *Men in Black*, Jerome thought to himself.

"Mr. Birchner?" the black agent addressed Jerome as he flashed his badge. It was Bushwell. At almost six feet, Bushwell was significantly taller than Jerome.

"Gentlemen, that's me. How can I help you?" Jerome answered.

"We need to ask you a few questions regarding the incident in North Korea. The Bureau has information that you were in the area a couple of weeks ago or so." Agent Bushwell said.

"I thought the CIA takes care of that?" Jerome replied hesitantly.

"Yes, sir, they do. It's basically their case. But we have our orders, I can't help it. And as you know there aren't too many witnesses. We just need you to tell us what you've told the CIA. See, there are four people dead—all U.S. citizens. Two helicopter pilots were killed, both were with the U.S. Army. And then there was a CIA agent, and of course, the Undersecretary of State. It's not that simple, see." Bushwell adjusted his sunglasses. "Based on all the facts so far, this wasn't just another unfortunate accident. From the evidence that had been gathered at the scene and which our lab has researched, it looks a lot like sabotage. We're talking a cold-blooded murder here, Mr. Birchner. Maybe even a terrorist act. That's where it gets kind of complicated," the agent explained in great detail, enforcing the need to ask Jerome some questions. "May we come in?" They had every intention to.

"Sure. I didn't know . . . I thought it was an accident. You know I was supposed to be on that chopper," Jerome said. "C'mon in, this way, gentlemen."

"Nice place, you've got here, Mr. Birchner," Agent Bushwell complimented as they entered the mansion.

Thanks for telling me what I already know, Jerome thought to himself. He wasn't fond of the FBI, CIA or any other government agency. Jerome hated bureaucracy while he was thankful for the work the FBI did in capturing criminals. Here they were, the two agents marching freely through his house. These guys probably made forty or fifty grand a year. Nobody could persuade Jerome that these guys weren't at least a little bit envious when they saw his stuff—everybody would've been. They hadn't seen the Porsche or the Jag yet. The mansion and the area alone was impressive enough and smelled to have cost at least a few million bucks. No vagrant living here—that was for sure.

They sat down in the living room. The other agent, a white fellow, hadn't said a word yet. He took a quick peek through the window to the outside across the lanai. He then came slowly walking over to the sofa where Jerome and Bushwell were seated.

"So you were in Korea too?" Jerome was interested to find out.

"No," the agent replied and chuckled a little bit.

"You said the FBI gathered evidence there."

"Oh, no. That's the same evidence the CIA has brought back to the States. We have access to it, of course," the agent explained. The agent who did the talking all along introduced himself now officially as Agent Oliver Bushwell. He continued his questioning, "Mr. Birchner, what was the reason for your visit to North Korea?"

"The Undersecretary of State had asked me to meet him there," Jerome answered.

"Was there any other reason for your visit?"

"For research purposes. I was interested in the Nicanor

project."

"All right. Let me ask you this, just for the record: Are you working for Nicanor Industries?" Bushwell got right to the point and asked the question bluntly.

"No, not really. I mean we haven't signed a deal or anything."

"What do you mean exactly, Mr. Birchner?"

"Do I need a lawyer for this?" Jerome inquired.

The two agents looked at each other.

"Do you need one? I don't think you do. I mean you have the right to have your lawyer present, of course, if you like," Bushwell answered, observing carefully Jerome's reaction.

"No, that's all right. I don't think I need one. To answer your question, I was in Dallas several weeks ago. I'd met with Mrs. Farnsworth as you probably know. We had lunch together and talked about her husband's estate. And that was pretty much it," Jerome replied in confidence. He couldn't tell these guys that he was doing whatever he was doing for Mrs. Farnsworth. With a false answer he would've blown the deal. On the other hand he was in the dilemma of committing perjury at this very moment. When it came right down to the letter of the law, he already proceeded with obstruction of justice, too. But at this time it wasn't an issue. Only if this case would ever make it to court, which wasn't a too far fetched probability, then things might become a little tricky, he thought.

"You're sure about that?" The agent was trying to establish a clear-cut response.

"Yes, Agent Bushwell. And the way things look I won't be doing business with them after all. Too many people dead, if you know what I mean," Jerome assured the agent.

"Well, I can't blame you. All right then, Mr. Birchner. What exactly do you do for a living?" Bushwell asked.

"I write books, and I'm a corporate consultant . . . mostly

European clientele. But I'm now semiretired."

"Jeez, you're barely forty years old, Mr. Birchner." The agent was shocked and showed it as he leaned forward, trying to lock his eyes with Jerome.

"It was hard work, you know. Had to work all my life, since I was fifteen. I thought it was time to take a break and relax a little bit." Jerome could feel the envy bubbling up inside Bushwell. The agent relaxed and sank backward into the sofa. He glanced at his notepad. "Did you see or hear anything when the explosion took place?"

"No, I didn't see anything and I didn't hear anything. A couple of CIA agents told me about the accident two days later. I really don't know anything about this tragedy."

"Meaning, you were a mile away from the scene, and you were a no-see-um no-hear-um kind of guy?" Bushwell paused for a second. "From the pictures that I saw and based on the evidence, it must've been some kind of explosion. It should've rattled the building or at least a few windows. But you say, you didn't see anything and you couldn't hear the bang?" Bushwell attempted to reinforce his question in a cynical manner.

"That's correct, Agent Bushwell. I just told you so. And there's nothing more that I can tell you about this event." Jerome felt agitated. "Gentlemen, I'm not a witness. Unfortunately I was there, but I don't know a thing about this incident." He purposed to stay nice, but the direction this inquisition was taking, it was hard for him to keep his cool.

"Mr. Birchner, I'm just doing my job. We don't have any witnesses. Four people are dead. And you were in the vicinity, almost in the middle of this, only a mile away from the crash. You must understand that we have to follow every lead and every single detail so that I can write a report, and so that we can assure the American public that we've done our job to the best of our ability. See, it's that simple."

Jerome felt like they were patronizing him. "All right. I understand. What else do you wanna know?"

"Are you a U.S. citizen, Mr. Birchner?"

"I'm both. I'm Austrian and a U.S. citizen."

"Are you traveling a lot, Mr. Birchner?"

"No, for the most part I'm right here in Naples. This is my home."

"Okay, sir, I guess that's it. Thanks a lot for your cooperation," Bushwell said as he stood up. The other agent followed Bushwell. They took another panoramic view of the interior of the mansion and headed toward the foyer.

"Here's my card. If you think of anything, call me. All right?" Bushwell turned around and handed the business card to Jerome.

"Sorry that I can't help, gentlemen," Jerome said with relief as he took the card from Bushwell. He opened the door for them and said goodbye.

Back in the FBI cruiser the white agent ask Bushwell, "What do you think? Is he telling the truth?"

"I think he is, but he ain't telling us everything, that's for sure. He knows something we don't know yet," Agent Bushwell answered. "I don't think he's dangerous, though. But let's keep an eye on him. Put him under surveillance, just for the next couple of weeks. Let's bug his phone too. We need to know who he's talking to."

"He has a nice place," the one agent said.

"Sure has." Bushwell agreed, as he leaned forward and through the windshield took one more look at the mansion. "I don't know this guy. I've never heard of him as an author. But he must be selling an awful lot of books to live in a place like this. Let's check him out. I'm sure the county recorder can tell us more about him—how much he owes on the house and how many other assets he has," Bushwell suggested.

CHAPTER

43

"ARE YOU still with us?" the male voice on the phone inquired.

"You know I am. We've got everything under control," Juliet Farnsworth answered, as she rolled over in the bed at her Dallas estate.

"Who is it?" the man next to Juliet in the bed asked, still somewhat drowsy. With his left hand he reached over, attempting to grab her and embrace her as lovers do. But he failed to accomplish this task as he dozed off again. She didn't answer him, but instead listened intently to the words of the man at the other end of the phone connection.

"Don't forget, Jewels, we need two billion and not a penny less. John and Baxter are out of the picture now. Does anyone else know about it?" The voice on the phone asked with a heavy British accent.

"No, only Birchner . . . but I'm taking over for him. And Trev, of course, he knows a little bit about everything. But that was the deal, you know about that," Juliet replied.

"Should we take care of Birchner?"

"No, I guess he'll be all right. After I hang up with you, I'm going to call him with the news. The next transaction is due in a couple of days and I don't want him to be involved in this one anymore. He already knows too much."

"Well, my dear, do you want him gone?" He was eager to kill

him. Anyone who comprehended too much was a threat to the operation.

"He'll walk away without a problem. He's made twenty million, George. I don't think he'll talk. There are already enough people dead. I understand that it was necessary to kill the others, but him, I don't think it'd be a smart move right now. They're already checking on Trev and are watching every move he makes. He can't keep them away much longer, George."

"Don't call me by my name," the man interrupted Juliet, snapping at her.

"Okay, okay, relax, would you?" Juliet lowered her voice. "Let me say this, that Trev told me and you probably already know about it that the FBI is also snooping around. And we don't own them. I don't think they'll be a problem though, but there's plenty of commotion right now. We don't need another dead body," she emphasized the last sentence.

"Don't forget, there are no dead bodies," George declared with relentless certainty in an attempt to assure her of the utter destruction of all evidence in this regard. He paused, then continued, "All right then. But let me know when he seems to become a problem."

"Don't worry. I have it under control," she ended the conversation with this affirmation.

Juliet turned to Gates and kissed him gently on the forehead. He was still asleep when she cuddled up to him.

44

"HELLO. YOU'VE reached the Birchner residence. Sorry, we're not home right now. But please leave a message, and we'll get back to you as soon as we can," the answering machine at the Birchner mansion responded every time Juliet placed a call to Jerome. For the past four hours she'd been trying to reach Jerome over three dozen times. Time was crucial now.

While Jerome still carried his cellphone and kept it in the car, he no longer turned it on. Too much stress, he argued. He was already retired and he prepared himself mentally for this reality. The Nicanor deal was almost like a hobby or an exciting travel adventure, more something like that than anything else, even though the money was the most he would ever make on a single deal, he thought.

This morning he went shopping with Birgid. For himself, Jerome bought a lot of things over the Internet. He bought books, DVDs, clothes, even his shoes on the Internet. It went so far that Jerome was now in charge of purchasing towels, sheets and everything else that had to do with the bedrooms and the bathrooms. Of course, he was already familiar with the right sources for these products and bought these particular items at specific Web stores. Almost daily the acquired merchandise arrived via UPS at Whitecaps Island.

But Birgid didn't like shopping on the Internet. For one thing, she didn't even know how to turn on a PC and furthermore, she had not the least interest in learning about computers either. Therefore, when she wanted something from the Web, it was always necessary for Jerome to sit by her side at the computer and to look things over with her. And then whenever she had made her selection he would order the items that she wanted.

Considering everything, the shopping experience with her on the Internet was a very time consuming endeavor and usually would take hours in each instance. She didn't want to bother Jerome too often with this.

When Birgid went shopping she didn't even use a credit card. She hated these things. Her plastic was locked up in a safe at home. And whenever she'd carried a credit card several years ago, she continuously complained about spending too much money and her inability to control her spending habits.

Aside from this little detail, Birgid preferred to touch stuff before she made a purchase. Regarding apparels, she most certainly wanted to try these on in order to make a proper decision. She was of the opinion that clothes had to look good and feel comfy. While she'd ordered stuff occasionally from Lands' End, she purchased most of her things at the local Wal-Mart, Target and sometimes at J.C. Penney in the mall. Birgid didn't care about designer brand name products. She was content as long as she was able to buy whatever she desired, go to the doctors whenever she felt like it, and had enough cash in her purse for whatever expense, and when she had plenty of money on her checking account.

For the past couple of years Jerome had written her a check for a hundred grand every Christmas. Last year she'd only spent about forty thousand. Birgid actually enjoyed saving money on all kinds of things. She searched for special sale events and would be one of the first customers there that day. Frequently, a couple of wealthy ladies accompanied her. They were all into crafts and stuff like that.

Jerome had a separate checking account and things were much easier that way. It was also Jerome who took care of the bills—he issued the checks. In exchange for taking care of the financial details, Birgid was in charge of the oil changes for all cars. This responsibility didn't bother her at all. She would take a book with her and read it in the waiting area until the car was ready.

AFTER THE short shopping spree, they ate *breakfast* at a café in Naples which was owned by a German baker. Then they drove up north to Fort Myers to check out the cars in stock at a local Cadillac dealership. Jerome asked Birgid to make a choice from the six brand-new Sevilles on the lot. A decision was made for a burgundy one with beige leather interior. The vehicle had been furnished with chrome wheels, a sunroof and a CD changer. It was fully loaded and it was a pretty set of wheels indeed. The color and interior was exactly the match his dad had requested as his first choice.

Jerome went for a five-minute test drive and the purchase was completed in less than thirty minutes. He was glad that he didn't have to waste any time to negotiate a deal—the manager of the Cadillac dealership was courteous and sold the car to him, without too many hassles, for dealer invoice. Jerome wrote a check for a little over fifty grand which included taxes and all fees.

Jerome drove the Seville back home and Birgid followed him in their Mercedes. The Cadillac would be stored in his garage for six months and then shipped from Miami to Bremerhaven in Germany, and from there forwarded to Austria. It would make a great Christmas gift, Jerome thought. His father would be elated to cruise in the new car through the winding Alpine roads of Austria.

* * *

IT WAS already early afternoon when Jerome and Birgid returned to Whitecaps Island. Jerome went over to the kitchen area where the red light on the answering machine flickered rapidly, indicating the number two for two messages. He pressed the *Play* button on the answering machine, but no message had been recorded. When he checked the caller ID unit, thirty-seven calls were registered. But no phone number was associated with any of the calls. For each call only the *Unavailable* message lit up on the display. Jerome was in the process of deleting all these calls from the caller ID when the phone rang. The caller ID once again was blank, except for the *Unavailable* indication.

The phone rang again. He picked up the receiver. "Hello."

"Is this Jerome?" Juliet inquired with a rather harsh underlying tone in her voice.

"Jewels, how are you?"

"Thank you, I'm fine. Where have you been this morning? I've been trying to get a hold of you at least a hundred times," she blared through the receiver.

"I'm sorry, I went shopping," he submitted the truthful reply.

"Well, it doesn't matter anymore. I have some bad news for you, Jerome. I don't need your services anymore," she said, grating.

He was dumbfounded for a few seconds. "Why? Did we do anything wrong?" he asked.

"No. Lots of things have come up over the past forty-eight hours. I have to deal with it. I meant to tell you about it earlier, but I couldn't get a hold of you."

"You don't want my help in this? Maybe I can assist you in one way or the other," he suggested as offered his expertise.

"Jerome, listen, we won't meet again. And you'd better forget everything you've done for me, and whatever we've discussed. You must put it all behind you and lose it somewhere in your mind. Scratch it, do you understand? It's for your own good, Jerome, trust me. You made twenty million and that's plenty. From here I have to take it by myself." She sounded guarded.

"Are you going to take care of the companies in Switzerland and all the other stuff?" he wanted to know, still stunned at the news.

"It's been taken care of, Jerome. Don't worry. You don't have to do anything anymore—it's all been taken care of." Then she brushed him off, "Thanks for everything—you've done a great job. Just forget about Nicanor, me and everything else and you'll be fine. Don't contact me again," she warned. "Also, don't mention to anyone that I've ever visited your place. It may sound cruel, but please go away, Jerome. I know you understand what I mean. It's much easier that way," she urgently insisted. Juliet was trying to stay calm.

Jerome stood in the kitchen, completely still, hardly breathing. "All right, no problem, Jewels. I just wanted to help, that's all. But, no problem, I'm gone. If you need anything let me know. Bye Jewels," he ended the conversation.

"Bye, Jerome," she said now with a gentle voice.

He sensed some sadness in the sound of how she said these two last words. Jerome was disturbed by Juliet's phone call. Thousands of thoughts rushed through his mind. Did he offend her? Was it because he didn't fool around with her at the atoll? Did he hurt her feelings somehow? What did he do wrong? Or perhaps she was in trouble, he contemplated. Well, the whole deal was too good to be true anyway. Sure, twenty million was better than nothing, but it was a far cry from a hundred million in the bank, which had been his goal.

"What's wrong?" Birgid asked.

"I got fired," Jerome said. He still held the dead phone in his hand.

"Fired! What's that supposed to mean?"

"Well, Juliet Farnsworth cut me off from the Nicanor deal."
He finally returned the receiver where it belonged. "I don't
know why and I can't figure it out just yet."

"Didn't she like it here?"

"She didn't say. I don't know what it is." Jerome was shaking
his head.

"Maybe it's time for you to relax and stop doing business
altogether. We've got plenty of money and there's always some
sort of trouble with these deals. You've made money on this
deal, haven't you?" she asked.

"Yeah, twenty million. I guess you're right. We should enjoy
the rest of our lives . . . eat good food, watch television, have sex
and grow old," he said, somewhat worried, but with a smirk on
his face. What the heck, it was an easy twenty million and his net
worth had just increased to eighty million in a matter of weeks.

*Let's forget about owning a Gulfstream—it's too dangerous any-
way,* he thought, terminating his desire for owning a jet perma-
nently. Eighty million in the bank would yield almost three
million in annual interest after taxes. Two hundred fifty gee a
month would work out comfortably, his mind calculated the
figures in no time. Currently, he only spent about fifteen thousand a month, and occasionally he'd squandered twenty or
thirty grand, especially during the Christmas season. Eighty
million was enough, he concluded. He also considered acquir-
ing some more of his favorite stocks which could potentially
increase his net worth down the road. With eighty million he
wouldn't make the Forbes 400, but who cared about it anyway?
It was a listing studied intensely by the criminal element. *No
thanks, I don't have to be on that roster,* he said quietly to himself.

Birgid smiled as she came closer and put her arms around his
neck. She kissed him hard on the lips as he grabbed her firmly
around the derriere pressing their bodies together. There was
still plenty of time until the kids would come home from school.

A sexual encounter would certainly provide relief to this situation, and produce a cool head afterwards to think things over. They undressed in the living room and made love on their favorite couch.

CHAPTER

45

JEROME PLACED an urgent phone call to Switzerland. He had
to check up on things. He called the Swiss Bank Corporation
and spoke with Heinz Richter. Once he got Heinz Richter on the
phone, he quickly identified himself and discussed the three new
accounts he'd just opened several weeks ago in connection with
the Nicanor deal.

"Did Mrs. Farnsworth contact you?" Jerome asked.

"Yes, Mr. Birchner, she did and everything is in order,"
Heinz Richter said, offering only this rather meager reply.

"That's good to hear. You know I'm no longer in the picture
regarding these accounts. Mrs. Farnsworth is now the only one
responsible for all three. I have nothing to do with what she's
doing now. Also, you may wanna make a note of the fact that
Mr. Walter Kalkmeier is no longer a director either. He, too, is
out of the picture. If you prefer we can Fedex you an affidavit,"
Jerome said, with much effort to persuade the bank official that
he was no longer involved. This was very important, because
once a client took over, Jerome wouldn't take a chance with
their limited ability to manage sophisticated transactions. Mistakes were too easily made and could've jeopardized everything.

"Yes, that's how we understand it. Mrs. Farnsworth is the
sole signatory. She faxed me a Power of Attorney detailing all
the particulars earlier this morning. Regarding the affidavit,

Mr. Birchner, I'd appreciate it if you could fax me a copy sometime. I don't need the original—a fax will do," Richter requested.

"All right, we'll do that. You've probably seen how much money has moved through these accounts. Not that there is anything wrong with it, but we just can't be connected to this anymore. Mrs. Farnsworth is no longer one of my clients," Jerome stressed the point vigorously.

Heinz Richter assured him again and again that things had been taken care of and that he didn't have to worry about it. None of the accounts in question were associated with Jerome anymore.

46

"HERE'S ANOTHER thirty grand. The deal is off. She fired me," Jerome said to Walter Kalkmeier and handed him a $30,000 cashier's check. Both men stood in Walter's driveway. Walter needed still to be paid off for his minor part in the Nicanor deal. He took the check and looked at it. "You said two hundred thousand. Now I only get fifty?" Walter complained waving the check, firmly clenched between thumb and index finger, wildly through the air. He was out of breath as he had just returned from his daily bicycle exercise routine. Usually, he would perform this workout in the early morning hours before the sun took its course to burn down from high above with crushing heat. The surrounding waters intensified the effect. Today, Walter had gone through the agony later in the afternoon for some reason. Sweat poured off of him freely. It was a smelly affair. His hair was wet. It almost seemed that he had just taken a shower, but that wasn't the case.

"Well, like I said, she fired me. The deal is off and she didn't pay me in full. You can understand that, Walter. At least you made fifty grand for nothing. That's a brand-new Corvette . . . don't forget that," Jerome said half jokingly.

"That's the last time I'm doing a deal with you," Walter said, disappointed, but it was obvious that he wasn't all that serious.

"I'll bet you on that, because it was my last deal. I won't do another one. I'm retiring. How about you?" Jerome was in the financial position to go through with it.

"That's easier said than done. But I've got all these developments and my construction business. It's not that easy for me," Walter offered the reply with regret. He could only dream about it and that's why he hadn't entertained such a thought with enthusiasm. Based on his fancy lifestyle and the way he went through the money, he wouldn't be able to retire for another fifteen years.

"You'll be all right." Jerome slapped him on the shoulder. "You've got a nice house and lots of fun toys for big boys. And you won't end up in the poor house either." Jerome draped his arm around Walter, sweat and all. "Listen, I've really tried to get the most out of this deal, but she just let me go with a phone call the other day. And that was it. She's a nice lady, but I can't figure her out. You know she was here recently. She stayed overnight at our place and she said that she had the time of her life. I don't know what's going on, Walter. She's a little weird. But then, we're all crazy, right? At least you got yourself fifty thou and I made some money, too. I'll make it up to you next time. Let's go out and eat—it's on me," Jerome encouraged him.

"Just the two of us? Let's leave the family at home," Walter suggested, feeling a little uncomfortable glancing at his mansion.

"Did you have a bad day at home?"

"No, Valerie isn't feeling good. The women thing, you know," Walter said. But it was more than that and it was rather obvious that they just had a fight or an argument about something. No wonder Walter was out in the heat of the day.

"How about the Outback? I haven't been there in awhile," Jerome suggested.

Walter agreed. "Sure, that's what I call good thinking. Let me take a quick shower. It'll only take a minute." He headed for the garage.

"I'll get the car in the meantime. See you in a few."

WALTER WOULD'VE preferred Hooters instead, which was his usual hangout. Jerome knew that and therefore quickly suggested the Outback. Hooters wasn't a place Jerome was interested in visiting. Walter had a different moral understanding. Valerie and Walter lived by the *Look, but don't touch* philosophy. Walter was a frequent guest at many nightclubs, strip joints and the like. He'd travel up all the way to Tampa and even over to the Miami area. To most bartenders and owners of such clubs, Walter was no stranger, but had befriended virtually all of them. He loved the girls, but purposed to remain faithful to their pithy standard of just looking and not touching. He had expanded the limits consistently. But, while Valerie didn't appreciate it, a lap dance was supposedly still acceptable and within the set boundaries.

Ever since Monica Lewinsky's statement about what in her opinion a sexual encounter really was and which behavior constituted only fooling around, Walter's standards had broadened immensely. He had told Valerie that only intercourse was actual sex and could be categorized as adultery. And he'd promised her he'd never do that—he would never cheat on her in such a manner. Kissing everybody was certainly normal and had no special intimate meaning in his understanding of things.

Valerie once became very upset when he told her that an act of oral étude that some bimbo had performed on him had absolutely nothing to do with love or sex. It was just fun as he put it, comparing it to a swim in the pool or a jog around the block. Then he added, in a failed attempt to appease the situation, that if these bimbos did these things to him, Valerie wouldn't have to do a blow job on him. Evidently, Walter didn't understand women at all. He was just preoccupied to satisfy his ever-present burning desires.

After he made these statements to Valerie, she got so angry that she stayed at a hotel for the night. Valerie took revenge by getting a little drunk and fooled around with one of Walter's contractor buddies. She recognized the guy in a local bar and it was she who approached him. He immediately recognized the opportunity as he saw what was going on and he supposedly understood her perfectly—that's probably why he screwed her.

There were many occasions when Walter drove off in his yacht with young girls aboard. Valerie never came along and wouldn't say anything. She was seemingly too naive and was convinced that Walter wouldn't go out on her. But out there in the Gulf on isolated atolls where nobody could see them, who knows what took place?

In most instances, Walter was unable to control his libido. He always put himself in the most awkward situations. In addition, he also had a slight drinking problem. Not once, but many times Walter had been found asleep in his car by local police and highway patrol. His car was parked on the side of the road or in some empty parking lot in front of a mall. Often a young chick in a skimpy outfit was with him, and his pants were open or even removed. The law enforcement officers, to whom Walter was no stranger, would call Valerie in the early morning hours. They would inform her at which station she could pick up her husband and his car. For whatever reason she'd put up with it for years.

In public, Valerie was a very kind and quiet lady. Birgid had often tried to break the ice and befriend her. There was seemingly no effective inroad to get through to her in a more cordial way. For instance, she would never give her kids or anyone else a hug. Valerie was introverted and had no real friends. She had established her own little world and lived in it all alone. She had no hobbies to speak of. Valerie was mostly occupied with raising the kids. Her life appeared to be dull.

One thing Valerie was preoccupied with, was her weight. No doubt about it, Valerie suffered from anorexia nervosa. She'd been rushed to the hospital four times within the past year. In the beginning of her sickness, she was able to hide the obvious signs of her eating disorder by coordinating certain clothes in a cleverly fashion. But, of course, the high humidity and the constant heat in the Naples area made it a burden for her to continue with this strategy. Since Valerie didn't think that she was really skinny enough, after a season she began dressing again according to the local fashion. This meant short skirts or shorts and airy tank tops or sport bras. As her sickness continued, outward signs of her anorexia became more frequently evident.

Several dark spots had developed on the surface of her skin. Her depressions increased too, and earlier in the year she'd been diagnosed a manic depressive. She locked herself in the bedroom and would lay for hours on her bed moaning and groaning, and finally with the help of some pills would cry herself to sleep.

Because of her anorexia she only went into public places during the evening hours. In the dark, her body appeared slender and even athletic. Walter and Valerie went out to dinner occasionally. She was a red head and her hair added some flavor to her jizz during such occasions. After dinner though, she'd often take a cab home, and Walter went on his tour through the night clubs.

Once she'd cut her hair very short in a boyish manner. That's when Walter booked a trip to Africa to join a safari. He was gone for a month. Before he left he told her, that he would return whenever her hair had grown back to normal. Jerome and Birgid felt sorry for her.

47

JEROME HONKED the horn in the Porsche. "Get in," Jerome commanded.

Walter was dressed up in his usual attire, which consisted of a pair of black shorts and a white silk shirt. Sandals, of course, was the obligatory footwear in this part of the country. His shirt was still unbuttoned and hung loosely over his shorts when he got into the car.

"Hungry?" Jerome asked.

"What do you think?" Walter answered with a big smile across his face. "I'm ready to eat a cow."

"Good."

They sped away in Jerome's Porsche to the Outback. The place was bustling. A young female greeter told them that the wait would be forty-five to sixty minutes. Walter and Jerome had plenty of time, but it was more a matter of principle not to waste an hour waiting for dinner. Immediately when he heard the announcement and as the greeter handed a pager to Walter, he requested to speak to the manager, who was his friend. Jerome was more reserved and was almost embarrassed when Walter did that. Of course, Walter was already interested in the lovely greeter, and was going about to establish first physical contact as he rested his hand gently on her shoulder when he told her his request to speak to the manager. She was new at the place.

"Walter, Walter," the manager screamed through the crowd gesturing with his hand in the air for him to come.

Walter beamed with satisfaction. "C'mon, Jerry, let's go. Do I have to take you by the hand?" he said jokingly, obviously pleased with the outcome.

At first Walter shook the manager's hand violently, then put his arm around his shoulders. He made some remarks and talked nonsense. Both men laughed.

"I have a table for you over there," the manager said.

Walter and Jerome thanked him. They ordered some juicy Aussie cheese fries, a Bloomin' onion, and hearty steaks. Walter ordered his Outback special medium well with a Caesar's salad and grilled mushrooms on the side. Jerome desired his steak very well done, burnt and charred as usual. A baked potato with everything on it and a house salad with ranch dressing were also served. Jerome requested A-1 steak sauce.

"I'm glad you established a couple of offshore companies for me several years ago," Walter spoke through mouthfuls of food. "I'm not sure if you remember. At first I didn't use them, but now most of my assets are in these companies. Are you sure that nothing can happen to those assets?" Walter inquired.

"If you've done everything right, nobody can touch it," Jerome answered.

"I mean, are you sure that the courts can't touch it? Meaning Val can't do anything about it, right?" Walter was close to a disclosure about this afternoon.

"No. If it has been done right, nobody can do anything about it. Of course, there's always a remote chance that someone digs up all the dirt and figures the whole thing out. But then, you're the only one who knows the exact particulars of your case." Jerome rested his knife and fork, then continued, "If I were you, I would have some money stashed away in a bank in Canada or Switzerland. But only if there was some immediate danger or for an emergency, or whatever." He began to cut into his delicious, charred steak again.

"You know, it's possible that Val and I may split up. I'm not sure, but sometimes I just have this gut feeling." Walter never missed a mouthful with particles of food clinging to both corners of his mouth.

"Walter, I'm sorry, I didn't know about that. Of course, I wouldn't be surprised to learn that Val had finally had enough of you—and that she doesn't wanna put up with your escapades any longer."

Walter looked hurt.

Jerome quickly added, "I mean, of course it's your personal thing, but honestly, she's putting up with a lot, isn't she? You know that, right? Are you talkin' divorce or just separation?"

"Hey Jerry, I'm not that bad, it could be worse," Walter said, not serious about it, still desiring to be goofy as he looked around the restaurant. "You know, I don't know about divorce and all that. Maybe it's just a phase . . . we'll see." Walter looked directly at Jerome as he continued, "I just wanna be prepared, just in case. People change over the years. I always thought that she'd get used to me, but she has these rages and throws dishes and everything else at me . . . I don't know. I just wanna be certain that she can't take the money," Walter explained now, more in a solemn manner.

"Didn't the money come from her originally?"

"Only the first couple of millions."

"You don't wanna leave her anything?"

"Of course I wanna leave her a little bit, but you know me, I don't want her to get into the way of things. But that's only if things get ugly. She can have a million or so, but I don't wanna cut everything in half, if you know what I mean. I wanna keep the house and everything. You must understand that, Jerry."

"What about the kids?" Jerome was curious.

"I know that's the tough part. At least they're teenagers now. I mean I don't really want a divorce. But you know me, I like to fool around—that's just me." Walter shrugged. "And she just has a hard time living with the reality of things. I love Val, of course, and I really mean that, but hey, I can't explain myself." "You're a mess Walter. Look at you." Jerome paused, then made a suggestion, "How about some counseling? Have you tried counseling?"

"Are you crazy, I'm not going to a shrink. I'm not throwing plates and glasses through the kitchen—she is," Walter argued defensively.

"I know, I know. I'm sure it's difficult and it's not my business, but you have to realize she ain't fooling around, and she does what she does because of your behavior. Maybe there's a chance so that you two can work it out somehow. I know it won't be easy, but maybe counseling can help. You don't wanna throw away your marriage. Maybe it's time to calm down a little and live a normal decent life." Jerome hoped Walter was hearing him.

"Jerry, you should be a preacher. I know you're right, but I just can't help it. Look at the girl at the door. Isn't she cute? I can have her just like that." He snapped his fingers. "See that's how I think, that's me."

"Well, whatever. It's your life. Regarding your offshore companies I only set them up for you, and you've managed them by yourself for all these years. I remember when you told me back then that you wanted to make sure these things really hold tight. Remember?"

Walter nodded.

"Under normal circumstances these things are waterproof. Nobody can bust them open, unless you've made major mistakes. My guess is: you'll be all right. Anyway, for my part, I'm no longer in that business." Jerome leaned back for a second and took a deep breath.

"The Nicanor deal is over, thank God, and I'm herewith officially announcing my retirement. It's all history for me. A couple of years ago I closed down my last offshore company. I mean, I still have one overseas, but here in the U.S., no more. There's too much heat for guys like me . . . I don't wanna get busted. From now on I just wanna live a quiet life. Relax, you know, and really enjoy a sunset. I don't wanna worry about all this crazy crap anymore. Even my house is no longer owned by an offshore . . . it's now all in my name. The same is true for my boat, the cars and everything else. The Navigator is in Birgid's name though, but nothing else, except her checking account. That's it, no more." Jerome attempted to make himself clear that he didn't wanna be involved in their marital bout, especially if it got ugly. In the course of things, divorces would always get down and dirty, especially when lots of money was at stake. What a mess, Jerome thought.

Walter listened as he canvassed the waitresses walking by swiftly in their short skirts. He couldn't change, and he knew that it was a matter of choice. It was up to him to rearrange his priorities. But he didn't wanna make a change in his life. He would have to give up his personality, and that was difficult because he was in love with himself, he thought. Every skirt presented itself a potential notch in the scorecard. Walter was a lost soul. Plagued, yes even obsessed by his consistent sensual desires.

48

JULIET FARNSWORTH wasn't aware of what kind of people she was messing around with. They wanted their money. It was payday. She could've had her share of one hundred million. She could've even doubled her portion as she was entitled to John's allotment, too. But two hundred million wasn't enough for Juliet Farnsworth—she needed more, much more. Her partners in crime were eager to lay their hands on two billion dollars— actually subtracting her two hundred million, they only required a solid one point eight billion. That was the plan from the beginning.

So far, everything had worked out fine. It was her partners overseas who shipped the nuclear material for the supposed power plant in North Korea. They had used Nicanor Industries as a cover. And going through Nicanor had been the perfect disguise. It was the only way to pull off this heist of such gigantic proportions in a proper and safe manner. And having the U.S. government's blessing on the deal couldn't hurt—it virtually sanctioned and almost legitimized the coup. In the end it would make a small group of people very rich.

OF COURSE, the intentions for the plant in North Korea were by no means peaceful. No peace mission here—this plant had a different purpose. China had every intention to reinforce their defenses in Asia. North Korea had been their closest ally for ages. While China was wealthy, North Korea had always been broke and needed the money desperately.

The government of North Korea didn't care if China had plans to build a nuclear power plant on their soil, which would have produced much needed energy, or if China decided to erect some silo for launching one nuclear ICBM after the other. North Korea depended on China's support in many ways. They needed their food, money, supplies and even their intellectual properties. Most of all, North Korea offered a strategic geographical position and aside from this crucial fact, it had cheap labor. China could use North Korea as a perfect front for its nuclear defense program.

China was allowed to do anything they wanted in North Korea. Somehow the U.S. didn't get the full picture. Aside from the occasional escalations and outbursts of the altercation between North Korea and South Korea, the region didn't post an immediate danger to the national security of the United States. The U.S. government was even careless to the point by providing billions of dollars in funds to the enemy. In effect it helped China and North Korea to construct this most dangerous weapons facility with the potential of mass destruction. Not only did the Nicanor facility constitute a significant hazard to the U.S. itself, but to the whole population of planet earth.

Was it greed, carelessness, stupidity, naivety, pride, arrogance, madness, or a combination of several factors, or something else? The reality of the existence of the only serious nuclear threat to the U.S. and the Asian realm, even to the world, couldn't be changed anymore. It was insane, a substantial menace to mankind. Now after the fact the world had to learn to live with it and its potentially ubiquitous perils.

It wouldn't make much sense to put the blame on somebody, even though political candidates, world leaders, and the media would eventually pursue that course. But the harsh reality couldn't be changed anymore—that's what most folks in governments all around the world simply didn't realize. It was established, ready to destroy the world. No James Bond, Batman, Superman or other superhero could help to dismantle the monstrous Nicanor plant in North Korea. No Special Forces, no Marines, no Navy SEALs or the like had the capability to infiltrate and destroy this project without blowing up our planet at the same time.

Worst of all, while the U.S. government had suspicions about the Nicanor facility, it was absolutely unaware of the devastating danger that lurked at this location. Only a small group of people knew about it. A few high ranking officials in the Chinese and North Korean government had hatched the plan together with the input and assistance from the greedy ones and the megalomaniacs, which were the capitalists from Western civilized nations. Even some top Muslim leaders in the Arab world were initiated to their vicious scheme. But most of the world didn't have a clue.

And the monstrous killing machine was proudly paid for by the United States of America. The dough came right out of taxpayer pockets. It wasn't just a little bomb put together by some tinkers. The world's top experts had constructed ten of the most powerful Intercontinental Ballistic Missiles crowned with the most potent nuclear warheads ever built. Big money had been spent. And the technology was the best ever manufactured anywhere in the world. The end of the world was at hand. The world was now ready for the true Armageddon. Nobody could stop it now. It was a time bomb already ticking, ready to explode at any moment.

49

JULIET FARNSWORTH had successfully completed her transactions. In the end she had been able to siphon off double of what she'd originally mentioned to Jerome. A total of one point two billion instead of the six hundred million dollars were now stashed away in her Swiss account. She'd spread some of the loot over a few other accounts at different banks in various countries. She'd made some mistakes along the way, but the $1.2 billion were a much better deal than the hundred or two hundred million she had been initially entitled to, she thought. She did it her way and wasn't afraid of paying a high price for it. The end was near. She couldn't see it coming. Juliet was proud of her accomplishment. She'd pulled it off, she thought. And it was all her doing.

THE FARNSWORTH estate in Dallas was put on the market. A high profile Realtor by the name of Wanda Cook from Prudential listed the property. Juliet planned to sell the ranch quickly and offered it for sale below market.

"That's too low, sweetie," the Realtor said. Wanda Cook was a flamboyant lady in her fifties. Her parents had immigrated to the U.S. from Poland in the twenties. She was of Jewish descent. Her enormous wig consisted of silver and white hair with an overall interesting hairdo. It made her head appear much bigger than her body. Even though she was only a little over five feet tall, her gift of gab seemingly exceeded her height significantly.

Long, fake finger nails colored in bright red, excessive arrangements of jewelry with dozens of rings on her fat little claws, and tons of bracelets around her wrists, as well as one chain after the other locked around her neck was a definite guarantee that she would never become friends with Juliet Farnsworth. Her obese body on short legs predicated this conclusion. The Realtor had packed her corpulent physical stature into a white and yellow knit suit—not a pretty sight. High heels, thick makeup with inordinate red lipstick and an undue amount of perfume made her appearance even worse.

Nevertheless, Wanda Cook was a hustler and the number one hotshot Realtor in Tarrant County. Her annual sales were always at least double and often triple that of the Realtor in second place. Year after year she'd been first in sales for well over a decade now. It's often the little people that achieve a lot and leave their mark upon history: Napoleon, Aristotle Onassis, Mother Theresa, and hundreds of others.

Wanda Cook wasn't modest about her success and showed off in a chauffeured brand-new white twelve-cylinder Rolls Royce. She assured Juliet that it wasn't the only Rolls that she owned. Matter of fact, she'd just bought two new ones of the same kind, each for a quarter million. And this was supposedly a pretty good deal. She made a failed attempt to convince Juliet as she rambled excessively.

Juliet wasn't impressed, but looked at her rather in disgust. She would never become like her, she said to herself as she patiently listened to the unending jabber that came out of the mouth of the Realtor. The lady told Juliet every reason in the world to list the estate at a much higher asking price—she could always lower the price later, Wanda argued.

Weeks after the initial listing with the already low asking price, still nobody had inquired about the estate. Juliet called Wanda and reduced the price even more. The Realtor freaked, but did as her client had requested. At first she was tempted to buy the place for herself and quickly calculated how much money she would make by reselling it later at a much higher price. She may even make a bundle in the process, Wanda thought, and potentially much more than the three percent commission she'd negotiated with Mrs. Farnsworth.

JULIET HAD decided to live most of the time in Europe, for the next year or two. Month after month the SEC filings revealed her shrinking Nicanor ownership, until her stake dropped below the five percent reporting requirement. Juliet had sold stock week after week. She'd sold practically all her Nicanor stock in the open market. Her selling rampage depressed the price of Nicanor shares even more, and sent it plummeting down to under a buck. Except from the SEC filings, her selling of the stock was virtually unnoticed. Hardly any institutional investor owned the stock anyway. The majority of shareholders were small individual investors and they had treated the stock as a speculative investment all along. Tens of thousands of former and current employees owned stock in Nicanor due to the company's ESOP and they were the biggest losers in all of this.

Juliet planned on keeping her luxurious chalet in Vail, Colorado, and an opulent ocean estate in Bermuda. On her shopping list she'd been eyeing a cozy château in Southern France.

She hadn't been seen at the Nicanor headquarters for several weeks, as she conducted most of her business out of her Dallas ranch, or when she was on the go. The day she turned her letter of resignation in, an emergency executive management team was put in place by her and Fred Hancock, for the time being. It wasn't a surprise to Fred Hancock—he knew it all along. He and a couple of other Nicanor VPs took over. Juliet no longer wanted to be the President and CEO of the company. At first, they thought of appointing her alternatively to the position of Chairman of the Board, but she showed no interest, and distanced herself even more from Nicanor operations. In all reality, Juliet Farnsworth didn't care what was next for Nicanor. She was now a billionaire. Rich enough to do anything she wanted and to fulfill every desire she had, Juliet thought.

CHAPTER

50

WE NEED the money! it read on the screen. The e-mail was
unmistakably clear, and there was no misunderstanding that the
patience of the sender had been exhausted. But Juliet didn't
respond to the demand and that made things even worse. The e-
mail messages kept flooding into her mailbox. Each e-mail
notice contained no text, but only headlines such as:

> *We need to talk!*
> *Where are you?*
> *We've gotta meet!*
> *Don't play games!*
> *It's time to talk!*

. . . and so on.

Most of her money was in the Swiss bank account and some
in the other accounts—it was safe there. So far, she'd barely
spent a dime of the loot. For two hundred grand she'd purchased
a Ferrari for Gates and that was it.

A FEW weeks ago, Trevor Gates had resigned from the CIA.
The pressure was too much, he argued with the director. And
obviously he'd messed up big time. A couple of months after the
North Korea incident, which had resulted in the death of the

Undersecretary of State Robert Baxter and CIA Agent Hank Taylor, the CIA had no leads whatsoever. Juliet and Gates weren't hush about their relationship either. They openly admitted to it. They were seen on the streets of Paris and Gates had moved in with Juliet at her Dallas estate. He had sold his house in Virginia. It was only three weeks on the market until it found a buyer. Gates sold his house for top dollar.

Before Trevor Gates left the CIA, he took the bulk of Nicanor files and shredded every bit of it. The CIA initially thought that the extensive file was simply misplaced. On the day Trevor Gates resigned, the CIA put him under surveillance, but the CIA couldn't detect any suspicious behavior. Sure, he was banging a rich widow, but that wasn't a crime—at least not necessarily. Maybe he was even in love with her—most of the agents at the CIA believed that. Some of the agents would've loved to be in his shoes, they acknowledged openly in conversations among themselves. They said that Gates had made it. In a sense he was their hero. He had made the jump from poor government employee to high roller with all the fancy toys that were absolutely out of reach for every other agent. And it was all just because she was seemingly in love with Gates the hunk. On many occasions, some agents would joke about it, while the others didn't pay attention to the scuttlebutt.

The CIA's view of Juliet Farnsworth was one of an innocent widow who sought comfort in the arms of a younger lover. She had no criminal past, and in fact, actually the opposite had surfaced. She had studied law and once served as an intern at the Texas Attorney General's office in Austin.

At John Farnsworth's death, Juliet had been married to John for many years. If she'd been married to John at his passing away for only a year or so, it may have given rise to some suspicions. At least it would've concerned the CIA and forced the Agency to look more closely into the relationship and the private lives of John and Juliet Farnsworth. But even then it was only a big *Maybe*.

Currently, things were fine concerning Juliet Farnsworth. Meaning, the circumstances regarding the deaths or murders in the Nicanor case were definitely strange to say the least, but based on all recent findings the CIA had excluded Juliet as a possible suspect. They had checked pretty much everything concerning her background, habits, lifestyle and so forth. Even the life insurance policy in the amount of two million dollars wasn't extraordinary. In comparison it was a rather meager policy and because no body had been recovered it would take at least a couple of years, according to the applicable terms of this specific insurance document, until she would even see a cent of it. John had arranged for it years ago, and Juliet didn't even know about it until their attorney informed her of the existence of the document.

One thing the CIA didn't know anything about were the fat accounts in Switzerland and other countries that brought sweet Juliet's total credit balance to a staggering one point two billion bucks. If they had found out about that, it would have certainly led to extensive digging, and may have evolved into a truly enormous case, and put the spotlight on Juliet immediately. But for now, they were ignorant of these accounts, and had no suspicions in this regard.

Also, Nicanor was seemingly financially not in trouble and quite honestly was doing very well in completing the North Korean project. No rumor of a scandal made the rounds nor was one on the horizon. Things were fine while not absolutely perfect. But there were no reasons to suspect foul play in the accident over the Pacific with John Farnsworth. Due to technical difficulties of the aircraft the FAA had ruled it an accident, even though they were unable to investigate any part of the crashed airplane, as they never found a piece of the Gulfstream.

Only the North Korean helicopter crash gave the CIA lots of reasons for trepidation. But then, it could've been an unfortunate incident, caused by the North Korean army, or an attack by terrorists, or some sort of radicals. So far, the findings of the investigation into this mishap were inconclusive.

CIA Director William B. Tish didn't like it at all, but had not much to go by. He swore to himself that he'd solve this case before he'd retire. Things didn't look good—they didn't run across any new leads, but the agents kept on searching. Was it the perfect crime? Or was there nothing to worry about, and had it all been just a series of some unfortunate circumstances? Tish mulled over these questions again and again. By nature he had to question everything and it was his duty to be suspicious. He was paid to be sceptical and would never take anything people said at face value. Director Tish trusted his agents, though—this was the holy fraternity.

He considered Gates a loser. Someone he'd put much hope into but turned out to be a failure. Gates had it all, Tish argued, and he saw himself in Gates. Trevor Gates was doing great until this Nicanor thing. Tish couldn't figure it out. Sure, people change, but maybe Gates had just a couple of bad months. Maybe Gates fell prey to novice traits, became big headed, and was simply not careful enough. Tish was trying to see the situation in a somewhat positive light as he stood by his man. As much as he attempted to convince himself of that, his gut feeling told him that something just didn't fit. They had overlooked something. Time would reveal it, but the clock was ticking fast and time was running out.

51

THEY MET in a café in Paris. She was alone, it seemed, and she sat in a corner in the back of the café. He jumped out of a silver Mercedes. He quickly stepped through the rain, successfully avoiding puddles, entering the café via the revolving portal which demanded some pressure to turn. Water ran from his head down over his beige trench coat splashing onto the carpet. The man had gray hair and stood well over six feet tall. It took him only a second to locate Juliet Farnsworth in the rear of the café as this was the designated meeting place.

"Bonjour, Madame Juliet," he said, not at all a Frenchman, but with a thick British accent.

"Hi, George, how are you?" she responded, taking another sip of her coffee. Juliet Farnsworth didn't get up and only glanced at the man in the trench coat.

"We need the money, Jewels," he came right to the point. He didn't hesitate to sit down in a chair next to her and George cocked his head forward attempting to inch his face very close to hers.

After smelling his bad breath, she turned and looked at the raindrops splashing against the window of the café. "I know you do. What would you say if I told you it didn't work out?" she suggested.

"Don't even think about it. Don't play games with me, Jewels. I didn't come here to be made fun of. I don't live around the corner, you know. I had to fly in from Vienna just to see you. Only because *Madame* doesn't feel like going there. You know I'm very positive that you have the money. There's plenty of documentation on all the wires. Where did the money go, Jewels? I didn't come here for nothing," he insisted.

"You'll get your money," she made a vague attempt to assure him.

"Not good enough, Mrs. Farnsworth. We've waited long enough. We need one point eight billion right now." He spoke each word precisely. "You can take your little chunk, and I'm sure you already have."

Juliet Farnsworth continued to stare from her seat at the raindrops splashing against the window now more frequently. She didn't look at him as she blew thick loops of smoke into the air. She didn't care what George wanted—she was in charge, she thought. She had the money and she was desperately trying to keep her cool. Juliet clenched her teeth and took all the guts that she had to prepare for a bold statement. "So what? I have every right to take my share. I did most of the work anyway." She looked directly at him. "Don't forget my husband. You've killed John just because of this stinking money. I'm telling you, the deal didn't work out the way y'all thought it would," she said, taking a firm stand and making her position clear.

George let go of a chuckle. "You don't care about your husband. You're not kidding anyone. You've already got yourself a new one. And you don't make a big secret out of it either. And don't talk to me like that. You're not in charge here," he scolded her.

"That's enough. Get the heck out of my face," she demanded.

"I want my money. Pony up, lady. It's not just me, you know that. Maybe you've forgotten, there are lots of people in this and they wanna get paid. I give you twenty-four hours to get me the money," he threatened.

"I can give you a hundred million for your hassle and that's it," Juliet offered.

"Sorry, sweetheart, you already took your chunk. Now I need one point eight billion by tomorrow noon. I've told you, people need to get paid. And they'll be very angry if they don't see the money by tomorrow," he warned Juliet. "Don't tell me any stupid stories, Jewels. You know I'm not kidding. I'll blow you away just like that . . . like everybody else." George looked at her dead seriously.

"What exactly do you mean by that? Get real, George. Without me you don't get anything. Without me you don't have access to the cash, remember? Why don't you get lost, George. Take your cronies and get out of my life," she said in a defying manner, frantically moving her lips up and down, and her chin back and forth.

"Wake up, Jewels. This ain't no game. This is the real world. Bad guys, good guys. You mess up, you lose."

"I can give you two hundred million and that's all there is," she insisted with finality, in a failed attempt to brush him off.

He grabbed her with his hand tightly on her arm and stared intensely into her face. "Look at me, sweetheart," he spoke between clenched teeth. "This is no time to bargain. It's one point eight billion by tomorrow or you can kiss your lovely ass goodbye." George briefly tightened his violent grip on her arm. "You understand? Did I make myself clear?"

Juliet had no choice but to look at him. He was so close that she could feel the spray from his infuriated mouth. She didn't answer. Even though he was red-faced, he tried very hard to control himself. George let go of her and got up. He took wide, decisive steps toward the exit, crushing through the revolving portal which continued to turn a minute after he'd left the café. The rain was now heavy. George swung through an open door into the backseat of the Mercedes.

JULIET WAS shaken, but still didn't realize the dilemma she was in. Gates emerged from a corner near the entrance of the café. He'd witnessed the scene and was ready to get up if things would've gotten out of hand.

"Did he hurt you? Are you all right?" He took her hands in his and tried to make eye contact as he sat down at her table in the same chair George had occupied until ten seconds ago.

"I'm all right," she quietly said. "They want the money. They didn't take the deal."

"Are you gonna offer them more?"

"No, even if I give 'em half a billion they won't rest until they have everything. And even then I'm positive that they're still going to kill me, and maybe you too, honey," she said, finally looking at him.

"We'll see about that. Won't we? We can live somewhere in South America or get lost in Canada," Gates suggested.

"No way. Do you really think that I'm gonna hide for the rest of my life? I'm not going to live in fear. As long as they don't have the money they won't kill me. Believe me, without me they won't see a penny."

"Gee, Jewels, by now you should know these guys," he cautioned her. "They're cold-blooded killers. They don't take prisoners. No matter if they find the money or not, sooner or later they'll try to kill you anyway."

"As long as they don't have the money they won't kill me. We'll disappear to Bermuda. It'll take them some time to find us there," she offered without much conviction as the only solution to the problem.

"Are you serious? In Bermuda? They'll find you in no time. We have to think of something else. We need a good story to create a diversion. They need to go after someone else," Gates insisted.

"Who's going to take the rap for this, honey? It's not about a million bucks, but it's one point eight billion U.S. dollars. Hello, anybody home?" This sum was staggering, especially when spoken out loud.

"Yes, I know. How about if we say that someone involved in the deal screwed up? Maybe the bank, or someone else just simply screwed you," he suggested, sincerely looking at her.

"We could put some blame on Baxter, but eventually it won't work because they won't find any money with the Baxter folks. And that's easily explained because he didn't have anything to do with the money. Sure, he was involved, but he chickened out just like John, remember? And only John and I were supposed to handle the money . . . nobody else even had access to it," she reasoned.

"How about Birchner? He helped you to get the ball rolling and he did the complete setup for you," Gates said, excited about his recommendation.

"You know he's going to get killed in the process. That's too much." Juliet shook her head. "We can't do that. You're pretty cold, Trev," she replied, disturbed at his casual attitude.

"It's either you or him. I don't see any other way. You didn't have anything going with him while you were at his place, or did you?" Gates narrowed his eyes at the thought.

"Are you crazy? Of course not. What is that question supposed to mean? Look, if you can't trust me, we can call it quits right now," she reacted furiously.

"Jewels, don't make a scene. I was just asking. I'm here to help you." Gates tried to get her back on track.

She got up and hurriedly left the café. Gates followed her, but was stopped by the waiter who requested payment of the check. Juliet vanished inside a taxi—it would take her back to the Ritz.

Through the window of the café, Gates saw her enter the cab and the car sped away. He handed the waiter a few bills and ran out the door, but was too late to catch her.

Gates was out on the street hailing his own cab. Several cabbies shot by him without even slowing down. From the puddles on the street he was badly splashed from head to toe. It was their first significant argument ever. She'd never run off before. But Gates wasn't insecure. He was convinced that she needed him, and most definitely he wouldn't get the boot. Gates knew too much. In fact, he knew everything—or so he thought.

52

JULIET AND Gates got out of a taxicab in front of the international terminal at Charles de Gaulle airport near Paris. Someone watched every move they made.

Late last night she ordered the wire for a hundred million U.S. dollars into a designated account at a bank in London. In the attached note of the electronic money transfer it read:

Thanks. There's no more. This is everything.

They had received confirmation of this particular wire from their bank earlier in the morning. The boss was infuriated. He'd told her yesterday in the café to wire one point eight billion U.S. dollars—not a penny less. A hundred million wasn't good enough. It was his job to pay every participant in this scheme his due share. His life could've been at stake too. Some of the folks in on the deal were not toying around. These people were real terrorists. In the past they had blown people into pieces for no good reason at all. George only imagined what they were capable of doing to him if he would fail to pay each one of them for their services rendered. Double-crossing these guys was certainly no fun. George understood that. It was his reason for playing tough on Juliet. The issue was no longer just his personal share from the deal, but rather the dough for the goons.

* * *

AS SOON as Gates and Juliet left the check-in at the Air France counter, the Arab, wrapped in a black leather jacket, approached them swiftly.

"The boss wants to see you," the man in the black leather jacket said in broken English with his Middle Eastern accent.

"We have a plane to catch," Gates answered unkindly in a harsh manner.

"No, that's all right." Juliet placed her hand on Gates's arm as she turned to the man. "We've gotta take care of it right away. Where is he?" Juliet hadn't told Gates about the wire from last night. Gates had been out on the town and arrived at their hotel suite after midnight. Juliet was already asleep.

"He's upstairs, in the bistro. Follow me," the man demanded.

"I'll meet you at the gate," Juliet said to Gates.

"No way, I'm coming with you," Gates insisted.

"No, you aren't," she said firmly. "I'll meet you at the gate. It's going to be all right. Trust me."

Juliet followed the tenebrous Arab on an escalator to the next level up. On the escalator she distanced herself about ten feet behind the Arab. The bistro was located diagonally across the escalators. The boss sat in an empty section of the small bistro. When he saw Juliet approaching, he got up and offered her a chair.

"I've received your note," the boss said. "I'm sorry about yesterday," he added the apology.

"Did you get the money, too?" she responded as she sat down in the chair across from George.

The Arab stood outside the bistro eyeing both of them. He also looked around to secure the area.

"It's not enough though. I told you yesterday that I need one point eight. So far, it's only five percent of that. Where are the other ninety-five percent?" He was deadly calm.

"Can't you read or hear what I've said? There is no more money. I gave you everything I had. I just want to get out of it. I don't need my share—you can have it. Maybe later, at the end of the year I can get some more." Her hands were tightly clasp in her lap. "There's still two billion the government hasn't paid us yet, remember? Maybe I can think of something and then you get another cut. But for right now, there isn't anymore," she was trying hard to convince him of her lie.

"Jewels, there's no time to play games. I've made myself clear to you yesterday. It's over. You've gotta pony up. Otherwise, I already see the ice melting under your feet, sweetheart. I assure you. I will get the money," George explained with definite intentions.

"Things didn't work out the way we had planned. Things went wrong, George, I told you. I know some of it was my mistake, but that's the way it is. There's no more money, George. I wouldn't know where to get it from right away."

"What went wrong? Who took you for a ride, Jewels? I have full documentation of all the wires and every transaction. I'm sure you know where the money went. We've tracked the account balances of Nicanor day by day. We saw every single penny that was deposited. And frankly, there's quite a bit missing, Jewels. Let me say this one more time, it doesn't make much sense to play hide and seek. It's over." He was speaking slowly and deliberately. "You've gotta pay up. I know you've got the money somewhere . . . I know it, Jewels. How much did you pay this financial consultant of yours? Birchner, was that his name? Did he hide the dough for you? It's at least over a billion bucks, Jewels. This chunk of money doesn't disappear like that. And I swear I'll find it—even if it's locked into a treasure chest on the deepest spot of the Atlantic."

"George, the money is gone. I had to pay transaction fees and engage people like Birchner for the transfers. You can't wire five billion around the world for nothing. It costs money." Juliet leaned forward, both hands gripping the chair. "Hundreds of millions just in fees, a charge here and there, and it all adds up. And I didn't take a billion in the process. I couldn't do it even if I wanted to. And you couldn't do it either—it's obvious. Nobody can hide a billion bucks. These people who handled the wires deducted their fees automatically. And it was a substantial amount. Hundreds of millions of dollars. You must believe me, George," she begged him.

"All the fees and charges were much more than what I had agreed to," Juliet continued. "That's why I had to fire Birchner right away. But it was too late and the money was gone. I don't know where he put it. He's a pro and I'm positive he didn't act alone." Her speculations grew. "Maybe he worked together with the guys in the bank in Switzerland. You've read his file. He's dangerous. He's done these for years. I don't know why he's still out there. But I can't call 9-1-1. Can I? What should I tell 'em? Maybe that we wanted to skim two billion off the U.S. government, but in the process we got screwed? Sorry, can you help us?" She leaned back in the chair. "I was glad to rescue what I could and you should thank me for that, George. I've wired you a hundred million. George, I beg of you, you must believe me," Juliet continued with her lie. She had worked hard and desperately to invent a believable story.

The boss listened intently. In a sense her story made sense. "I must admit it's conceivable. But who is working with Birchner? Who took little Juliet for a ride?" he inquired.

"It's Birchner, Jerome Birchner. I don't think he's alone in this. But based on the calculations I've made he took at least over a billion. I had those numbers checked by our accounting department, and they said the same thing," she said in her final attempt to convince George of the truth of her tale.

"Birchner? Well, we don't know too much about him, do we?

But he'd be crazy to steal the money, unless he knows something we don't know. Maybe he works for someone. We've gotta find out, Jewels."

With the stage now set, Juliet took the limelight. "He was very upset when I told him that he was fired. I didn't trust him from the beginning, George. Birchner did all the setups for the accounts. And it was he who initiated the incorporations of all these offshore companies. And when the wires came from over here and over there he took a big chunk out of it." She was feeding George the whole story. "I didn't find out immediately, but when we added everything up in the Nicanor accounts, it was obvious that quite a sum was missing. We waited a few more days, but no additional funds were wired. It was too late then. Birchner knew what he was doing. I've tried to get the money back from him, but he didn't respond."

"I hope your story is right, Jewels. If not, I swear to you, I'll kill you myself, make no mistake about it."

"George, you must believe me, it's true. You can find him in his mansion in Naples. He rarely ever travels. I know you can get to him," Juliet continued with the final trap.

"Who has hooked you up with this guy? I know we considered him in the early phase of our evaluation, but he sure wasn't the first choice on our list. I've checked into it and it was your call, Jewels."

"One of our suppliers brought Birchner with him. I think Dermont was his name. He operates out of Baltimore . . . some kind of laser company. I can e-mail you the details when I get back to Dallas," she offered.

"Dermont. Who's Dermont?"

"He's just a supplier. He's kind of new. I don't know him. I guess anything is possible. This guy, Birchner and for whomever he works really screwed us, George. I mean that's obvious. And based on his history—I mean I've read the whole file on him. Anything is possible."

"I'm gonna get this sucker. Is his place a fortress?" George inquired.

"I can help you, George. I've got lots of pictures and a video from inside and outside his mansion. There are no guards, no protection whatsoever." Juliet's plan was now in progress.

"Good. Get me those pictures. I'll think of something. This better be true, Jewels. You know I don't wanna hurt you. I'm gonna get this guy," he was determined. As they spoke, the whole picture seemed to unfold and George began to comprehend it little by little.

Juliet stood up. "I'll get you those pictures, George." She wanted to get out of there fast.

Juliet hoped her lie would hold up. She knew it wasn't as solid as she had wished it would be. But the story was conceivable. It made sense and Jerome could've siphoned the money right into his accounts. Nobody knew all the details about the accounts aside from him and her. The ominous account could've been easily his. That account was not only empty by now, but closed. Her billion point two was first transferred from Switzerland to a bank in Liechtenstein, and then forwarded to yet another bank in Luxembourg. Later the sum was divided and sent off to numbered accounts owned by offshore trusts in Bermuda and the Cayman Islands. Another chunk of the loot was put into a bank in London. Juliet had done her homework as she'd read all books by Jerome Birchner.

"George, I've gotta catch a plane. Do you mind? Get him, George. Let's keep in touch," she said, running off to the gates.

"Betcha, girl," he said quietly so that she couldn't hear it.

Juliet headed swiftly to the departure gates. Flight 001 from Paris to New York on the Concorde was getting ready for takeoff. She ran through the terminal, carelessly bumping into people along the way, passing other passengers at the security checkpoints. Juliet was in good physical shape as she kept running, but still barely made it to board the aircraft. Gates had told them to prepare for her late boarding. This wasn't unusual. Many busy executives were often late and got on the plane at the last minute. Time was money and most passengers on the Concorde were always in a hurry as precious time was slipping away.

"I didn't think you'd make it," Gates said as he approached her, waiting at the gate.

"I think he bought it." Juliet was out of breath and fell into his arms.

"He bought what?" Gates asked, holding her, feeling her breath in his neck.

"Birchner. I think he bought the Birchner story," she said as she pulled away from him, to look him into his eyes.

"You think it's really gonna work?"

"I sure hope so. Believe me, they want the money. They won't go away unless they have the money. At least it buys us some time," she rationalized, as both stepped into the aircraft now.

The Concorde was first class throughout and their two seats were the ones in the fifth row on the left of the aircraft. It only took them about three and a half hours to arrive in New York. At JFK the Nicanor Gulfstream was waiting to fly Juliet and Gates to Dallas.

SO FAR, still nobody had put in an offer for the Farnsworth ranch near Dallas. Juliet longed to be out of the picture and to finally enjoy her billion. She couldn't wait to squander some of it. Things were basically still going according to plan. She thought that the hundred million would pay George and his cahoots off, and she hoped that they would go away. But Juliet didn't realize the viciousness of these people. They were evil and nothing could stop them to get their fair share from the Nicanor deal. Most certainly they wouldn't stop killing, not even after they got hold of the moolah.

IT WAS dark. Dawn was yet a few hours away. As expected, the night sky over Naples was clear and stars sparkled brilliantly across the firmament. A highly sophisticated surveillance helicopter hovered quietly over and around the Birchner mansion for about ten minutes. It was one of these new high-tech, so-called whisper choppers. When they made their approach it was almost inaudible. At least it wasn't the usual loud annoying sound of such an aircraft, but more at a noise level similar to an air-conditioning unit.

Their intentions weren't to wake anyone. Everybody had to be sound asleep in the house, otherwise their plan would've been off that night. The chopper was equipped with special night vision gear. The gear was the newest type of its kind with an extra high level of heat sensitivity guaranteeing the best possible monitoring capability available. This allowed the men on board the helicopter to survey and detect any movement in the house beyond any walls and levels. They strategically checked the building a few times and didn't discover any movement at all—everybody was seemingly sound asleep in the Birchner mansion.

After the surveillance maneuver, the crew from the helicopter signaled a simple *okay* through a radio control unit to the ground forces. The aircraft left and positioned itself approximately three miles out over the Gulf. There, in a southwesterly direction off the Gulf coast, the crew waited patiently in the air for the next step in the well-prepared and thought-through procedures of the crime.

Six powerful engines of two forty-three-foot Fountains in black camouflage paint bubbled in the water. Both boats made their approach slowly toward the private beach of Whitecaps Islands. So far, their sophisticated endeavor had been handled in quite a professional manner.

When they landed at the beachfront of the Birchner estate, a group of six men jumped into the easily accessible grounds. The Birchner home was somewhat isolated at the far end of the development. This aspect made it vulnerable to intruders who had intentions to access the property from the water. The perpetrators were therefore tremendously helped by this circumstance. Neighbors couldn't see them either since there were none at this location of the development. It was up to the Birchners to detect and identify a potential intruder.

All men were dressed in black and carried night vision gear. Two of the men held automatic assault rifles. These two acted as lookouts and positioned themselves near the powerful motorboats. The other four moved swiftly toward the mansion. With a sharp cutting tool one man made an incision into the screen of the cage. The opening had been cut out in a matter of seconds which led the men into the lanai. With another precision instrument the same man cut out a huge piece of glass from one of the sliding doors. This section of glass was fastened by large suction cups and removed noiselessly by two of the thugs. It was cautiously put to the left into a nearby corner of the house. Through the cutout hole the goons were led from the lanai into the living room and the attached kitchen area.

A SOPHISTICATED alarm system with infrared detection units

had been installed in the Birchner mansion. But Jerome rarely ever activated the system. Only when all of the Birchners went on a trip for a few days or so, they would, as a practice, switch the complete security program on. Jerome was always confused by the many features of such an intricate system. During the first month when they had just moved into their dream house, several times police patrol units with sirens showed up at the gate, just to learn that it had been a false alarm.

In order to prevent false alarms in the future, Jerome simply didn't activate the security program in the house when they were at home. For their protection they counted on the heavily secured walls around Whitecaps Island. The gate too had been highly fortified. Along the inside walls and the gate an elaborate infrared web had been installed. Through specialized sensors it went up automatically every evening until the early morning hours. Initially, this infrared web detection system caused plenty of false alarms until it was fine tuned. The adjustments for the fine tuning were subject to the climate, the game that was in the area, and various other aspects. The technology was so sophisticated that half a dozen technicians from the manufacturer in Cincinnati had to be flown in to do the job right. What in the beginning seemed to be a one-day assignment, turned out to be an ordeal for a full week.

Access through the gate to the development was only possible with the use of certain remote control units, virtually custom-made for this specific development. These certain remote control units changed the access code with every use. The unit would select one random code from over a billion possible combinations each time the gate was opened. From the four homes in Whitecaps Island, only the Birchner and Kalkmeier mansions were occupied. One house was empty and Hubert Neumann, the owner of the fourth house, rarely ever lived there. Neumann left his remote control units in the mansion and contacted either Jerome or Walter before he arrived in Naples. Either one would go to the airport and pick Neumann up to drive him home to his estate.

The Birchners felt safe within the development and even safer within their house. Even without activation of the alarm system for their specific house, they couldn't contemplate that someone could violate their privacy. How could it be possible? Regarding the access area by the water, they initially gave it some serious thought, but in the end dismissed the imagined scenarios and considerations as nothing more than paranoia. The first obstacle for a potential intruder from the water was that such a perpetrator had to come close to the private beach area of Whitecaps Island. During daytime hours, any would-be intruder would've been spotted immediately. The huge bay windows afforded a vast view of the Gulf at all times. In the dark it was more difficult to see anyone, and that was the only soft spot in their protection against the criminal element—they all agreed on that.

But then there was the cage which created the next obstacle. The door to the cage was always locked. Any cutting of the screen around the cage would generate some noise, they argued. Therefore the cage was considered a hindrance to a potential intruder. Secondly, when everybody went to sleep, the glass door to the lanai was locked and presented therefore another impediment. To enter the Birchner home, a stranger had to cut the glass, which once again would generate some noise and would probably wake the inhabitants, they thought.

All the huge bay windows around the house were of no concern as those were substantially above ground and not easily accessible. Additionally, those windows were equipped with Rolladen shutters which were the most secure protection for windows. Even outside the sliding doors on the lanai, Rolladen shutters had been installed. But these were rarely ever let down at night. These Rolladen shutters in this particular location were put in not only because such shutters were installed all around the house, but because Jerome's primary objective was to avoid any penetration of natural light into his personal movie theater which was attached to the living room.

Thirdly, the sophisticated alarm and security network would scare away any intruder that did make it inside the house anyway—they were confident about that. They had thought of everything, they assumed.

Of course, then they were only joking about a scenario that was now actually in progress. Neither Walter nor Jerome were afraid of such an episode to ever take place in Whitecaps Island, as it was more likely and typical to befall only drug lords, war lords and the such. And neither Walter nor Jerome had anything to do with illegal drugs or weapons. And no drug lords or war lords lived in Whitecaps Island. But such crazy potential events were pure speculation—stuff movies were made out of, they reasoned. It would never happen to them, they assured themselves.

THE FOUR intruders speedily and methodically made their way upstairs into Vivian's bedroom. She was asleep. The solid steel and concrete construction didn't allow for any kind of vibrations or cracking noises like houses made out of wood.

Two men grabbed Vivian—one putting a sleep-inducing sedative into her face. There was no struggle. The other two men silently moved into Dennis's bedroom. They grabbed him. One of the two men put the same narcotic substance into his face. The four men carried Vivian and Dennis swiftly downstairs. Then they transferred the bodies through the opening of the glass door to the outside. They were careful to make absolutely no noise. From the lanai through the cutout area in the cage it only took ten more seconds. In all, from entering the slit of the cage to the kidnapping of the Birchner kids, until they were back on the boat, it took only about three minutes for the whole operation. They hauled the two children away in one of the Fountains. Both boats left slowly, so as not to generate any disturbing noise. Once far enough away from the beach, they opened to full throttle and raced a few miles out into the Gulf.

About three miles out on the sea, Dennis and Vivian, still unconscious, were airlifted by the hovering helicopter which had waited for them. The Fountains disappeared in the dark of the night. The chopper journeyed off toward the coast of Cuba.

54

AT SIX in the morning, when Birgid went to check on Vivian, she thought it was strange to not find Vivian in her bed. She searched the bathroom and then Dennis's room. He wasn't there either. This was completely out of the ordinary. Birgid's heart began to race. She ran to Jerome, shaking him violently with both hands.

"Get up! Get up! I can't find the kids," Vivian screamed.

It took a minute for Jerome to open his eyes. "What's going on?" He wasn't yet aware of her fears.

"I can't find the kids. Get up, Jerome!" She was frantic.

"Maybe they already went to school?" Jerome suggested.

"No, it's only six," she screamed, pointing at the clock. Birgid was on the verge of totally losing her composure.

"Maybe they're down at the beach?" he said half asleep. Jerome was getting just a little perturbed at Birgid's histrionics. All Jerome desired at this moment was to sleep a little longer. Birgid was emotional and sometimes freaked out about a little detail just because she couldn't explain it at the moment.

"All right. I'll do it myself," she said angrily and left to search upstairs again for the kids. Once again she looked into every bedroom and bathroom. When she was unable to locate the kids she ran downstairs. Only when she walked into the kitchen area, things became especially eerie. There was a huge hole in the sliding door.

"Jerome!" she screamed. "Jerome! Come on down, Jerome!" Birgid was frozen in place, unable to fathom the scene before her.

He rolled out of bed and wiped his hands over his face. Jerome was certain that there had to be an explanation for all of this, yet the tone of her voice was unnerving.

"Honey, what is going on so early in the morning? I really need some more sleep. It's too early." He entered the kitchen and stopped dead in his tracks.

"Jerome," Birgid sobbed. "The kids are gone. Look at this." She showed him the hole in the sliding door.

Jerome was speechless as he looked at the opening. It was now obvious that something strange had happened.

"Check the house one more time," he commanded her.

They searched the residence as they called out the names of their children. Then they checked outside. Birgid phoned the Kalkmeiers to see if they had any clue about the whereabouts of Vivian and Dennis. Walter and Valerie were sound asleep when the phone rang. The Kalkmeier kids too, were still in dreamland at this early hour. Sometimes, the Birchner kids would go over to the Kalkmeiers for an early swim in their pool together with the Kalkmeier kids. And occasionally they ate breakfast over there. But this was rarely the case and usually Birgid would've known about it in advance.

When they heard the news, all four helped search for the Birchner kids. Jerome, Birgid, and the Kalkmeier family ran their private beach up and down, frenetically calling out the names of Vivian and Dennis. They also looked over the Gulf, calling, calling. Walter started up his yacht and swept quickly across the shoreline around the area of the development.

While it was only a remote possibility, it was conceivable that Dennis had taken the boat for an early morning cruise. But then Vivian's disappearance couldn't be explained as she would never drive with Dennis out to sea. He was a maniac with the boat, running dangerously over the waves and often jumping almost completely out of the water. But they found the Scarab securely docked at the pier.

Jerome finally called 9-1-1. "Something happened at our house last night. I'm not sure what though," Jerome said shaken and upset.

The 9-1-1 operator went through the routine of taking Jerome's name, address, and other inane details. "Sir, you have to calm down. Now tell me what exactly has happened," the 9-1-1 dispatcher continued.

"I don't know exactly, but it seems that we had a break-in or something. Maybe even a kidnapping. I can't find my kids and there is evidence of a forceful entry," Jerome explained, irritated.

"I'll send a patrol unit to your location, sir. It will be there within a few minutes. Is the address an apartment? What are the cross streets or any other important points that may help to locate your exact address," the operator inquired.

Jerome provided a detailed description to Whitecaps Island. He didn't understand why she needed all this detailed address information. When he stopped by at the local county fair a year ago, the mayor had proudly announced that every emergency vehicle in Collier County was now equipped with a GPS unit. With the GPS they were immediately able to locate any address in the area at a touch of a button. For a brief moment her address inquiry was mind-boggling to him and he wanted to argue the point, but he let it pass. He just wanted them to get here.

The dispatcher also asked for the name, age, gender, height, and weight of Vivian and Dennis. It only took two minutes for the police to arrive at the gate.

"Sir, the patrol car is now at your address. They're telling me that there's a gate. Can you please open the gate," she requested.

Jerome pushed the button to open the gate. "Thank you," he said and hung up. He ran to the front door to signal to the officers.

The police cruiser came to a halt in Jerome's driveway. "Hi, sir, good morning," one officer said. "What seems to be the problem?"

"Good morning," Jerome replied. "Please, come in, officers. Let's go through the house. It looks like a break-in." Jerome went ahead and led the way.

Both police officers followed him. He showed them the hole in the sliding door. Then he directed their attention to the cutout opening in the cage.

"I think there are footprints beyond the cage." Jerome pointed.

"Sir, you're saying that your kids were kidnapped?" one officer inquired.

"I'm not sure, but it looks like it. I mean, I can't find my kids." Jerome waved his right arm wildly through the air in the direction of the openings.

"Did your kids have problems at home?" the officer asked.

Jerome was taken completely by surprise with this question. But he knew that some families were not as fortunate as his. The Birchner home was sheltered and it had a loving atmosphere. "No, officer, that's not the case here. I mean we're somewhat wealthy people and it's conceivable that perhaps an abduction took place . . . at least there's a potential for it. But we've never received any threats that I know of. I agree that it may sound like a wild story, but I have no other explanation for this. It doesn't look like a joke to me." Jerome had a lump in his throat.

"All right then, sir. I have to call in our violent crime unit, if you insist that such a crime may have occurred," the officer said. He wasn't at all convinced that such a crime could happen in peaceful Collier County. But he followed procedures and called

Jerome's suspicions in to the station through his attached radio unit.

The other officer retrieved a register with a legal pad from the police cruiser. "Sir, we need some details," he said.

"Sure, my wife can help you. Can you start with her?" Jerome showed them back to the house.

Birgid went into the kitchen area. The officers began to explain to Birgid the necessity to record a statement and several particulars regarding a variety of important facts. They sat down with Birgid at the kitchen table to relive the events of the morning.

Jerome's mind was racing to find an answer.

JEROME THOUGHT of FBI Agent Oliver Bushwell, who had visited him once before. He went into his office and removed a pack of business cards from the top drawer of his desk. Over a hundred business cards were neatly put together and a rubber band secured the stack. Jerome went through the pile until he found Agent Bushwell's card. He phoned Bushwell in his office in North Miami Beach, which was one of three FBI field offices in Florida. The attempt to reach Bushwell in person failed. Jerome had forgotten that it was barely seven A.M. Instead, the answering machine urged the caller to leave a message.

"Agent Bushwell? Hi, I don't know if you remember me, but I'm Jerome Birchner from Naples. It appears that a crime has been committed at my place. Can you please help me. I think it's a kidnapping. Please call me back at 261-5337 in Naples. Thank you! It's extremely important." Jerome's heart sank as he cut the connection.

It took half an hour before the sheriff with additional officers arrived at the Birchner mansion. In the meantime, one of the officers had taken a statement from Jerome. In the report, Jerome insisted that his kids had been abducted.

Jerome retold the same story he had shared with the police officer in his earlier statement. The sheriff didn't know what to make of Jerome's bizarre tale. After all, at this time the kidnapping was just speculation according to the sheriff's assessment of the crime scene. The breaking and entering was obvious, although nothing was apparently missing from the house, except the children. The evidence was compelling enough to believe the suspicions about the break-in. But an abduction, while a probability, was at this point only the result of a paranoid presumption of an overly protective parent, the sheriff concluded.

Agent Bushwell called the Birchner house just as Jerome finished his report to the sheriff. Jerome explained his speculations and fears to Bushwell. Agent Bushwell listened intently. He promised to be in Naples around noon or at the latest in the early afternoon. In the meantime, he would call the FBI field office in Tampa to see if any agents were in the Naples area to stop by the Birchner estate. All agents at the North Miami Beach field office were currently engaged in another exigent case.

As a final question, the sheriff asked Jerome if he had been contacted by the kidnappers yet. Bushwell had asked the same question over the phone. But Jerome had to deny that. So far, no demands, no messages, no nothing.

Around eleven-thirty two FBI agents arrived at Whitecaps Island. They were in the Fort Myers area when they received the call from their superior in Tampa. The agents came down to Naples to gather fresh evidence before the alleged crime scene was contaminated. The FBI agents conducted routine procedures. They had first stopped at the sheriff's office to see if a copy of the file was already available. So far, no file had been established. The only reference at hand was the tape of the recorded 9-1-1 call from earlier in the morning, but nothing else. The police officers wouldn't write their reports until later in the afternoon.

The gate to the development was now open and patrolled by officers of the local police department. Both FBI agents were polite as they introduced themselves to Jerome. They went through the house as Jerome explained his fears and suspicions. He showed them the footprints outside the cage leading down to the water. The sheriff made a copy of Birgid's and Jerome's statement and gave the copies to the agents. As they slowly gathered evidence, the FBI agents considered Jerome's story a potential probability. His story became more conceivable as the day went on. Neither Dennis nor Vivian had showed up at school. Their pajamas weren't found. Due to the high humidity in the area, the ground was soft. The footprints from the cage to the beach showed an interesting pattern, which made it even more believable that someone had been carrying someone or something heavy. Of course, nothing was conclusive at this point. Experts from the crime lab had to determine whose footprints those were and if indeed the subject had been carrying something heavy. But at least they were working on it, Jerome thought.

Agent Oliver Bushwell appeared at the Birchner mansion at two o'clock in the afternoon. One of the two FBI agents filled him in on the findings and the status of the investigation. Jerome was friendly and actually relieved to have the agents around in this time of need. He didn't know what to do in such a situation. By himself, Jerome was helpless, he thought. At least initially he couldn't do more than what he was doing. It was now the kidnappers turn to reveal their demands.

The morning had been very busy and Jerome hadn't turned on the television to glance at the news yet. He hadn't checked his e-mail log either. Finally, when things calmed down a bit, he switched his computer on. He checked the e-mail log. It listed three dozen new messages. A few notices were only the regular spam which he discarded after briefly checking each message for its content.

Thirty e-mail notices didn't contain a text, but each e-mail showed only a headline. Jerome instantly noticed a pattern. His heart stopped.

You love kids?
Where is the dough?
Life is beautiful
One point seven
Pony up, buddy!
We need it now!
Wanna see your kids again?
Get us the money
Like to play?
Who screwed who?

Jerome printed each headline. He called for Bushwell, "Agent Bushwell, take a look at this." He handed the printout to Bushwell.

Bushwell took his glasses out of his coat pocket. He scanned through the roster as he was also trying to look at the computer screen at the same time. "Birchner, it looks like you were right. Someone has your kids," he asserted.

Birgid heard Bushwell's statement. Sobbing, she fell into the couch in the living room. Birgid covered her face with her hands. She began to rock.

"Looks strange to me," Bushwell said as he handed the printouts over to one of the two FBI agents. Both agents stood next to him and looked at the list.

"What do you mean, chief?" one agent inquired.

"Either these kidnappers are cocky professionals, or stupid beginners. They talk a lot and they don't care if he calls in the cops for help or not," Bushwell said.

"What do they want?" Jerome asked.

"It's obvious: they want money. I just can't figure out how much though. I guess they'll get in touch with you again later.

Did the trace on the e-mail log return any results?" Bushwell asked Jerome.

Immediately after receiving the e-mail notices, Jerome had initiated a trace to locate the original sender or a mailbox of each ominous e-mail.

"No, Agent Bushwell. Nothing. It's all going nowhere. The usual deal like with all the other spam." Jerome continued the search. "Same thing—you just can't find 'em," Jerome responded not really surprised. These e-mail notices came from all over the world and from nowhere. Every lead in search of the original sender resulted in a dead end. They ran through all kinds of servers, portals and networks. The high tech hide and seek game was amazing.

"Mr. Birchner, we may need to take your PC with us," Bushwell told Jerome.

"Is this really necessary?"

Bushwell nodded.

"What if they wanna contact me again?" Jerome asked.

"Do you have another computer that you can hook up to this?" He pointed to the outlet in the wall.

"Yeah, I can use my notebook and plug it in. Let me just save some files from this one, all right?" Jerome said. He sure didn't want Bushwell take his PC and then go through his most sensitive files. Jerome quickly connected his notebook to the cable modem. Then he put virtually everything except the Internet files from the PC into a few Iomega 250 MB Zip disks. It took Jerome about five minutes to complete the procedure and secure the data. He not only saved most of his files, but also deleted anything that appeared to be sensitive material.

Bushwell watched Jerome's actions carefully, but didn't bother to confront him. He wondered why he didn't just simply hand the PC over to him, especially when he recognized the steps to delete various files from the computer. *Did Jerome have something to hide?* the thought crossed his mind frequently. By now he'd looked over Jerome's extensive dossier which included everything Juliet Farnsworth had received before she'd hired Jerome Birchner. From that, Bushwell concluded that Jerome Birchner was certainly not a saint.

AGENT BUSHWELL sat down in the living room and began conducting a routine interview with Jerome and Birgid. Later in the questioning, he said, "I have to ask you a few personal questions. Did you have a fight recently?"

"No." Birgid shook her head.

"Can you think of any enemies that may wanna do this. Somebody that may wanna cause you harm?"

"I don't think so," Jerome quickly replied, his mind racing over countless contacts and deals.

"Someone has your kids, Mr. Birchner. I need to know everything. Did the kids ever talk about running away?"

Birgid looked at Jerome indicating that he should answer the question.

"No," Jerome insisted. "They are happy kids. They have everything. What else can I tell you."

"Did you owe somebody money?"

"No, not that I know of. I'm pretty sure that I don't owe even a penny to a single soul."

"If there is something you haven't told me, Mr. Birchner, then now is the time to tell me. Is there a business deal that has gone wrong somehow? Or is there something we don't know of? Think hard, Mr. Birchner, I need to know," he insisted.

Jerome was desperate. "Agent Bushwell, I really can't think of anything right now. I just want my kids back. No matter the cost, we want them back." Jerome held Birgid tightly and buried his face in her hair.

Neither Jerome nor Birgid had heard or seen anything during the night hours. They woke up and the kids were gone. They had found the hole in the door and in the cage. And that was it. The evidence confirmed their suspicions that the intruders had accessed the property through the water. All security systems around the gate and the walls of Whitecaps Island were fully functional and without interruption in service last night. Only the alarm system of the Birchner mansion hadn't been activated.

CHAPTER

56

DURING THE day, FBI agents had also questioned Walter and Valerie. Once they came home from school, the Kalkmeier kids were to be interviewed by the FBI too. Walter told the FBI that he too, rarely ever activated his alarm system. It wasn't necessary until now, he continued to explain to them the various reasons why he wouldn't turn on his security system in the house. Walter led them to the gate and demonstrated the extensive security measures with the infrared web installed around the whole property. The FBI agents, together with Agent Bushwell, were impressed and concluded that Whitecaps Island was substantially fortified, almost in a manner that could've competed with any *State Pen*.

IT TOOK less than thirty minutes from the time the FBI agent called the kidnapping into the headquarters in Washington, D.C., until the press showed up at the front gate of the development. The abduction of an individual was a felony and a federal offense. CNN and units from the local television stations had arrived early in the afternoon. Later in the afternoon, reporters from all kinds of newspapers, magazines and the tabloids arrived at the scene. All were kept at bay. Jerome didn't wanna deal with the press at this time, except for a few words to the kidnappers.

"We want our kids back. We'll pay whatever ransom you demand. We'll purpose to fulfill your demands immediately. But please don't harm our kids. Please, I beg you, get them back to us unharmed and healthy," Jerome pleaded. He looked tearfully into the cameras.

After Jerome's cri de coeur, Bushwell said a few short sentences about the investigation and the fact that the ransom demands were not clear as of yet. He also explained why Jerome involved the FBI immediately since the abductors had not communicated any wishes in this regard. Bushwell assured the kidnappers that Mr. Jerome Birchner would pay any price to get his kids back healthy, unharmed and as soon as possible.

CNN interrupted their regular broadcast as a *Breaking News* story for the live feed from Naples. The network received photographs of Vivian and Dennis from the FBI. Birgid had given those pictures of the two teenagers to the sheriff's office and to the FBI earlier in the day. The network also showed a picture of Jerome taken from the back cover of one of his books. Commentaries and pictures about the Lindbergh kidnapping were inserted and comparisons made. It was a media frenzy.

Later in the afternoon, CNN produced a special report on abductions and mysterious disappearances of individuals in the U.S. The feature also documented the Patricia Hearst incident of her kidnapping on February 4, 1974 and her arrest in San Francisco on September 18, 1975. So-called experts provided their far fetched comments, opinions and often wild theories about the Birchner abduction.

Birgid had stayed in the house throughout the day. Valerie was by her side to comfort her. Jerome called in special guards from a local security firm to provide extra protection for the property. It was their job to keep the media outside the front gate and to secure the area around Whitecaps Island.

Jerome checked the e-mail log every fifteen minutes. Several publishers contacted him directly with offers on the publishing rights for the story. Also a major agency from L.A. attempted to get in touch with him via e-mail. It all made Jerome kind of sick. The Birchner mansion was bombarded with phone calls since the story first aired in the afternoon. Valerie had volunteered to answer the phone until seven P.M. Then a temp agency had sent a secretary to handle the continuously incoming phone calls. People from all over the country called in to express their sympathy. Media folks called to arrange for exclusive interviews. Wackos called, gloating over the Birchner tragedy and cursing the rich family.

FINALLY, AT ten o'clock, the telephone rang with a seemingly important caller. The caller requested to speak only to Jerome Birchner. Jerome picked up the phone and the conversation was automatically taped.

"I only tell you this once. Do you have a pen and a piece of paper?" the devious voice said.

"Are you holding my kids?" Jerome inquired.

"They're all right—for now. But we need the money right away," the male voice demanded.

"What money?"

"The one point seven billion, you idiot."

"I don't have a billion seven." Jerome could not connect this caller with anything in his past.

"Stop playing games with me. You pay the money or we'll kill your kids. Do you understand?" the caller screamed through the receiver.

"But, where should I—" Jerome was desperate to answer the question when the vicious party disconnected the line.

The FBI was unable to trace the call. The trail was probably lost with some satellite over the atmosphere. At least they had the conversation on tape. It would take days to compare stored voice pattern files from known criminals. If these comparisons were negative, chances of finding a match were slim.

A final resource were tens of millions of recorded phone conversations by a special CIA outlet in New Mexico. They had stored information from the past three to four years in an attempt to find matching voice patterns of drug dealers and other international criminals. The CIA had an elaborate filing system for these intonations.

Millions of civilians were also recorded in their database. A couple of years ago, they began attaching mug shots to these recorded inflections. It was much easier to identify wanted individuals in a more expeditious manner. The massive database also helped to locate such individuals with great speed, in case the CIA or FBI needed to. This computer filing system stored all kinds of information from regular folks who had never committed a crime, to the worst serial killers who were as guilty as they could be. From birth records to driver's licenses, passports, credit card applications, even some job applications, dental records, tax information, payment records especially regarding credit card transactions, and about everything else that created a common paper trail was easily accessible and logged in the database. All privacy had disappeared. Big brother was watching and knew virtually everything.

Jerome was still in shock regarding the amount. He had no clue how the kidnappers came up with this sum of one point seven billion dollars. Without hesitation, the FBI affirmed that this unusually high ransom was obviously an odd number. This sum may have not been directly associated with the abduction of the Birchner kids, the FBI assumed. It wasn't just an odd number, but the highest amount ever demanded in U.S. kidnapping history. Something didn't click here. There was a part missing in this picture. The FBI was certain of this. Bushwell asserted that Jerome held the crucial answers to the missing piece of the puzzle. Jerome Birchner had to talk. No more secrets. It was time for the truth.

IT WAS after midnight when Bushwell and two agents knocked on the door of the Birchner mansion. Birgid had already gone to bed. Jerome was fully awake, watching television. He didn't count on getting any sleep that night anyway.

"We have to talk, Mr. Birchner. You better tell us everything right now, or we gotta take you with us," Bushwell gave Jerome fair warning.

"Then I've gotta call my lawyer," Jerome said as he led the agents into the house.

"Why would you need a lawyer now, Mr. Birchner?" Bushwell inquired.

"Because this is getting out of hand. My kids are gone and in the hands of some maniac, and all you wanna do is arrest me?"

"No, no, Mr. Birchner," Bushwell assured him. "We don't wanna arrest you. But we need answers to some important questions. But it seems as if we're missing something here. To be honest, Mr. Birchner, I don't think you've been thoroughly truthful with me."

"All right. What exactly do you wanna know?" Jerome assumed a defensive posture, crossing the arms around his chest.

"Tell me about your last business deals. When was the last one. Think about it, Mr. Birchner. Were there any problems? Maybe there was something that didn't work out and your client wasn't fully satisfied? Or maybe something else, I don't know. Tell me, Mr. Birchner, you can trust me," Bushwell worked on getting through to Jerome and he insisted on the truth.

"You're right. I wasn't absolutely truthful with you." He

took a deep breath.

Bushwell frowned and looked with the *I told you so* expression at the two agents.

Jerome didn't look at Bushwell, but had his eyes fixed, beholding the dark outside. "I was involved in a deal with Nicanor. But only for a few weeks." He shook his head lightly. "That's why I was in North Korea. Mrs. Farnsworth fired me for no reason a few weeks into the contract. But it's history and it's all right with me. Too many people dead, if you know what I mean. I planned on retiring anyway," Jerome explained, now focused on Bushwell.

"Besides Nicanor, was there another deal before this one that for whatever reason didn't work out okay?" Agent Bushwell phrased the question carefully.

"No, the last deal before Nicanor was quite some time ago and it worked out perfectly. There were no serious problems and in the end everybody was happy, and we've all made lots of money. The biggest deal I've ever participated in was the Nicanor deal, because it was billions and billions of dollars. I was sure sad to see this one slip away. But, whatever, you can't win 'em all. Right?" His attempted lightheartedness fell far short of the mark.

"That's right, at least we all try. Okay, Mr. Birchner, we're getting somewhere. How much money did you make on the Nicanor deal?" Bushwell continued the midnight interview.

"Gee, I can't tell you that. I mean it's not really an issue." Jerome was in no mood to answer this frivolous question. Answering trap questions like that could've opened a whole can of worms. He couldn't tell them that he had made twenty million. They would demand to know where the money was now. Jerome couldn't tell them, because it was in his secret Swiss bank account, and not even Birgid knew anything about it. He didn't wanna lie either and say that he didn't get paid, because the truth may catch up with him rather sooner than later. Jerome didn't know what Juliet's story was. Maybe she would cave in and lose it, and tell them everything. She'd cut a deal with the FBI or the CIA and they would surely give her immunity in no time, and in the process hang him and everybody else involved in the racket.

"Mr. Birchner, it's the life of your kids that's at stake here. We've gotta know and we will find out somehow anyway. Somebody is gonna talk. Try to be straight with me right now, Mr. Birchner, and we can help you to free your kids. Chances are much better now to recover them. Every minute counts—there's no time to waste. You're in a tremendous heap of trouble right now, Mr. Birchner, if I can say this. If you don't get our help right now, it looks a little grim to say the least to recover your kids." Bushwell spoke quieter now, trying to nail him slowly to the cross.

"It's more like quicksand, if you want my honest opinion. One point seven billion dollars is a whole lotta money. I wouldn't know what a million looks like, but almost two billion bucks I can't even comprehend such an amount. There's something big going on, Mr. Birchner. I don't know what to say, but my gut feeling never disappoints me." He looked directly at Jerome. "You must cooperate, Mr. Birchner. You're playing with fire. The life of your kids is at stake. Don't think that these guys are blessed with the gift of patience, if you know what I mean. We must act now," Bushwell was hard at work with the intimidation game.

"Tell you what, Bushwell, I have to talk to a lawyer first. I don't know what's going on. All right? Can you do your job and find my kids? I'm gonna try my best to see what I can do. After I've talked to my lawyer I'll give you a complete statement. Is that fair?"

"You're not in a position to cut a deal here, Mister. Every

minute counts. Every hour we don't get your kids back reduces our chances to find them alive. I wanna help you. I'm not the enemy, you must understand that," Bushwell continued without any intentions to break up the interrogation now.

"I understand. And I don't wanna be unkind. You're doing a great job, but I've never been in a situation like this before. And I don't wanna do anything stupid," Jerome countered.

"Tell the truth, Mr. Birchner. That's all there is to it. Don't play hide and seek with me."

"I must ask you to leave now, Agent Bushwell. As I've just said, I don't wanna be unkind, but I've gotta do a few things. I need to find my kids. And if you can't help me . . . I've gotta do it on my own." Jerome was past the point of politeness. His exhaustion was working on both his body and mind.

"All right. We'll go. If you change your mind let me know. I hope it's soon enough to save your kids. You know where you can get a hold of me." Bushwell stood up. He and his men let themselves out.

JEROME TRIED to reach Juliet Farnsworth. There was no response, neither at her Dallas ranch, nor through her satellite phone. Jerome remembered that CIA Special Agent Trevor Gates had questioned him in North Korea. He searched the stack of business cards for the card that Gates gave him. When he found it, he immediately called the CIA. At this hour chances were slim to none to reach anyone at the CIA headquarters. But he gave it a try anyway, maybe he would reach an answering machine. The receptionist told Jerome to call back at eight A.M. Eastern.

He checked his e-mail log one more time. Besides the junk mail, he found one e-mail which only had a number in the title. At first it appeared to be just another spam, but when he read the message things became more obvious. The eight-digit number indicated what appeared to be an account number. In the text, the number from the headline was repeated. Underneath the words *Bank Routing Number* were printed with the number attached. Under the bank routing number it read:

US$1.7 billion

Normally, wire information had to include the name of the bank and at least a city with zip code and country. Sure with the bank routing number and through the common search functions it was rather easy to determine the location of the bank. It was Barclays in London. So far so good, Jerome thought.

He tried to call Juliet Farnsworth one more time at her Dallas estate and once at her satellite phone. But there was no answer at either number. As a last attempt to contact her, he sent her an e-mail. It read:

Hi, Jewels. Maybe you've already heard in the news that my kids have been kidnapped. The kidnappers want $1.7 billion. You think it's possible that perhaps Nicanor could help me out with a short-term loan? Sorry, if this sounds funny, but I'm desperate. Please let me know if you can think of something. Thanks!

Jerome was exhausted. He went upstairs to try to get some sleep. It was impossible. As his mind raced, he thought about every feasible way to find and free his children.

IT WAS five o'clock in the morning when a woman was on the phone, demanding to speak with Jerome. The temp secretary knocked gently on Jerome's bedroom door. He was awake and picked up the phone.

"Hi, Jerome." The southern drawl identified Juliet Farnsworth.

Jerome was surprised. "Hi, Jewels. How are you?" he inquired.

"I'm all right. But how about you? Who are these people that have your kids?" She was curious.

"I don't know. Dennis and Vivian were abducted about twenty-four hours ago. We've been working with the FBI on the case. But, so far, they have no leads."

"It's a lot of money they want, Jerome."

"Sure is, you're telling me. Even if I tried everything I wouldn't know where to get that much cash. And I don't know who these people are. I just want my kids back unharmed, that's all. And I know it's a lot right now. I don't know where I can turn, Jewels, that's why I contacted you. Nobody has that much money in the bank. I mean I could do something crazy and maybe ask one of our great billionaires, Bill Gates, Warren Buffett, or maybe even Ted Turner, but that would be a last desperate long shot if nothing else works. So I thought maybe Nicanor has some spare change that I can borrow. I don't know where else to turn, Jewels," Jerome said with obvious despair in his voice.

"Jerome, Nicanor doesn't have that much money either. And even if we did, I don't know if it would be a smart idea to give the money away to some crazy terrorist. What does the FBI say about this? Maybe the abductors will take less?" she suggested. She knew who was behind the kidnapping. It was George and company, and they were desperate too. But she couldn't tell him that she'd been responsible for the mess. Juliet couldn't worry about the lives of others. She had enough things to take care of in her own life.

"Well, how much do you think you could loan me to pay these suckers off?" he asked.

"Tell 'em a hundred million—that's all. A hundred million is a lot of money. They'll take it. They would be stupid not to, otherwise they'll never see that much money again."

"Really, I appreciate it. Maybe I can negotiate a deal with them. They've already indicated an account number for the wire transfer. I'll e-mail it to you. But wait until we're sure that the kids are all right."

"Okay, e-mail me the account number. Whenever things seem to work out, send me another e-mail to give me the go-ahead for the wire."

"Thanks, Jewels. I really appreciate it. Can I always get a hold of you?"

"Yeah, via e-mail or the sat phone. I'll be waiting. Good luck, Jerome." It seemed that every step in the plan made her heart harder.

"Thank you so much," he said. Jerome didn't worry about her agreeing so easily to the hundred million bucks. He thought that's what friends were for in such a crisis situation, although he appreciated her gesture deeply.

JEROME ENCOUNTERED one major problem, namely that he was unable to get in touch with the kidnappers by any other means than through a television statement. Initially, CNN didn't take his phone call seriously. They thought he was some weirdo seeking notoriety. It took the folks at CNN almost ten minutes to verify Jerome's identity and to confirm that he was the genuine deal.

They showed a picture of Jerome Birchner on the screen and played the message Jerome had recorded for the kidnappers. "We're able to pay a hundred million dollars immediately. This is a lot of money. It's more than what I'm worth. And it's a miracle that this money has been made available. Whoever you are, please get in touch with me. I know we can work this out somehow. Based on the information you've sent to me, I can place the full amount into that location immediately. Please contact me." The picture with the message was played every fifteen minutes twice in a row.

"You've got some nerve," the familiar devious voice said on the phone. "It's the life of your kids, and you're trying to negotiate a deal?"

"It's all the money I can get. There's no more. Even the

hundred million is a miracle," Jerome explained.

"Tell you what. To show you my good will I'll let your girl go for a hundred mill. You show me your sincerity and I show you that I'm not such a bad guy after all. All I want is my money, doesn't anybody understand that?"

Jerome didn't think much about it, but had no choice than to accept the deal. "Where can I pick her up?"

"You'll get her. Just get me the money, all right?"

"I need some assurance that she's unharmed and that you'll really release her."

"Buddy, you get me the hundred million and the girl is back. You've got my word on that. She's not hurt—we've treated her like royalty. And your boy, too. All I want is my money," the devious male voice repeated in its British accent, but the intonation was certainly distorted.

"I'll wire you fifty million right now and another fifty million when I see her."

"Birchner, you're really driving a hard bargain." The caller's voice got hard. "Don't you understand? You neither have the time nor are you in a position to cut a deal here. Just fulfill our demands and let's get it over with."

"Please, I beg you. I'll put fifty million right now into your account, and as soon as I have my daughter the other fifty million will be there. Guaranteed. Please."

"All right. I want the first fifty mill credited to my account, but no later than thirty minutes from now. If the banker doesn't call me by then, the deal is off. Get the other fifty mill ready too. When you see your kid put the money in the account immediately. If something goes wrong, your boy dies. Do you understand? Did I make myself clear?" The man hung up.

Jerome immediately dialed Juliet's satellite number. "Jewels, I need fifty million in their account right away. I can't explain everything right now. Did you receive the account number?"

"Yes, I did," Juliet Farnsworth responded with a sleepy voice. "Fifty million?"

"Yes, it's fifty million right now, and another fifty million when I get Vivian," Jerome explained.

"Fifty million it shall be. I'll make arrangements for the transfer right away. It'll take an hour or so. Is that okay?"

"Jewels, he wants the money credited to his account within half an hour. Is it possible that you can work that out somehow?" His desperation was evident.

"Let me check with my bank. I'm going to call them right away."

Juliet Farnsworth arranged for the wire immediately. It was a different account than where her first hundred million were sent. But it was the same bank and she had an account there too. The wire was credited to the ominous account of the abductors within less than ten minutes.

58

JEROME PHONED the CIA after speaking with Juliet about the fifty-million-dollar wire. "I'd like to talk to Special Agent Trevor Gates," he said.

"May I ask who is calling?" the secretary responded.

"My name is Jerome Birchner. Agent Gates gave me his card when he was in North Korea. Remember, when the Undersecretary of State, Robert Baxter, I think that was his name, was killed in a helicopter crash?"

"Yes, sir. Agent Gates is no longer with the Agency," the female voice said calmly. "Would you like to talk to someone else, sir?"

"Oh, he is no longer with you? Sure, I can talk to someone else, that'll be fine." Jerome was stunned.

"Just a moment, please," she said. After a couple of minutes she got back to Jerome who waited impatiently, counting the seconds. "Sir, I've got the CIA Director William B. Tish on the line. Let me connect you."

"Hi, sir. What can I do for you?" Director Tish asked.

"Mr. Tish, I'm Jerome Birchner. I don't know if you've heard of me or not. My kids have just been kidnapped down here in Florida."

"Let me think . . . Birchner?" The phone was quiet for about half a minute. Then he said, "Birchner. Sure, I remember. Oh, I saw it on the news last night. I thought the FBI is working the case?" he posed the question.

"Yeah, that's true, sir, but they're not making any progress. At least not so far. I don't know if I can tell you this, but I've negotiated for the release of one of my kids," Jerome shared the good news with the director.

"You have? Well, that's good news. Has the child been returned to you, sir? Does the FBI know about it?" Tish inquired.

"No, not yet. See, it's kind of complicated. We've just paid them some money and now they're supposed to release my daughter. I thought that I should get the CIA involved, because you're all doing highly sophisticated intelligence work. Maybe there's a chance you can help me. Whatever." He continued, "See, Mr. Tish, they only gonna release my daughter for now, but the abductors will still hold my boy captive. And I wanna know who these people are and where they're hiding my kid. I think these people are possibly terrorists. They might be operating on an international level. And that's a matter of national security. Isn't it?"

"Mr. Birchner. That was your name, right? I understand your concern. But the CIA usually doesn't get involved in domestic crimes like that. I mean we could provide some intelligence, but I still have to talk it over with the FBI and then we'll see what we can do. But, I tell you what, you can tell 'em that you paid the money. Tell the FBI agents that you paid the perpetrator money. Where are you located?"

"I'm in Naples, Florida," he replied.

"Tell you what. I'm gonna talk it over with the FBI as soon as I get off the phone with you. And depending on what they have to say, maybe we can cooperate somehow. But I can't guarantee that and I don't know. Let's figure it out first and go from there, okay," Tish offered.

"Sounds good to me, sir. Thank you, sir." Jerome wasn't in

the *sir* business, but in this case he'd made an exception. Things had to move forward fast. He needed to find Dennis as soon as possible.

FIFTEEN MINUTES after Jerome had talked to CIA Director William B. Tish, he called his office again. "This is Jerome Birchner. I just called a few minutes ago, and I'd like to talk to the director, Mr. William Tish." He was put on hold for about ten minutes.

"Tish here."

"Mr. Tish, it's me again, Jerome Birchner from Florida. I don't wanna bother you, sir, but I have an idea that may work."

"Mr. Birchner, I've just talked to the FBI and they're working the case. I can assure you that you're in good hands with them."

"Sir, I need your help and it may sound like a wild suggestion, but I want my kids back. Please hear me out, Mr. Tish. Maybe, if at all possible, could you send a few of your special agents down here? And whenever my daughter is released, maybe they can follow the perpetrators. I'll pay for the whole operation and then some. We need a few top professional people to bring this situation quickly to a peaceful end. I don't really wanna hire paramilitary troops or private individuals. The CIA has surely the most qualified people for such a task at hand." Jerome's mind was working overtime.

"Mr. Birchner, I can see your desperation and I feel for you. But, this is certainly not within the realm of work the CIA does," the director replied.

"Sir, I'm willing to pay millions for the services of the CIA in this matter. Meaning I can cover all expenses and provide a donation to some CIA related causes or whatever. Please remember, Mr. Tish, that these kidnappers have asked for one point seven billion dollars. That's the largest ransom ever demanded. They must have something much bigger in their wings. It's definitely more than just the abduction of my children. Nobody in their right mind makes demands like this, unless those terrorists have a serious and dangerous agenda."

"Mr. Birchner, we'll keep in touch. Let's see what's next. I'll follow the case closely. I really have to go now. People are waiting for me," the director said and hung up before Jerome could say another word. It was a wild idea, Tish thought. What did this Birchner think, even though he understood a father's desperation to get his kids back, did he really think the CIA was for hire? No way he would allow his agents to be demoted to barbaric mercenaries. He dismissed the offer as he rushed to a meeting with the President and the National Security Advisor. This meeting was unrelated to the Birchner or Nicanor case, but other important issues of international concern were on the agenda.

59

AN FBI agent knocked loudly on Jerome's door. He didn't go into the house when Jerome opened the door, but remained standing at the door. "Sir, we've found your daughter. The U.S. Coast Guard has just spotted her. They're gettin' her out of the water right now."

"Thank God. Where did they find her? Where is she? How is she? What is her condition?" Jerome peppered him with questions.

Birgid came running to the door.

"The Coast Guard found her drifting on a raft south of the Keys. I don't know anything about her condition though. But we should get word of it any minute now," the agent said.

"Where will they take her?" Birgid could finally get involved.

"Ma'am, I really don't know for sure. But my guess is that they'll fly her to a hospital in Miami," the agent answered. "She's fine. They say she's fine," he repeated as he heard the comment from another agent in his earpiece.

Jerome and Birgid smiled. "Can we talk to her?" Birgid desperately wanted to verify the news.

"Not right now. They say that they're taking her to the hospital," the agent continued to repeat what he heard through the FBI communication system.

"We need to get to Miami as quickly as possible. You don't have a helicopter available, do you?" Jerome said half jokingly.

"Sir, I'll have to ask the chief."

"Can I talk to Agent Bushwell? Where is he?"

"Sir, he's over there where the crowd is." The agent waved in the direction of the various groups of media folks.

Through his hidden microphone the agent repeated Jerome's request. He received a negative response with the suggestion that probably in Fort Myers a chopper might be available for hire. "Sir, we don't have a helicopter at your disposal. But our agents in Miami will take care of your daughter. They told me that you may wanna check into a private helicopter service. There should be one available in the area."

Jerome went into the kitchen and retrieved the yellow pages from a drawer beneath the phone. He quickly located a flight service out of Fort Myers and dialed the 800 number. "Hello, yes, my name is Jerome Birchner and I need a helicopter immediately down here in Naples. We need to fly to Miami. Could you please send one? It's an emergency."

"Yes, we have a chopper available, but I just need to find a pilot," the female voice said. "Let me check on it. Can you hold?"

Walter Kalkmeier came through the door and had overheard Jerome's inquiry about a helicopter. "Jerome, who are you calling?"

Without a word Jerome showed Walter the ad in the yellow pages.

"I know this place. It's owned by a Swiss guy. I used to rent airplanes up there. Let me talk to them," Walter said.

Jerome handed him the receiver.

"Hello. Hello. Hello. Is anybody there?" Walter asked impatiently. "Yes, hello, this is Walter Kalkmeier. I'm a member of your flight club. Is Joe Steinbichler around?"

"Let me see. Just a moment please," the female voice never realized that the caller had changed.

"Walter, we really gotta go. I think I have to stay here in case the kidnappers are trying to get in touch with me again. Birgid has to be in Miami as quickly as possible," Jerome urged Walter to speed up the process. "Just a second," he bid Jerome to calm down. "Don't worry. I know these people. Hello, Joe, how are you?" Walter spoke into the receiver now, much louder. "We need your chopper. A friend of mine has to be in Miami really fast. It's about the Birchner kidnapping. Have you seen it on television?" Then Walter listened for half a minute while Joe Steinbichler was talking. "Yeah, just come on down to Naples as quickly as you can. They gotta go to Miami to pick up their little girl," Walter concluded the phone conversation.

Then Walter turned to Jerome, "It's all done. They'll be here in about twenty minutes. It's best if Birgid gets to the airport in the meantime. That's where they'll be landing."

"Thanks, Walter."

Jerome addressed Birgid, "Please get your things. You've gotta get to the airport fast. A helicopter is coming to take you to Miami," Jerome hollered through the house.

"Val can take her to the airport," Walter offered.

"Thanks, Walter. That's great," Jerome said as Walter went to fetch Valerie.

Birgid left the house a couple of minutes later. Valerie waited in her Ferrari in the driveway of the Birchner mansion. In typical Valerie Kalkmeier fashion, she put the car in reverse and backed out of the driveway without even a glance into the rearview mirror. Tires spinning and burning white smoke, the Ferrari came to a screeching halt at the front gate.

Birgid asked one of the FBI agents which hospital they had taken Vivian to. An agent had to make several phone calls to find out. The Ferrari moved through the crowd of reporters and as Valerie ignored the speed limit, they hurried to the airport.

Only minutes later a chopper landed and flew the two ladies to Miami. They could not receive clearance to land directly on top of the hospital. The nearest private airport was too far away, therefore the pilot landed the chopper in the grass near the hospital before he received permission to do so. Birgid and Valerie ran over the lawn to the main entrance of the hospital.

60

"JEWELS, IT'S done. They've released Vivian. Please put the other fifty million in the account. I can't thank you enough." Jerome had reached Juliet on her satellite phone.

She was in the middle of fooling around once again with Trevor Gates. "Consider it done, Jerome," she said, breathing heavily only seconds away from her orgasm. Immediately after climaxing, she crawled out of the bed. Still naked she walked over to her desk and ordered the second fifty-million-dollar transfer. Gates remained laying on his back, satisfied.

ABOUT FIFTEEN minutes later, Jerome called Juliet again. "Can I talk?" he inquired.

"Sure, shoot."

"Do you know anyone that is for hire for special services? You know people that are like paramilitary troops or a private little army or something? Or maybe some professional merce-naries, soldiers, you know what I mean?"

"I'm at a complete loss concerning things like that. I've never done this before. Jerome, I can't help. I wouldn't know where to start searching," she said.

"What does he want?" Gates inquired.

"He wants some mercenaries or something."

"Let me talk to him," Gates requested. "Hi, Jerome, this is

Trevor Gates. We met in North Korea. Remember?"

"Sure do. I was looking for you." Jerome was surprised to hear Gates's voice.

"Really. Where were you looking?"

"At the CIA. They told me that you had quit and no longer worked for them."

"Yeah. Too dangerous. I'd like to remain in one piece for awhile, you know," Gates commented.

"Trevor, when you were at the CIA, did you ever meet some mercenaries? You know, people for special projects. I'm sure the CIA must have hired folks like that for special missions. That's what they always show in the movies. I need to get my kid out of there. Maybe Vivian can give us some details. And from there maybe we'd be able to locate the hideout of these kidnappers. I just need some rough guys that can handle stuff like that in a professional manner. I'll pay good money."

"Well, we've used lots of people like that for special missions. It's all classified though." Gates thought for a few seconds, then continued, "You know there are a couple of special units at the CIA. All former Navy SEALs and guys like that. Don't tell 'em I told you about them, but ask for Osteen, Chuck Osteen. He might be able to help you. He was there in North Korea when the helicopter crashed—you saw him. I'm sure he knows quite a few capable men, and if he can't get involved himself, I'm sure he can give you a contact or whatever. Jerome, I'm not a soldier anymore. Sorry about your kids though. I hope things work out all right." The conversation ended with Jerome asking Gates one more time about the exact name of the contact at the CIA.

JEROME CALLED the CIA headquarters in Langley, Virginia once again. First, he requested to speak to Chuck Osteen, but received a negative response. The secretary was unable to locate

Osteen in any of the official CIA directories. Then Jerome asked to talk to CIA Director Tish one more time.

William B. Tish picked up the phone ten minutes later. He was on his cellular phone and the meeting in the White House was just ending. The secretary had explained to him that the call was of great urgency as she told him who the caller was. "Yeah," he said, gruffly.

"Mr. Tish, it's Jerome Birchner again. I'm sorry to bother you again. They've found my daughter. She's all right. But I just got a tip and I'm looking for a gentleman by the name of Chuck Osteen who works for the CIA. He might be able to help me. The secretary was unable to find him in the directory. Can you tell me where I can find this man, sir?"

"Um, Birchner. I'm in the middle of a meeting with the President," he answered.

"Sorry, sir, I didn't know. But you know my situation. Every minute counts," Jerome apologized, but wasn't really sorry for interrupting him.

The director sat next to the National Security Advisor. He got up and walked away from the sofa where they were seated. "Excuse me gentlemen, Mr. President, just for a second," he excused himself from the company of the President and the meeting. "I'm not supposed to tell you anything about Osteen. It's all classified. Who told you about Osteen?" the director asked.

"Sir, a former agent of yours by the name of Trevor Gates told me about Osteen. I'm not supposed to tell you this, I've promised him."

"Gates! Where is he? What is he doing?" Tish wanted answers. "Don't worry, it'll be all right. You know what, Mr. Birchner, let me see what I can do. I'll get back to you, okay? What's your phone number?" he asked as he looked for a piece of paper to write on. The director took the napkin next to his coffee cup on the table by the sofa.

Jerome provided the director with his phone number. "When can I expect to hear from you?" Jerome had lost all sense of decorum.

"I'll get back to you. Give me a few hours, all right?" The director couldn't make a commitment. He didn't even know if he was able to get in touch with Osteen right away. First, he had to conclude the meeting with the President, which was almost over anyway. Tish was disturbed by the fact that Jerome had contacted Trevor Gates and that Gates was trumpeting classified information. Despite the fact that it was a unique situation in the Birchner case, Gates was not supposed to do that. Without further ado and without niceties, a goodbye or anything else, the line was abruptly disconnected.

JEROME CHECKED the e-mail log on his notebook and found, aside from dozens of useless messages, only one that was obviously from the perpetrator. It read:

Well done!

in the headline—no text. Jerome frowned—he didn't need a pat on the back by this weirdo.

Hours later, four CIA agents arrived in two cars at the front gate of Whitecaps Island. The private security officers notified Jerome via intercom of the visit.

Simultaneously with the arrival of the CIA agents, a camouflage helicopter landed loudly on one of the larger lawns in the development. From the chopper emerged a man clothed in fatigues—he was about five eight in height. Disturbed by the commotion, Jerome opened the front door to check on it. The four CIA agents parked their vehicles in the driveway of the Birchner mansion. The five-eight military man approached the house from across the street, together with two more men dressed in fatigues.

Then the five-foot-eight man took the lead and advanced toward Jerome. "Are you Mr. Birchner?" he asked.

"Yes, that's me," Jerome confirmed.

"I'm General Osteen," he declared.

For a moment Jerome was speechless, but then immediately invited Osteen, his men and the four CIA agents into the house. Except for two CIA agents, all other men sat down on the two sofas and the love seat in the living room. Jerome explained the things that had occurred since the abduction. He also told them about the money transfers and that Mrs. Juliet Farnsworth had provided him with a hundred-million-dollar loan to free Vivian.

BEFORE OSTEEN'S arrival, Jerome had filled in Agent Bushwell and other FBI agents about the monetary transaction. One FBI agent said that based on his experience, the whole thing of paying off these criminals was a bad idea. Bushwell didn't comment. The FBI now concentrated on investigating the area where they found Vivian in the rubber raft. FBI agents were at the hospital in Miami and had already interviewed Vivian in the presence of her mother.

Vivian was a little shaken, but not harmed. She had been more afraid of the sharks in the infested water around her rubber raft than of the abductors. Vivian told the FBI agents what she remembered from the time of the kidnapping to the time of her rescue. She couldn't recall anything from the night of the abduction. Her account of the incident started when she woke up on a mattress in a house somewhere. Next to her was Dennis, also sleeping on a mattress which had been placed on a wooden floor.

The FBI agents had asked her about some specific particulars of the building and her kidnappers. Vivian described it as a two-story house with tropical surroundings. From her descriptions they concluded that it must've been an island property where she had been held captive. But the details regarding the perpetrators were not of much help as she said they all wore either camouflage fatigues or black overalls. Their faces were covered all the time with a black cloth that served as a mask. There were about six to eight guys, Vivian recalled. On their heads were black cloths which had been bound around their skulls. The men didn't talk much, Vivian reported, and whenever they said something it wasn't in English, or only sometimes there were fragments of broken English. She described their language with a lot of *chs* which may have hinted to Arabic or a similar vernacular, one FBI agent suggested.

How she got into the raft was a more spectacular story. Vivian told the agents that she had been lowered from a helicopter into the yellow rubber raft. She was in her pajamas and blindfolded. Before she was taken from the house in the islands, the blindfolds had been put on. During her stay in the house neither Dennis nor she were restrained or blindfolded. They had the opportunity to look out a window. And a man with an automatic weapon stood in front of the open door to their room. They were told to keep quiet and that the ordeal would soon be over. She was also assured by the kidnappers that neither Dennis nor she would be harmed if everything went well.

She was left alone in the raft. After the chopper left, afar off she heard the sound of an engine from a motorboat. "The boat took off with full throttle," she said, and the engine sounded similar to her dad's boat—the Scarab, Vivian remarked.

OSTEEN LEFT Whitecaps Island in the camouflage helicopter. Over a satellite phone he requested a tape copy of Vivian's testimony as well as a transcript. The chopper took Osteen to Miami to the hospital in which Vivian was kept for medical observations. He too, was out to interview Vivian in order to receive some answers to his specific questions. They landed right on top of the hospital.

As Osteen jumped out of the aircraft, an FBI agent

approached him with a tape player and a folder. They ran down a flight of stairs—their boots making a thundering noise as they hammered down the steel stairs. An elevator took the men to a lower level. The FBI agent and Osteen with his two soldiers entered a small room which served as a temporary FBI command center.

Osteen read the transcript and scanned the tapes. Then he went to Vivian's room. She was ready to be released from the hospital. Osteen sat in a chair across from Vivian. Birgid sat next to Vivian holding her hand. Vivian was now dressed in shorts and a T-shirt.

Osteen spoke with a very calm and gentle voice. He went through the transcript and added information as Vivian answered his questions and retold her tale. It took about half an hour to conclude the inquiry. He was kind, almost empathetic. Osteen needed every bit of information in order to find her captors and to locate Dennis. The gathered intelligence seemed curious. While some aspects of the abduction indicated professionals at work, other details didn't warrant such an assumption. Parts of the kidnapping even appeared to be improvised.

After the interview, he rushed toward the roof of the hospital. Within less than a minute the chopper lifted off with Osteen and his men aboard. They flew south to survey the surrounding area where Vivian was found in the raft. They penetrated Cuban airspace for only a moment.

62

"GEORGE, WHAT are you doing?" Juliet was irritated. She was at her Dallas estate using the satellite phone. "Are you crazy?"

"I told you we need the money. By the way, thanks for the other hundred million. We've checked your info on Birchner. And I must admit you've fooled me again. Not bad, Jewels. You really set him up. He left his mark all over the place in several major money transactions. You even used his name in all the other transfers too. Your story made a lot of sense. Very good, Jewels. The only problem is that my sources have just confirmed that Birchner doesn't have that kind of money. You've set him up, Jewels, and in the process you've set me up too." George was infuriated. "You're not telling me the truth, sweetheart. You're lying. You know I hate liars. What kind of fool do you think I am?" His tone was menacing.

"Well, well. Big George, big mouth. You made two hundred million on that deal. And that's not enough?" George was the last person on earth she wanted to hear from. She thought she'd lost him. Now she felt hunted.

"I told you, I still need another one point six billion. I've gotta pay these people. And it's my neck just as it's your sweet little pumpkinhead. We're together in this, Jewels. Our heads are gonna roll if we don't pay. These people don't play games. Nice try, though, Jewels. I need the money now." George spoke those last words with an air of finality.

"What are you going to do with the other Birchner kid?" Juliet wondered.

"I don't know yet—I'll keep him for leverage. I'm gonna think of something. You should be more concerned about your own neck, Jewels. The time is up."

"I don't know what to say anymore. I have told you, and I don't know how many times, that there's no more money." Juliet sounded just as final.

"Jewels, let me tell you this. I want my money. You've fooled me more than once. My patience is exhausted. With your stupid games you're getting us both killed. You just don't understand that the plutonium and everything else to make the nukes costs a lot of money. And it had to come from somewhere. But remember, we're not dealing with DuPont or Johnson & Johnson. Honey, it's not only the Russian mob, we're talking about ruthless wheeler-dealers that control the world market with this stuff. And if you don't pay, you die—that's the rules. Why is this so hard to understand? You knew it from the beginning." George was losing patience quickly—he wanted to kill her.

"I don't have to tell you anything. You've forgotten that I've given you plenty of MOX fuel. And don't forget that we've built the plant. Your cronies didn't do a thing. All they want is money, money, money," she countered.

"Your stuff wasn't the pure thing, Jewels. The other party provided the enriched plutonium—that's the expensive stuff. You couldn't get your hands on it, remember? Without the pure stuff we never would have had a deal in the first place. I had to take care of it. That's how Nicanor even got the contract, and that's how you were able to make billions. You're so greedy you even had to raise the price by several billion dollars. That was quite a stunt. And now you're telling me that you don't wanna pay the crazy guys? Girl, wake up. This is not some monopoly game we play. This is real." George communicated the urgency to pay off the syndicate.

"All right, George. I hear you. But I can't help you on this. I gotta go, George," she said and hung up.

"What was that all about?" Gates asked.

"It's George. He wants the money. I think we should leave the States for awhile. I guess Bermuda will do until things cool down." Juliet hated for other people to determine her schedule.

"I can handle George. I'll get rid of him in no time," Gates offered.

"Trev, you stay out of this. I need you alive. I need you for myself all alone," she said, as she slipped her arms around him.

"When you wanna leave," he asked.

"How about right now? I think we should get outta here immediately. I don't trust him anymore . . . he may nuke us."

"Well, one more round and we're ready to go." They embraced and couldn't get enough of each other as they fell back into bed.

63

VIVIAN AND Birgid arrived back home in Naples later in the afternoon. Both were exhausted. After a wholesome lunch, Vivian went to bed early and locked her bedroom door.

During the evening hours, Chuck Osteen arrived once again in the camouflage helicopter at the Birchner mansion. The aircraft landed on the broad avenue in Whitecaps Island. Sand blew everywhere. It was a noisy affair. Vivian woke up, screaming. Birgid stormed into Vivian's bedroom. She held the sweaty girl in her arms. Birgid embraced her, protecting her daughter from any harm. She assured her that the disturbing commotion was carelessly caused by a special agent from the CIA who landed his helicopter in front of the house.

Osteen came to the house alone. Jerome bid him in and he showed Osteen to the lanai. Both men exchanged small talk as they ate sandwiches and drank iced tea. Osteen shared combat stories as Jerome listened intently. The purpose of Osteen's visit that evening was primarily to gather some more intelligence. Maybe there was something they had overlooked, or perhaps Jerome hadn't told him everything. Chuck Osteen couldn't offer a solution to free Dennis just yet.

Currently, all efforts centered on locating Dennis. They had extensively gone over the gathered information that stemmed from Vivian's recollections of the ordeal. During the interview earlier that day in the Miami hospital, interesting particulars

had transpired. Most speculations regarding Dennis's whereabouts hinted to a possible hideout somewhere in the Florida
Keys. The only piece that didn't fit the puzzle was the part in
Vivian's description regarding the location of the house. It
seemingly indicated somewhat of an elevated area, maybe a
slight hill or an ascent along a coastline for instance. Such a
landscape was foreign to the Florida Keys, but could've been
possible in some areas along the Cuban coast.

"The CIA has a satellite flying over Cuba during daybreak.
The satellite will be searching for a helicopter and a Scarab-like
boat," Osteen informed Jerome. These two details were basically the only two clues the CIA had to go by. They would focus
in on the supposed area. The satellite would search the Cuban
coastline, hoping to pick up an image of a helicopter, preferably
one hidden in an odd location. If they would find a Scarab-like
boat near by this could turn out to be a hot lead. The FBI hadn't
been filled in on their plans yet and probably wouldn't be,
because apparently it was no longer a domestic matter.

Osteen stayed for a couple of hours and looked over the e-
mail notices from the perpetrator. He also paid attention to the
money transactions and the conversations with Juliet Farnsworth
to which he listened over and over again. Osteen filled his
notepad with all kinds of particulars.

EARLIER THAT evening, Jerome had offered a reward of one
million dollars to anyone who could provide information on the
whereabouts of Dennis Birchner. The announcement was aired
against the recommendation of the FBI. CNN broadcasted the
announcement once every half hour on Headline News.

George disapproved of this measure, too. He'd sent an e-mail
to Jerome and informed him that this was a stupid idea and that
it had to be discontinued immediately. He threatened to kill

Dennis if he didn't see immediate compliance to his request, which was more of a command than anything else. Jerome called CNN and demanded that they would no longer broadcast the announcement. George instructed Jerome, once again via e-mail, to arrange somehow for the wire of the remaining one point six billion. George informed Jerome that he now definitely knew that Jerome hadn't taken the money. He suggested that Jerome cooperate with Juliet Farnsworth because she would most certainly know how to get hold of this kind of cash. From this last e-mail it was confirmed that the kidnapping of his children had everything to do with his involvement in the Nicanor deal. Now Jerome was used and Dennis was leveraged by the syndicate to get to Juliet.

As soon as Agent Bushwell read that last e-mail he became even more sceptical of Jerome. He knew all along that Jerome Birchner hadn't told him the full story, but so far only bits and pieces. Bushwell was convinced that Jerome withheld crucial intelligence about something very important. Nobody could raise a hundred million with a phone call from outside sources just like that, Bushwell argued. Something big was going on in the background and Jerome was part of it. Bushwell was anxious to learn the whole story. But Bushwell would wait a little longer to make his move. Just a little bit more evidence had to be collected and he expected to nail Jerome soon.

64

THE PHONE rang at the Birchner mansion at six thirty in the morning. "I don't wanna get your hopes up too high, Mr. Birchner. But they've found something that looks interesting. At least it's worth checking out." Osteen had some key information.

"Where?" Jerome asked.

"I can't tell you that, sir. I can only say that the satellite has picked up various images that could perhaps match what we were looking for. Right now I'm on my way there to take a closer look. We'll be in touch. I'll keep you posted."

JEROME AND Birgid waited for hours watching the CNN reports attentively. No phone call, no e-mail, no fax, simply nothing. It was a maddeningly quiet day, except for hundreds of requests from the media to broadcast an exclusive interview with Vivian. By the end of the day some networks had offered a million bucks for the exclusive with Vivian. Jerome didn't respond to any of the inquiries. Other, more immediate issues were at hand. Dennis had to be found and he had to be brought back to Naples unharmed.

THREE HELICOPTERS advanced toward the Cuban coastline.

Osteen was in command. They approached the supposed site from an angle so that it would've been very difficult to detect them. The Cuban government wasn't asked for cooperation or permission in the pursuit of this covert operation. The CIA invaded Cuban airspace. All three choppers landed in an opening in the jungle near the beach. It was virtually impossible for the people at the targeted site to hear any noise from the air. Also from their low positional approach, nobody at the suspected hideout would be able to see the helicopters coming.

Eighteen troops closed in on the location. They found only one guard with an automatic weapon outside the two-story building. But it was reason enough to shoot the guy immediately. They weren't a hundred percent sure yet if this indeed was the proper target. But based on gathered intelligence, everything hinted that this was the critical site. The CIA didn't wait long to classify these thugs as international terrorists. This, of course, justified their involvement in the matter. A kidnapping was the FBI's sole business. But in this case there was a connection to Cuba, billions of dollars had been demanded for a ransom, and these abductors acted more like international terrorists as they didn't fit the typical kidnapper profile, the experts at the CIA reasoned.

BACK AT CIA headquarters in Virginia, the puzzle was put together, piece by piece, in a tedious fashion and it slowly began to take form. A multibillion dollar deal, nuclear material, a popular industrialist dead, the Undersecretary of State dead, a CIA agent dead, an outrageous kidnapping, a wealthy widow, a thirty-two-year-old former CIA agent that had just quit the *Force* out of the blue, North Korea, Europe, and the web spun on and on. Many pieces didn't fit together at first glance, but certain common particulars were evident across the board.

* * *

TEN OF the eighteen special agents made their approach swiftly toward the ominous hideout. They stormed the house from all four sides. They found Dennis dressed in his pajamas, upstairs. He was still asleep and rolled up on his mattress without a blanket.

Each of the soldiers had a picture of Dennis Birchner. Before they took off in Miami they had memorized his face thoroughly. They had made two dozen modifications to the picture: Dennis with beard, Dennis with black hair, Dennis with blond hair, Dennis with long hair, Dennis with a shaved head and so on. All kinds of altered images were generated on a PC to make sure the rescue crew wouldn't kill Dennis by accident in the shuffle or in a moment of confusion.

Inside the structure only two guards were present. Both goons were shot instantly. Things went smoothly and Dennis was rescued within minutes. At first, he was confused and didn't know who these camouflaged soldiers were. They had black and green painted faces, black shirts and jungle camouflaged pants. Each one was armed with an assault rifle and they carried huge knives at their sides. Every one of these special agents was also equipped with a Glock in their open holsters around their waists. Upon arrival at the ready helicopters, the soldiers identified themselves to Dennis as members of a Special Forces unit of U.S. law enforcement.

Dennis was relieved to hear the news. His parents hadn't given up on him. They had done everything to rescue him from his captors. Dad had surely mobilized everything possible to save his son. Dennis cried as a barrage of thoughts shot through his brain.

They took him to the same hospital as Vivian the day before. As soon as Dennis was on board one of the three rescue choppers, Osteen called Jerome to report the results of the successful rescue mission. It was early afternoon.

"It's done, Mr. Birchner. We have Dennis with us. He looks all right to me," Osteen said loudly through the phone as he looked at Dennis, smiling.

"Hi, Dad," Dennis screamed into the receiver.

"Dennis, how are you? Are you all right, boy? I'm so glad to have you back." Jerome felt like crying.

"I'm fine," Dennis answered.

"I see you in a little bit, Dennis."

"Mr. Birchner, we're on our way to the same hospital where they cared for Vivian yesterday. Can you meet us there?"

"Thank you so much, General Osteen. Thank you. We'll meet you at the hospital. Thank you!" Jerome beamed and everybody around him rejoiced as they heard the exciting news.

THE HIRED chopper from yesterday was still on standby at the Naples airport. CNN hadn't brought anything new on the kidnapping. Right after the call from Osteen, Jerome and Walter raced in Jerome's Porsche to the airport. They flew to Miami to see Dennis. Birgid stayed home. A private security firm continued to secure the area around the Birchner mansion and for that matter, around the whole development. This time the water access areas were also patrolled by officers of the security firm.

Once again, the private helicopter wasn't allowed to land on top of the hospital, so they used the nearby lawn. When Walter and Jerome arrived at the hospital, Dennis was still in ICU. He was shivering and sedated. The doctors said that it was probably physical exhaustion in addition to a few symptoms of shock from the whole ordeal.

Jerome went into the room where Dennis received medical treatment. He held his son. "I'm here, my boy. I love you. It's okay now. It's all over now. We'll take you home," he didn't want to let go as he gave him a kiss on his forehead.

The shaking stopped within half an hour. Dennis opened his eyes and was glad to see his Dad. They embraced for a long time.

Walter, always in the mood for a joke said, "You've passed the test, buddy. You made it."

Jerome looked at him with a smile and told him to shut up. "I love you, Dennis. I'm glad you're home, boy."

"Where am I?" Dennis asked.

"You're in a hospital in Miami right now. Vivian was here yesterday. She's all right too. We'll get you outta here as soon as the doctor signs the papers," Jerome answered.

"I'm all right," Dennis said. "How is Vivian. Did they hurt her? I'll kill 'em if they did."

"She's okay, Dennis. Don't worry. She's just a little shaken up, but she's unharmed," Jerome assured him.

"Okay, can I get out of here?" Dennis inquired. "I wanna go home."

"Well, you look okay, son. Let me ask the doctor to make sure we can take you right away. Walter can you get me a doctor?"

Walter fetched a doctor from nearby.

The doctor came into the room and was relieved that Dennis was doing better. "He looks okay, but we gotta do some tests before we can release the young man. We need to check him out for internal injuries and for some other potential complications. It's just a routine procedure. It won't take long," the doctor said.

"How long will it take, doctor?" Jerome inquired.

"I guess a few hours. Yeah, I would say give me at least two to three hours, all right? We just wanna make sure everything's okay."

"Sure, doctor, whatever you say." Then Jerome turned to Dennis, "I'll stay right here with you. When we're back home we'll go out for a really good steak, and we'll spend more time together. I'm retired now, you know." Jerome smiled. He couldn't take his eyes off his son.

"You've said that before, Dad," Dennis said weakly, but he was smiling.

"No really," Jerome insisted. "We'll spend lots of time together. You'll see. We'll go golfing. You like golfing?"

"Oh, yes, that sounds like fun," Dennis said.

They had to wait a total of four hours before the doctor was convinced that Dennis was stabilized. He was only hesitantly inclined to finally sign the release. Dennis was okay, except for some slight physical exhaustion.

In the rush, Jerome had forgotten to bring a fresh set of clothes for Dennis to the hospital. So during the four-hour testing period, Walter ran over to a nearby Wal-Mart and purchased a pair of sweatpants, a sweatshirt, a pair of sneakers and underwear. Dennis wasn't overly thrilled about Walter's taste, but it certainly didn't matter at this moment and the new outfit sure beat the pajamas he had worn for nearly three days. Walter, Jerome and Dennis walked across the hospital grounds to the helicopter, and enjoyed the short flight back home to Naples.

Birgid, Vivian and Valerie waited at the airport. Jerome had phoned the house just before lift-off to let the ladies know the approximate time of arrival. Upon arrival, they all gave Dennis a big hug. He was a little embarrassed by it, but was happy to be home again. The nearly two days of captivity for Vivian seemed like an eternity, she said. But the nearly three days for Dennis were like a really long time, he admitted.

Jerome stood back and took a good look at his family. Life was precious. I can't take it for granted, Jerome mused. They all swore to live much richer lives from now on. They made plans for an extensive summer vacation. They vowed to spend more quality time together.

YOU'RE NEXT! the e-mail read on Juliet's e-mail log. But she wasn't there. And neither had she taken her laptop to Bermuda. Before she left Dallas she requested a new call number on her satellite phone. The unit had been reprogrammed. Most of the time she didn't even turn the unit on, but only carried the phone for emergencies. Juliet went so far as to disconnect all phones in the vacation home in Bermuda. She was no longer interested to think about reality or to be confronted with the facts in her own life. It was all left behind in a different world, a different life.

Here in Bermuda, Gates and Juliet would simply relax and spend time together. They would enjoy the beach, good food, the romance and sex. It may have been wishful thinking and for a while it would probably work out okay. This was what she imagined and longed for. The billion bucks would make her invulnerable, she thought.

AFTER A couple of weeks, Juliet would find herself crying for hours every day. She laid on her bed rolled in a fetal position, sobbing. At first, Gates comforted her during these times of need. But soon he was asked to leave and stay away from her during these bouts of severe depression. Tremendous guilt came over her and plagued her day and night. She had helped to kill her husband and in the process she was responsible for the death of several other innocent people. These impressions became a psychological torture. These thoughts rushed through her conscious mind now more frequently and became mental escapades which turned into agonizing nightmares. Juliet could not escape her thoughts.

She'd arranged for incredible pain and heartache for the Birchner family. These things were weighing on her conscience. The inner tumult and conflict was a painful experience. Juliet contemplated suicide as the torment by her inner demons intensified.

After all, Juliet Farnsworth wasn't the heartless, tough, cool business woman she initially had portrayed. It was only a facade, a role she had absorbed for a season to pull off the billion-dollar heist. It was greed that drove her to do the unthinkable and go over the edge.

She couldn't really explain why she reacted in such a way, but there was a war inside of her. Her conscience wasn't seared yet, as she'd hoped for and mentally trained for. This unbearable pressure threatened to rip her apart into millions of tiny pieces—her blood vessels rupturing, and the blood gushing out of her veins. Her heart was pounding heavily, pumping that blood forcefully through her body, over and over again. Yes, she had all the money in the world, it seemed. And she had a young lover, but even now he couldn't distract her from the ever-present throbbing guilt.

Was it all really worth it? Seeds of suicide crossed her mind—it was an alternative, an option to end it all, she thought. In her hallucinating nightmares, she saw herself leaving her physical body and watching horrible things happen to her: demons from hell lunching on her intestines; black shadows slashing her body; a train crushing her as she stood on the rails trying to stop it; jumping out of a high rise in a attempt to fly, but instead crashing like a stone to the ground, and her body smashed like a potato. Had she become a monster? These intense dreams were way beyond a nightmare.

Juliet was often delirious and believed that there were all kinds of creatures attacking her. She would scream and act insane by throwing lamps and things against the mirrored walls in her bedroom. She had trashed her room more than once. In the process, she'd hurt herself with cuts and scratches all over her face, her hands, legs and thighs.

She finally began to drink heavily. First it was champagne and she smashed the flutes against the wall. Then she resorted to whiskey and bourbon right out of the bottle. Initially, neither Gates nor Juliet were into drugs and they kept away from such stuff. Gates joined her in the drinking rituals, though.

As he watched the rapid and vast deterioration of Juliet's mental health, he obtained some morphine and heroin. A doctor at King Edward VII Memorial Hospital sold the drugs to him. The hospital was only a short distance away from their hideaway mansion along the Bermuda coastline. Eventually, the drugs, of course, made everything worse and caused further decay in her mental stability.

The illegal substances affected Gates too, as he experimented with the heroin himself. He purposed to try it just a little bit to show Juliet that it was a harmless affair, and that these drugs would help her make it through the day without pain. In the beginning it brought relief, but within a short period of time, Juliet was dependent on these drugs and steadily required more of it.

She lost quite a bit of weight as she rarely ate any solid foods. And whenever she consumed a bite here and there her body reacted violently. As the first signs of the reaction began to show, Gates had to drag her into the bathroom. During the convulsions the vomit sprayed all over the place. Whenever they ran out of drugs, she would be totally out of control and physically attack Gates.

Soon, the beach was deserted and they remained only in the house. Juliet very rarely took a shower and otherwise didn't take care of herself in any way. A foul odor had penetrated the mansion. Her hands shook so severely that she was unable to put on any makeup. Except for Gates, she didn't want to see a soul and even him only when she needed his help for a few minutes here and there.

They didn't have too many friends on the island to start out with, and when the few found out about Juliet's irrational behavior they quickly distanced themselves. The maid was not welcomed in her room. Gates finally told the maid to come to the house only once a week. Within weeks Juliet had aged by a decade.

Gates had stopped shaving and looked like a bum. His hair was long and he was rarely found without a bottle of booze in his hand. The atmosphere around the house was tense as never-ending shouting matches took away every flicker and source of potential peace and harmony from the paradisiacal surroundings of the tropical island.

Sex had been nixed completely. Only Gates occasionally felt the urge to be animalistic, but because of his drunkenness and the drugs in his bloodstream didn't get very far. Juliet had no interest in sexual encounters whatsoever. She preferred to lay her head on his chest while smoking a joint and shooting heroin as he gently stroked his fingers through her oily hair.

A FEW days after Dennis was rescued, Jerome Birchner had been asked to come to Washington. A CIA Learjet was sent to Naples and flew him to D.C. They had sent the CIA Director's black Lincoln Town Car to the airport to transport Jerome to the CIA headquarters.

At the CIA headquarters he personally met with CIA Director William B. Tish. Chuck Osteen was also present at the meeting. Jerome thanked both men again for their heroic act and help in the rescue operation of his children. He offered again a substantial payment for their services. The CIA Director rejected the gesture without hesitation, but suggested to Jerome to perhaps place donations to a variety of CIA endorsed scholarships and causes. His secretary would get back to him with a list of such available venues, the director assured him.

After the niceties the director addressed Jerome with a more serious demeanor. "Mr. Birchner. We've read through your extensive file. It's impressive, I must admit. I'm sure you know about the existence of such a dossier. I must also assume that a man of your caliber and with your resources most certainly knows everything that's in that file. All the reports from the INS, the IRS, FINCEN, the FBI . . . it's all in there." The director tossed the thick folder casually onto the desk to his right. It made quite a bang when the file hit the table.

Jerome could only imagine bits and pieces of various facts

about him in the folder, but he had never read the thing and neither had he ever obtained a copy of that stuff. And honestly, he didn't care what was in the dossier. Sure, some particulars might have been of interest, he thought, and it may be great material for a novel, but basically he wasn't even remotely interested in all the intelligence collected about him in this folder. Jerome had no desire to be disturbed by stuff that was written about him, maybe it was misinterpreted, or even false, or for that matter, maybe even true. He didn't care and he wouldn't give anything for the opportunity to check it out. Instead he was reluctant to even look at the dossier from several feet away.

"Let's have a seat, gentlemen," the director said.

All three men walked to an area with two sofas, a chair and a low coffee table. Tish sat in one sofa while Jerome took the seat across from him. Osteen was seated in the massive chair on one end of the coffee table.

"Look, Mr. Birchner. You may not know this, but just like North Korea, even France and Germany are considered what we call *Hard-target countries*. Now, you don't have to panic. We don't wanna recruit you as one of our agents. We know you're very wealthy and you're at the brink of retirement, at least you wish to do so pretty soon. But anyway, we still have a little problem and we need to solve this case. I'm sure it's in your interest too that this thing is put behind us.

"But there is one missing link to reach our goal and to bring a conclusion to this matter. Mr. Birchner, I must tell you that you won't be safe for the rest of your life unless we can bring the people that are responsible for the kidnapping of your kids to justice. Believe me, once we catch these suspects, they won't get out of the slammer ever again. I'll make sure of that. If it was up to me, they would get the death penalty, guaranteed," CIA Director Tish emphasized.

"Tell me, what do you have in mind, exactly? How do I fit into the picture?" Jerome inquired.

Osteen turned to Jerome and opened his mouth. "We want you to make a collection for us. That's what we call the process of gathering raw intelligence information. You're a research guy, Mr. Birchner. You're a pro at this. It's not going to be hard for you to get what we want. We just need to find out a few more things to make sure we're on the right track. You speak German—that's important in this case. We suspect that our perpetrator acts from Vienna, Austria. Remember, we're not sure yet who it is, but we're very close," Osteen explained now in detail.

"But what can I do? I'm not a spy nor an agent. And I don't wanna become one either. Why do you think that the suspect is located in Vienna?"

"Well, we have suspicions about a certain agency that is headquartered there, the IAEA to be precise. It is located in the UNO-City complex in Vienna. When we went to North Korea during the investigation of the Undersecretary's helicopter crash, we took the opportunity to check out the Nicanor plant. It was pretty obvious that the IAEA was running the show over there," Osteen elaborated.

"So why don't you ask Juliet Farnsworth? I'm sure she knew what was going on over there," Jerome commented.

Osteen glanced at the director. "We sure would like to. The CIA would love to talk to her." Osteen now faced Jerome again. "But we have a slight problem with our Juliet Farnsworth. We don't know where she is. I think she knows quite a bit. But so far, she has vanished from the face of the earth without a trace. We were able to eavesdrop on a few of her last conversations, which she conducted through her satellite phone from her Dallas ranch. That was before she changed her number and since then apparently her phone hasn't been turned on. And in addition to all this, of course, the conversation was scrambled for the most part. We were able to pick up only bits and pieces."

"Meaning, you wanna tell me, the CIA doesn't know how to find Juliet Farnsworth? C'mon, that's impossible. You have plenty of intelligence and you can't find her?" Jerome interrupted.

"I can see you're gettin' the picture, Mr. Birchner. Well, anyway. Our research lab in New Mexico found a perfect voice match. She was talking to the same guy who communicated to you about the abduction of your kids. The suspect was called *George* which obviously isn't his real name. It's only some sort of a decoy. We ran extensive checks on everybody with the name George in the IAEA and at USEC, and nobody qualifies even remotely as a subject. We want you to find out who it is. We think that George is in Vienna and I'm positive that he'll contact you when you're in Vienna. He'll be eager to talk to you, believe me," Chuck Osteen said.

"In short, I'm the bait," Jerome replied, trying to follow things the best he could.

"No, not at all. See, you're an Austrian citizen. You can enter Austria without a visa or anything. We have a few agents there, but Austria too, in a sense, is a *Hard-target country.* We've got people in Hungary, Italy, Poland, you name it, and they'll assist you. Unfortunately we don't have a resident agent in Austria at the current time. The whole thing is only for a few days, Mr. Birchner. You'll be back in no time. We have a first-class ticket on TWA for you from JKF for Sunday night. You'll stay at the same hotel like on your last visit."

"Oh, that's cool." Jerome wasn't stupid and got the picture immediately. "So everybody knows me there already. I'm a real easy target," Jerome said.

Osteen tried again to help Jerome understand his part. "Several months ago when you were in Vienna, you may have been under surveillance. We have strong evidence of that. To make things easy for George we get you into a tour at the IAEA. That's scheduled for Monday noon. Don't worry, you won't be alone. We'll be watching. We expect George to contact you once you're inside the IAEA during the tour. He will probably try to arrange a meeting," Osteen explained.

"Why would this *George* be interested in talking to me?" Jerome asked.

"It's a feasible consideration that you might be the only bona fide link for them to find Juliet Farnsworth. I'm sure they wanna get hold of her just as badly as we do. That's also why they won't kill you. It's a low-key covert operation, Mr. Birchner. We're ready to go. If the suspect doesn't contact you on Monday, you'll go on the tour again on Tuesday. And if he doesn't contact you by Tuesday, we have a backup plan. I'm positive he's going to go for that. But we hope that we don't have to implement the backup plan. Anyway, I'm absolutely certain that he's gonna show himself one way or the other." Chuck Osteen lit up on the inside. To him this was serious business. It was the cat-and-mouse game he loved so much. It was war. He was thrilled.

"If I do this, what do I get out of it?" Jerome asked.

"You'll get your life back. And no more hassles from the IRS, or anyone else. You can retire without fearing that your assets will be seized, or that you lose your U.S. citizenship, or that anyone will be threatening your life or the lives of your family. Do you get the picture, Mr. Birchner? All you gotta do is go there and wait. And then come back home and enjoy your retirement. We'll take care of the rest," the director answered, dry and right to the point.

It was a shock to Jerome to hear the director's statement, which was more like a threat than anything else. *Do as I say, or else,* that's what it meant, Jerome thought to himself. He paused, looked up to the ceiling, and finally said, "I have to think about it."

"Well, don't think too long, Mr. Birchner. The trail is hot right now—we've gotta make our move now. That's our only chance," Tish continued to stress the point.

67

JEROME HAD no real choice. There was no leverage for him to strike a bargain or to negotiate a deal. The CIA made it pretty clear to him that in the case he wouldn't cooperate it would be better for him to leave the U.S. They probably had found out about the twenty million he'd made in the Nicanor deal, Jerome thought. They also knew that he was perhaps the key figure in funneling hundreds of millions of dollars into a Swiss bank account controlled by Juliet Farnsworth. Money laundering convictions were usually subject to hefty penalties and carried long prison sentences.

The apparently incriminating conversation between Juliet Farnsworth and ominous George, which the CIA was able to tape, was obviously a scary piece of evidence. Maybe they knew everything. During the investigation of the helicopter crash, Kensington was questioned by Osteen in North Korea. Maybe Kensington had told them everything, and maybe he had cut a deal with the CIA and was now the mole inside Nicanor. Jerome was worried about these little details.

In reality, Kensington wasn't going to rat on anyone. He remained tight lipped and played the part of the innocent scientist exactly by the book. He knew nothing about this tragic incident and was only concerned about his work at the plant. But something smelled real bad down there.

For Jerome it was the last time he'd do anything for someone else. He requested that the CIA put everything in writing. Jerome demanded absolute immunity for any wrongdoings that may surface during the investigation of the Nicanor deal or during a potential trial involving certain suspects. But the CIA in turn couldn't guarantee anything in writing, CIA Director Tish explained. The only thing Jerome had to go by was the director's word, witnessed by Chuck Osteen, that he wouldn't be prosecuted.

Jerome considered himself a little fish in a big pond. There were people that probably had stolen billions of dollars. But even worse, there were high ranking U.S. officials that had betrayed the confidence of the U.S. and had committed treason. They had potentially helped a communist nation to obtain significant nuclear resources.

THE SUSPECTED North Korean nuclear site had no peaceful intentions at all. As some evidence surfaced, a little here and there, it manifested itself even stronger that Nicanor had built a state of the art nuclear missiles facility near Yongbyon. Worst of all, the U.S. government had supplied at least ten billion dollars in aid to create this threat to world peace.

Within a few years, the U.S. government would urge for the formation of a Senate Intelligence Committee regarding this matter. The Committee would then be chaired by a Senator and they would conduct some hearings about the matter. But it would take years for this to take place and even then it wouldn't produce any significant results, except a media rumble. There was insufficient evidence to prove anything. In the end, Baxter's helicopter crash would be filed away as a tragic accident.

With the Nicanor plant under control, China was now even mightier than before. Before the construction of the plant, they were in possession of only two dozen ICBMs with nuclear warheads. Now their nuclear arsenal had been increased by ten long-range supernukes, no other government on earth had in its possession yet. Technically, it would take quite some time to manufacture additional supernukes for any other nation in the world. The U.S. controlled six thousand of the standard missiles, but was not in possession of even one supernuke.

These new supernuke missiles were capable to fly from Asia not only to the West Coast of America, but had a reach as far as New Mexico. One of these supernukes was able to devastate everything from the coast of California to Memphis. No longer was the effective radius limited to only five hundred miles, but with these types of warheads the radius had been extended to a gigantic two thousand miles. In short, with the detonation of only one supernuke one third to even half of the United States of America could be wiped out. The country would become a radioactive wasteland within minutes. At the point of detonation, tens of millions of people would be burned alive after the air had been sucked out of their lungs within seconds. Survivors wouldn't live long either—cancer would devour their bones and organs within a few months, or perhaps even within weeks.

Everybody in their right mind would agree that the nukes on Hiroshima and Nagasaki were devastating and horrific. But these traditional nukes back then were nothing in comparison to the new supernukes built by Nicanor Industries. Once launched, even destruction in the air would produce a deadly nuclear shower of ash rain lasting several days. A detonation on the ocean floor of the Pacific would create a tidal wave over a hundred feet high flooding the U.S. West Coast effortlessly, taking out Hawaii along the way, killing millions in San Francisco, L.A. and San Diego. Billions of fish and other maritime life would die instantly. The Pacific would be a polluted sewer for tens of thousands of years to come. The implications were staggering.

* * *

JEROME BIRCHNER had no choice. He had to cooperate with the CIA. Maybe there was a remote chance to somehow get the bad guys. It was too late to stop the construction of this monstrous facility because it had already been built and was now operational. It stood there, ready to destroy the world. But maybe it wasn't too late to stop the madness of application and implementation in the real world.

Because the nuclear facility existed, all kinds of treaties had to be negotiated. It would take years to do so. These treaties had to be signed to take effect, which wasn't an easy task. China already laughed at the United States. They compared their population to the amount of individuals living in the U.S. To China people were power. China had already more than five times the population of the U.S. They were able to instantly mobilize an army of two hundred million troops if necessary.

Security measures needed to be installed to prevent a launch of these supernuke missiles by accident. The site would require consistent monitoring. It would take years and hard work of diplomacy to negotiate such treaties. It was absolutely up to China and North Korea to cooperate voluntarily and they didn't have a history of doing so. Why should they care about the rest of the world, when China had killed tens of millions of their own people over the decades.

Sure, China wanted to be a fully integrated member of the World Trade Organization, but not at all costs. They had their own system and their own philosophy about life. The right for freedom of speech, for instance, had not found a place in their constitution. China had a totalitarian government and wouldn't change their way of life ever. North Korea followed in the footsteps of China and practiced the same. This was pure communism in its unadulterated form.

There was a slim chance that the people responsible for this mess could be brought to justice, Jerome thought. Most certainly it was only the tip of the iceberg, but it didn't matter at this point. Whoever wasn't caught in the raid would come after him in the end anyway. From the desire and comfort of a relaxed eternal retirement at the age of forty, it felt as if scales were removed from Jerome's eyes, as he began to comprehend the whole picture and he realized how fragile his life was. It wasn't just his life, it concerned everybody in his family.

On the other hand there were these menaces who had toys to take billions of lives within hours. Lunatics who endorsed their wicked, evil Marxist philosophies. Maniacs that thought they were God in the flesh, because they didn't believe in The God. Vicious political leaders who robbed the people of their personal freedom. Under their tyranny people were not allowed to verbalize their thoughts—and preferably shouldn't even think them. Their humanity with all its creativity was curtailed and reduced to nothing but dirt. These leaders desired absolute mind control. Everybody had to conform to their rigid and ridiculous standards of communism.

Anyone who rebelled against this system was burned at the stake so to speak. They had killed their own. It was nothing new because it surfaced all throughout history. The Romans did it. It was done in the former Soviet Union, Rumania and in Iran. It was happening today in China and in North Korea. Castro did it in Cuba and Saddam Hussein in Iraq. There were many places throughout the world that had a violent history in murdering their kindred.

Jerome had never planned to deliberately become a part of it. How could he have been so blind?

CHUCK OSTEEN arrived in the obligatory CIA Learjet in Naples at nine o'clock on Sunday morning. Jerome awaited him at the airport. As usual, Osteen was all dressed up in his camouflage fatigue. Judging by outward appearances, the war for General Osteen seemingly never ended. Until noon that Sunday they sat outside on the lanai around the pool at the Birchner mansion. Osteen explained over and over again the exact procedures in Vienna. He commented on emergency situations, if this or that would occur unexpectedly.

"What happens if they pull a gun on me?" Jerome was covering all possible scenarios.

"They probably won't. Rest assured, if they do it's only for intimidation purposes, but they won't pull the trigger," Osteen attempted to calm Jerome's concerns.

"So I just need to get George to agree to a meeting at some place in Vienna?"

"That's the plan. Make sure it's not in the UNO-City building, though. A meeting there wouldn't be as favorable to us because all his cahoots are probably around there somewhere. And we don't wanna be responsible for a bloodbath. If at all possible, try to get him to meet you at the restaurant in the Hilton where you'll be staying. This would be a perfect place. Don't forget we only have one shot at this. If he gets suspicious, it's over. He might shoot you right then and there," Osteen said.

"Jeez, this looks good—really good. You'd better be there when I need you," Jerome couldn't restrain himself from splattering some sarcasm.

"We'll be watching every move you make. The only weak point so far is the IAEA tour. It's going to be tough to get any of our men through the checkpoint without the alarm bells ringing like crazy. But we need the tour, unless George is going to contact you in the hotel before the tour. My guess is he won't because you'll only have an hour in the hotel before you leave for the tour. That's not enough time for him to make his move." Osteen smoked a fat Cuban cigar. Somehow the lanai seemed to be the ideal place to light a cigar, Walter once observed. Osteen blew thick circles of smoke into the air. He followed the circles with his eyes as they dissolved on their way up around the edge of the roof. Osteen remembered chasing after bubbles as a kid, and compared the game now to the circles of smoke.

Jerome had some concerns, but nothing that posed too big of an obstacle. Worst case scenario, he thought, was that he'd be catching the next plane home. Couldn't they all just leave him alone? That's what he wished for. After all, he was a civilian now.

EARLY ON Sunday afternoon the CIA Learjet took off in Naples. It flew Jerome and Osteen to JFK airport. In New York, Jerome boarded a TWA airliner with a direct flight to Vienna. Chuck Osteen was scheduled to board another plane with a different airline, just thirty minutes after Jerome was in the air. Osteen changed into a pair of jeans, a T-shirt, sneakers, and a bomber jacket. Even in this outfit he looked somewhat suspicious. He couldn't shake the tough-guy image.

FOR THIS trip, Jerome had brought only a tote bag. He wore khakis, Timberlands, a polo shirt, and an oversized dark brown leather jacket. Vienna was always cool at this time of the year. Birgid had put a pair of leather gloves in his bag, just in case. She'd also reminded him to take a pair of socks as he usually ran around without such footwear. He'd forgotten about the socks, but she had stuck a pair into the bag together with the gloves.

The TWA airliner touched down in Wien-Schwechat at eight-thirty in the morning. Jerome had slept at least five hours during the flight. He went through customs without a problem. In the terminal he went to a booth with the letters *Maztours* written all over it. At the sales desk he hired a Mercedes with a driver.

"The car with the driver costs five hundred Euros for one day," the receptionist at the Maztours sales desk said. As she strove to speak formal German, her tongue continuously slipped into a heavy Viennese dialect. She was overweight. Her chest was squeezed into an orange T-shirt. The contour of her over-sized breasts was a significant distraction. Not that this sight was stimulating, but rather that the enormous bust must have created a tremendous hindrance to her movements. She leaned over her desk and rested her pendulous chest on top of the counter as she finalized the transaction with Jerome.

Orange was the choice company color of Maztours. Maztours

also operated VW vans as shuttles, which were also painted in orange. Maztours was written in big black letters over these VW vans—on the sides, in the front and back, and even across the roof. The whole Maztours booth was dominated by the colors orange and black. Thick red lipstick emphasized the sensual full lips of the receptionist. It was obvious that her very light blond, almost white hair wasn't her true hair color. Her hair was bleached to the max, that was for sure. She may have been in her late thirties, but based on her appearance, she still longed to be eighteen.

If he hadn't known this company, Jerome wouldn't have done business with Maztours. The appearance of the booth was terrible. But the owner, Freddie Mazzor, had been a former client of his.

FREDDIE HAD made so much money with his business that he didn't know what to do with all the lucre. On top of making a fortune, he considered paying income taxes an unjustified burden and for years he refused to pay taxes. In the process he also withheld a big chunk of the customary VAT which he received with every sale and was supposed to forward to the Austrian government. Mr. Mazzor had bundles of actual cash laying around in his residence. He converted one bedroom into a gigantic safe with stacks of bills stored in cartons and in plastic bags everywhere.

In the late eighties Jerome had set up a few offshore companies for him and his wife. The money vanished into Swiss bank accounts within weeks. Mr. and Mrs. Mazzor each had a big Mercedes. They drove together with the two cars to Zürich. Both automobiles were packed with cash in the trunk and even in the passenger cabin. They had to make two trips to deliver the cash to the banks in Zürich.

When the Austrian tax authorities audited Maztours head-quarters, they were unable to find any wrongdoing. Then the tax agents searched the Mazzor villa in Hietzing, which was Vienna's thirteenth district, and they couldn't find anything incriminating there either. Freddie's conscience was so tormented by guilt that he even offered a bribe to one of the tax officials so that they would leave his lavish estate. But the tax agent refused the baksheesh and was kind enough to let Freddie know that he had nothing to fear. Everything had turned out to be perfectly clean and in proper order.

Even Freddie was flabbergasted. He counted on their expertise and that he'd be found out to some degree. Freddie was convinced that he would have to go to trial and pay at least a hundred grand in fines. He was prepared for it. But nothing like that happened. The tax authorities did a thorough probe which lasted for nearly two weeks and they walked away with nothing. They only provided a few harmless suggestions to the accounting office, but that was it.

Jerome couldn't believe that things had worked out all right at the Maztours audit. Their accounting department was an unbelievable mess to say the least. Back then, most of the business was done in cash, and record keeping was an unknown practice to Freddie Mazzor and his employees.

Proud as Freddie was, he told everybody in town on his excessive trips through the taverns, bars and nightclubs about how he had duped the Austrian tax authorities. Soon a statement for a fine of an equivalent of five hundred thousand dollars arrived at the Maztours headquarters. He contended the fine for years. His legal fees were soon half of what the original fine and the dispute was all about. Freddie made it clear that he would never pay this fine—it was a matter of principle. Through his lawyers he suggested that he'll be willing to settle for a hundred grand—this was the sum he had prepared for and had always in mind.

JEROME PAID the five hundred Euros for the car with chauffeur. The receptionist explained to him the designated exit to where the Maztours cars were parked. "You go through the door and keep right. Always to the right."

She also instructed him to hand a special ticket to another employee at the Maztours desk near the designated exit. Once Jerome got there he handed the ticket to the stocky guy at the specified counter. The man didn't say anything to Jerome as he reached for the ticket. Then the stocky gentleman said something into his walkie-talkie. Another stocky man with a superficial smirk on his face came through the door of the exit. He introduced himself as Jerome's driver.

Suddenly, a tall man hurried by the exit. He was accompanied by another man much shorter than he. The two men were engaged in a discussion as the tall man gestured with his hands, obviously trying to explain something to the other. Jerome couldn't believe it—it was Freddie Mazzor himself. He knew that Freddie had always hung out at the airport some ten years ago, day after day, but he didn't count on Mr. Mazzor still doing the same thing today. Freddie's body was arched forward and his shoulders were raised tensely. It didn't seem that these would relax momentarily.

"Hello, Mr. Mazzor. How're you?" Jerome said, as he approached Freddie Mazzor when he came through the door. He stretched out his hand to greet him.

Freddie turned to Jerome and his facial expression showed surprise. *"Ja, Guten Tag,"* he said and clutched Jerome's hand, almost unconsciously just to be friendly. Then he walked away as he obviously didn't recognize Jerome and couldn't even recall ever having met him.

Inside, Jerome was just excited about seeing Freddie and knowing that he was still around. He simply appreciated his former clients, and in his own way, Freddie had already become a legend. Jerome understood his behavior since Freddie was known as a rather cool type and not at all as cordial. He let it go and turned his attention to following his driver to the car.

IT WAS almost ten o'clock when they arrived at the Hilton across from the Vienna Stock Exchange. It was the same hotel he had stayed in during his last visit to Vienna. Jerome told the driver to wait in front of the hotel and to be prepared to leave in about an hour.

"Do you mind if I go for a cup of coffee in the meantime? I didn't have breakfast this morning," the chauffeur said politely with a hungry look on his face.

"Sure, go ahead. But we must leave in an hour. Please make sure you'll be waiting over there," Jerome answered, pointing to a spot across the hotel entrance.

"If you need me before that, then you can find me in the coffee shop over there," the driver explained as he now pointed to a building across the street next to the hotel. A sign was written over the entrance to the building that read *Kaiserwalzer*.

Jerome checked into the hotel and remembered that the gentleman at the front desk was the same guy as last time when he had checked into the hotel. Not many things change in places like Vienna. It wasn't unusual for people to keep the same job for thirty years and even longer. Rarely ever would anyone change from one employer to another. And if they did so, it was a big deal. A good job was a great employment opportunity—it was as simple as that.

Jerome rushed into his room and enjoyed a quick shower. In his thoughts he was already going back home to Naples and questioned himself over and over again as to why he had even caved in to the pressure to come here?

70

THE CAR drove him across the Danube to the UNO-City which was the home of the IAEA amongst many other international agencies. The IAEA occupied the top floors of the building—all floors from the eighteenth to the twenty-sixth.

He checked in at Checkpoint Charlie and explained that he was here for the tour. The guards asked him to step aside and they retained his Austrian passport. Jerome was told that he could pick up his passport at the same Checkpoint Charlie upon leaving the property again. They handed him a slip which was supposed to be signed off by the tour guide. He was shown to a separate area just in front of the entrance to the UN towers.

Jerome waited there for five minutes before a group of Japanese tourists joined him. Finally, the tour guide arrived. It was an elderly woman, dressed in a dark blue suit. She had a big tag fixed to her jacket. She explained in English that it was absolutely necessary that they had to stay together and follow her very closely. In case somebody got lost the tourists were instructed to return to Checkpoint Charlie immediately. To avoid any inconveniences she signed all visitor slips right then and there. They didn't begin the tour on the ground floor, but were asked to step into an elevator, which took the group to the twenty-sixth floor—right into the heart of the IAEA headquarters, or whatever part was made available to visitors on these public tours.

* * *

THE ARAB recognized Jerome immediately. He was surprised and called George to inform him of the intruder. "What's that supposed to mean? Why does he come here?" the Arab inquired.

"How the heck should I know? Run an immediate ID check on all visitors from this morning," George ordered the Arab. The Arab searched his PC and ran a matching program on all picture IDs from individuals who had passed through all four checkpoints within the last hour. Hundreds of regular UN employees had come through these checkpoints since eleven this morning. But Jerome was the only stranger that was identified with a perfect match. No CIA agent had entered the facility—at least none that were known to them. No matches were found on any of the Japanese tourists—they were just insignificant onetime visitors.

"Gotcha," the Arab said aloud, only for himself to hear. At once he got George on the phone, "It's him. It's Jerome Birchner," the Arab said.

"All right. Let me handle it. Did anyone else that we know come through or did he come alone?" George inquired.

"Nobody so far . . . just him."

"Where is he now?"

"Still on our floor. I guess they'll be heading down to twenty afterwards," the Arab suggested.

"What is he wearing?"

"A dark brown leather jacket and beige pants. I'll get you his mug shot. Wait just a second."

GEORGE LEFT his office hastily as the Arab approached him with a color printout of Jerome's picture. He hurried down the narrow hallway. It didn't take George long to find the tour. He glanced frequently at the photograph of Jerome which he held in his hand. George had never seen Jerome in the flesh before and except for that photograph he had no other visual depiction of him. As he looked at Jerome from behind, he compared the real Jerome with the photographic image several times. He was certain that he had identified Jerome Birchner. George followed the tour from a safe distance. It was easy for him to hide between people as a constant flow of traffic went in and out of offices and in both directions through the corridors.

Jerome was the last one in the group. He was lagging behind for obvious reasons. He wanted to be recognized. Jerome was eager to meet the perpetrator who had kidnapped his children. Subconsciously he had made plans to punch the guy in the face. He pictured the scenario in his mind over and over again. If they would arrest him, it wouldn't matter, he said to himself. Just the satisfaction of knocking the guy down was definitely worth it.

Before coming to Vienna, he had the chance to train a few days at home. At Sports Authority he bought a punching bag and boxing gloves to get in shape. For hours he'd been training to get the perfect right just right. A local boxing instructor whom he'd met at the sporting goods shop when he purchased the boxing gear was eager to help him out with private lessons. Jerome was thankful for his encouragement, but rejected the offer when the guy made some unkosher remarks. Meaning, the guy was probably gay. And homophobic Jerome, who was also a little paranoid, wasn't in the mood to bother with such personalities at the moment. But then, how hard could it be to hit someone in the middle of the face, he asked himself many times. He prepared himself also for every eventuality so that he wouldn't be startled once the suspect made contact.

George approached Jerome from behind. "I'll meet you in the cafeteria. Ground level. In five minutes," George said almost whispering. When he spoke the words, he was not even ten inches away from Jerome's right ear.

All the preparations didn't help as Jerome was surprised by the approach. In his mind he had thought how he would be contacted perhaps through a phone call or a note. Then he would meet George in some dark corner of a badly-lit café or restaurant—preferably at a late hour. He would march toward him with a friendly smile until George felt secure and comfortable enough. And as he got up and approached Jerome to shake his hand, Jerome would reach out and deliver the well-prepared and thought-through megapunch. He'd enjoy the blood gushing from his nose and looking at a stunned George. That's at least how he had imagined things would take their course—but dumbfounded now, as he heard the voice whispering the command into his ear to meet him.

This guy had a lot of guts, Jerome thought. Contact was established. He swerved around momentarily, but George was no longer there. Jerome was unaware of what George even looked like. He searched the crowd, but who was George? There were fifty, maybe a hundred people in the hallway. Most of them nicely dressed in suits, dresses and all kinds of professional attire. Nobody in particular appeared to be a kidnapper. *But what did a kidnapper look like anyway?* he contemplated. Potentially anyone could become desperate and turn into a wacko, and blinded by greed, could do the unthinkable. Thoughts raced like razor edges through his brain and produced migraine-like jolts in his forehead. The first priority on his mind now was to find an elevator to descend to the ground level.

Jerome searched every corner to find an elevator. Then he finally found one and the cabin was full. He squeezed himself into the elevator cage. People complained about him for a second, then turned their attention to the physical sensation of falling twenty-six floors to the ground. The dynamics and hydraulics of the elevator worked well as the elevator cabin proceeded to slide into its proper position at ground level without jerking. Smooth ride, he thought.

He left the elevator cage first and was glad to do so. Jerome searched for signs that would direct him to the cafeteria. There were none. He approached a man who was walking quickly in the other direction, "Excuse me! Where is the cafeteria?"

The man ignored Jerome, so he tried his approach again, this time with an attractive lady and her friend. "Excuse me ladies. Where may I find the cafeteria?" he asked the attractive woman politely.

"Over there," the female next to the attractive dame said as she pointed in the direction of the cafeteria.

"Thanks," he answered, focusing at the indicated line of fire. His full attention was now on entering the cafeteria to meet George. He got in line like everybody else. Jerome wasn't hungry, so he grabbed a donut wrapped in plastic and a Coke from the soda fountain next to the cashier.

"Seven Euros," the cashier said.

Jerome handed her a ten-dollar bill. What was this about these Euros anyway. They had no bank notes yet—the Euro was just an accounting system, but they all quoted everything in Euros. Sure most people already had their Euro currency cards, similar to a credit card, but Jerome didn't own such a thing. "I only have US Dollars. Is that okay? You can keep the change," he said.

The cashier nodded. Jerome concentrated now on finding an empty table to wait for George. This wasn't an easy task. Most people just sat next to someone else, and based on the crowd, it was lunch hour. All corner tables were taken. Then he spotted a person getting up from a small table in the central section to his right. With the tray and the donut and the Coke, he marched quickly to the empty table. Two chairs across from each other were placed at this table. He secured his tray on the table and placed the cup of Coke atop the tray. Then he sat down and began eating his donut and sipping his Coke. He looked around the cafeteria to perhaps notice George somewhere in the crowd. Ten minutes went by and George hadn't approached him yet. During this time, one man asked to borrow the empty chair across from him. At first he thought that this was George, but the voice was a completely different one from the one he had learned to fear. Jerome denied the man access. He also searched the cafeteria for CIA agents, but he couldn't make any out, although plenty of suspicious looking individuals roamed the area. The waiting was killing him.

CHAPTER

71

AFTER FIFTEEN minutes had passed, and Jerome had eaten his donut and emptied his cup of Coke, he made up his mind to walk over to one of the exits. The cafeteria had several exits and instead of solid walls, the whole cafeteria was enclosed in glass. He could no longer sit still. He had to do something. As he got up, a tall man stepped toward the table.

"It's free. I'm done. It's available," Jerome said.

"Great, you can sit down," the deep voice with its thick British accent ordered. It was George.

Jerome sat down and his plans crumbled. He wouldn't deliver his vicious punch that he had envisioned all along, at least not for now. Their eyes locked.

"Did you like your donut?" the man asked.

"It was good. You should get one too." Jerome was determined that this despicable creature would not get the best of him.

"Look, I'm sorry about your kids. I apologize, I'm really sorry."

For Jerome it was hard to gauge George's sincerity.

"But Jewels has set me up, just as she has set you up. You know that, right? You've been set up. She told me that you took the money. All of it."

Jerome could hear his blood pounding in his ears. "She did? Why would she say that?" Jerome was puzzled. He didn't believe a word the man said.

"Women . . . they're always a problem. Never do business with women, young man. You arranged everything for her, then she fired you and set you up. But really, I wanna apologize for what happened to your kids. I'm sorry. It may sound kind of strange, but really, I'll make it up to you somehow, some day," he offered as he stretched out his hand to initiate reconciliation with a handshake.

Completely taken off guard, Jerome clutched his hand and shook it. At this moment he couldn't figure out what this was all about. All of this was incredibly strange. It was true that his kids weren't really hurt during the whole ordeal, but still, psychologically the abduction had certainly left a negative impact. Vivian and Dennis may have to endure ridiculous counseling later in their lives as their psyche could perhaps cause various flashbacks. Nobody knows.

And Vivian had already begun to develop some phobias. She would no longer open her window and always locked the door to her room. They had become more watchful as they went down to the beach and never wanted to be left alone in the house. This was more true of Vivian than of Dennis. Although he too, had become more cautious and rarely ever went over to a friend's house to play ball or stay overnight. The Birchner kids were now more withdrawn and had become even introverted to some extent. The roving security guards at Whitecaps Island provided added safety. But for now it seemingly had no psychological consequence for the Birchner kids.

"So this is the face that goes with the voice," Jerome said.

"I have to make this short, but I gotta talk to you about a few things. Maybe you can fill me in on it. I know it may sound stupid to ask you for help, but you're probably the only one who may know the specific information that I'm looking for." George was dead serious. He was polite and apologetic.

The whole thing seemed ludicrous to Jerome. "Maybe you wanna meet me at my hotel, at the Hilton across the Exchange. Let's say tonight, for dinner?" Jerome suggested.

"No, that wouldn't be a good idea. There are only a few things that I need to know. Let's get outta here," he suggested hastily, looking uncomfortable.

They left the cafeteria and walked to a lounge area near an exit of one of the UNO-City towers.

THE ARAB watched both men closely. At first, he stood next to one of the doorways in the cafeteria. Then he followed George and Jerome at a safe distance. As usual, his outfit was dark—black sweatshirt underneath his black leather jacket, a black pair of jeans and black boots. He looked so obviously suspicious, but for whatever reason he blended into the crowd and didn't stand out. When George and Jerome sat down in the lounge area, he positioned himself in a dark corner.

"DO YOU mind if we go up to my office?" George asked.

"Matter of fact, I do. I need people around me. As you can imagine I'm a little paranoid to say the least. I don't know who you really are," Jerome replied. *Who is this guy?* Jerome said to himself. *Is he crazy? Does he really think I'm gonna go with him to some remote location to get killed? I'm not gonna make it easy for him and his cronies,* Jerome swore to himself, as he was tempted to deliver the vicious punch, right at this very moment.

"ALL RIGHT. As you probably know I'm with the IAEA. In fact I'm an Executive Director with the agency. We're here to prevent the illegal distribution of nuclear materials. We oversee things around the globe and we manage anything from nuclear fuel rods to nuclear waste. You name it, we're in charge of everything that has to do with nuclear stuff. Without our consent, nobody on earth has permission to deal with plutonium and other classified substances. Every nuclear power plant on our planet is inspected by us and virtually under our full control," George explained.

"That's interesting. But I heard that you were one of the bad guys," Jerome still didn't know if he could believe the guy. He anxiously fingered a quarter in his left pants pocket.

"Yeah, they always say that. Without us our planet would've gone up in smoke several decades ago. But we make sure that such a thing won't happen. The thing is that Jewels and her now dead husband had some plans to make billions of dollars with nuclear materials from China and North Korea. They were in a good position to pull it off. Nicanor is a reputable company and neither the DOE, nor the State Department, or the Defense Department had any suspicions when they signed a contract with North Korea a few years ago. They actually came to the rescue of the U.S. government which had made a promise to spend ten billion dollars in infrastructure in North Korea." George divulged this information without reservation.

"So you're lecturing me now on nukes and stuff?" Jerome cynically asked.

"Well, Mr. Birchner, I'm sure you wanna know about this. Listen, at first, the ten billion were supposed to be used to dismantle and secure existing nuclear sites. That's when the IAEA got involved to supervise the whole scoop. But John Farnsworth, naive as he was and eager to play the philanthropist, had the idea to build nuclear reactors instead. His intentions were good because he just wanted to help the poor folks in North Korea with electricity, as most of them didn't have any. He thought that in the process he could dismantle the suspected weapons sites, which were supposedly under construction, and then use some of the material to build his peaceful reactors. Of course, Nicanor would make a fortune in the process."

"Was John Farnsworth one of the bad guys or one of the good guys? I'm not sure I follow you."

"Well, let me explain, Mr. Birchner. I'm telling you this so that you understand why certain things went wrong the way they did. All dismantling and construction was supposed to be done under the careful supervision of highly qualified and trusted U.S. corporations. But it didn't work out that way. China didn't like John's idea. They were eager to get their hands on the cash. China suggested that the U.S. should simply deposit the ten billion dollars in the State Bank of North Korea. Then China would take care of everything else and this would help both countries to expand their infrastructures, they argued. It would create jobs in China and North Korea, they said."

"How about North Korea? Did they have no opinion about all this? I mean to me it seems like China was heavily involved in all these negotiations and North Korea just stood by and didn't say a word?" Jerome's mind was running ahead of George's explanation.

"I'll get to that in a second. Of course, the U.S. government wasn't interested in just handing ten billion dollars in cash to the North Koreans. That would've been crazy. Instead, the U.S. went with John's plan. It took a lot of negotiating and it dragged on for quite some time. Finally, the Chinese agreed as they made alternate plans for themselves how to make the best out of this deal. Funny, they rarely asked for the opinion of the North Koreans. See, the Chinese obviously had the North Koreans in their pockets. The North Koreans had to shut up and take whatever they would get. They were and they continue to be at the mercy of China," George elaborated.

"George, why are you telling me all this? Can I call you

George or do you have a real name, too?" Jerome posed the question with a healthy dose of self-confidence.

"Yeah, call me George. That'll be fine. I'm telling you this to explain that in fact we're the good guys, we're legit, but that it is Jewels who's the bitch in the story. You must understand that. Don't you?" Throughout his essay, George forged sentence after sentence into his ever thickening British accent.

"Well, I'm not sure about anything and I most certainly don't know who is who. If what you say is true, then why did you authorize that they have now a first-class nuclear weapons facility over there that is able to destroy our planet several times over? I mean, according to what you've just told me, the IAEA was in charge of supervising the whole scoop over there."

As he couldn't hear a word that the two men said, the Arab grew impatient. He had the impression that this conversation was going nowhere—it took too long. He retrieved a pistol from the right pocket of his jacket. From the left pocket he fumbled with another piece of metal—it was the silencer. At the moment he pulled it out, he lost the piece and it fell loudly to the ground. Instantly, Jerome turned his head in the direction of the hollow bang. George too, glanced down the hallway, but couldn't see anything suspicious and only imagined for a moment what this noise could've been. To regain Jerome's attention, he continued with his speech.

"No, Mr. Birchner, you don't understand. I can't tell you everything and I will only give you a glimpse into these international affairs. But there's more to this picture than meets the eye. It's a long story and you probably wouldn't believe me if I told you. All those things are connected to specific strategic national security interests in the White House. That's all I can tell you. The U.S. government is in charge of the whole thing. Rest assured of that. The IAEA is working very closely together with the Pentagon on this."

Jerome listened intently, but raised his eyebrows when he heard this statement. He couldn't believe it.

In the meantime, the Arab attached the silencer slowly to the front of the gun. As he continued to observe the two men, he was ready to kill. It was racing in his blood. It would be a quick hit and nobody would notice, he thought.

"But the issue that's important for you, Mr. Birchner, is the fact that billions of dollars have vanished. And you've set it up . . . your name is all over the map. Meaning, you've incorporated the companies in the BVIs and you've established the accounts for Mrs. Farnsworth. Therefore, what we'd like to know is: Where did she put the money? We need the exact location of her accounts. That's all and that's it. We just need to find out how much money she took," George explained his request. He was calm and spoke in a professional manner, just like a government agent would.

"I could tell you a few details, but it won't help you. Only Jewels has access to the accounts. And the way I know how the system works, you need to show up at the bank with her death certificate in your hands in order to receive any information about her accounts. That's what the bank officials will want to see. And even then you'd better have a solid Power of Attorney from the President of the United States or a court order from the Supreme Court, so that you'll even have a chance to get anywhere. It's very difficult to obtain any account information otherwise. It's virtually impossible to access the funds without her presence," Jerome explained.

"Well, that's all right. We just need a little hunch concerning how much money ran through her accounts. That's it. Tell me the location of her accounts and you won't regret it. I promise," George said with a cunning grin on his face.

"George, it sounds interesting. But I really don't have the time to listen to wild stories. I'll give you the details to her account. There's only one account that I've set up. If you think of it, let me know once you find out where the money went. Otherwise, I really don't wanna hear anything about this anymore. For me this is history." Jerome scribbled something on a piece of paper. He handed the paper to George and got up. "That's all there is. Just get yourself a court order or something and maybe they'll give you some information. But I'll betcha, you won't get the money. Everything you need to know is on that piece of paper."

"Thanks, Birchner. You won't regret it. I gotta go," George said now hastily.

"By the way, you're not going to touch my family again," Jerome said like a warning.

George stood up and Jerome hesitated for a moment. The conversation was over. As both men looked at each other, the Arab aimed at Jerome's head—waiting for George's signal to take him out. He could no longer feel himself breathe. The tension grew as adrenaline rushed through the killer's veins. Every hit was an exciting adventure and a thrill, he thought. It was a rush—he was born to kill.

"Of course not. I'm the nice guy, remember? I said I was sorry, and I truly am. Back then I thought you were one of the bad guys, Birchner, just as you thought that I was one of them. But we're the good guys, Birchner. Don't you get it? The government is on our side—you should know that." George laughed with a deep cough from his lungs as he said that. "All right then, see you around, Birchner," George said as he turned around.

The Arab stared at George. His emotions were stretched like a thin, highly sensitive condom around the delicate male organ at the immediate moment of ejaculation. Just one movement, one glance, and Jerome would be dead. But George simply moved away. He didn't give the signal. For the first time in what seemed like an eternity, the Arab took a breath. His disappoint-ment was evident as he lowered the gun reluctantly. He removed the silencer and put both metal pieces back into his pockets.

In the very moment as George swerved around, the bright sunlight that shone through the higher parts of the larger windows reflected on what appeared to be a lapel pin on George's sports jacket. For a split second, Jerome was able to zoom in on this small item, just enough to get a glimpse. It was the penny. The reflection though, was tainted because of the tiny little hole that had been shot with a laser through the surface of the coin. He was stunned, and when he realized what it was, he wanted to take a closer look at the lapel pin. But Jerome could only watch as George walked quickly toward the elevator bank and vanished behind a sliding door.

No, Randy Dermont couldn't be involved in this, he thought. It was probably just an odd coincidence, Jerome concluded and dismissed all suspicions instantaneously. Sure, the pennies were APL's trademark giveaway gimmick, and APL was involved in many government deals with defense contractors, but it couldn't be that Randy Dermont was part of this sinister scheme, or was he? Jerome was stunned at the thought.

72

HE WENT outside to the front entrance, where he'd waited for the tour guide before. Then he headed to Checkpoint Charlie. His passport was still there and he handed the visitor slip to a guard. Another security officer compared the names on the slip with the passports that were in a drawer. The officer returned the passport to Jerome.

His chauffeur was leaning against the Mercedes smoking a cigarillo. He apparently enjoyed the butt as he clenched the burning stump of tobacco without a filter between his lips.

"Take me to the hotel," Jerome ordered the chauffeur, as he entered the bench in the rear of the car.

The driver dropped the stogie to the ground, then sped away over the Reichsbrücke, the bridge that connects the Donaustadt district with the heart of Vienna over the Danube. They headed back to the Hilton.

At the hotel, Jerome ordered the driver to wait in front of the hotel. "I'll be back in ten minutes. Just gotta get my stuff," he said.

IT TOOK Jerome only a few minutes to grab his things and to check out of the hotel. Then he requested that the chauffeur take him to the airport as quickly as he could. It only took 'em twenty minutes to get there. At the airport, he paid the driver a hundred-dollar tip. He had no smaller bill, and didn't mind blessing the guy. Jerome was elated to get out of Vienna. And he was in a hurry. Jerome entered the terminal, his jaw set.

That was it. Jerome had to retire. He had done his part. George didn't want to meet him outside the UNO-City building complex. He'd given it his best shot to arrange such a meeting. But then, what if George was telling the truth? Jerome didn't know who to trust. It wasn't his call. The CIA had capable people to do the job right. Maybe someone in the CIA was playing a dangerous game—maybe a double agent or something. He considered this thought carefully. Former CIA Agent Trevor Gates had done so—he had crossed over. What about Osteen? Maybe he was in on it, too. *Who knows? Who cares?* Jerome contemplated the various possibilities. He was ready for retirement and as far as he was concerned, the Nicanor case was now history.

He was also convinced that the CIA knew nothing about the twenty million which he'd made in the Nicanor deal. George seemingly knew more about the whole thing than the CIA. Osteen and Tish wouldn't even curse Jerome, because at least he gave it a shot. Jerome was hoping that they would see the picture through his eyes. He'd traveled across the Atlantic and acted as the bait.

They'd portrayed George as a maniac. But what Jerome saw was a scientist who was highly regarded in his field. George held the office of an Executive Director at the IAEA—a position which carried a high level of responsibility. Nobody would get a job like this if he acted like a wacko. And most certainly nobody would keep such a job for very long, if that person was engaged in any kind of wrongdoing.

INSIDE THE terminal, Jerome went to the Lufthansa check-in

counter and inquired about the next flight to the States. Then he went to the KLM counter, to the Swissair counter, to Sabena. But every airline personnel at all counters told him that all U.S. flights had left for the day. It was only about three P.M. At British Airways the lady behind the *First-Class* desk told him that a flight was leaving from London to New York at seven A.M. the next day.

Air France offered him the earliest arrival in the States. They suggested he take a plane to Paris around five, and then in the morning they still had a seat available on the Concorde. This would be the speediest solution. Arriving early with the Concorde in New York could get him to Miami just before noon on Tuesday. Birgid would be surprised and on cloud nine about his early return.

Jerome booked the afternoon flight to Paris, including the ride with the Concorde from Paris to New York the following morning. Air France accommodated him generously. They treated him for the flight from Vienna to Paris at no charge, first-class, of course. They even provided him with a room at an airport hotel for that night, also free of charge. Sure, the one-way fare for the Concorde was $4,500. He could've taken an early flight from Vienna to New York the next morning, but he wanted to get out of Vienna as quickly as he could.

IT WAS time to say goodbye to Vienna, and not to return there for awhile. The city was beautiful, especially during the summer months. It was quite a sight to see *Fiakers* ride around the Ring. These carriages were pulled by two horses and were ideal for sight-seeing adventures in an old-time charm. Splendorous palais, well over a hundred years old, still from the era of the Kaiser, had been restored way beyond and above their former grandeur. These pretentiously elegant buildings decorated the

Ring in perfect order. But behind the gorgeous facades of historic treasures along the Ring and in narrow alleys of the Innenstadt lay many dark buried secrets.

VIENNA HAD been called *The Door to the East*. Ominous weapons deals and busted drug smuggling operations used to crown the daily headlines in local papers during the seventies and throughout the eighties. Corruption was also prevalent. With the decay of communism in the Eastern European countries and the opening of the Eastern European borders, a massive crime wave swept through Austria. Suddenly, especially violent crime had increased significantly. Things became even worse when the Russian mob began buying up most of the buildings and stores in the major shopping districts of Vienna, such as Mariahilfer Strasse and Kärntnerstrasse, during the early nineties.

Behind the disguise of *Gemütlichkeit* on the many pseudo-happy faces of Austrians, the crude reality of a lost identity was buried. They had been run over by the mighty powers of the East. And whatever the folks from the Eastern nations didn't take, the Germans and Swiss snapped away. Membership in the EU was supposed to rescue the Austrian heritage, but had exactly the opposite effect. Austria's farmers had it difficult enough without the EU, but once Austria joined the EU, most of them went bankrupt.

Tourism used to be a highly supportive industry of the Austrian economy, but it had collapsed utterly. Austria once was also proud of its technological advances and exceptional quality of products, but that edge had rapidly disappeared with the arrival of the high-tech era of the nineties. Japanese and U.S. companies had conquered the world with its low-priced, but high quality products. Austria still had its wine, its culinary excesses, and its cultural heritage with Mozart and other old masters. Liberalism had creeped in and had spread wildly throughout the Austrian society with sensuality prevalent.

IT WAS just before noon on Tuesday when Jerome arrived in Miami. Instead of calling ahead and having Birgid arrange for a chopper to pick him up in Miami, he rented a car at the airport. He'd been traveling too much that year and he wouldn't be in the air for awhile, he promised himself. Solid ground under his feet was now a high priority on his list.

At one-thirty in the afternoon the rented Cadillac drove through the stately cast-iron gates of the lavish development in Naples. He was home. Everybody else in the family was home, Birgid, Dennis and Vivian. They embraced.

CHAPTER

73

ONE DAY on a sunny morning, Juliet Farnsworth and Trevor Gates were found dead in the master suite of their Bermuda hideaway. Juliet and Gates had been shot in the foreheads at close range, causing a bullet hole in the front of the head and a big opening in the back of the skull. Their brains had been blown out. Angela, the native Bermudian maid, found them during her regularly scheduled visit—days after the crime had been committed.

The house stank already as the corpses had begun their natural course of decay. When Angela discovered the bodies, she screamed at a rather high pitch for a woman of her age and stature. She was also surprisingly swift as her voluminously short body ran erratically through the mansion. Even though Angela was heavily overweight, she looked kind of cute with her big brown eyes, staring out of her round, fat, dark face. She ended up in front of the house, standing in the middle of the circular driveway, jumping up and down. Angela continued to howl in utter disbelief at the terrible sight she had just witnessed. It was almost incomprehensible.

Several maids, all of them native Bermudians, hurried over to the Farnsworth estate. They came from nearby homes around this wealthy neighborhood as they heard Angela screaming. Finally, after about ten minutes, the ladies were able to calm Angela down. She was still in shock and sat down on the brick steps in front of the mansion. Tears ran over her puffy face. One of the maids retrieved a magazine from the foyer and used it as a fan to comfort Angela as she stood in front of her, waving this thing back and forth and up and down. Another maid called the police headquarters to inform them of the atrocious crime. None of the maids were eager or even interested to take a closer look for themselves at the horrible scene, as Angela had described it to them in every gruesome detail. They simply believed her report.

The local police did not charge anyone with the crime—they had no suspects. It was believed that the perpetrator had accessed the property from the water. Footprints were found leading from the beach to the house and back. Although, no violent entry was detected. The screen of the cage that led to the lanai hadn't been damaged. The sliding door that provided access from the lanai into the house, was unlocked and stood open.

They laid next to each other on their backs in a pool of blood, staring with fixed open eyes at the ceiling. No guns or other weapons were found. Due to the setting of the crime scene, from early on the police excluded the possibility of a murder suicide. The scene didn't indicate a struggle either.

The police report stated that they had found over four hundred thousand dollars in cash in a drawer next to the bed. It didn't seem that any jewelry or any other valuables had been removed from the mansion. Therefore, the police also eliminated burglary and robbery as a potential motive for the slaying. They were shot in cold blood at close range, and perhaps while they were sleeping, the forensic expert specified. Maybe they were drunk. It must've been a painless death, the coroner's report concluded which indicated an instant cause of death for both individuals.

CNN brought a short report about their murders and the

danger on the islands. "Vacationers beware of the mysterious rituals on the islands," the female reporter from CNN began her brief special report on the case. "Even in paradise the danger is lurking," she continued. "There is trouble in paradise." It was a bad analogy.

The local Chief of Police had tried desperately to keep the case low profile. Only after he was pressured by U.S. sources to provide information regarding the incident, he reluctantly agreed to communicate sparse details about the crime to the press. The police chief emphasized vehemently that this tragedy had been a random act of violence. It had been the most heinous felony ever committed on Bermuda. He would personally guarantee that the perpetrators responsil· 'e for this devious deed, would be brought to justice, he said r' .atedly over the airwaves and into the rolling television ca⁻ .s.

The media portraye .liet Farnsworth and Trevor Gates as innocent tourists. They ,howed a few pictures and a short video of Juliet in her prime as faithful wife of John Farnsworth. Most footage came from Nicanor's PR department and every image was carefully selected and edited as necessary. No photograph of Trevor Gates had been broadcast. The media referred to him as a wealthy playboy that hung out with the freshly widowed Juliet Farnsworth. Overall, most of the TV reports didn't last over forty-five seconds or so. The tragedy was only news for a couple of days and then vanished from the screen and from everyone's mind.

Some tabloids picked up bits and pieces of the story in greater detail several months later. Their emphasis and concerns, though, were more on the subject of warning tourists about the lurking danger in paradise.

OSTEEN CALLED Jerome's house on Wednesday. "What's going on, Mr. Birchner? I thought we had a deal," he inquired.

"I did everything the way you instructed me to do it. George just didn't wanna meet me anywhere else."

"So, you met George?" Osteen was curious and somewhat dumbstruck.

"He told me a few stories about the nuclear powers in the world and how they relate to each other. And that was it. Nothing of great interest though. I'm sure nothing you don't already know," Jerome offered the reply.

"Do you have a good description of him?"

Jerome considered his options. What should he answer? He decided to lie. The whole Nicanor thing was history for him. "Well, it's not that he walked up to me and introduced himself. And we didn't sit down for a chat, if you think that's what happened. Honestly, I didn't even see him. I heard his voice. The same voice you have on tape."

"Mr. Birchner, you're not telling me a story here, are you?" The General found his story hard to take.

"General Osteen, you're asking a lot of questions. I don't have all the answers. I did what you asked me to do. And by the way, not that it really matters now, but I didn't see any of your guys there either."

"Well, they were watching."

"Is that so?"

"Look, Mr. Birchner. All I want is an idea what our George looks like. Just a simple basic description so that I can write something into his file. Don't forget, he abducted your children. You're not forgetting that, are you?"

"I don't know Chuck—I can call you Chuck, right?" Jerome was pushing it.

"Sure, call me whatever you want, just tell me the truth, will you please?" The General's voice was taking on an irritated quality.

"This whole thing is a done deal for me. Do you understand, Mr. Osteen? I'm retired. You may wanna play war for the rest of your life, and that's all right with me, but you have to exclude me from all of this. I'm done with deals, wars and whatever. Chuck, listen, I greatly appreciate what you've done for me and my family. Really, we're all very grateful to you for that. Rescuing the kids, you know, it was remarkable what you've pulled off down there in Cuba with your guys. I'll never forget it and we thank you forever for that. Thanks again." Jerome made it clear to Osteen that he was out of the picture. Even though he hadn't celebrated his fortieth birthday yet, his retirement was well deserved, he thought.

"It's not over Jerome. Don't fool yourself. There's still Kensington. I'll get him as a witness sooner or later. He'll testify. I know what he looks like. I sure hope you haven't dug yourself a smelly hole there. You could get out of it now without a problem. But if I find out some day, down the road you know, that your shirt isn't as clean as you say it is, it's gonna be nasty. I guarantee it. You too, will go down with George and his cahoots, just like Braniff did in the old days. It's never over as long as you live. Don't forget that, Birchner," Osteen threatened Jerome. His last sentences almost evaporated.

Jerome was already absentminded. Osteen may have meant

well and may have desired to reach an imaginary goal at this point. But for now, it was only wishful thinking, Jerome was sure of that. That's all that it was, simple dreams and desires, wishful thinking. Nothing but vain words without a purpose. Osteen didn't have a lead, nothing to go by, Jerome thought. Kensington wasn't a threat either. He wouldn't be intimidated by Osteen's warning. No way, there was no reason to be alarmed by his saber rattling.

A FEW months before the Nicanor plant in North Korea was finally completed, it was necessary to close the American Embassy in Pyongyang abruptly. Urged by the Chinese government, the North Koreans decided to disallow any further diplomatic U.S. representation on its soil. The North Koreans didn't appreciate the suspicions which the U.S. had continuously floated to the world media about North Korea's supposed secret nuclear weapons arsenal, and that North Korea wasn't a government to be trusted.

Jo LeJeune must've been ecstatic beyond any imaginations to leave that treacherous territory once and for all. Finally, he'd be reunited with his wife and kids in New Orleans.

75

FOR JEROME, at the moment things were fine and would stay that way for quite some time, he hoped. Jerome had confidence in his dreams. Life was unpredictable, but it sure was precious. And often, in the pursuit of some superficial standard, it was so easy to miss out on the true treasures in life.

The nukes were waiting somewhere on the other side of the Pacific, waiting to attack the U.S. and perhaps the world some day. But Jerome wouldn't worry about it, at least not right now. He couldn't do anything about it anyway, he thought.

Yes, he was left with the puissant provision of prayer, just like everybody else. Prayer would strengthen his faith in God. Fear would only lead to a mental imprisonment for himself and his family. Fear would limit them. Fear would hinder them to live a fulfilled life within the realm of their own creative potential and even beyond their individual capabilities. God was in control—that was for sure. It was good to believe in God—He could be trusted. Too many vicious people were roaming the earth with their own hidden agendas, trying desperately to build their own little kingdoms at any cost.

AFTER THE scary events surrounding the abduction of the Birchner kids, with the glorious ending of their safe return, Walter and Valerie gave it one more shot at life together as a couple and a family. In fact, the whole nightmare radically changed their philosophies and outlook for life. "It was a rearrangement of priorities," as Walter had put it eloquently. He found a tremendous treasure by looking at his family. After all, life was short and it most certainly wasn't just a game. He swore to himself to stay home more often and to care for Val and the kids a lot more.

Val saw Walter change almost instantly, especially concerning some key issues that had bothered her so much, and that had almost forced her to divorce him. Now as a family they went out to eat several times a week and Val slowly gained some weight. She was soon back to a normal weight for her stature and looked healthy again. Val's body continued to be on the slender side, but now with athletic contours. Walter and Val worked out every morning. Jerome saw them often together riding their bicycles around Whitecaps Island and even into town. Instead of liquor, both drank lots of purified water now. They didn't touch alcohol anymore and even an occasional glass of champagne was no longer in the cards. Val joined Birgid's craft circle and she had begun to make some friends. They often went shopping together and gathered socially for this and that.

As Jerome, Birgid and their kids now attended church more frequently, Walter and Val, and their kids joined them occasionally on a Sunday morning. Their lives had definitely changed as they came in touch with redemption.

76

SIX MONTHS after Jerome met George at the UNO-City in Vienna, a Cashier's Check in the amount of fifty million dollars payable to Jerome Birchner was delivered by DHL to the Birchner mansion. No particular sender other than a bank in London had been specified on the airbill. Not even a note was inside the letter package envelope. The Cashier's Check had been issued by a bank in London.

It was a lot of money, Jerome thought. For a moment the acceptance of the fifty million was a strong temptation. It would definitely boost his net worth quite a bit, he continued the thought. Nobody in his right mind wouldn't appreciate that kind of money, he argued with himself. But taking it could mean another obligation to someone unknown as of yet. Maybe it was a trap. Or maybe it was a blessing. Whatever it was, it smelled like trouble. No, he didn't appreciate the money. Whoever had sent it, shouldn't have done so.

Maybe George had finally gotten hold of Juliet's billion in some bank account. Jerome pictured George sitting on a yacht in the sun, somewhere in the Caribbean. Jerome's gut feeling told him that it was George or one of his cronies that had sent him the check. But he didn't care. No, Jerome wasn't one of them.

Jerome took the check and ripped it into many tiny pieces. He went on the pier to his boat and scooted a bit out into the Gulf.

The sun slowly disappeared into the ocean. Raising his hands, he threw the many tiny pieces of paper into the air against the sinking sun, toward the Gulf. The fish would eat them, maybe. Or the salty waters of the Gulf would surely destroy every remaining piece of the check sooner or later. He didn't care. He didn't need the money.

During the last seven or eight months his selective stock portfolio had doubled. Right after he had received his payment for his involvement in the Nicanor deal, after Juliet fired him out of the blue, he had increased his holdings in his favorite stocks to forty million bucks. These shares were now worth eighty million—a rich and healthy forty-million-dollar profit. This money was much easier earned than any other dough he had ever gotten hold of in his life before. Because he only had to pay capital gains taxes on this significant increase in value, he was left with a nice chunk of a wholesome net profit. Through this investment his net worth had now well grown over a hundred million. Jerome was rich enough.

And most importantly, he had his wife and kids. They were all healthy and alive. *He was blessed—no doubt about it,* Jerome mused, as he stood there in his boat, the engines bubbling, and a tender evening breeze hugging him. Jerome looked out over the Gulf and a certain warmth came over him as he watched the sun on the horizon slip away into the sea.

AUTHOR'S NOTE

A REALLY big "Thank You!" to my precious wife who didn't get tired of encouraging me over and over again to write and complete this novel. Her continuous motivation was essential to bring this story unto paper. I love you, honey!

I'm also grateful to my agent who is a great coach. His firm professional opinion was always seasoned with kindness.

Thanks also to Gail for poring over the manuscript and making the book better. She's an excellent editor.

Visit Alec Donzi's Official Website at:

www.scherf.com/alecdonzi.htm

scherf.books

I Love Me: Avoiding & Overcoming Depression
by Dietmar Scherf
A Practical Guide for: Avoiding & Overcoming Depression,
Developing Proper Self-Esteem, Obtaining a Victorious Life
with Joy, Substance and Purpose.
More Info at: www.scherf.com/scherfbooks.htm
Available at most Internet bookstores like amazon.com,
bn.com, borders.com, and at your favorite local bookstore.

scherf.music

Nice To Meet Ya!
by Dietmar Scherf
Sixty minutes of contemporary instrumental music. A
musical journey to a place of relaxation and daydreaming.
More Info at: www.scherf.com/scherfmusic.htm
Available at: www.amazon.com

Visit the Official Scherf Website at:

www.scherf.com